NOISE™

Created by
Tsutomu Nihei

HAMBURG // LONDON // LOS ANGELES // TOKYO

NOiSE
Created by Tsutomu Nihei

Translation - Stephen Paul
English Adaptation - Nathan Johnson
Retouch and Lettering - Star Print Brokers
Production Artist - Mike Estacio
Graphic Designer - Tomas Montalvo-Lagos

Editor - Luis Reyes
Digital Imaging Manager - Chris Buford
Pre-Production Supervisor - Erika Terriquez
Production Manager - Elisabeth Brizzi
Managing Editor - Vy Nguyen
Creative Director - Anne Marie Horne
Editor-in-Chief - Rob Tokar
Publisher - Mike Kiley
President and C.O.O. - John Parker
C.E.O. and Chief Creative Officer - Stuart Levy

A **TOKYOPOP** Manga

TOKYOPOP and ⊙ are trademarks or registered trademarks of TOKYOPOP Inc.

TOKYOPOP Inc.
5900 Wilshire Blvd. Suite 2000
Los Angeles, CA 90036

E-mail: info@TOKYOPOP.com
Come visit us online at www.TOKYOPOP.com

ISBN: 978-1-4278-0303-0

First TOKYOPOP printing: December 2007
10 9 8 7 6 5 4 3 2 1
Printed in the USA

9/87

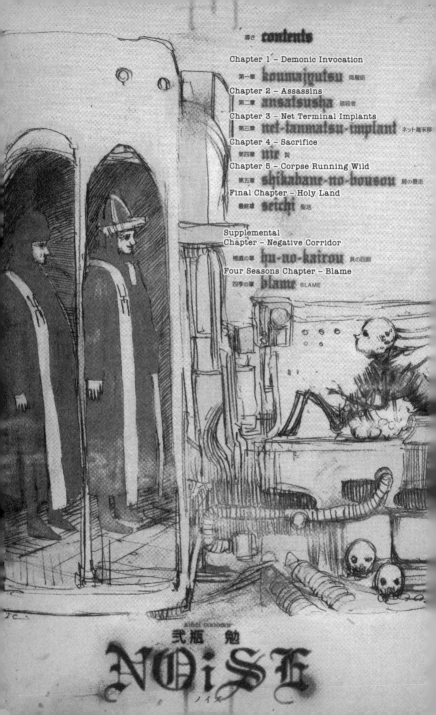

導き contents

弐瓶 勉 nihei tsutomu

NOiSE
ノイズ

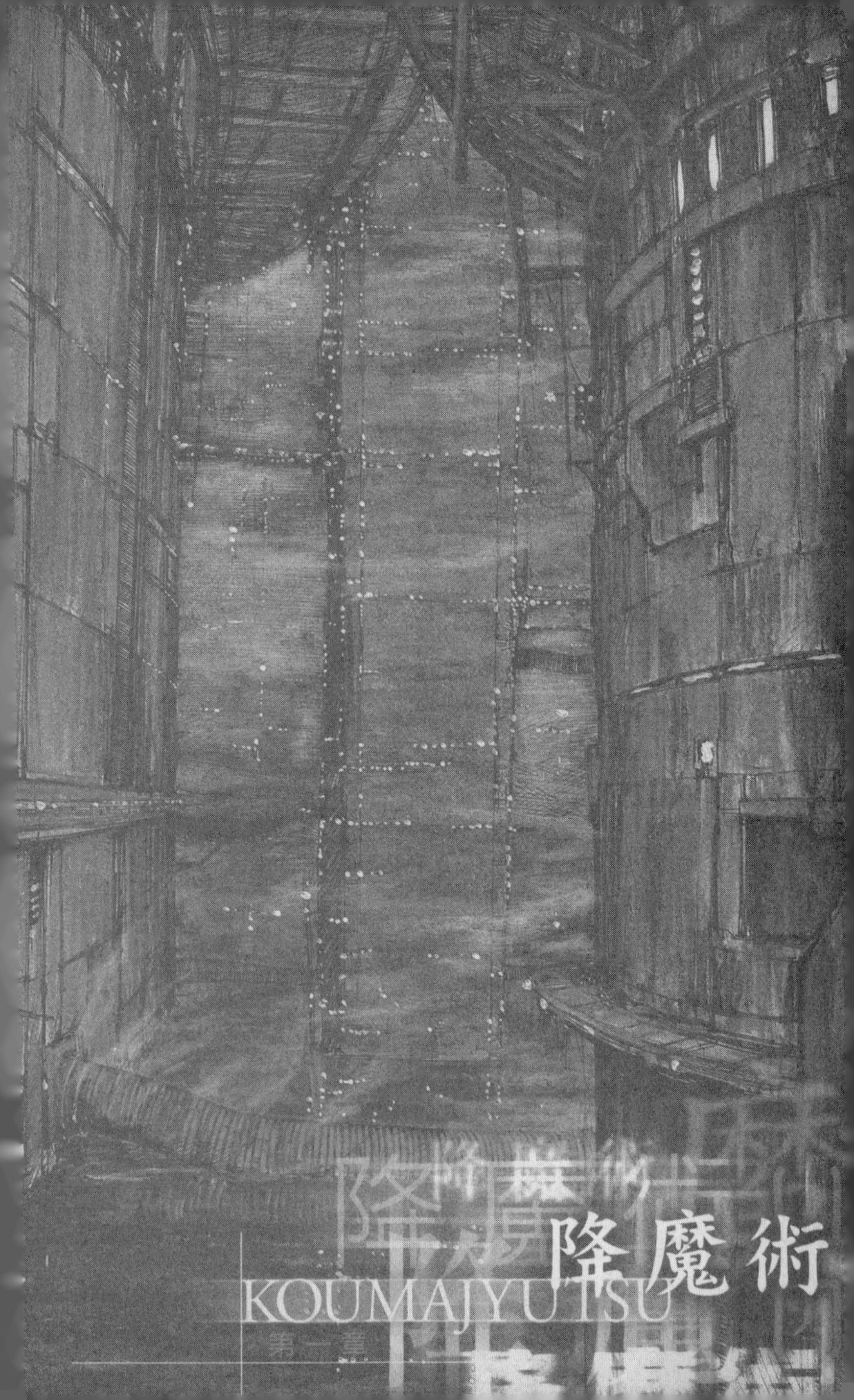
降魔術
KOUMAJYUTSU
第一章

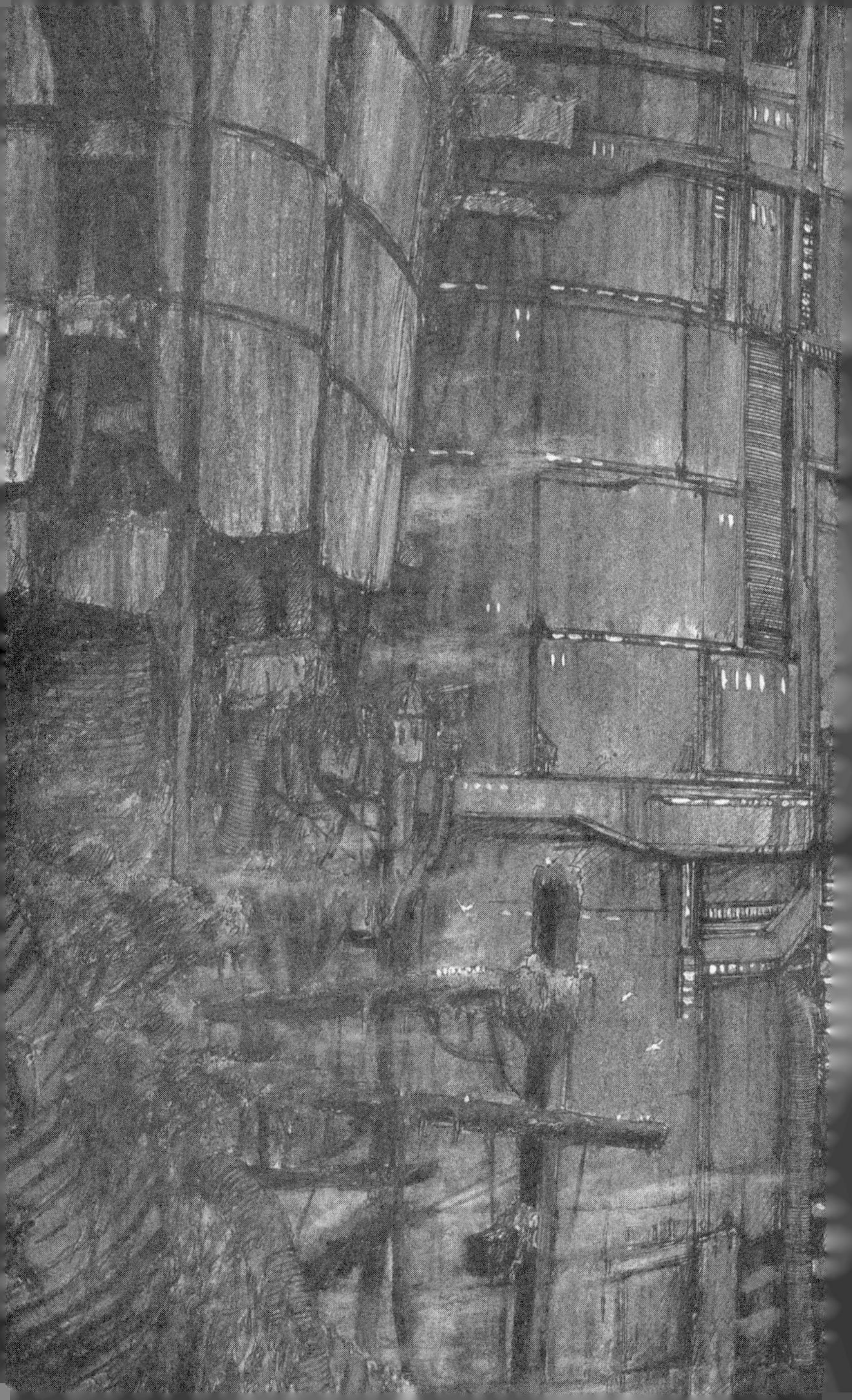

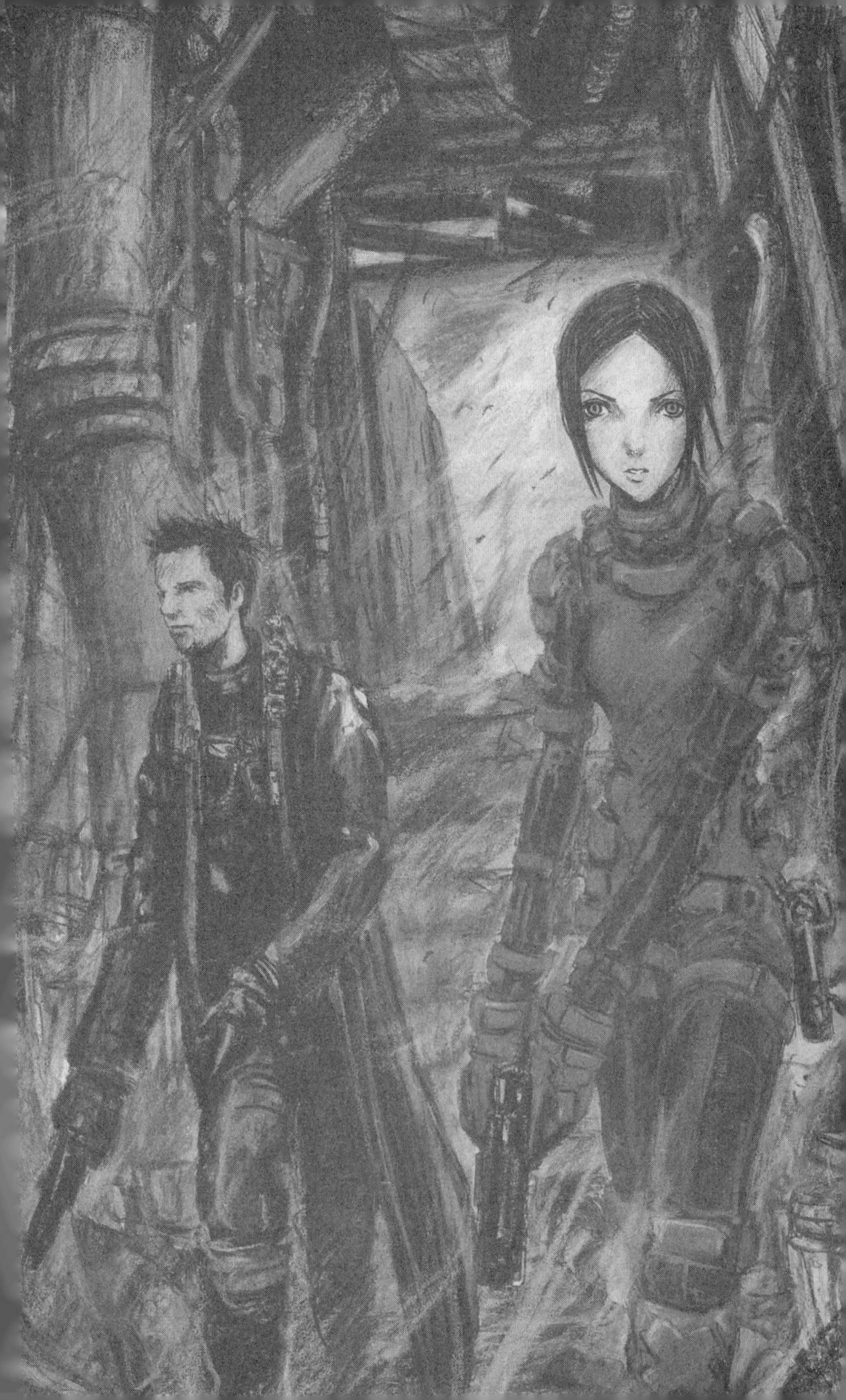

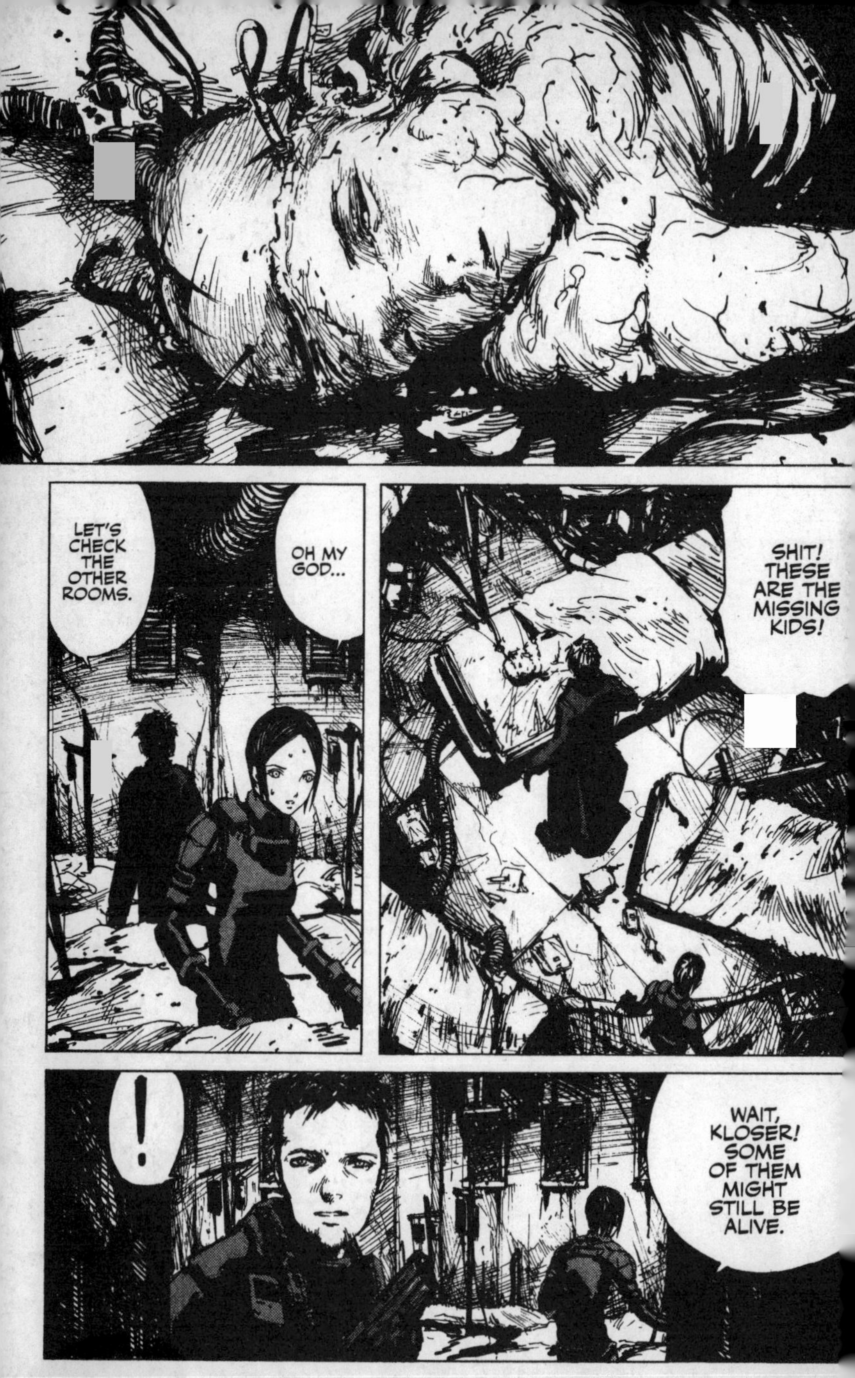
SHIT! THESE ARE THE MISSING KIDS!
OH MY GOD...
LET'S CHECK THE OTHER ROOMS.
WAIT, KLOSER! SOME OF THEM MIGHT STILL BE ALIVE.
!

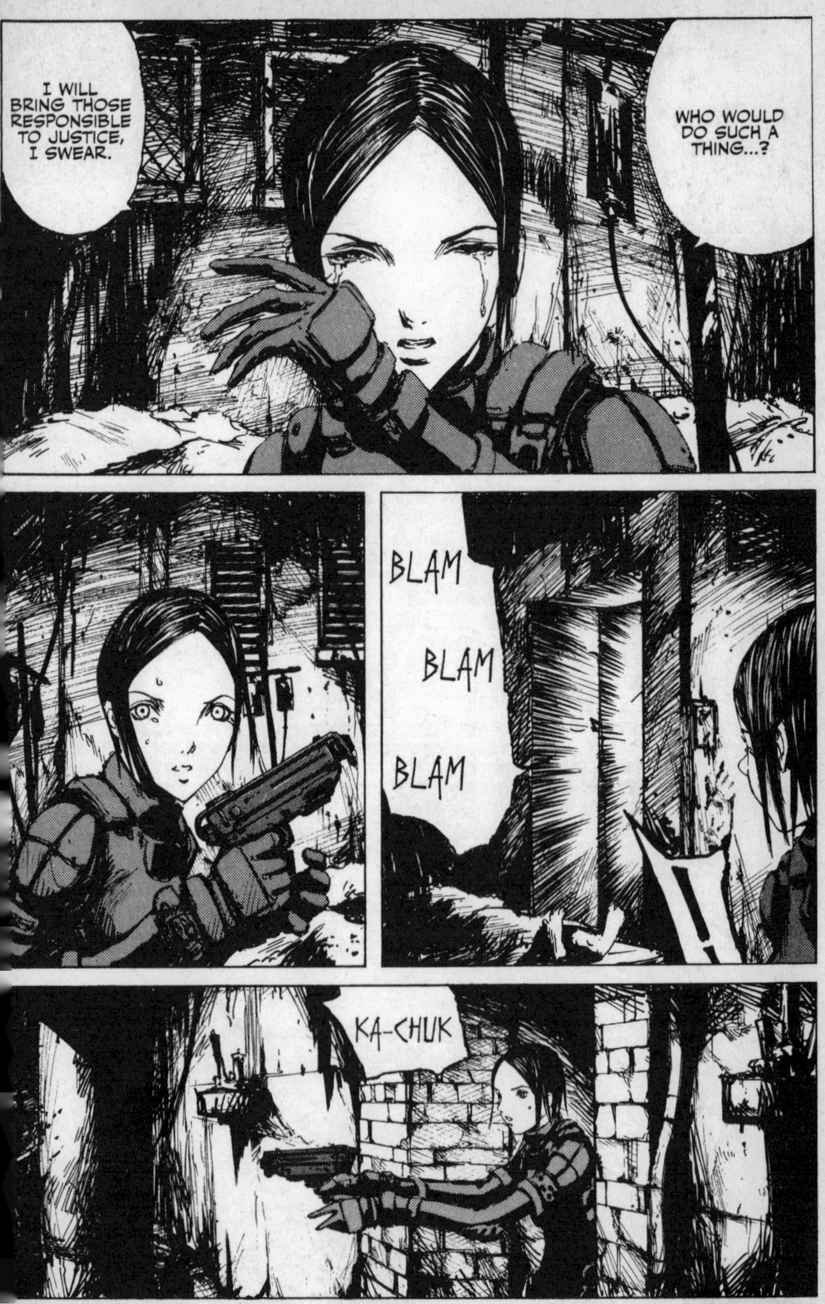
WHO WOULD DO SUCH A THING...?
I WILL BRING THOSE RESPONSIBLE TO JUSTICE, I SWEAR.
BLAM
BLAM
BLAM
KA-CHUK

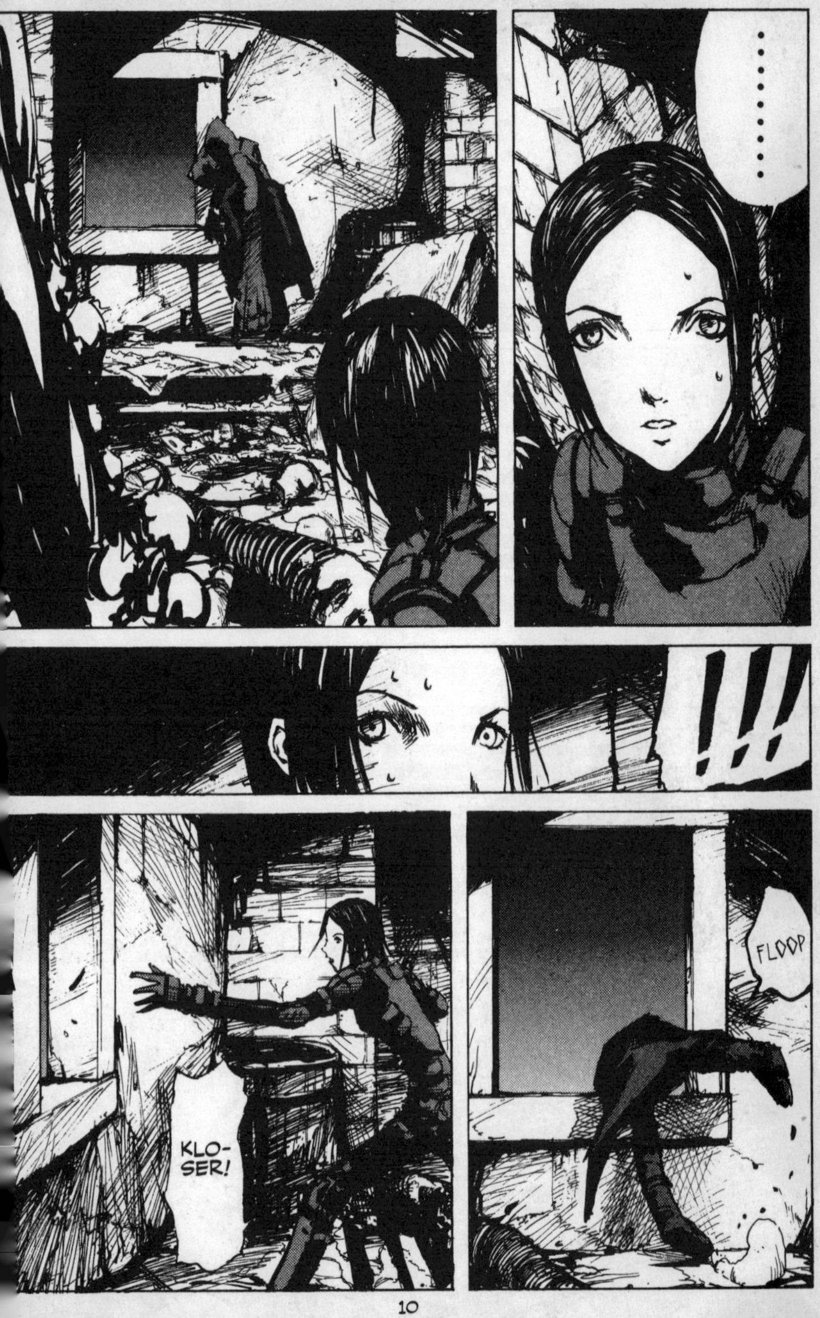
......
!!!
FLOOP
KLO-
SER!

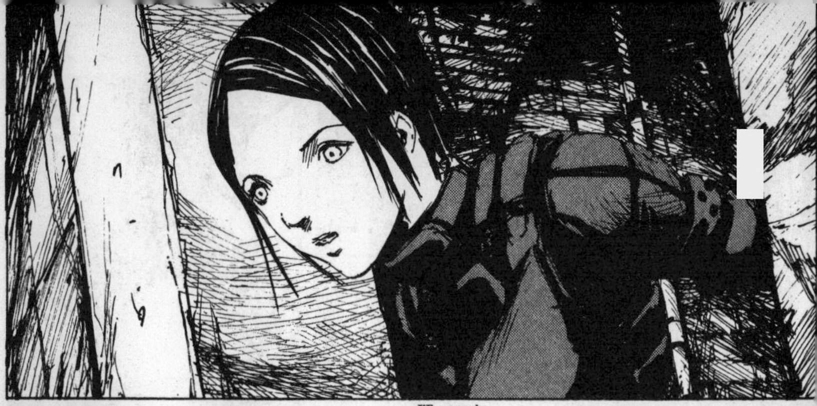

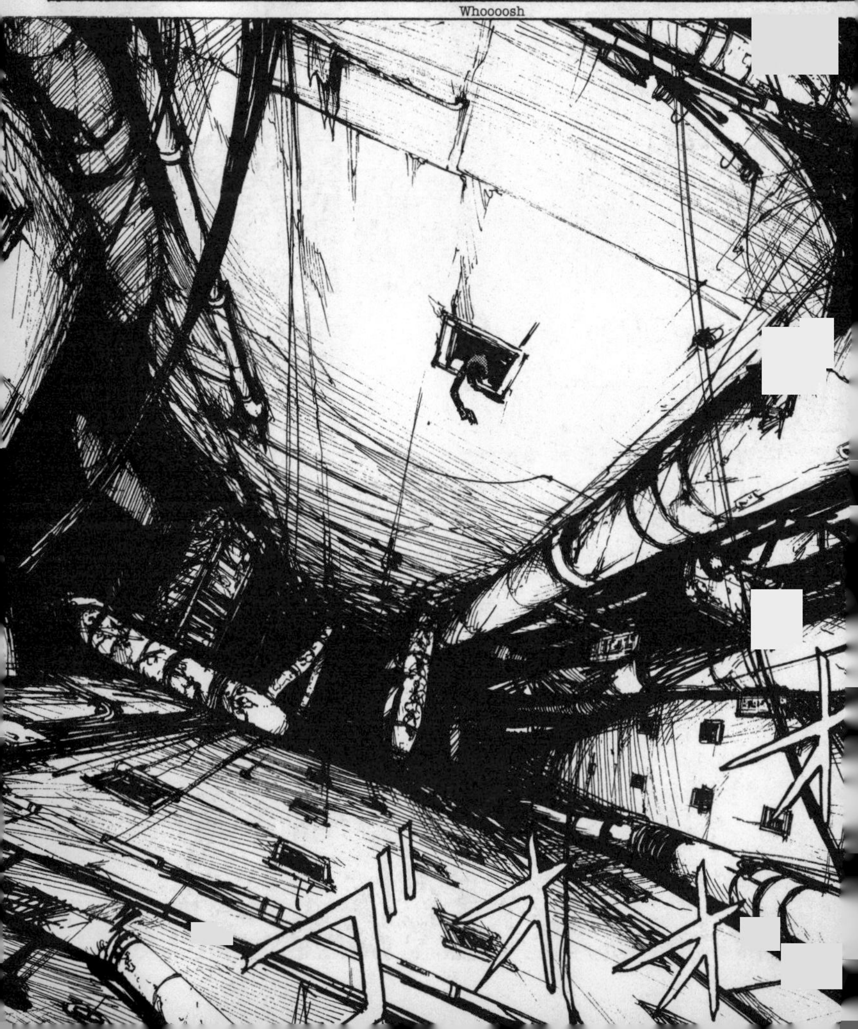
Whoooosh

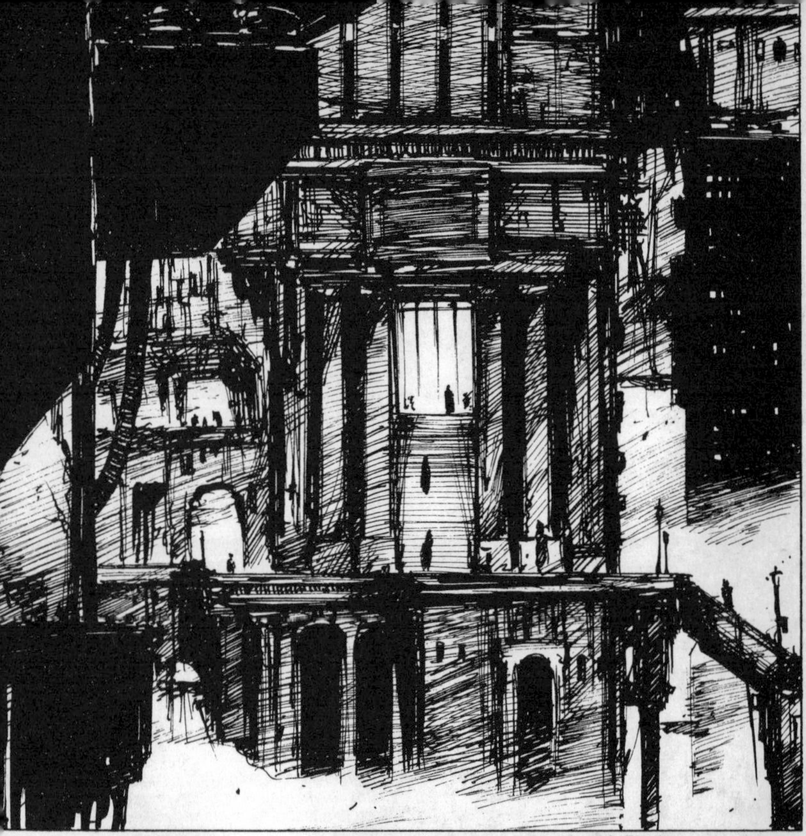

Sign: Juvenile Division

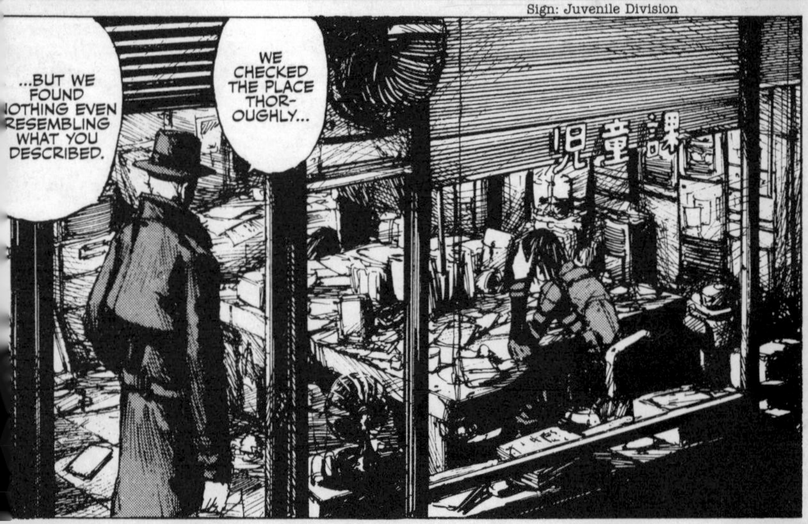
児童課
WE CHECKED THE PLACE THOROUGHLY...
...BUT WE FOUND NOTHING EVEN RESEMBLING WHAT YOU DESCRIBED.

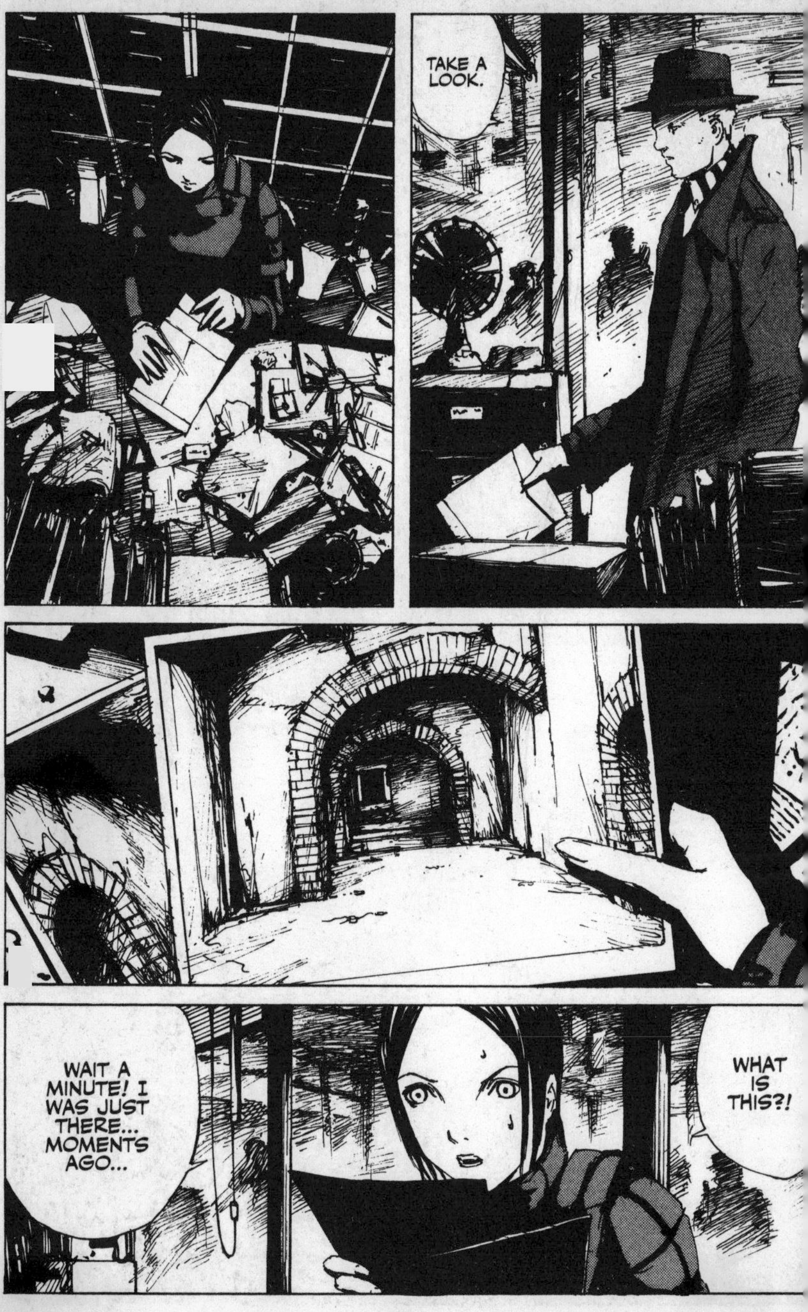
TAKE A LOOK.
WHAT IS THIS?!
WAIT A MINUTE! I WAS JUST THERE... MOMENTS AGO...

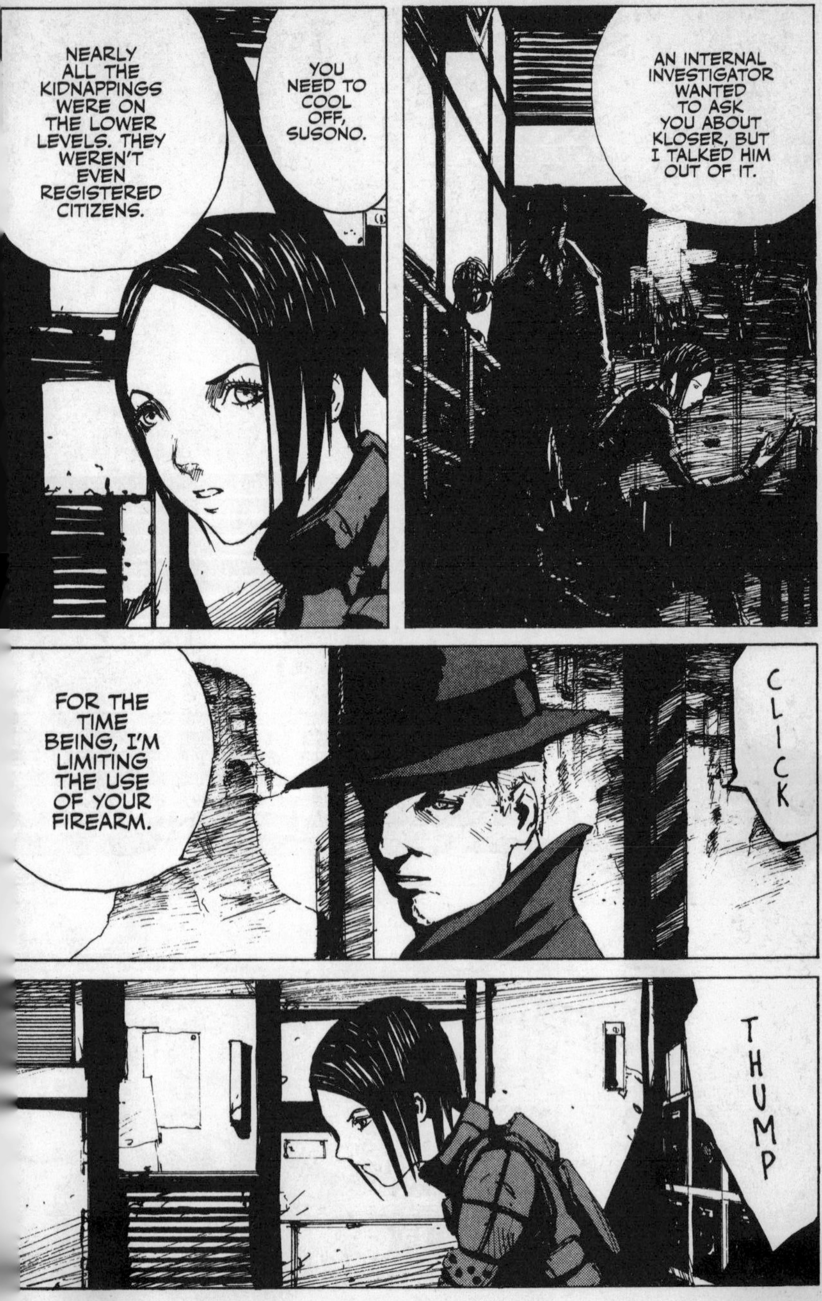
AN INTERNAL INVESTIGATOR WANTED TO ASK YOU ABOUT KLOSER, BUT I TALKED HIM OUT OF IT.
YOU NEED TO COOL OFF, SUSONO.
NEARLY ALL THE KIDNAPPINGS WERE ON THE LOWER LEVELS. THEY WEREN'T EVEN REGISTERED CITIZENS.
CLICK
FOR THE TIME BEING, I'M LIMITING THE USE OF YOUR FIREARM.
THUMP

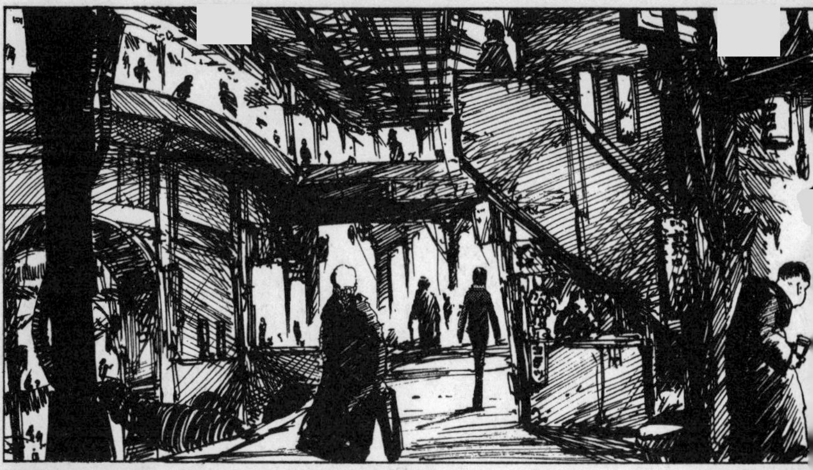
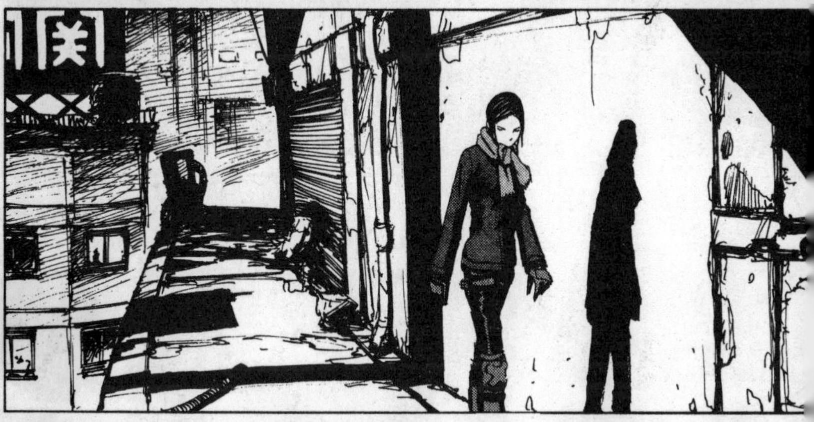
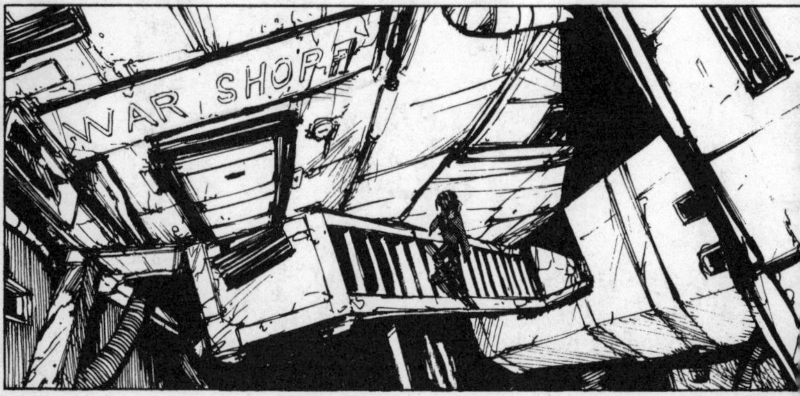
WAR SHOP

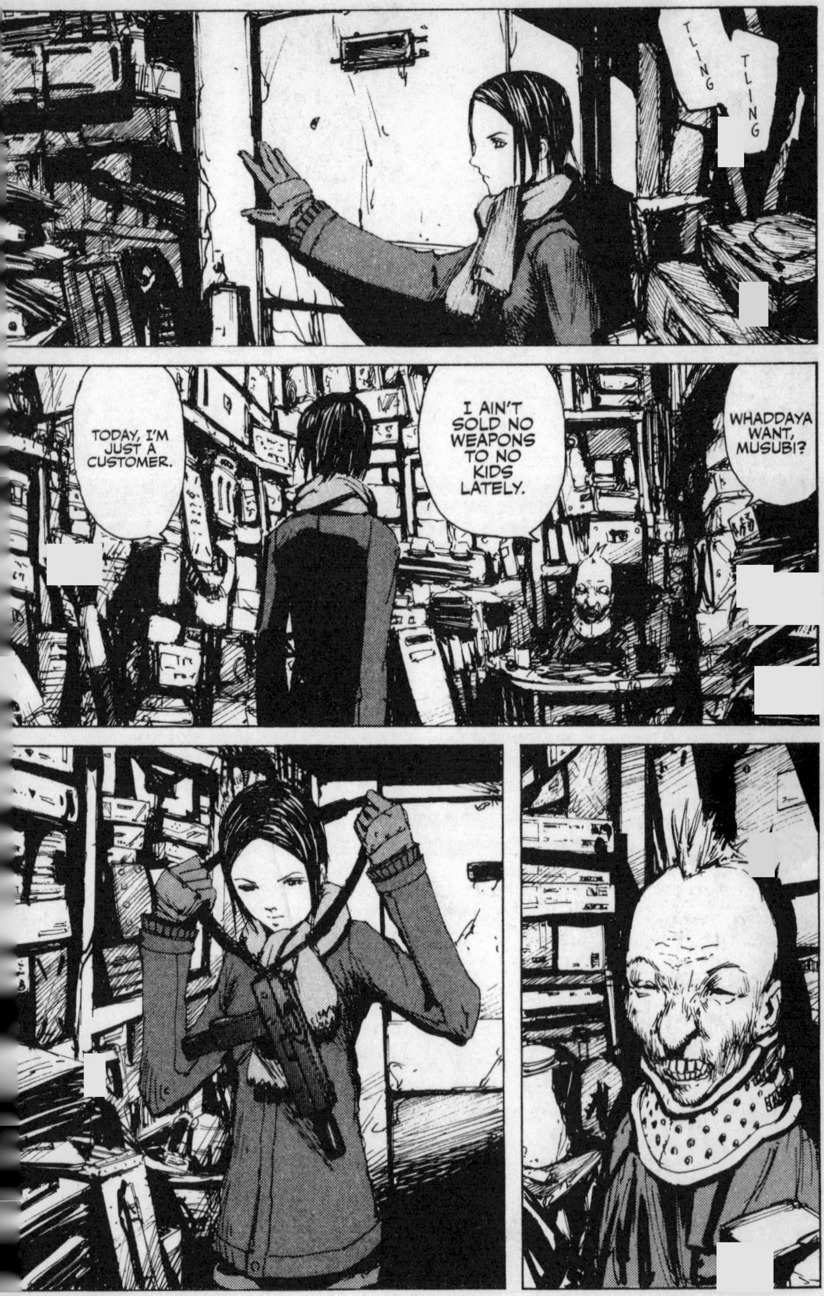
TLING
TLING
WHADDAYA WANT, MUSUBI?
I AIN'T SOLD NO WEAPONS TO NO KIDS LATELY.
TODAY, I'M JUST A CUSTOMER.

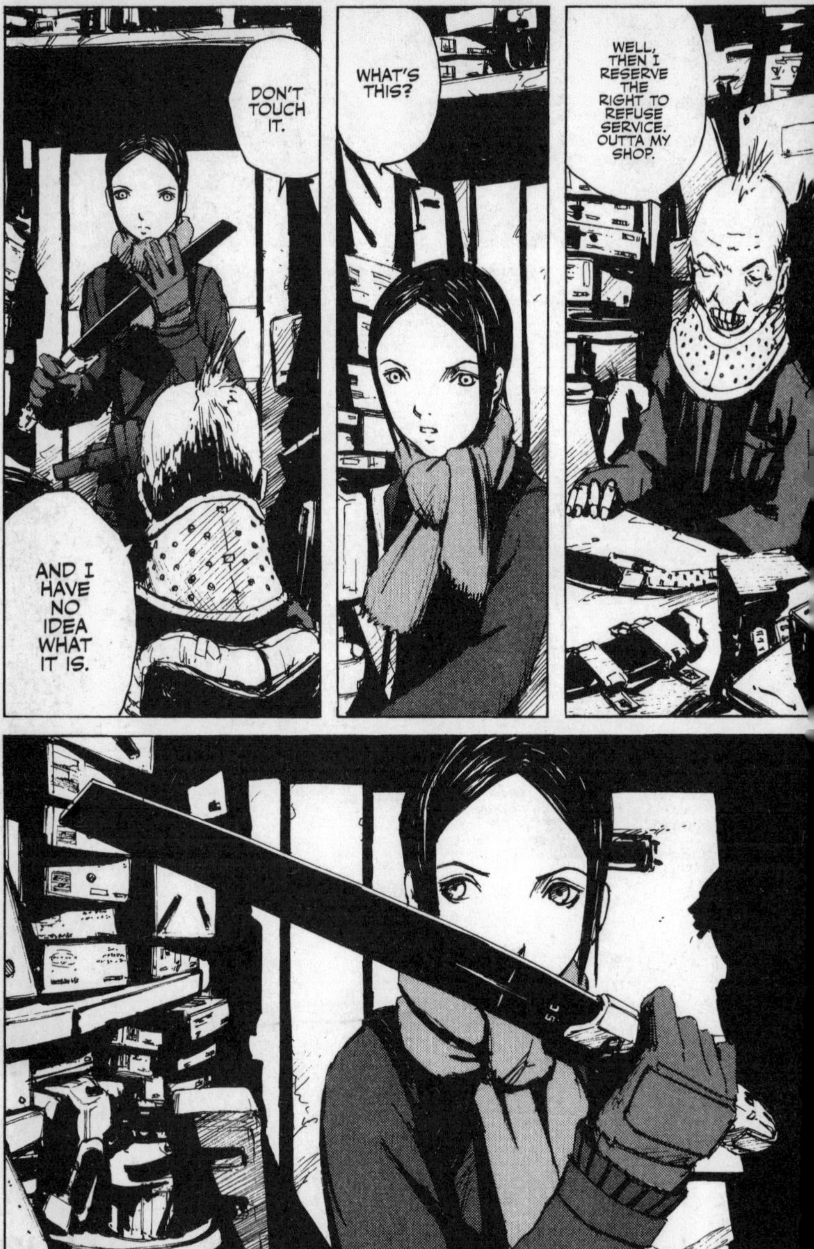
WELL, THEN I RESERVE THE RIGHT TO REFUSE SERVICE. OUTTA MY SHOP.
WHAT'S THIS?
DON'T TOUCH IT.
AND I HAVE NO IDEA WHAT IT IS.

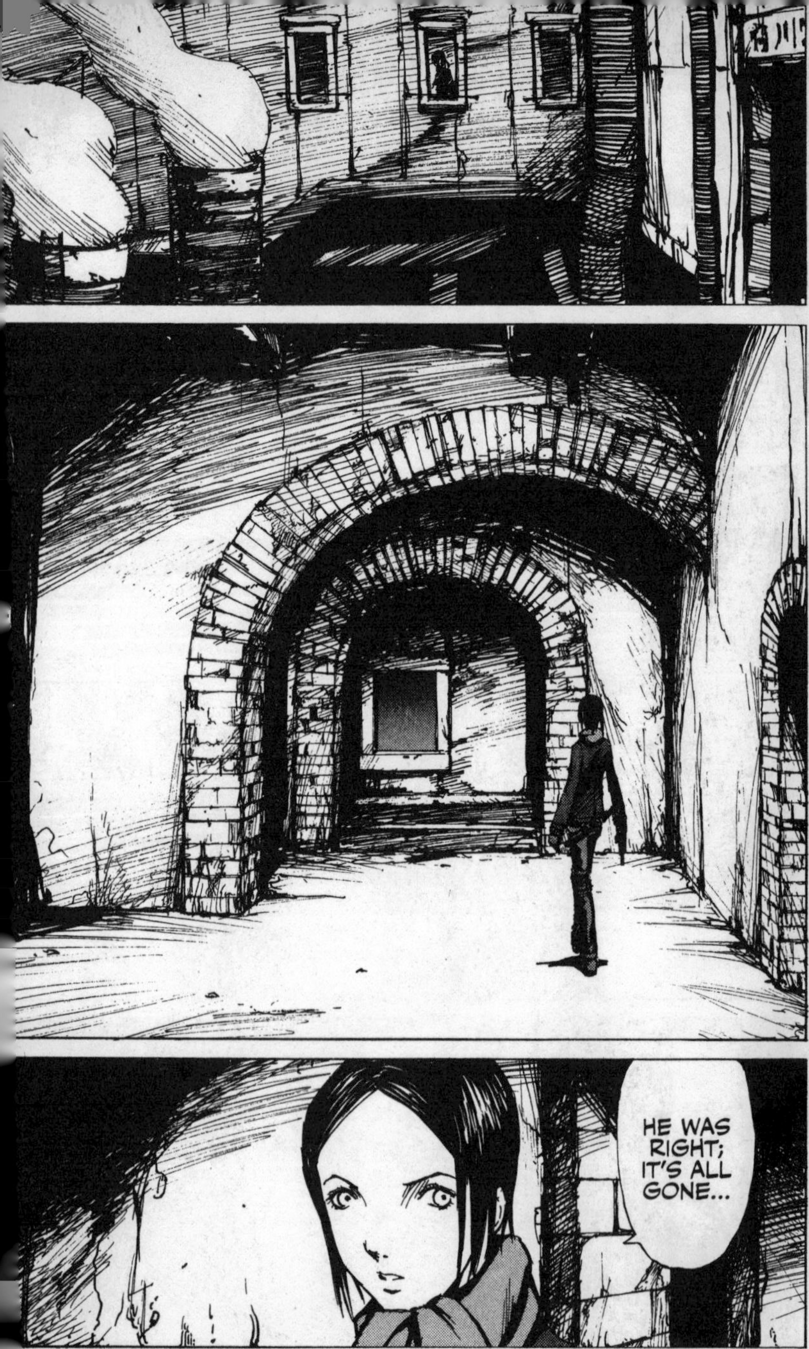
HE WAS RIGHT; IT'S ALL GONE...

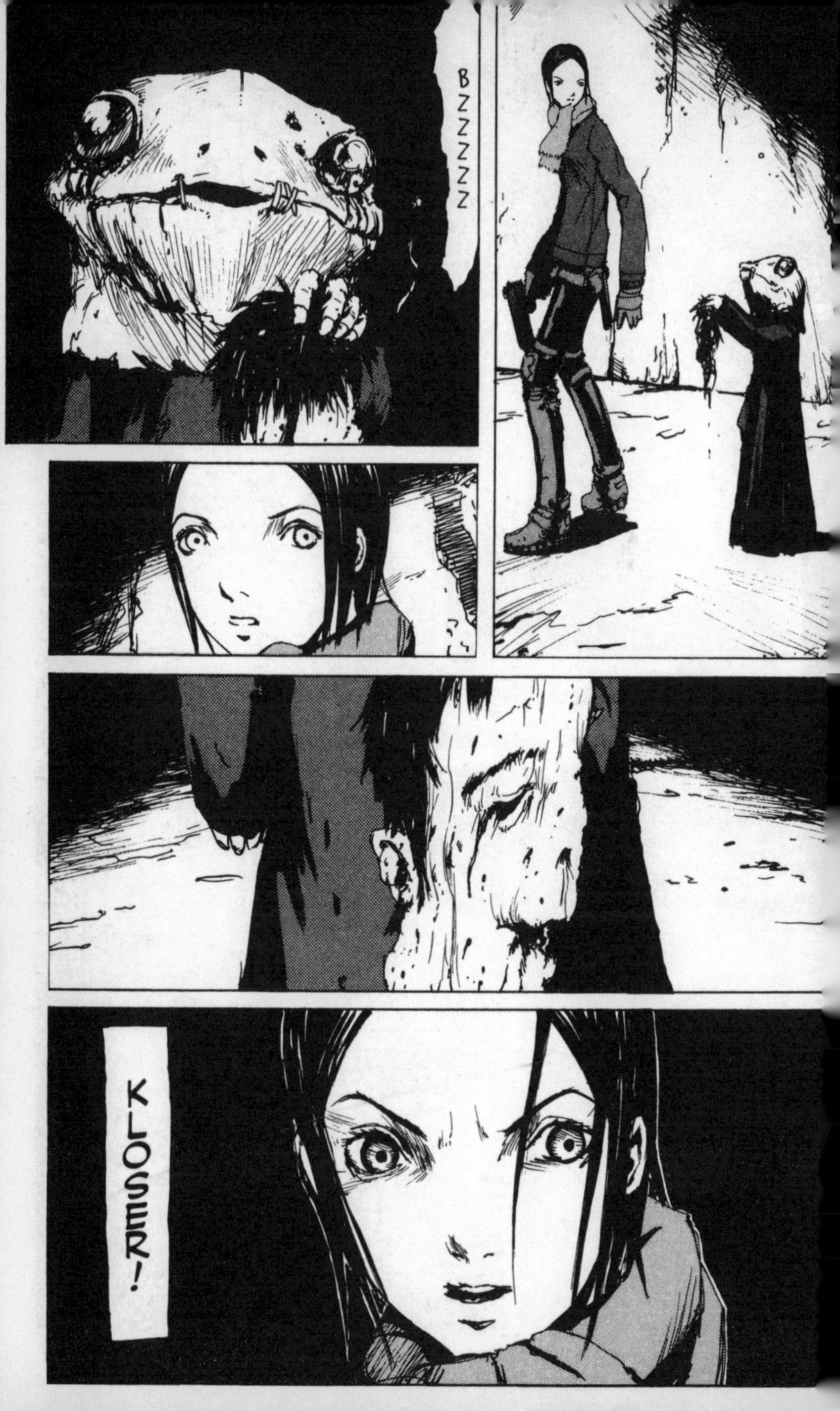
BZZZZZZ
KLOSER!

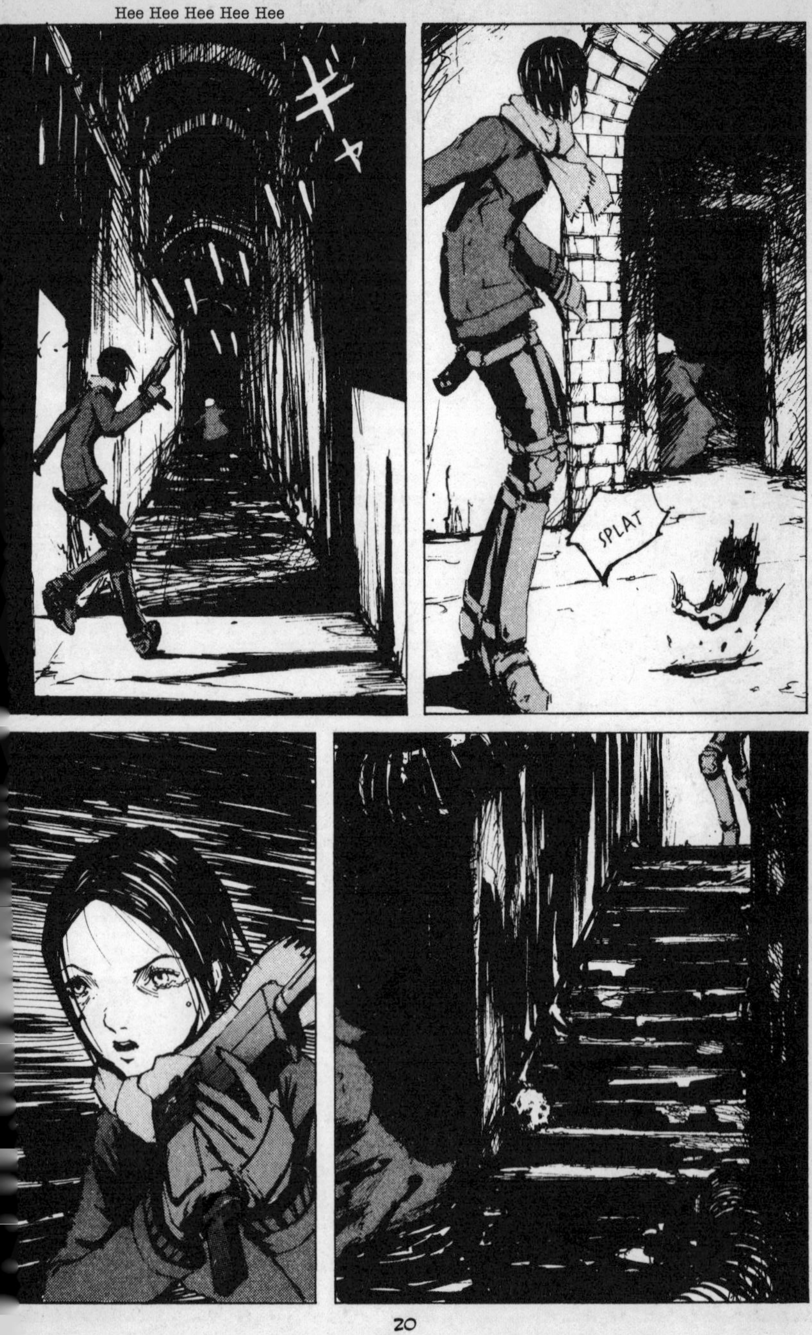
Hee Hee Hee Hee Hee
ギャ
SPLAT

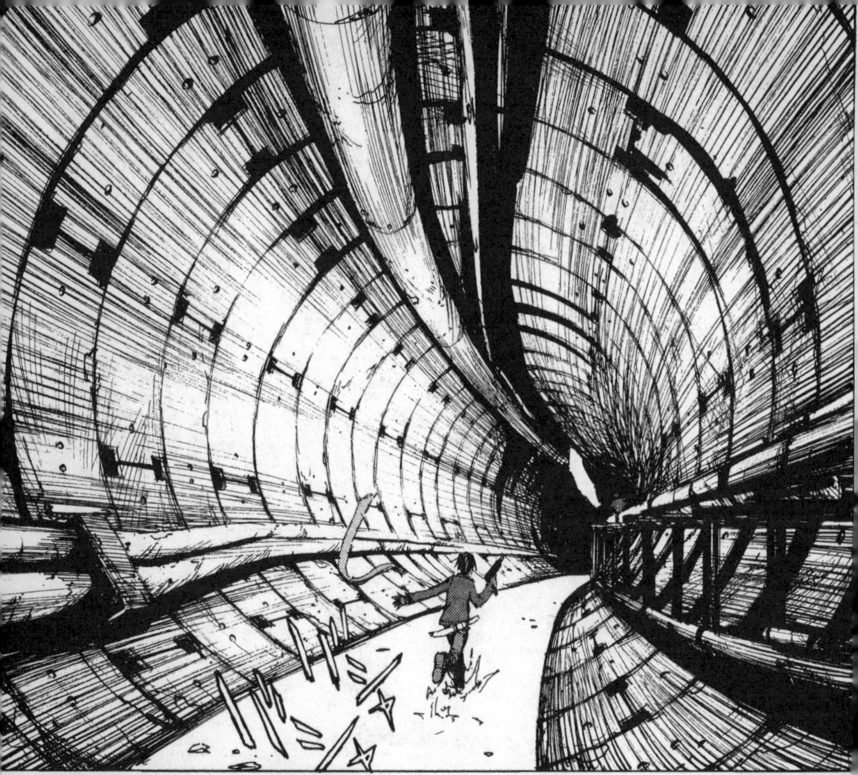
Splash Splash

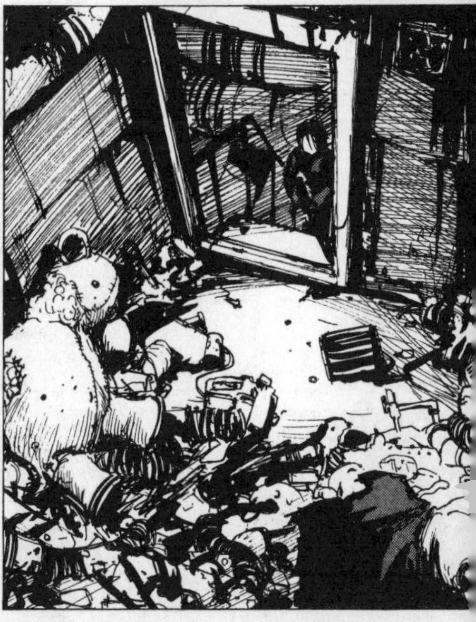

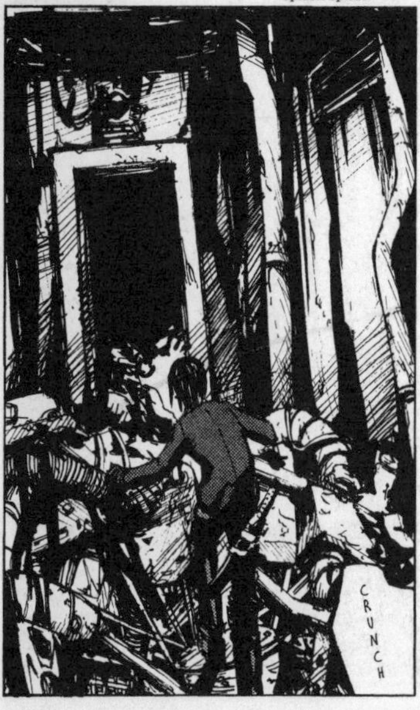
CRUNCH

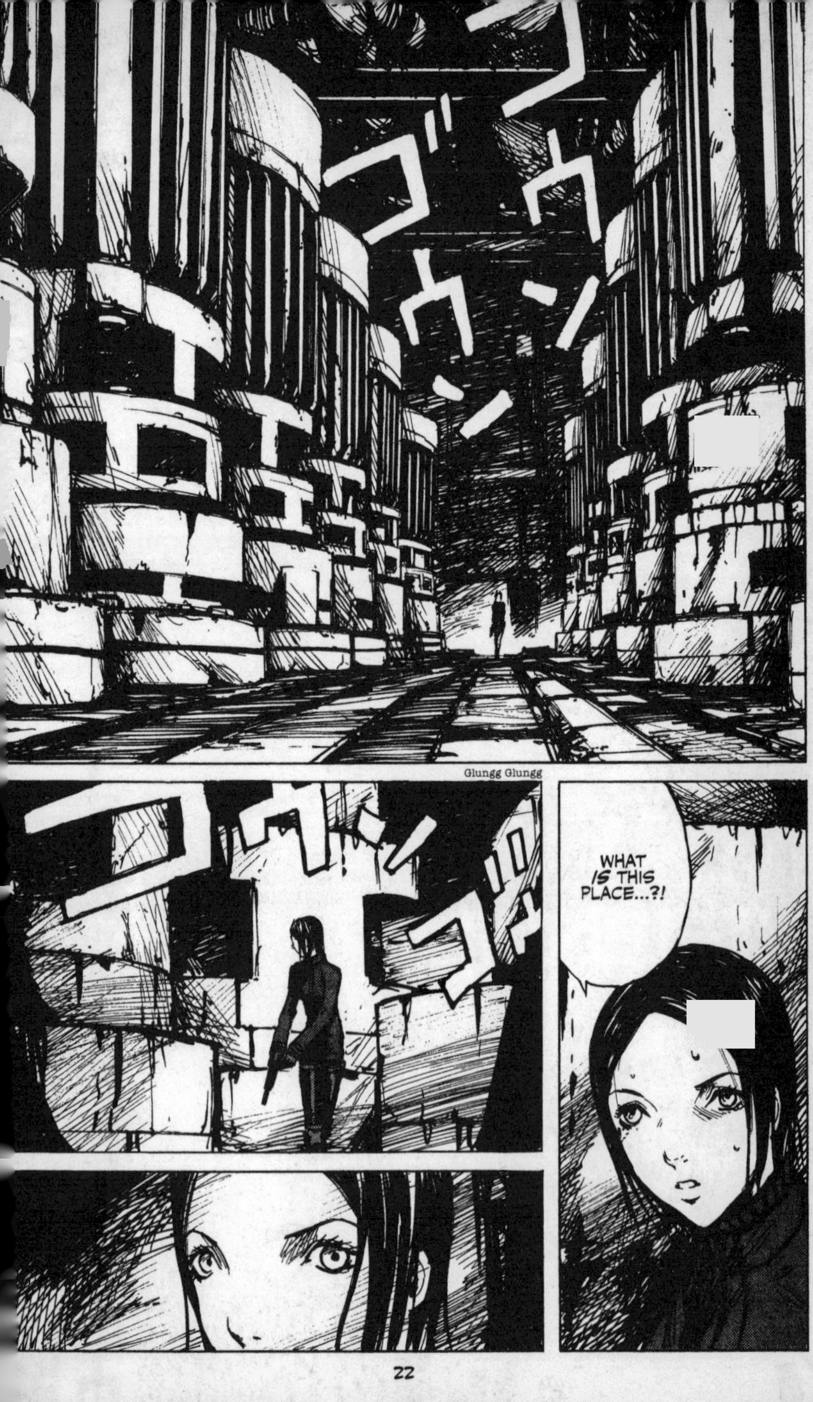
Glungg Glungg
WHAT *IS* THIS PLACE...?!

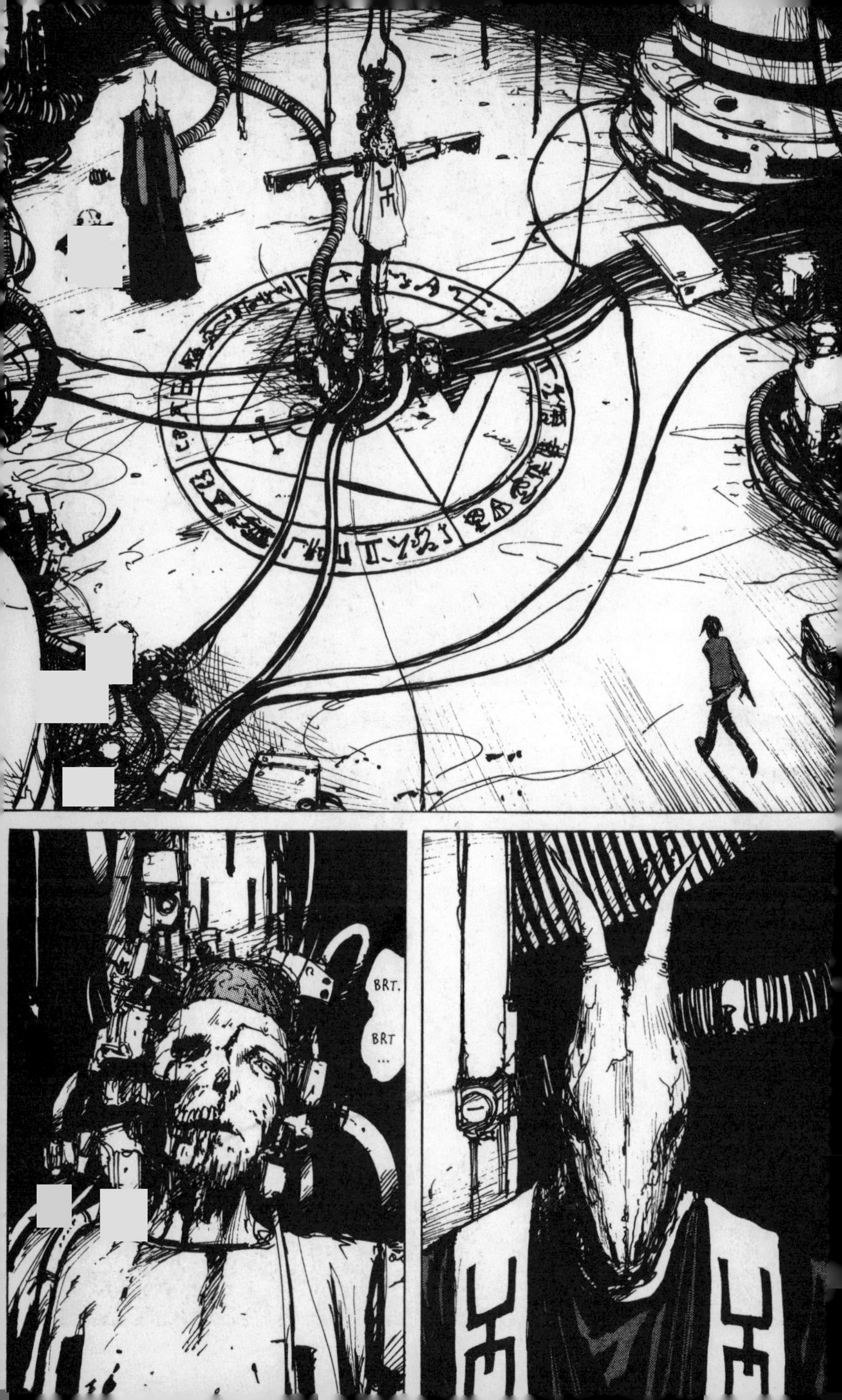
BRT.
BRT
...

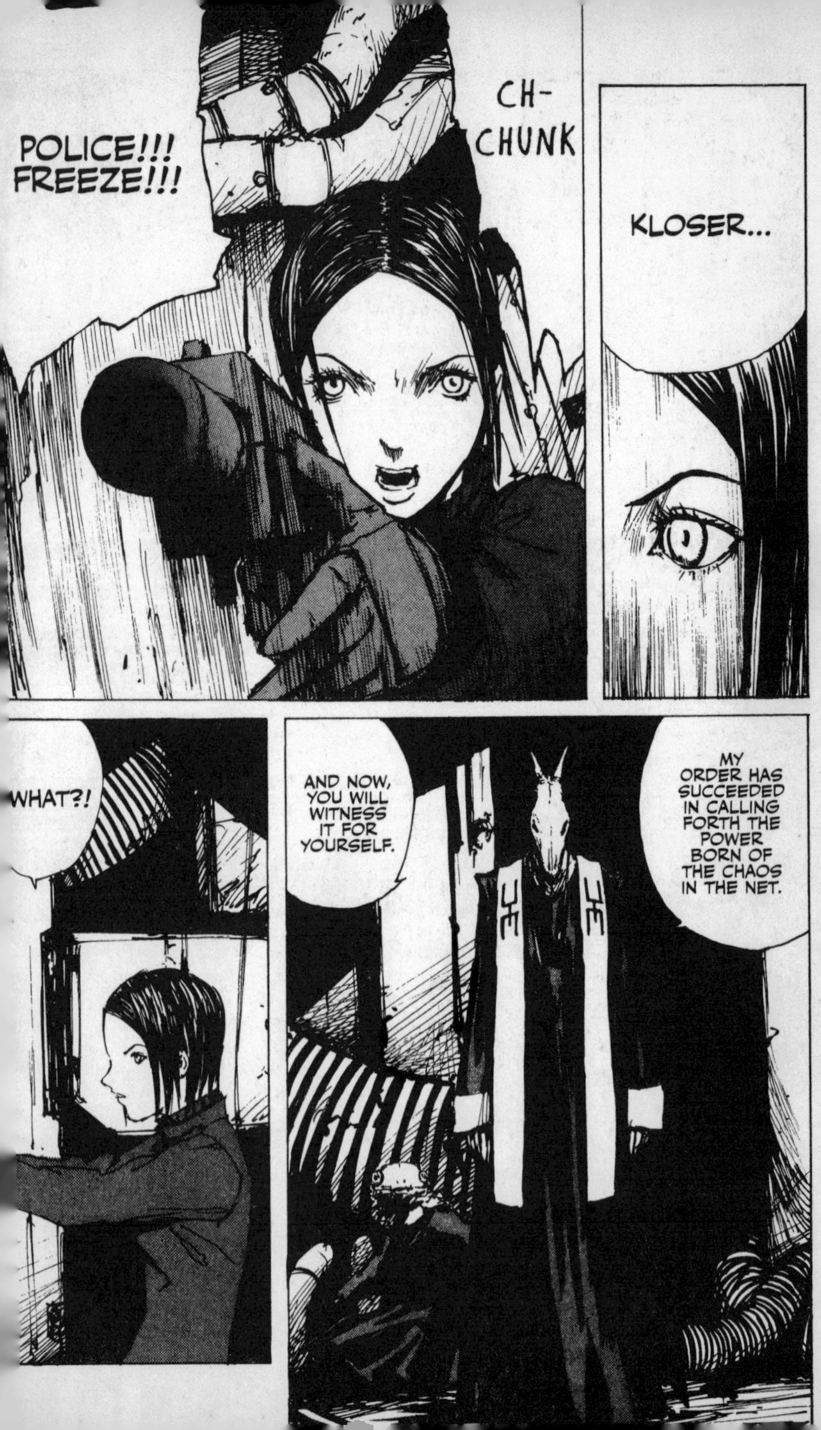
KLOSER...
CH-CHUNK
POLICE!!! FREEZE!!!
MY ORDER HAS SUCCEEDED IN CALLING FORTH THE POWER BORN OF THE CHAOS IN THE NET.
AND NOW, YOU WILL WITNESS IT FOR YOURSELF.
WHAT?!

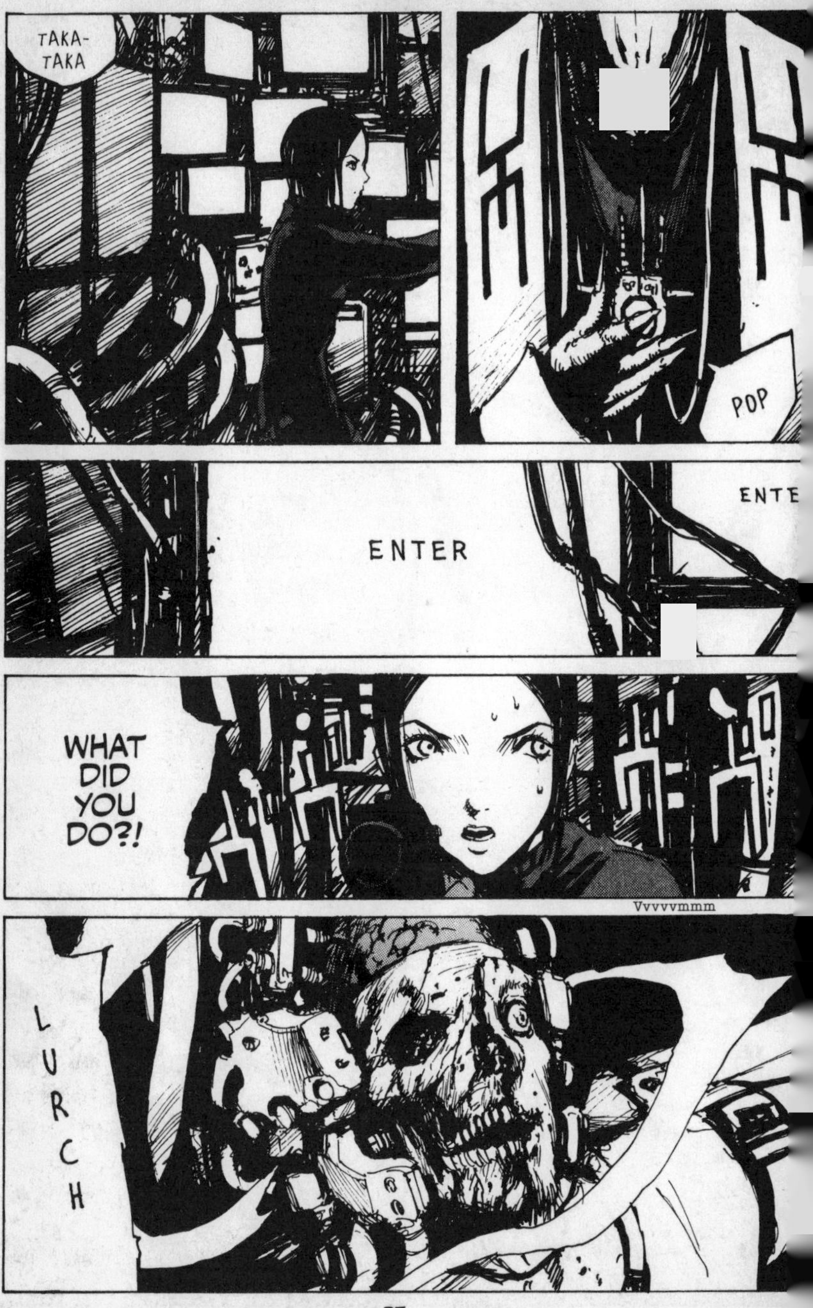
POP
TAKA-TAKA
ENTE
ENTER
WHAT DID YOU DO?!
Vvvvvmmm
LURCH

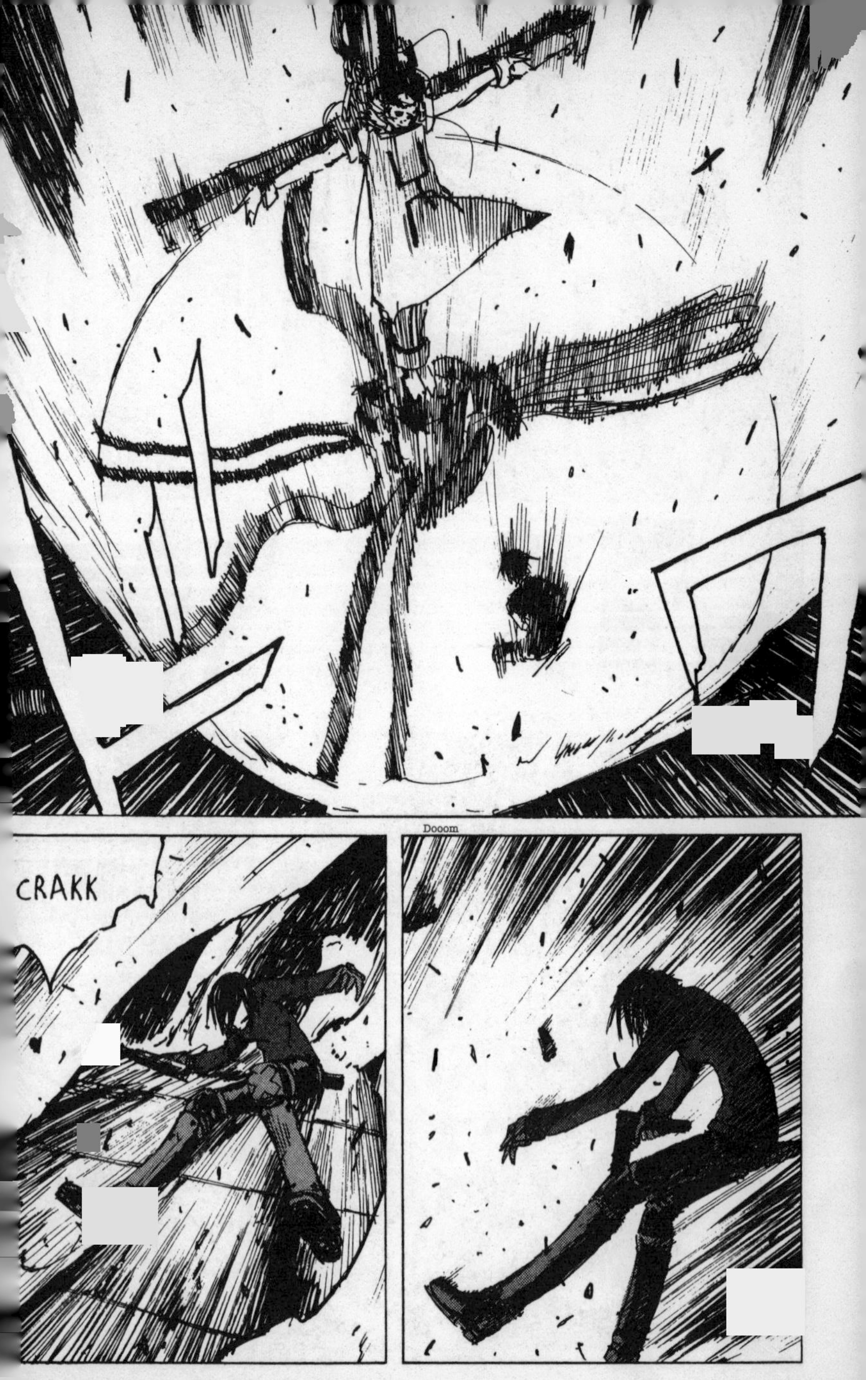
Dooom
CRAKK

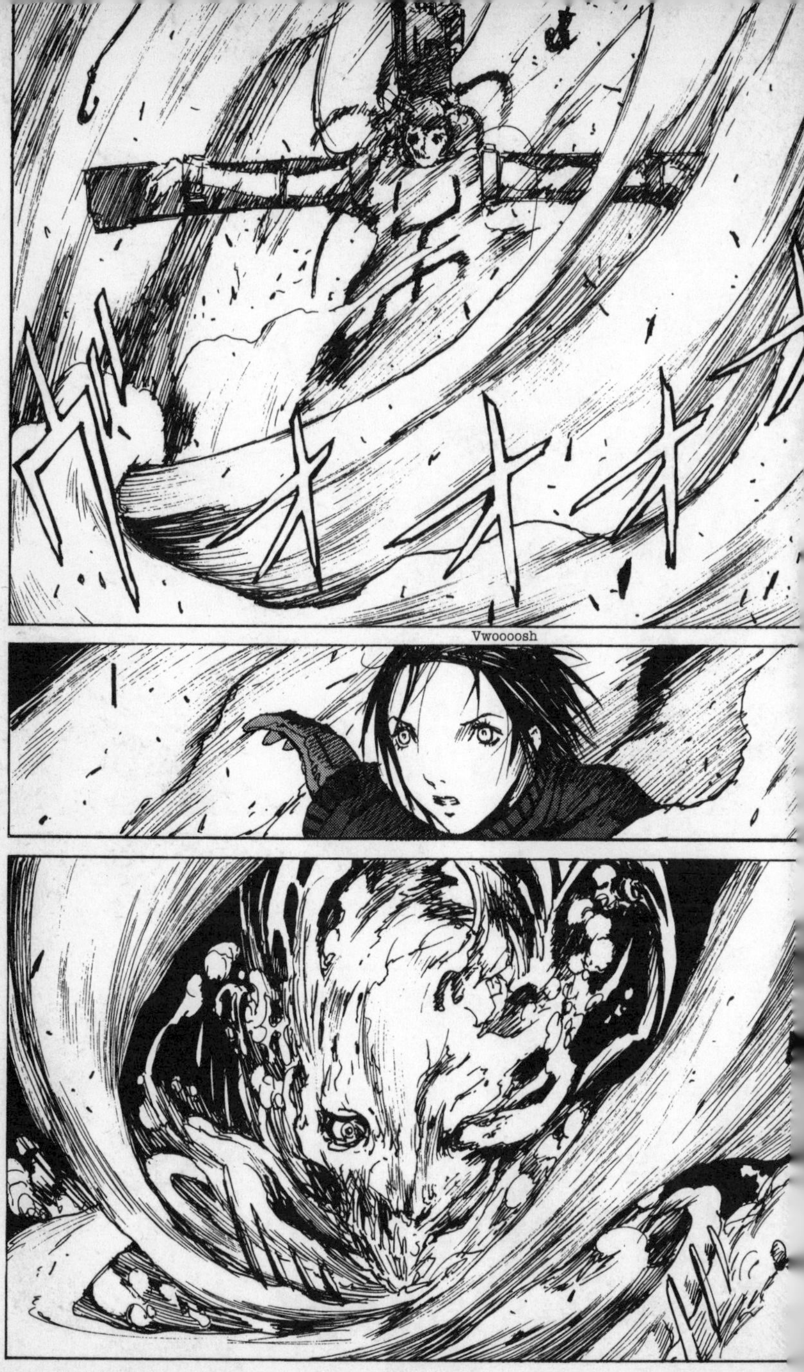
Vwoooosh

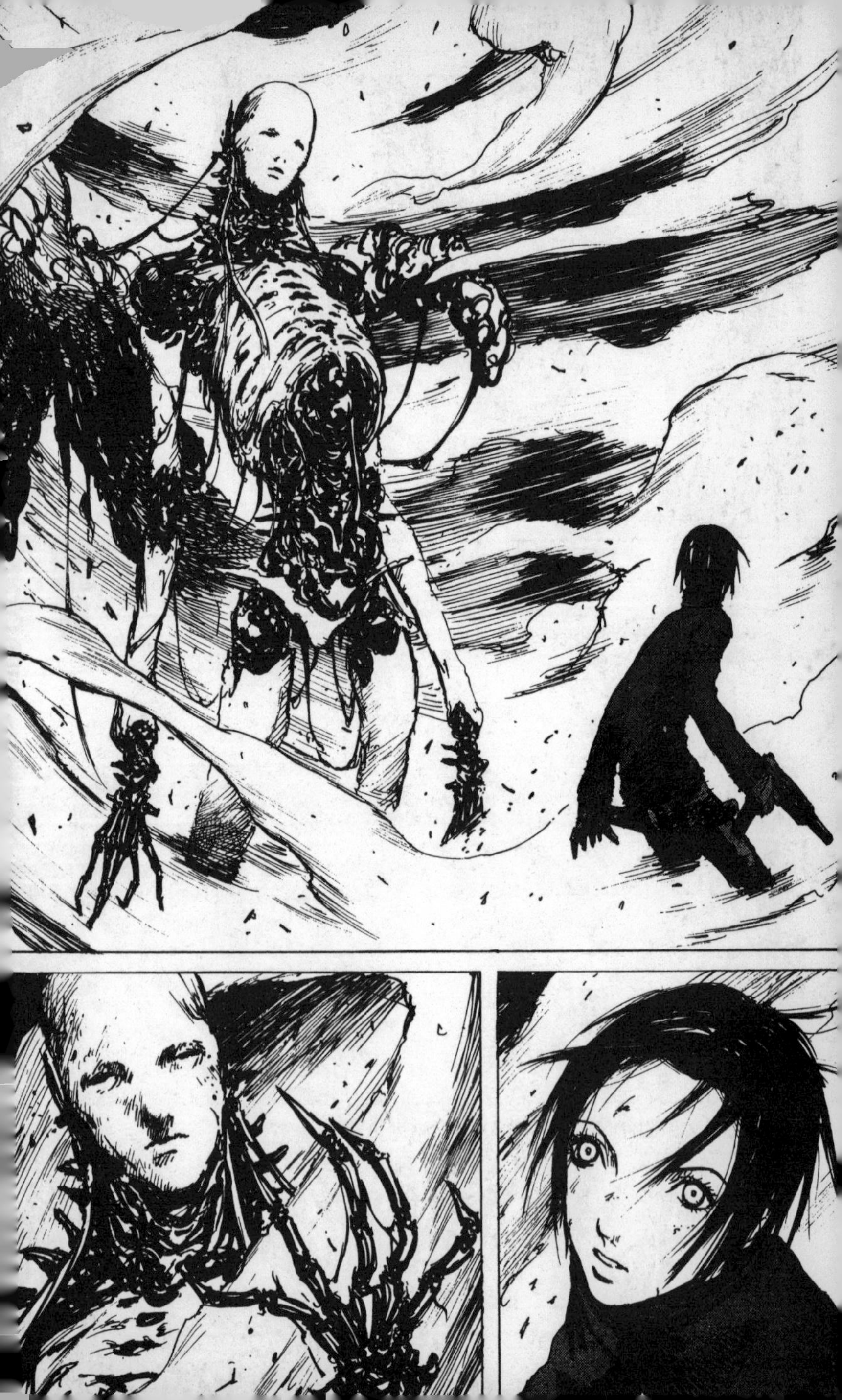

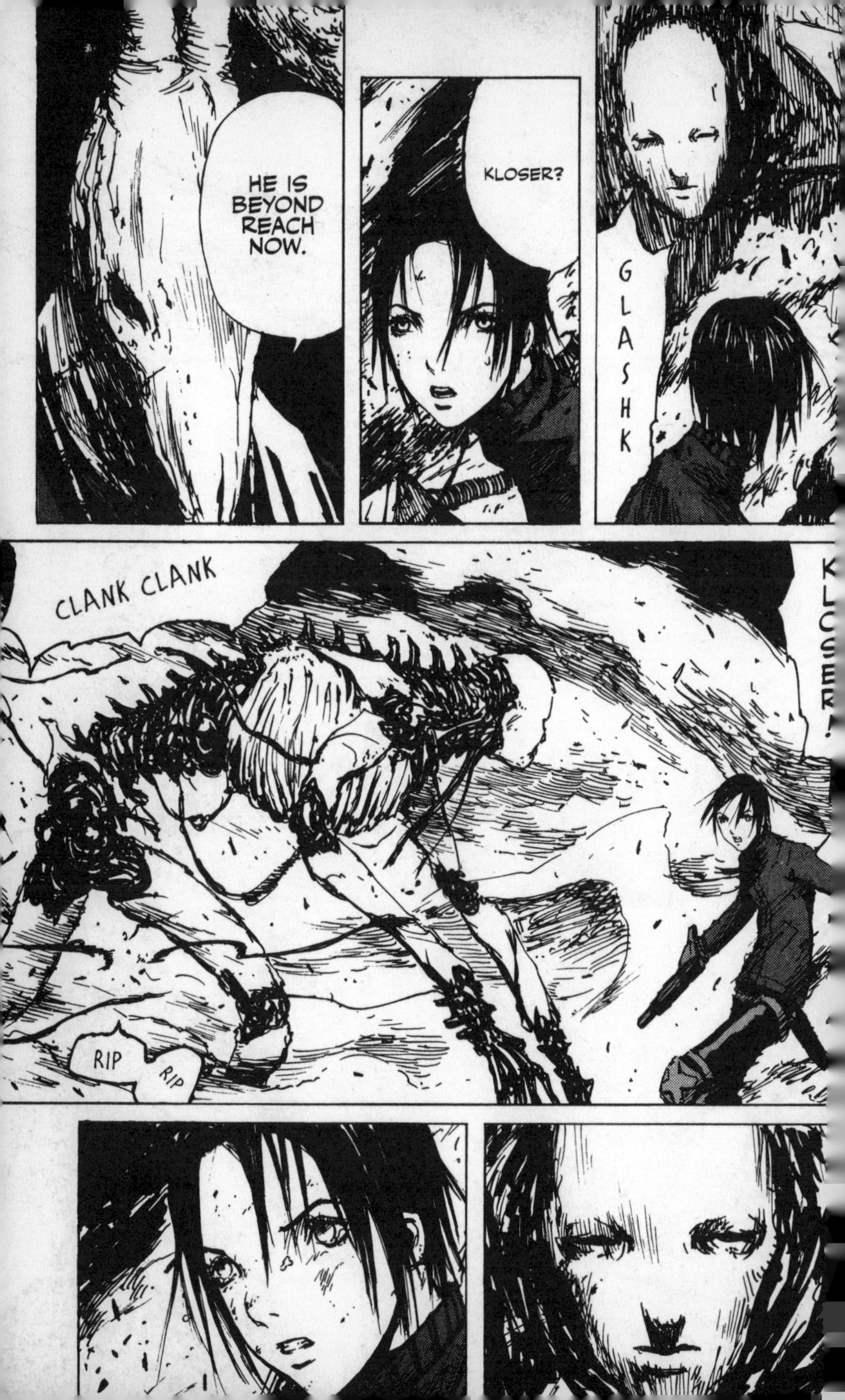
GLASHK
KLOSER?
HE IS BEYOND REACH NOW.
KLOSER!
CLANK CLANK
RIP
RIP

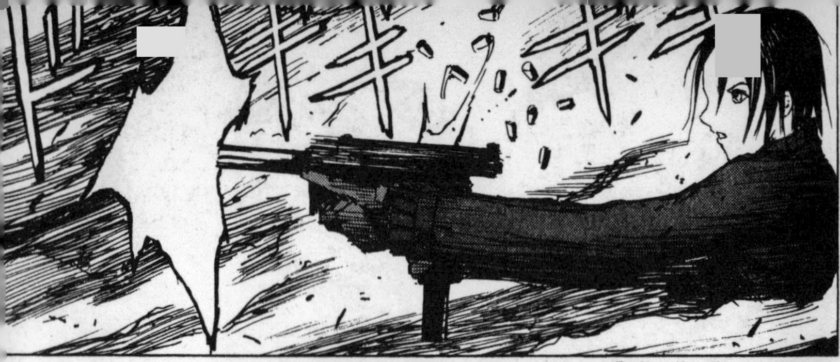
Brattarattaratta

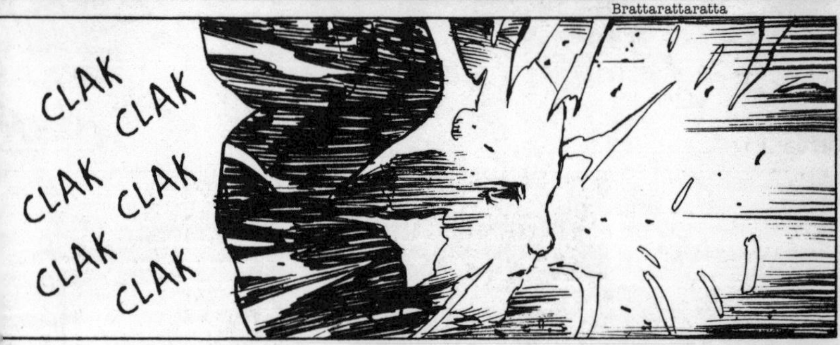
CLAK
CLAK
CLAK
CLAK
CLAK
CLAK

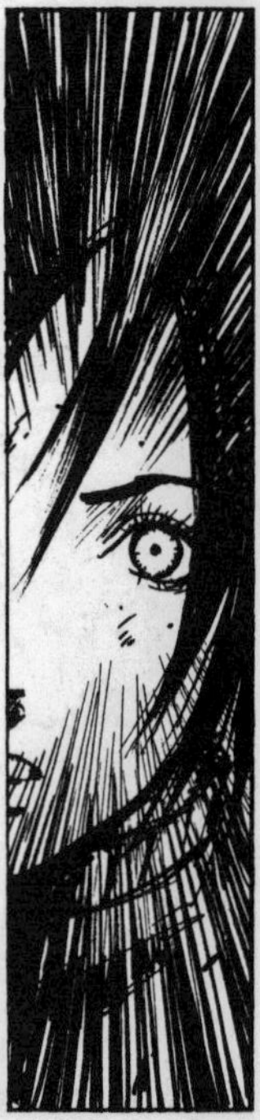

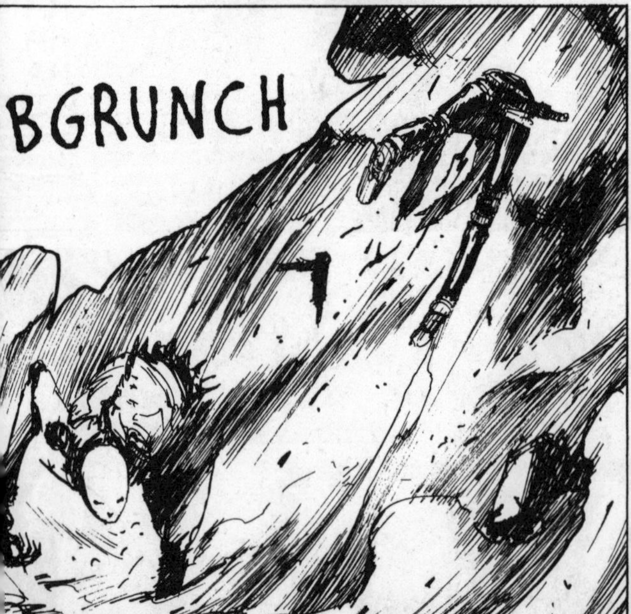
BGRUNCH

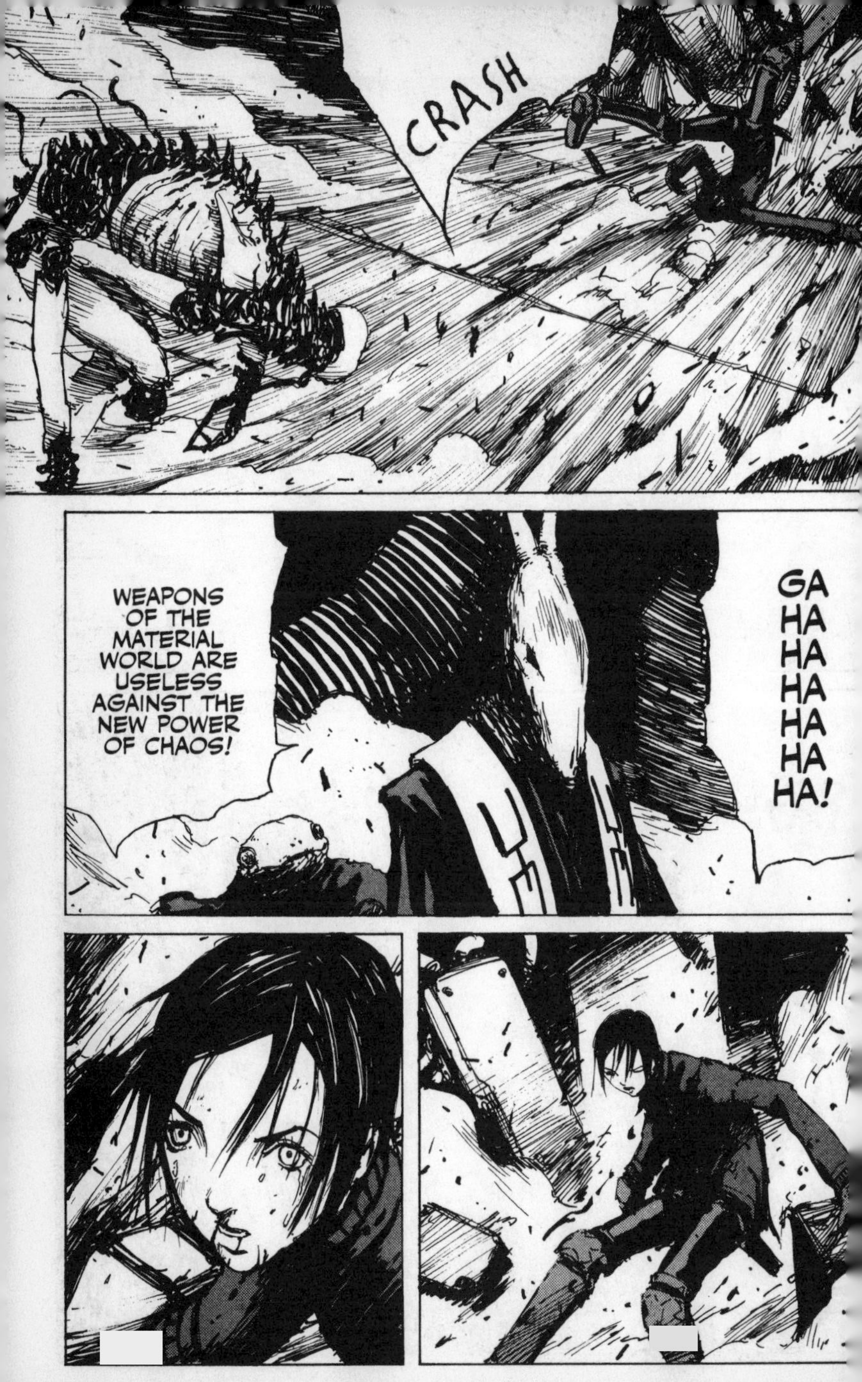
CRASH
GA HA HA HA HA HA HA!
WEAPONS OF THE MATERIAL WORLD ARE USELESS AGAINST THE NEW POWER OF CHAOS!

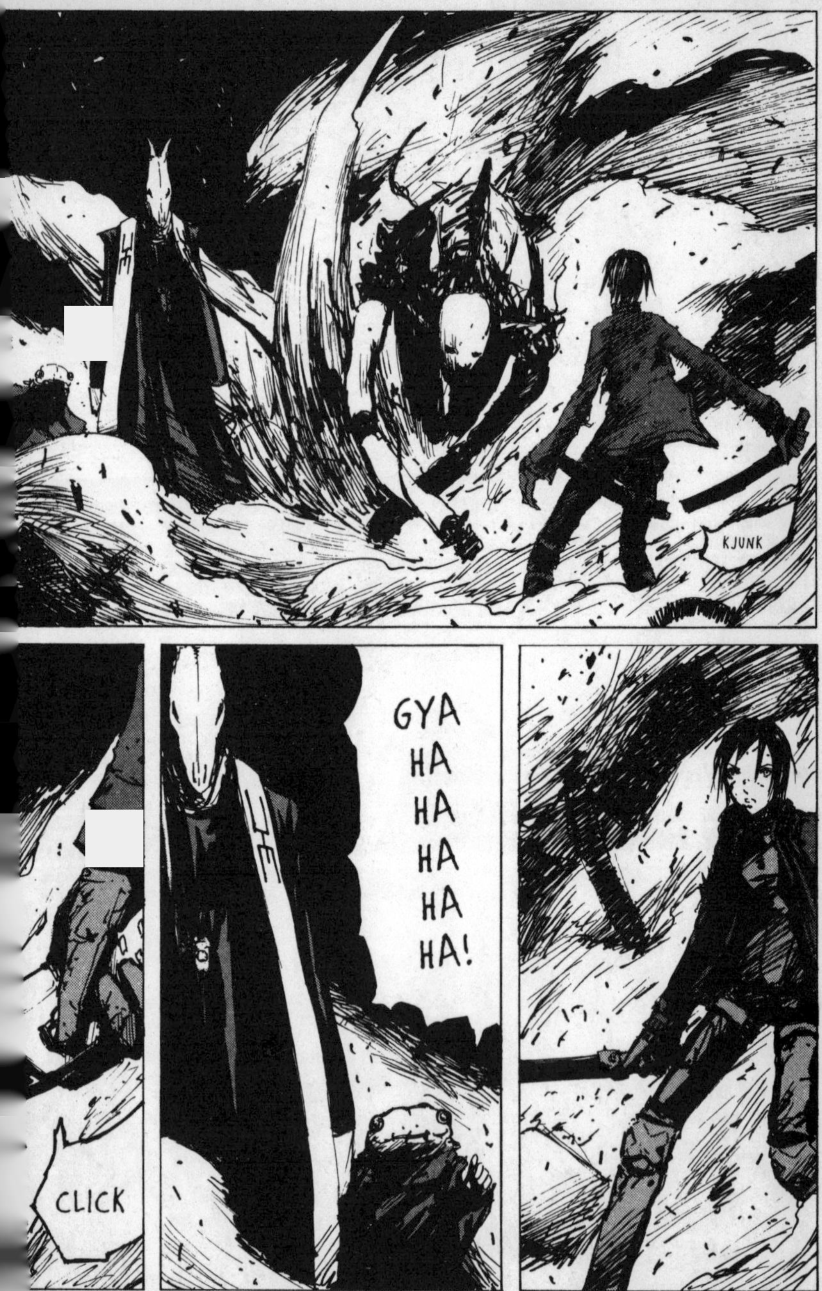
KJUNK
GYA HA HA HA HA HA!
CLICK

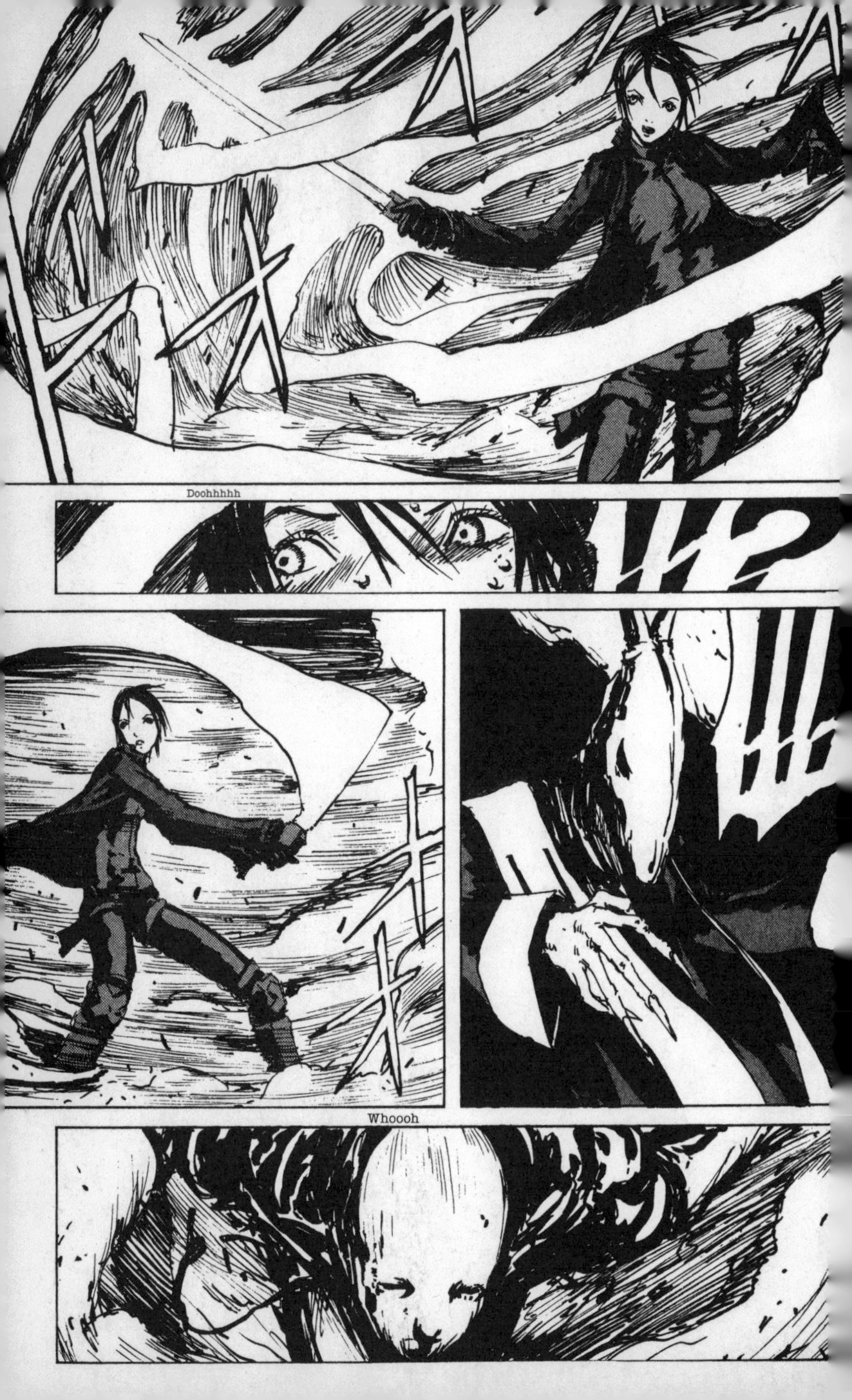
Doohhhhh
!!?
!!!
Whoooh

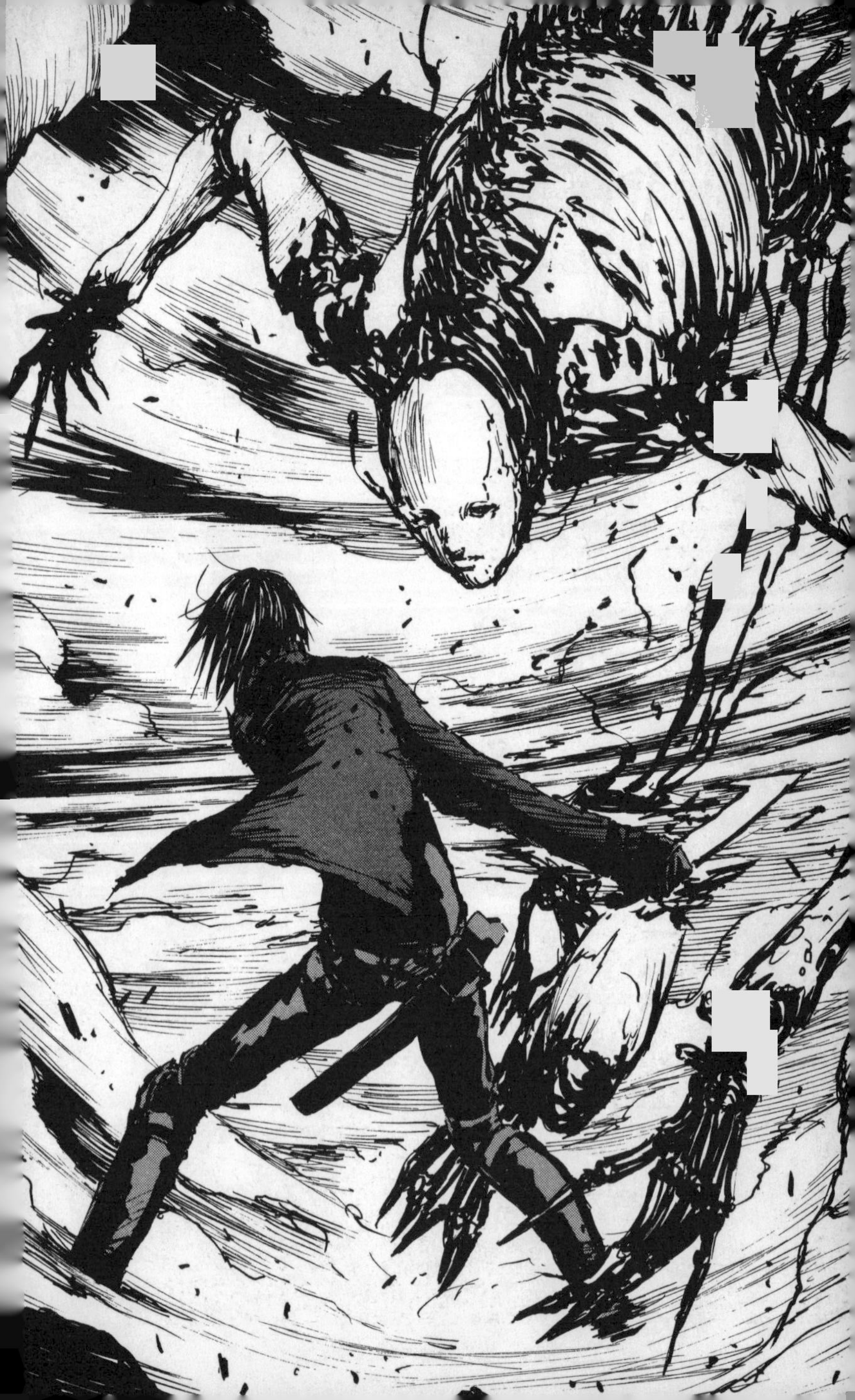

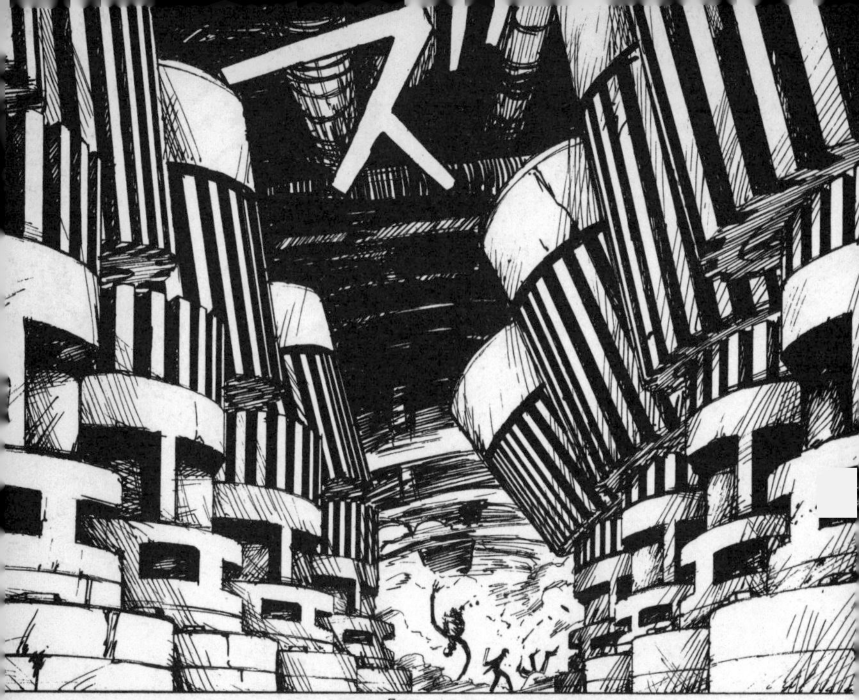
ス

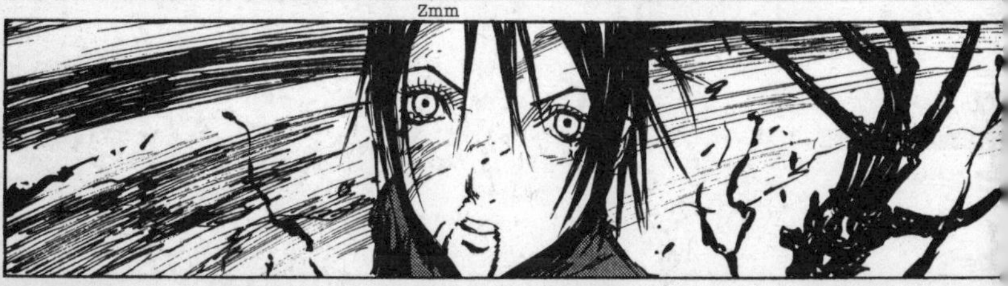
Zmm

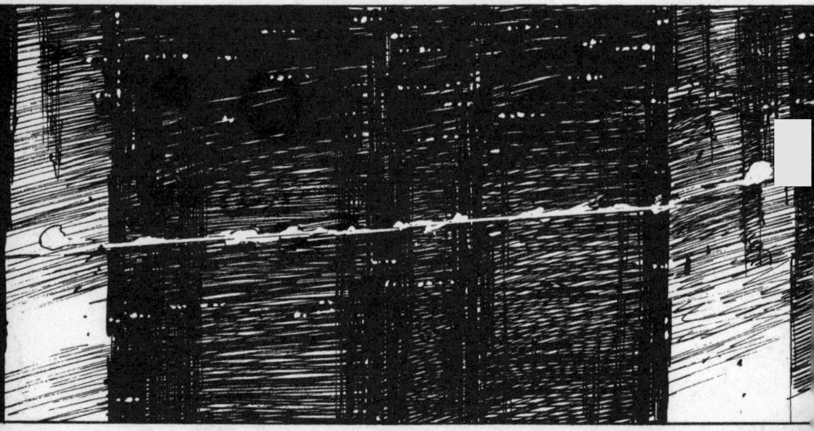

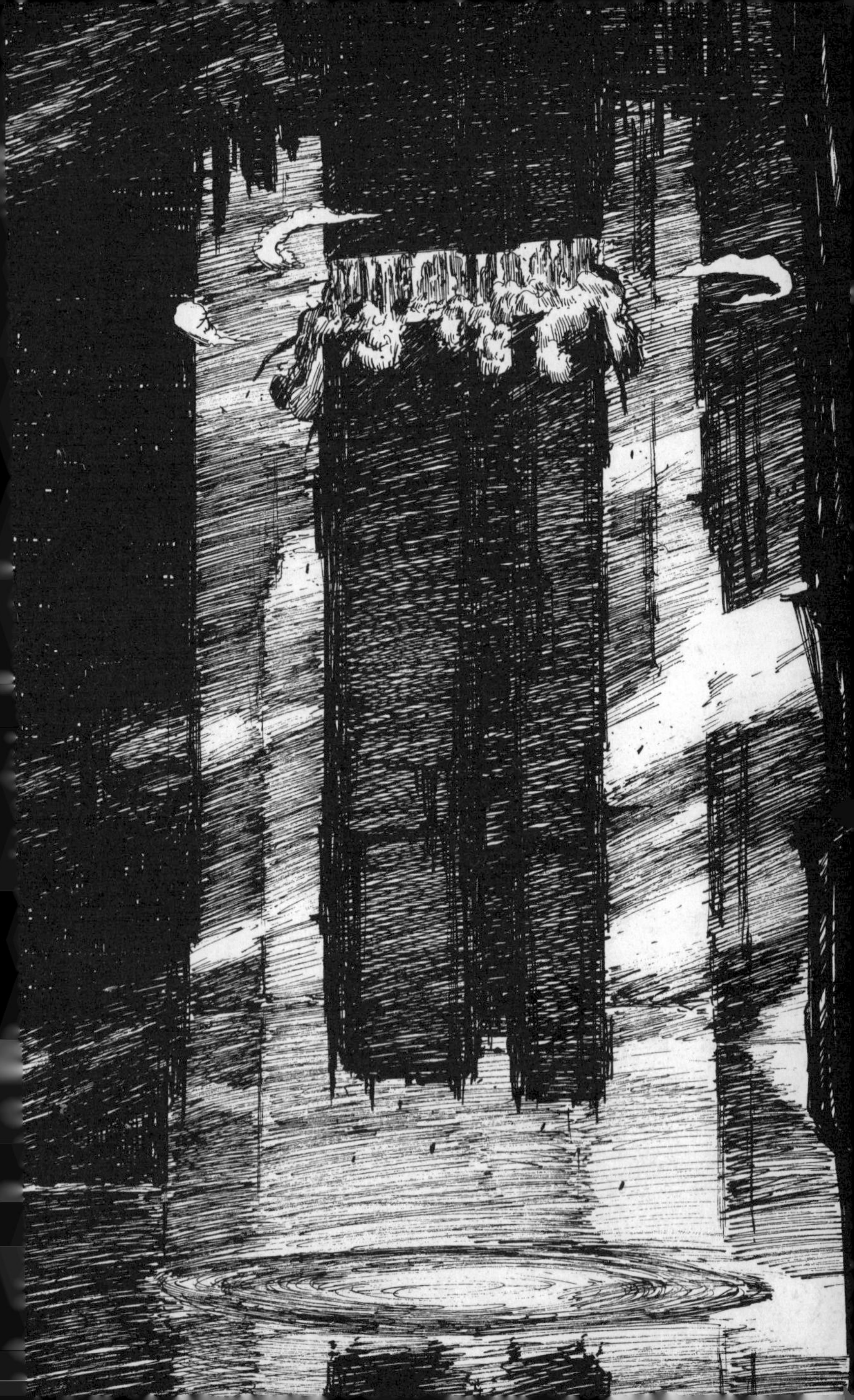

B-b-bmmm

Gohhh

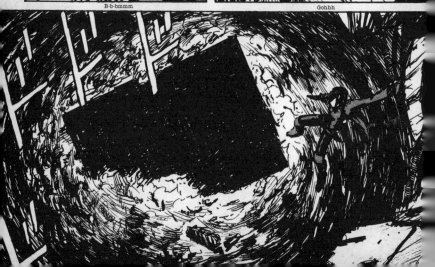

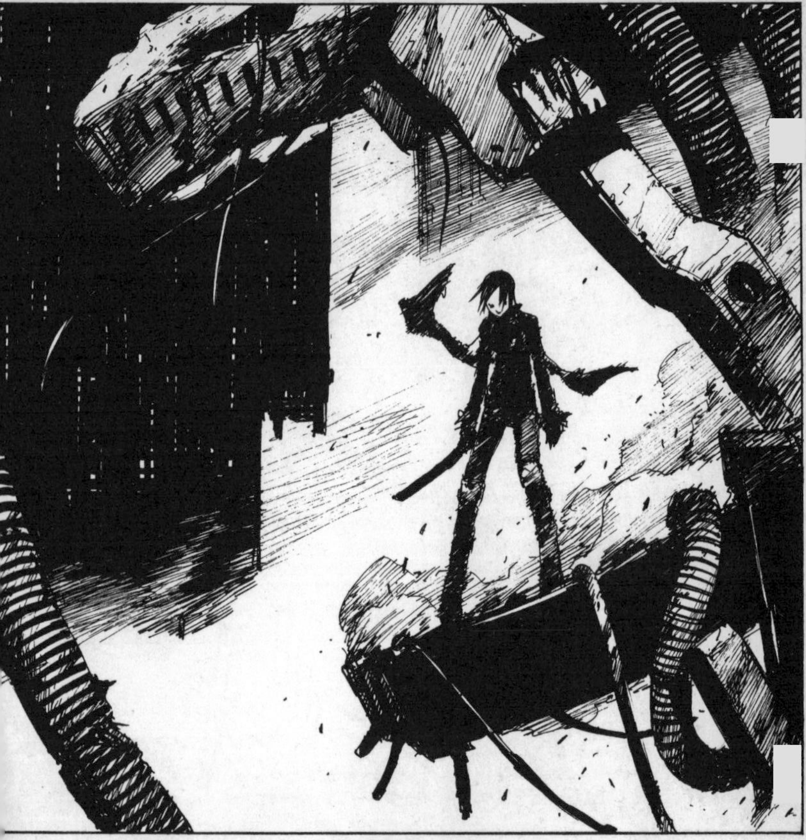

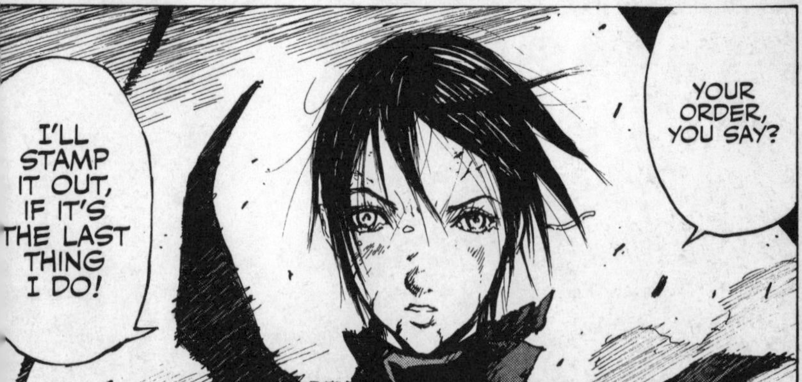
YOUR ORDER, YOU SAY?
I'LL STAMP IT OUT, IF IT'S THE LAST THING I DO!

Chapter 1 Demonic Invocation ~End~

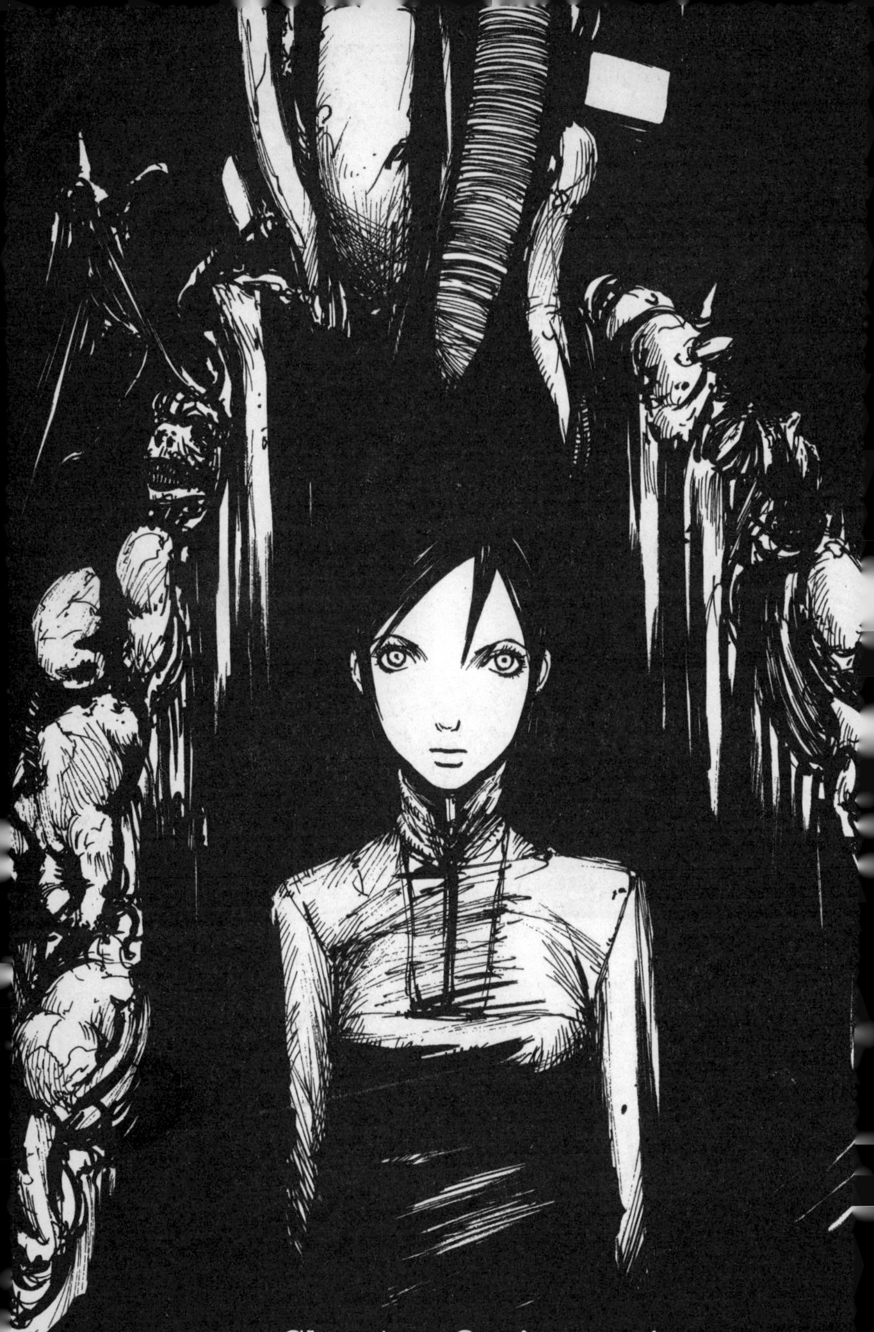

Chapter 2 Assassins
第二章 暗殺者

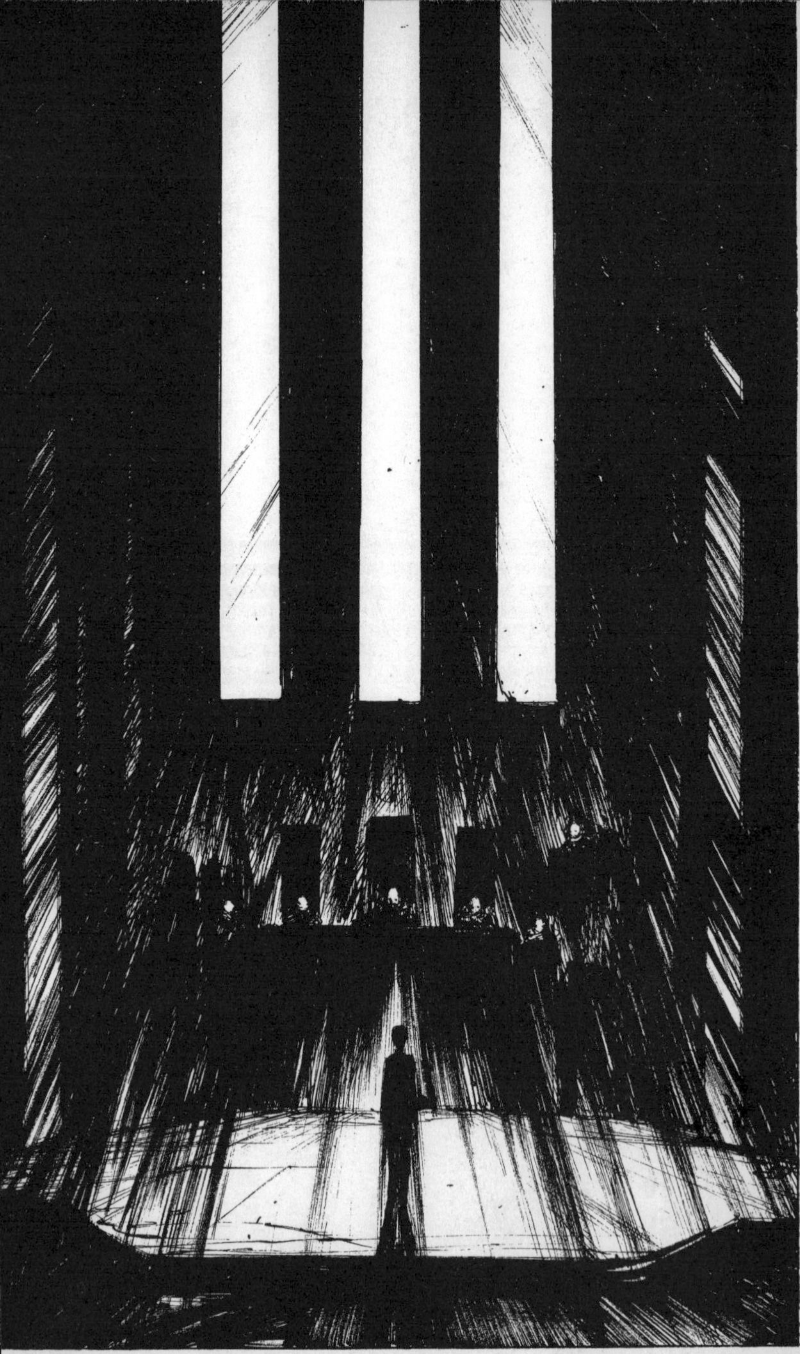

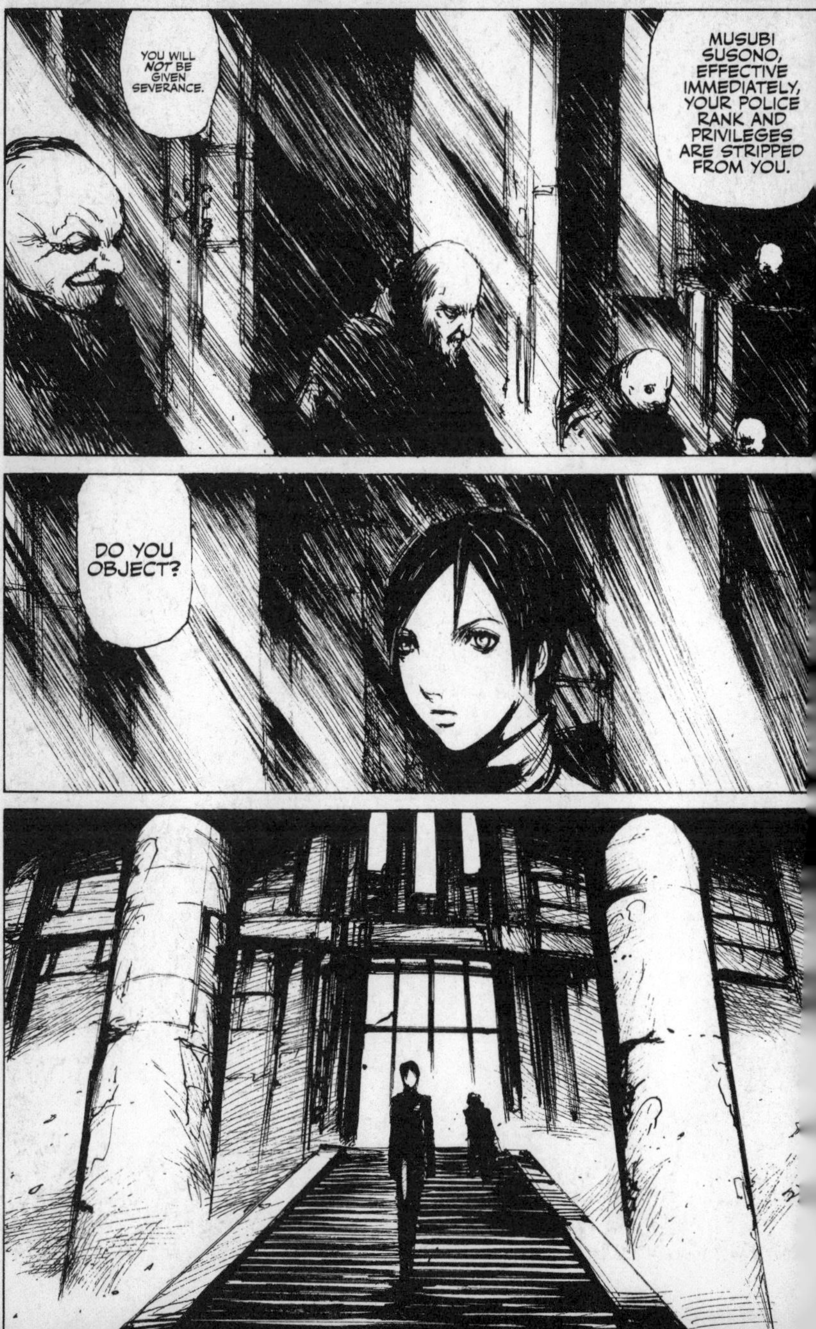
MUSUBI SUSONO, EFFECTIVE IMMEDIATELY, YOUR POLICE RANK AND PRIVILEGES ARE STRIPPED FROM YOU.
YOU WILL NOT BE GIVEN SEVERANCE.
DO YOU OBJECT?

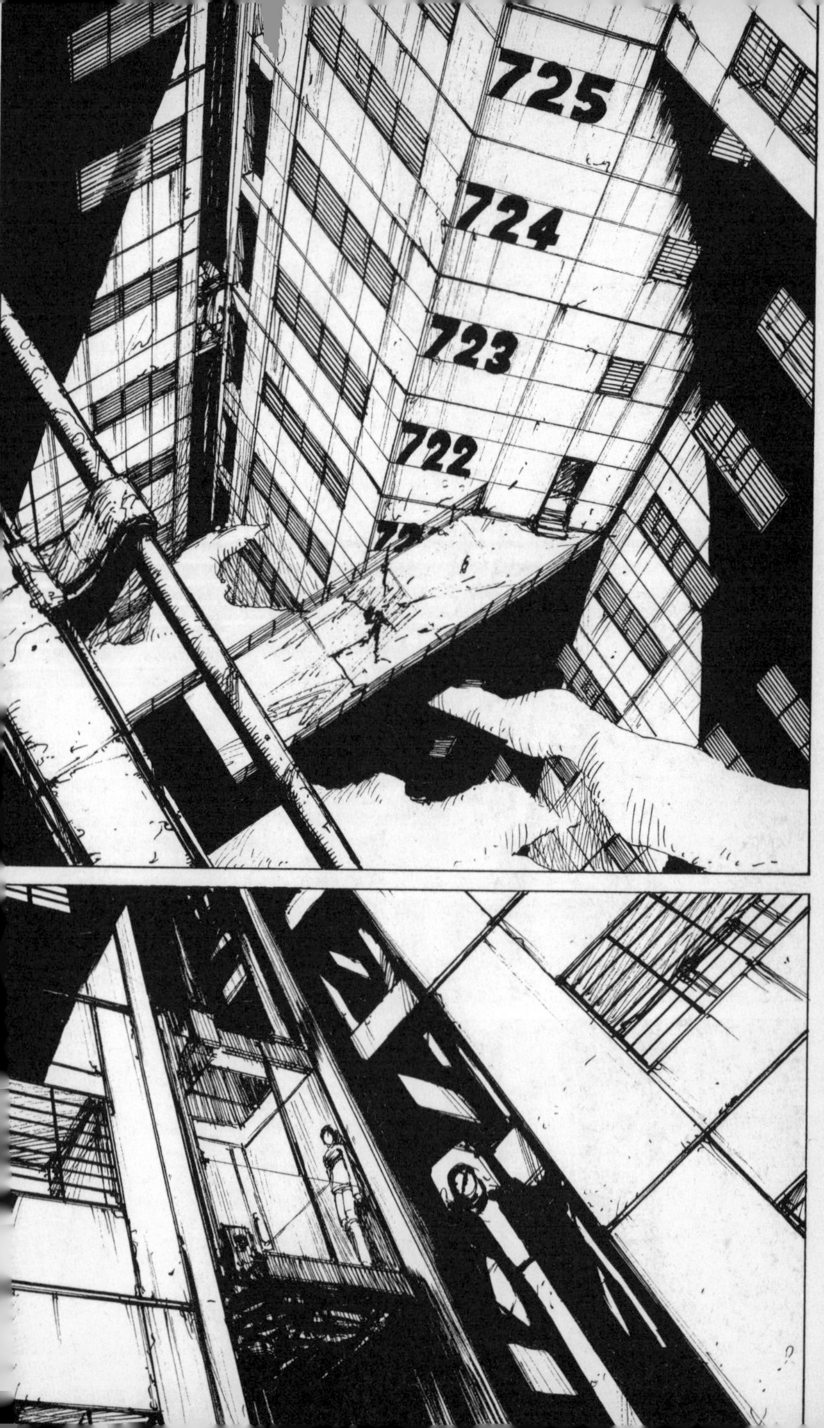
725
724
723
722

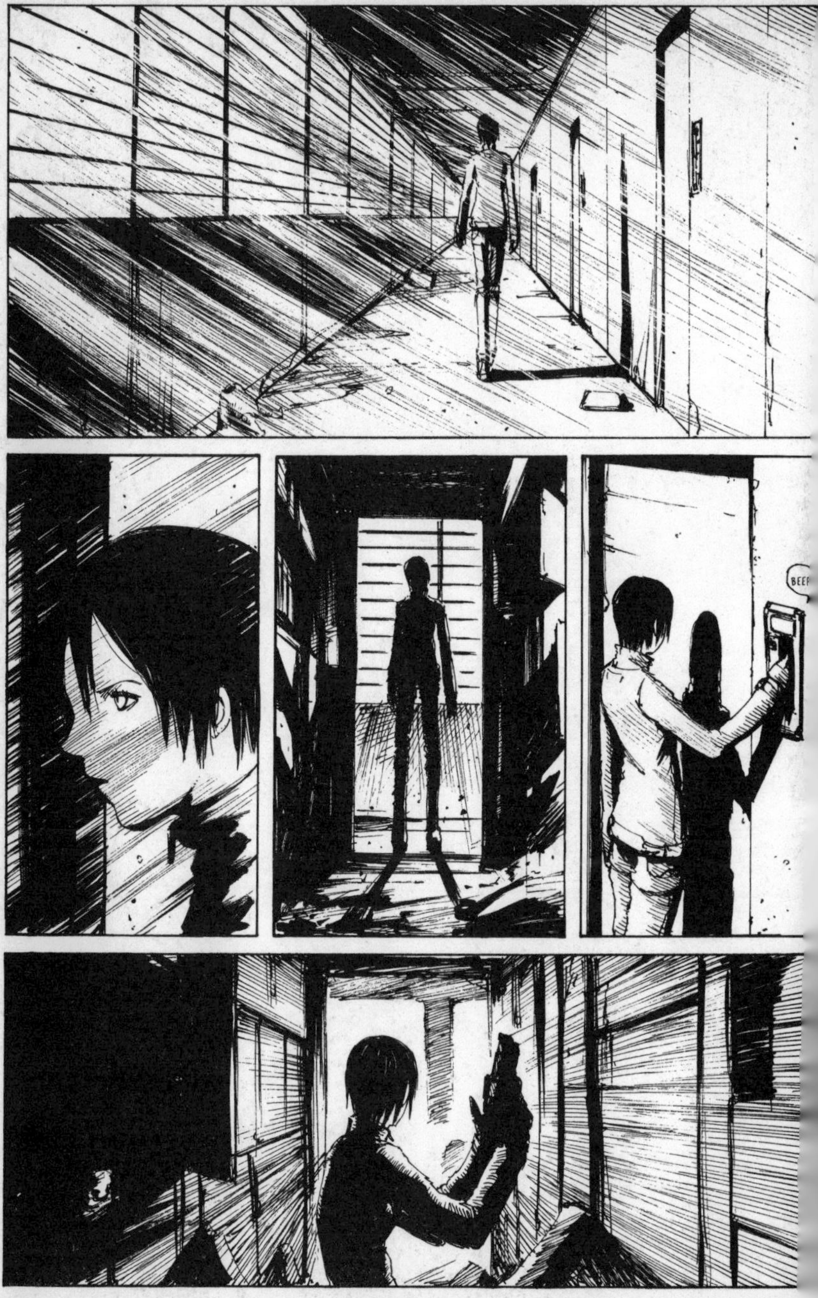
BEE

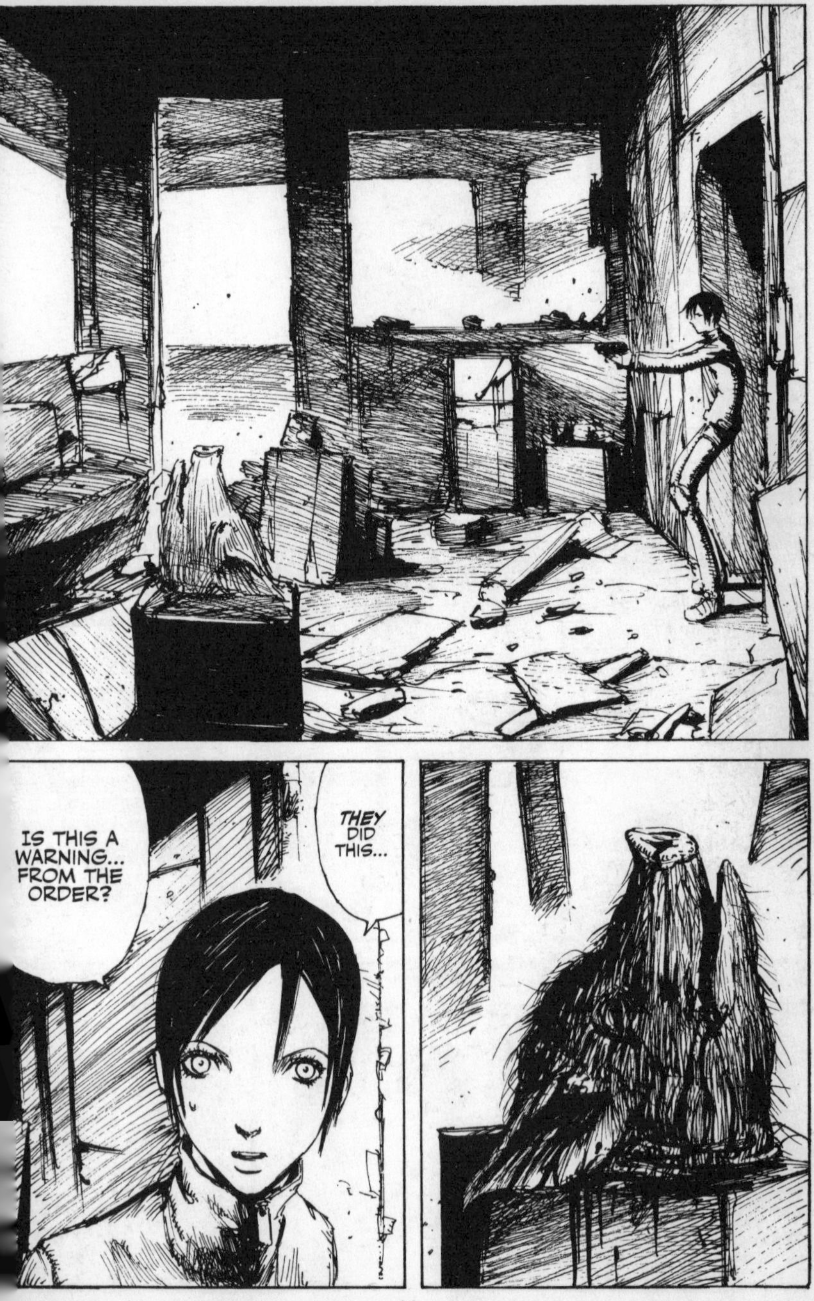
THEY DID THIS...
IS THIS A WARNING... FROM THE ORDER?

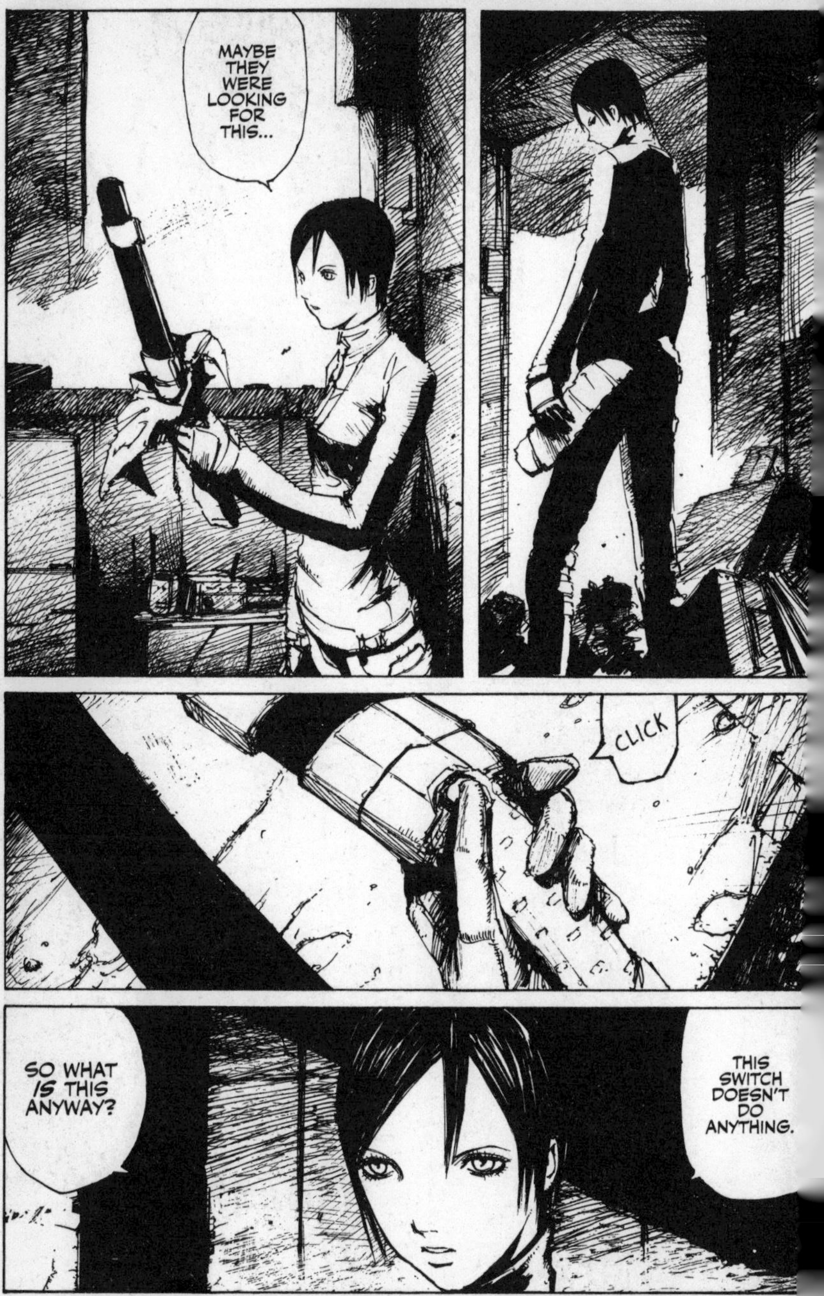
MAYBE THEY WERE LOOKING FOR THIS...
CLICK
THIS SWITCH DOESN'T DO ANYTHING.
SO WHAT *IS* THIS ANYWAY?

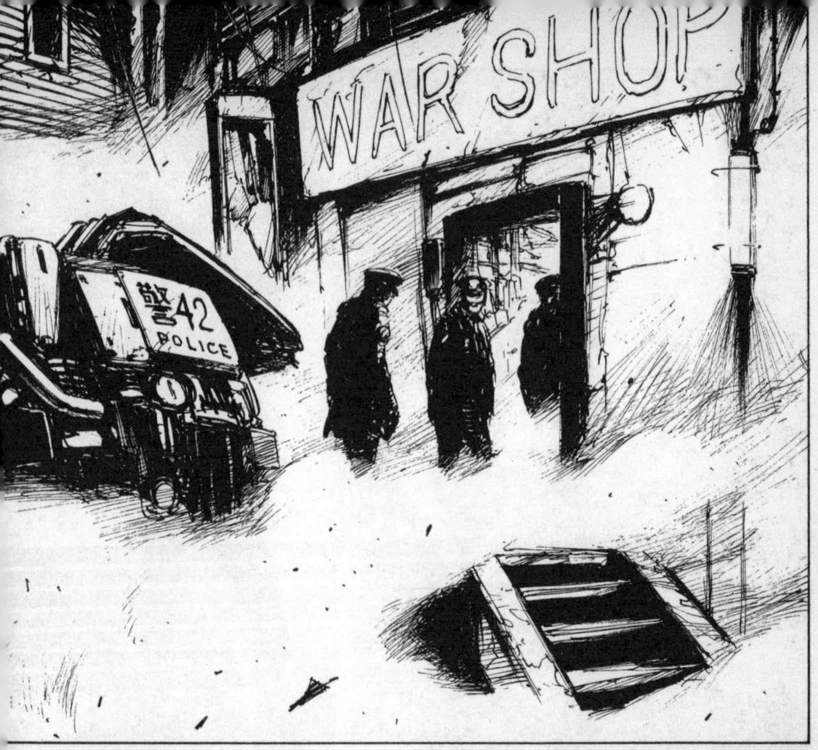
WAR SHOP
警42
POLICE

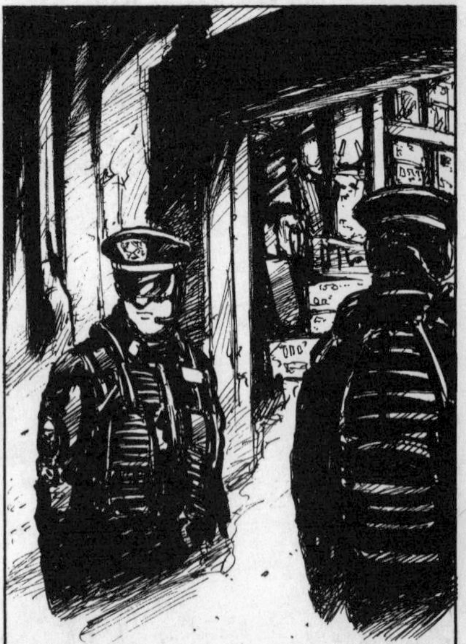

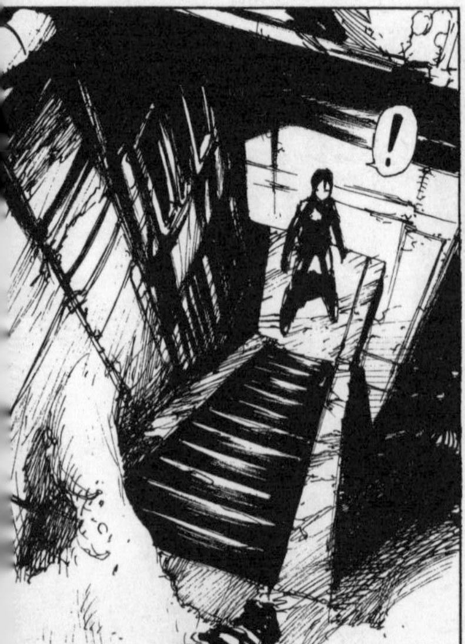
!

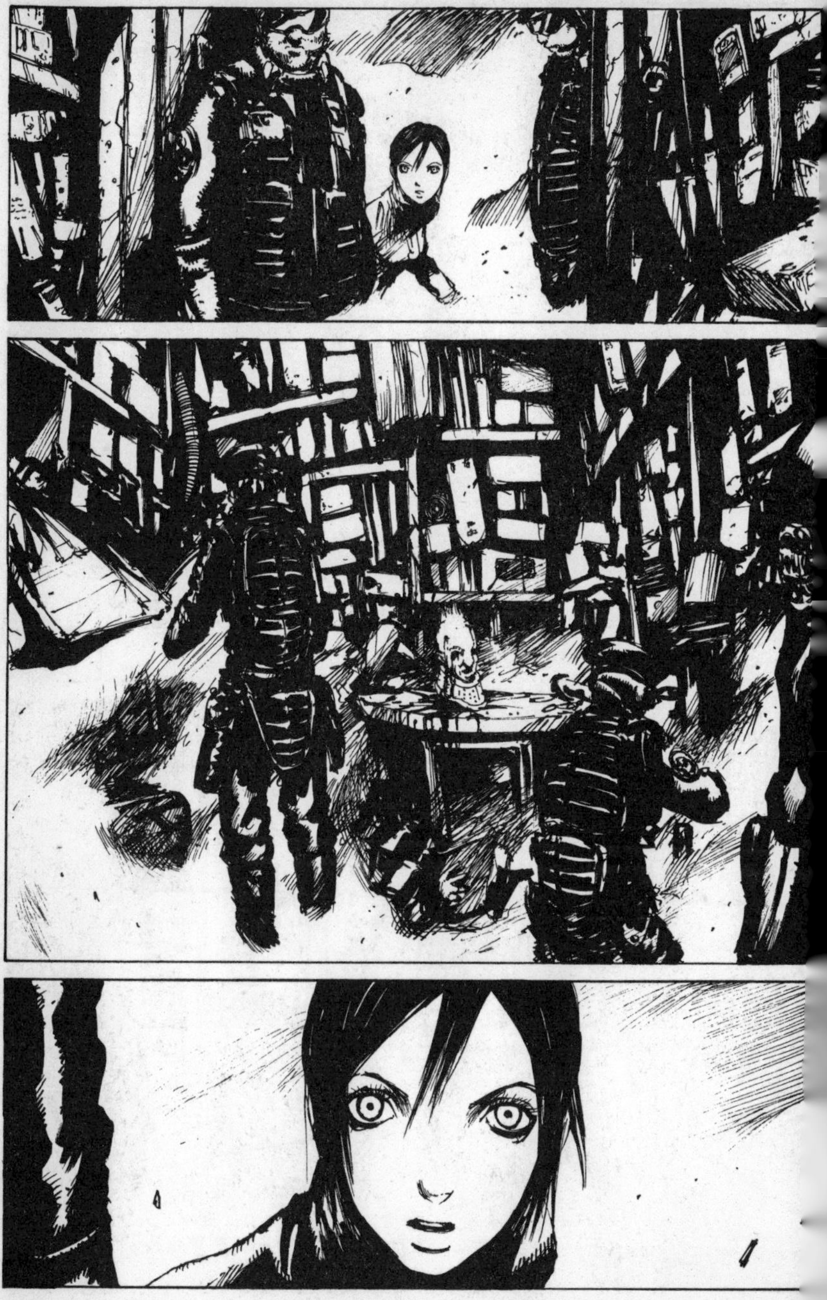

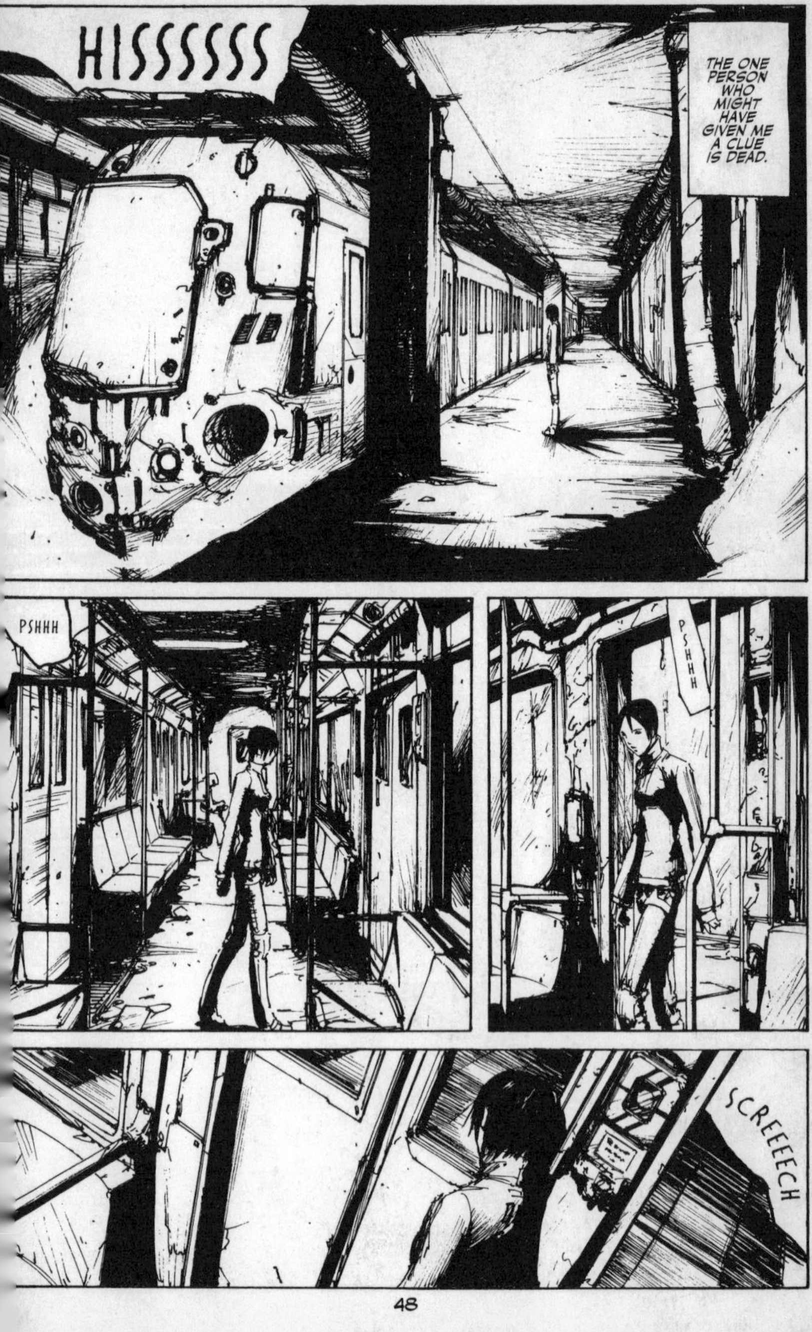
THE ONE PERSON WHO MIGHT HAVE GIVEN ME A CLUE IS DEAD.
HISSSSSSS
PSHHH
PSHHH
SCREEEECH

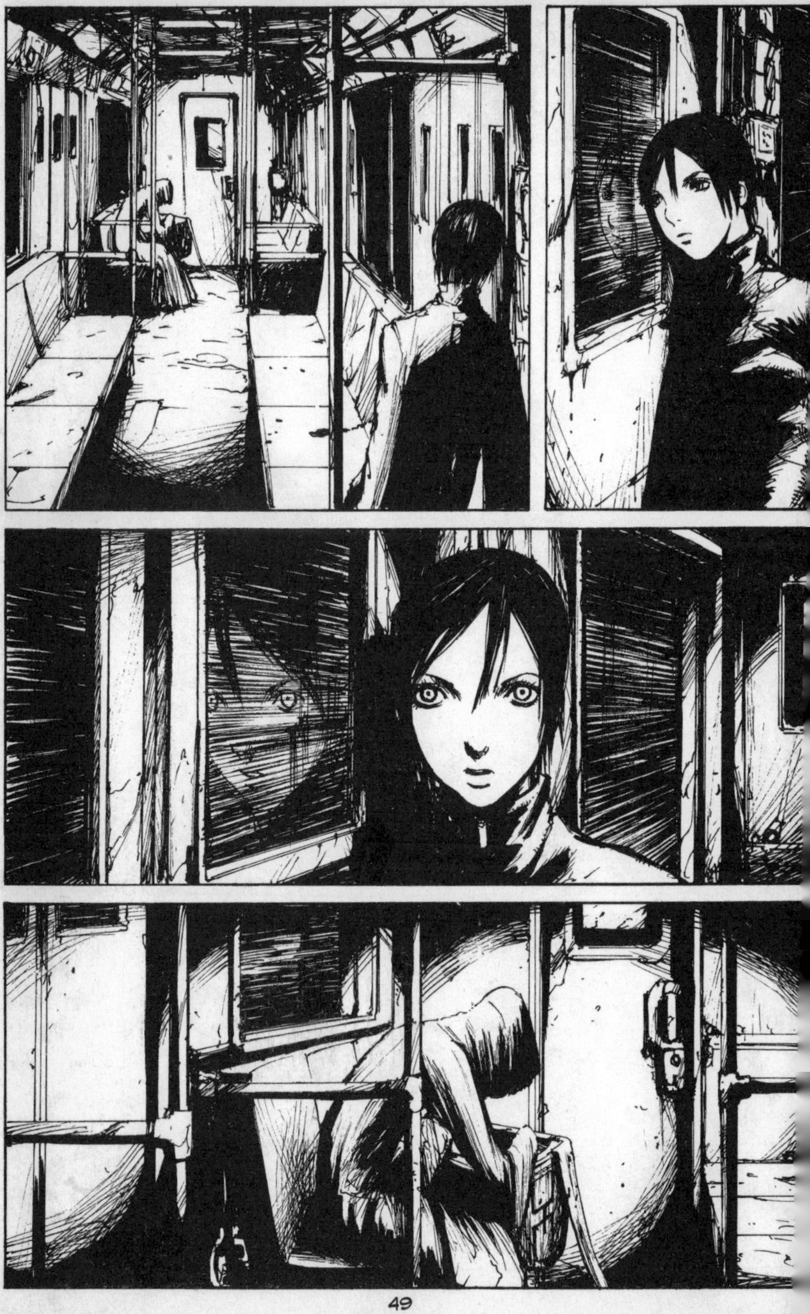

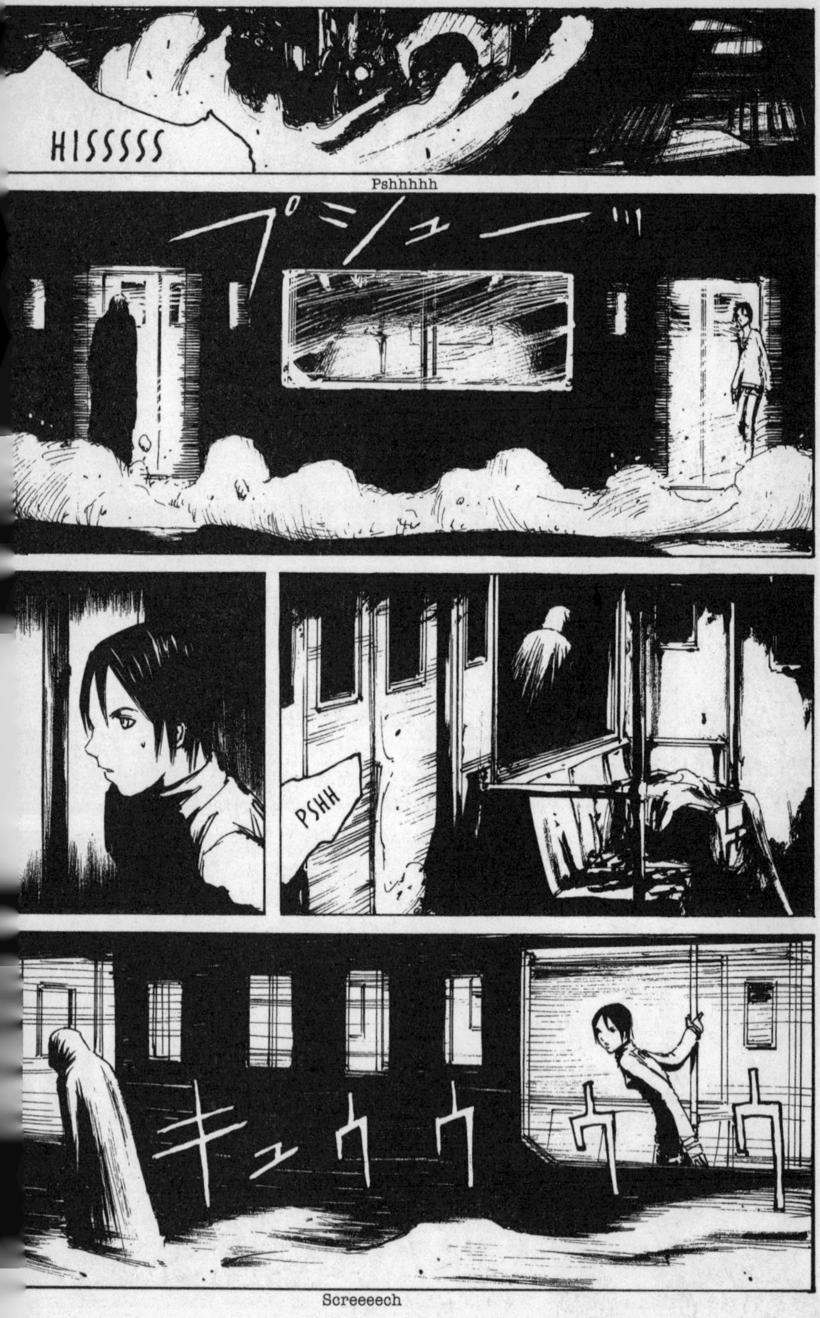
HISSSSS
Pshhhhh
プシューッ
PSHH
キュウウ
Screeeech

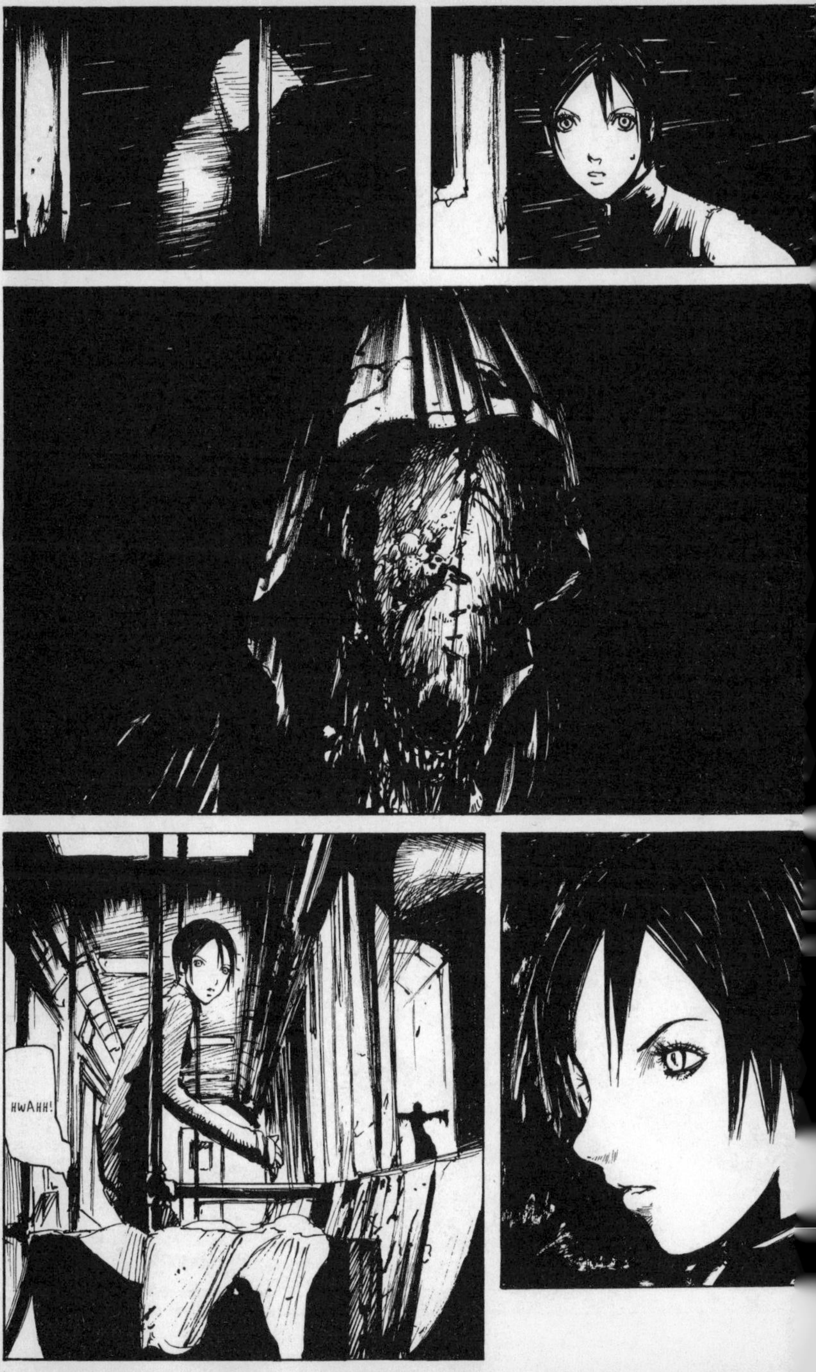
HWAHH!

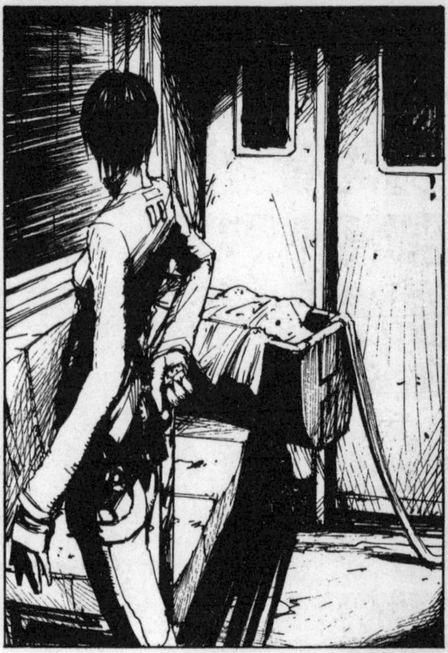
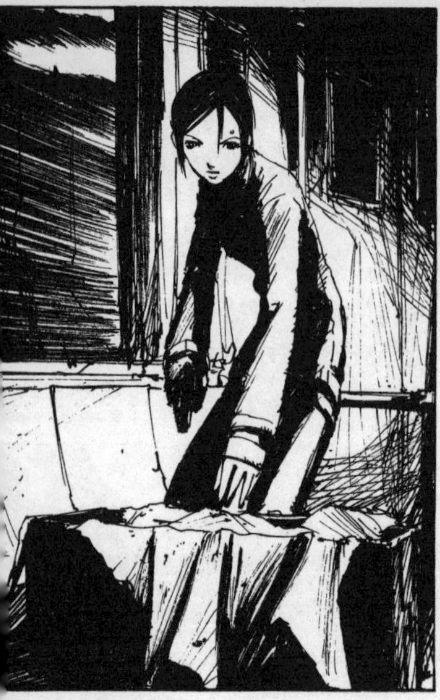
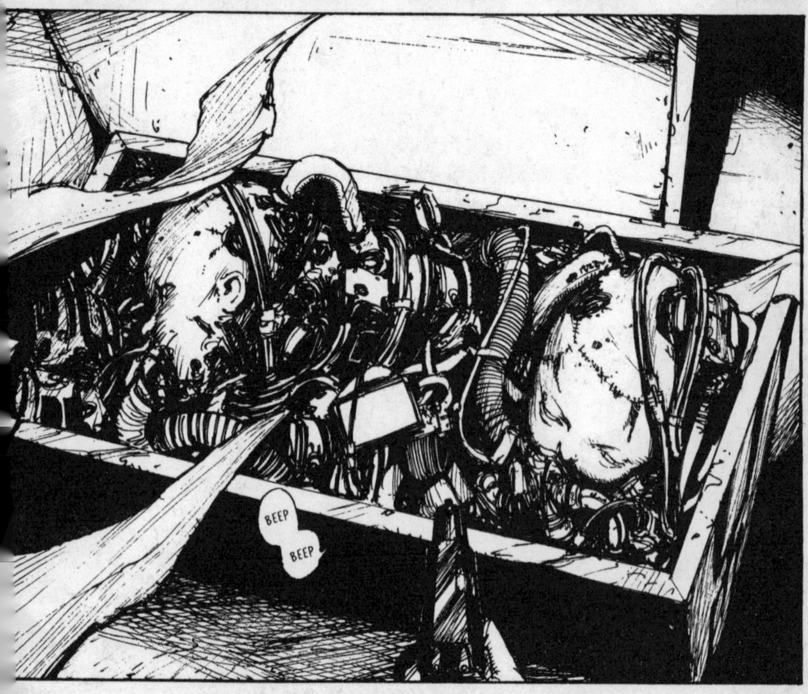
BEEP
BEEP

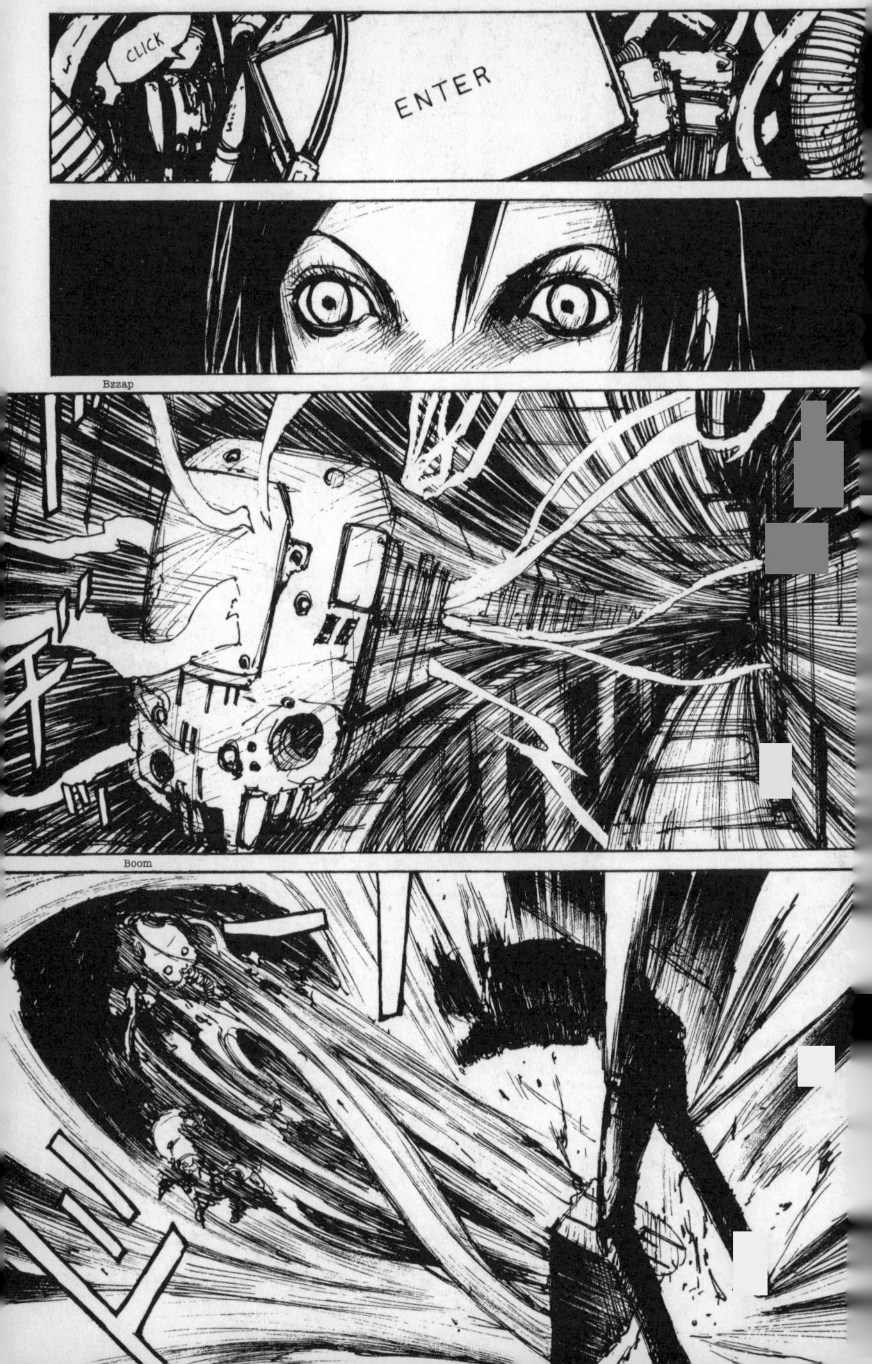
CLICK
ENTER
Bzzap
Boom

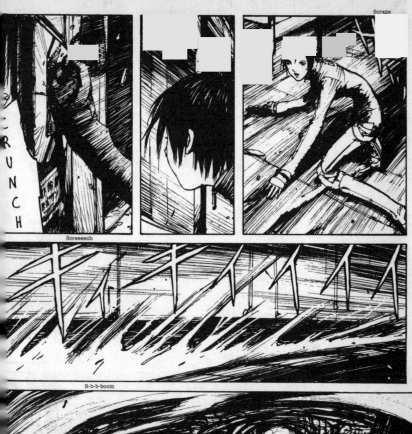

Scrape

CRUNCH

Screeeech

B-b-b-boom

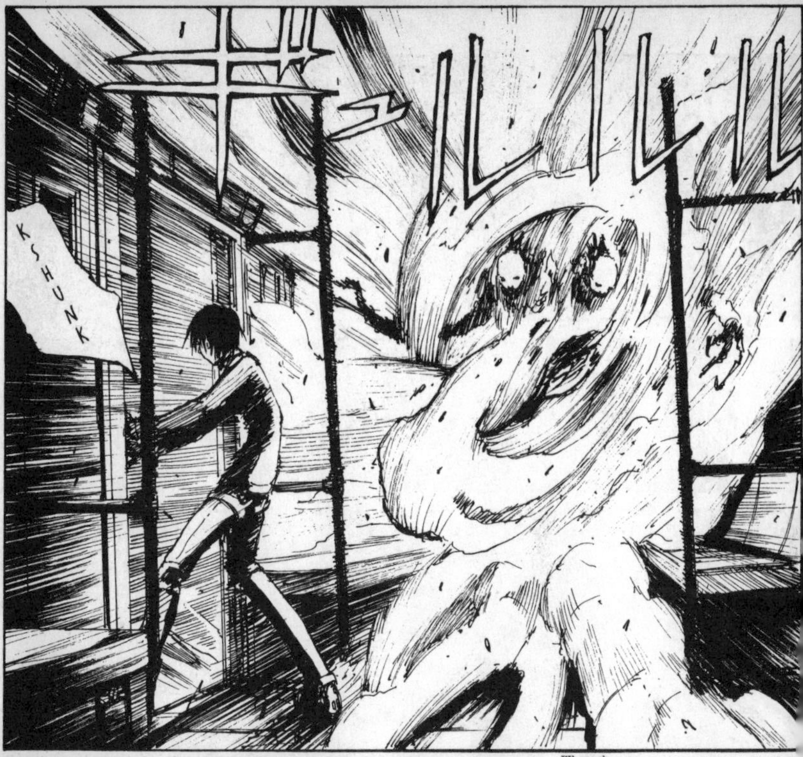
Shwurlll
KSHUNK

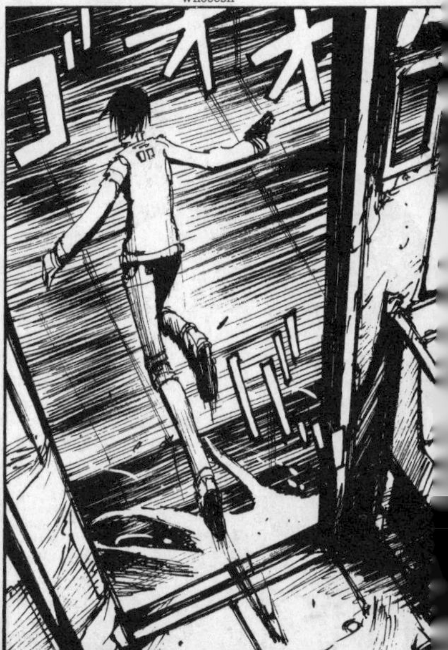
Whooosh

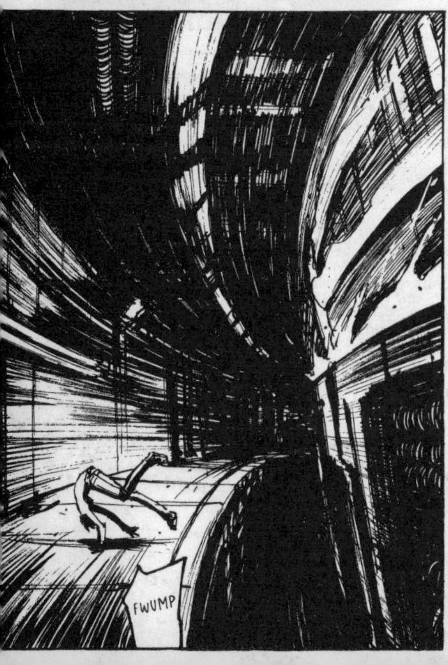
FWUMP

Baboom

Crashh   Bjank

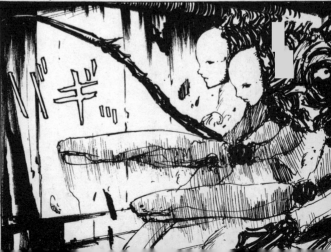

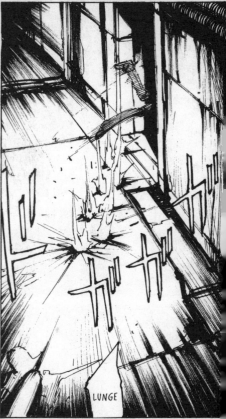

Gagagagaga

Damdamdamdam

Dbambambam

LUNGE

Dbam

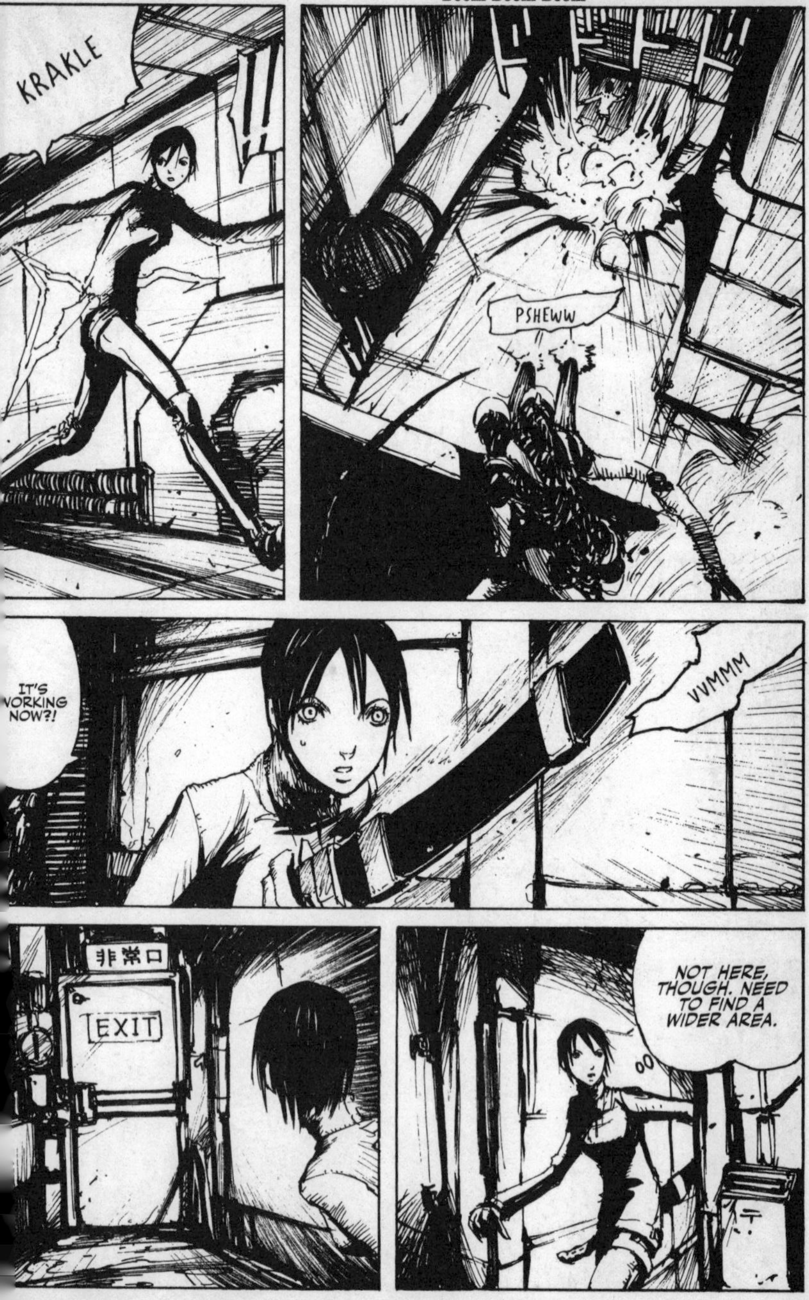
PSHEWW
KRAKLE
VVMMM
IT'S WORKING NOW?!
NOT HERE, THOUGH. NEED TO FIND A WIDER AREA.
非常口
EXIT

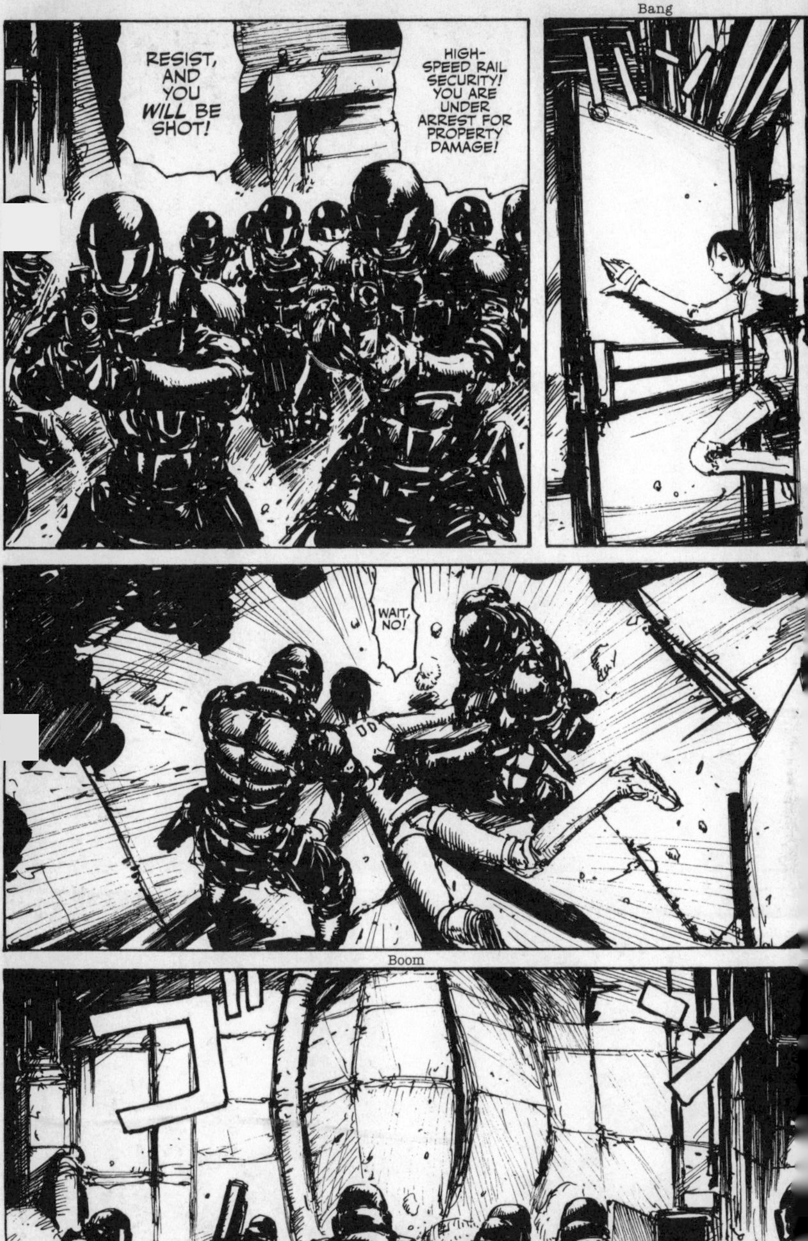
Bang
HIGH-SPEED RAIL SECURITY! YOU ARE UNDER ARREST FOR PROPERTY DAMAGE!
RESIST, AND YOU *WILL* BE SHOT!
WAIT, NO!
Boom

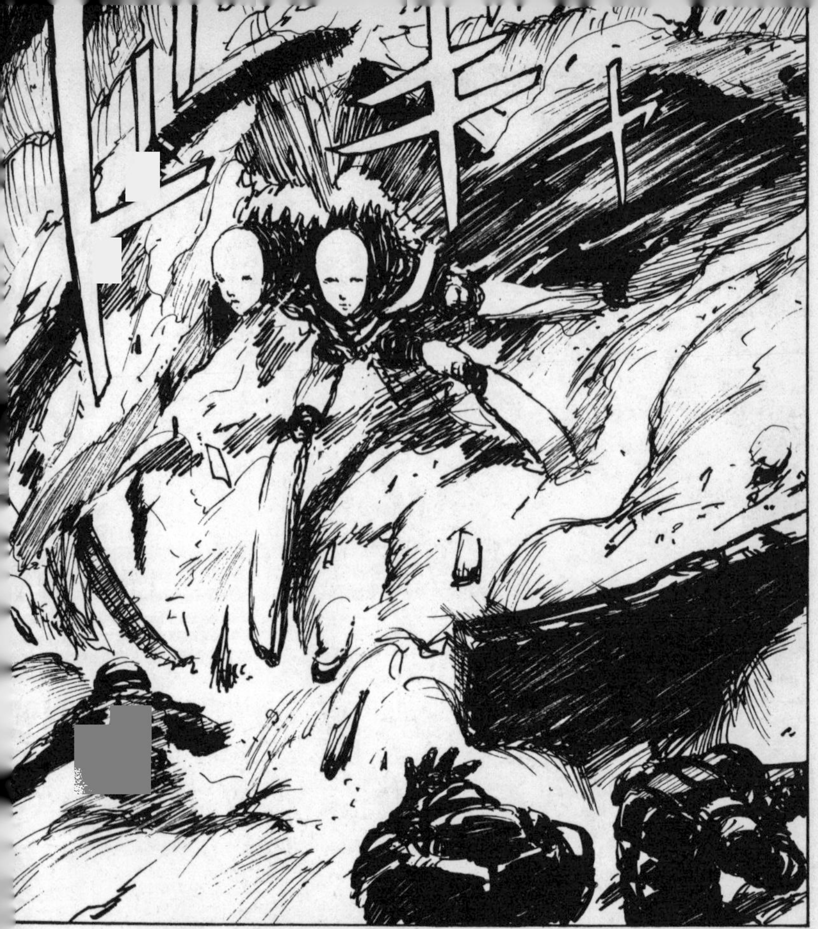

Kraaash

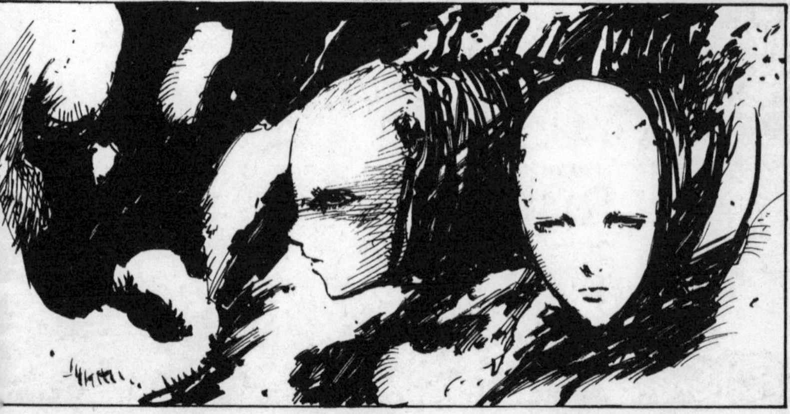

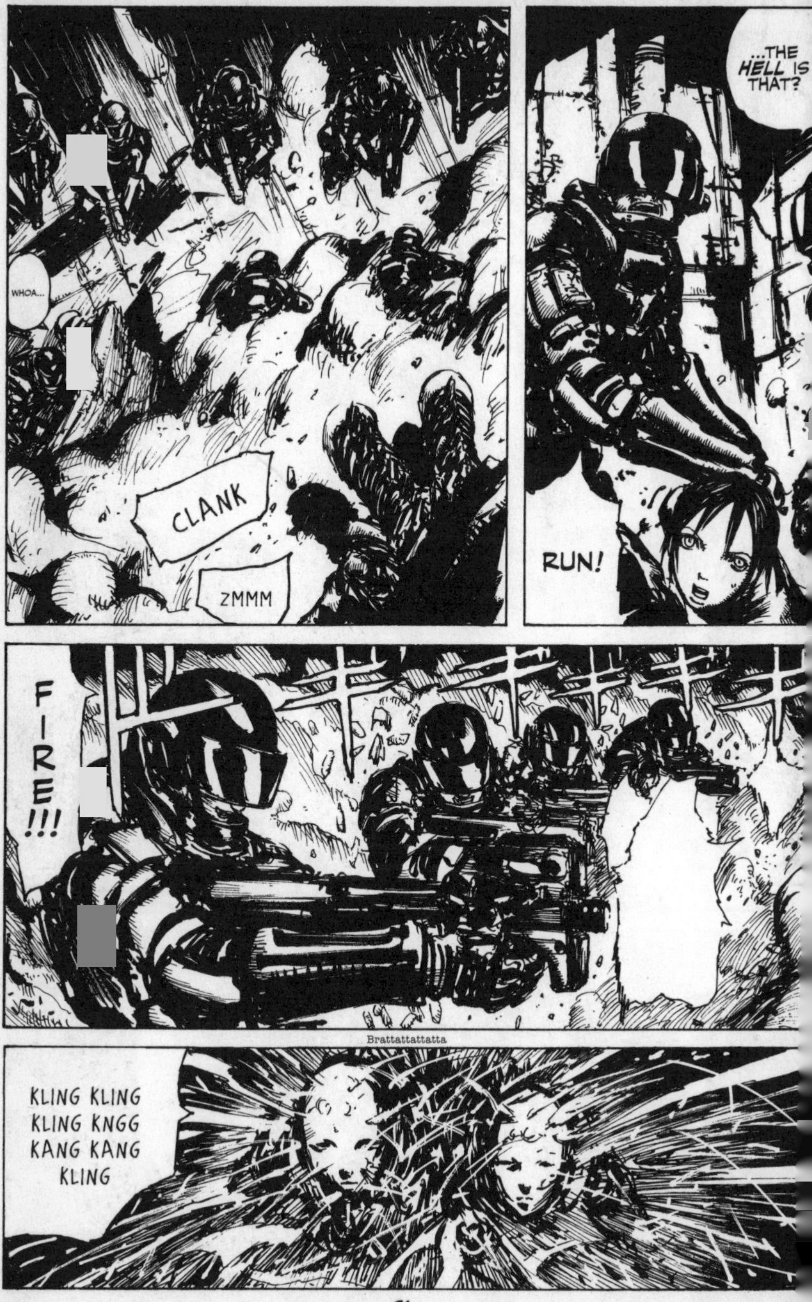
...THE HELL IS THAT?
RUN!
WHOA...
CLANK
ZMMM
FIRE!!!
Brattattattatta
KLING KLING
KLING KNGG
KANG KANG
KLING

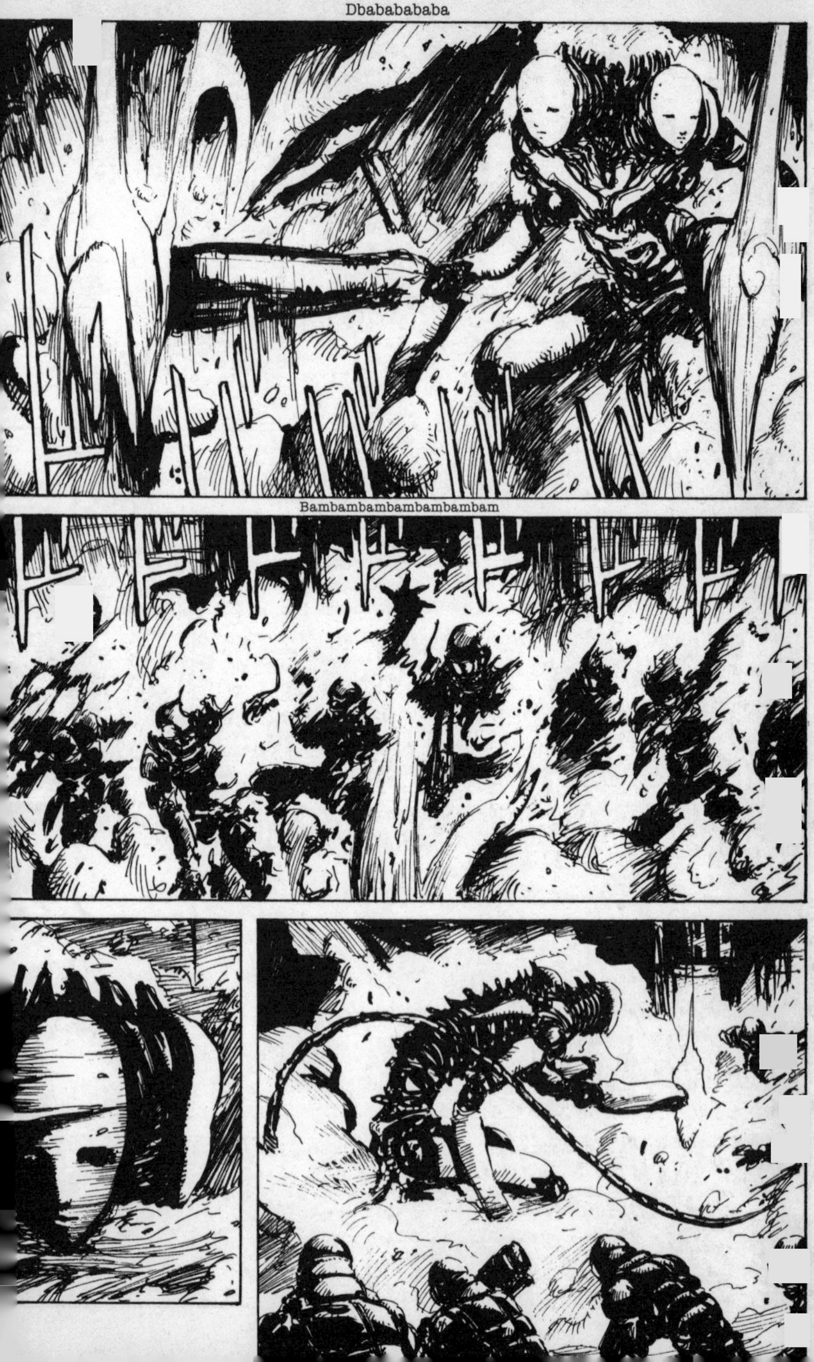
Dbababababa
Bambambambambambambam

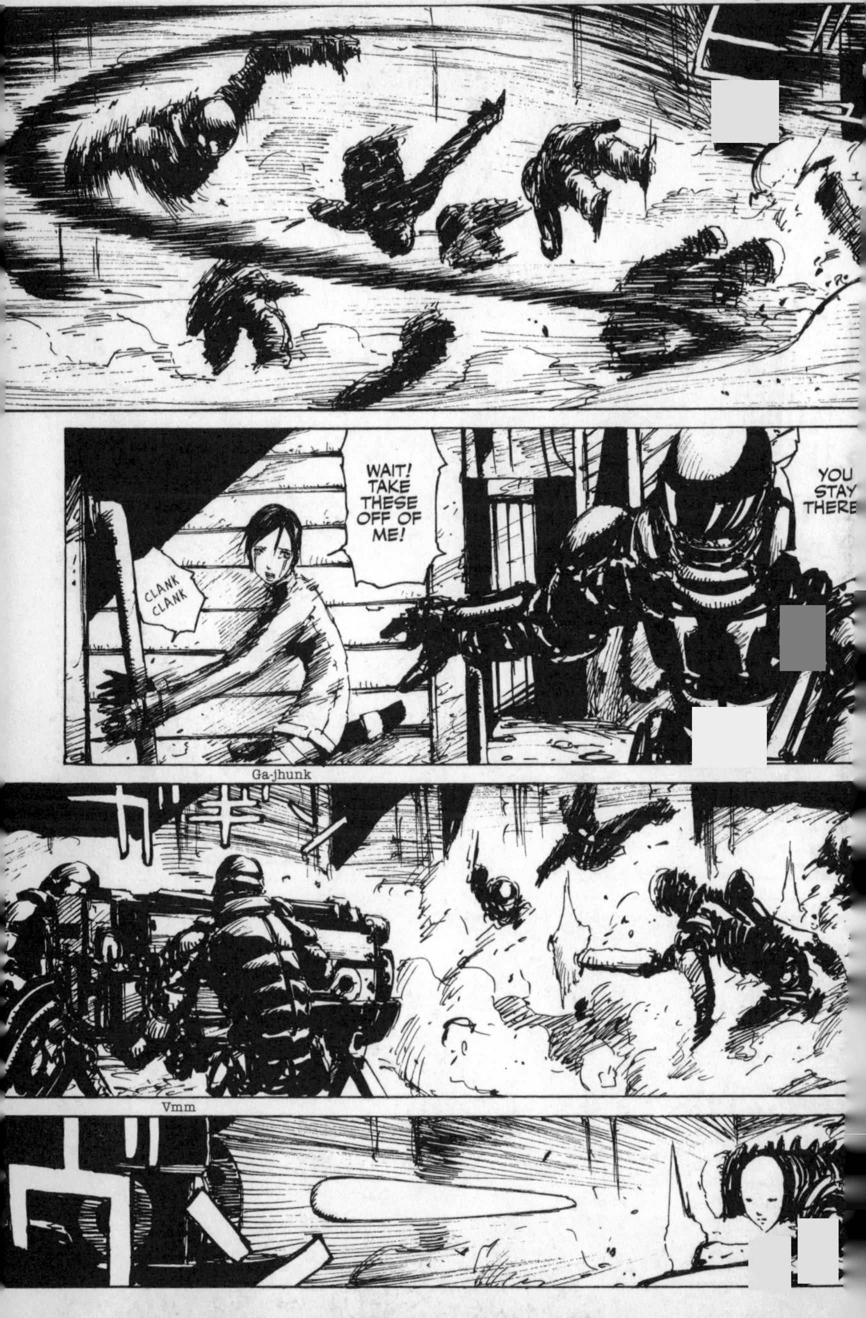
Whip
YOU STAY THERE
WAIT! TAKE THESE OFF OF ME!
CLANK CLANK
Ga-jhunk
Vmm

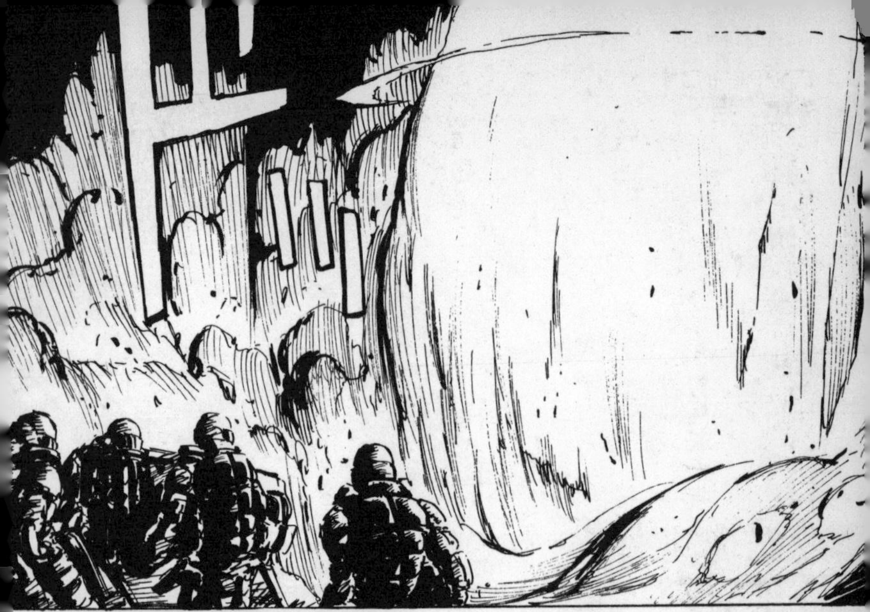

Booom

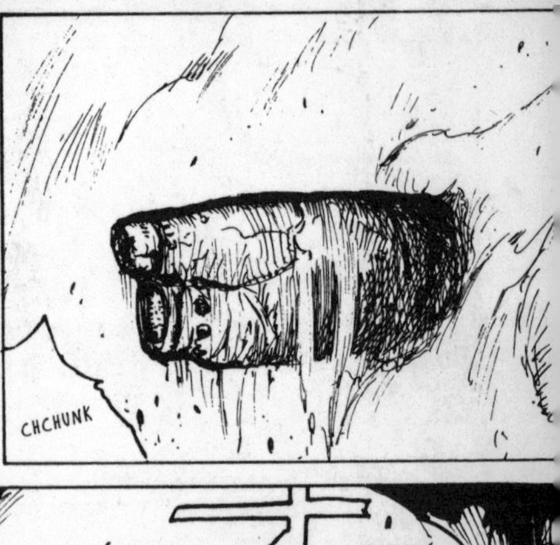
CHCHUNK

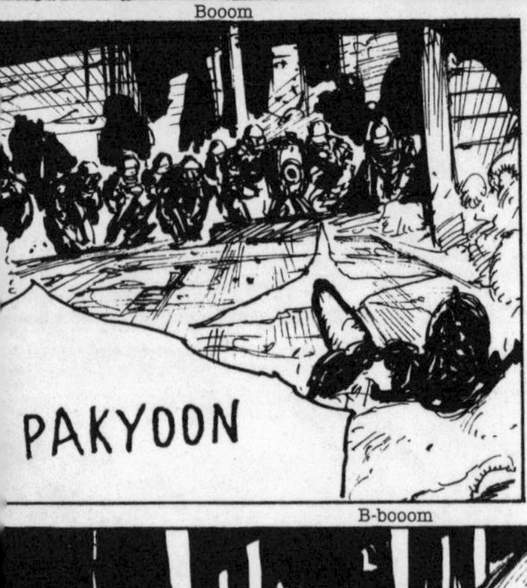
PAKYOON

B-booom

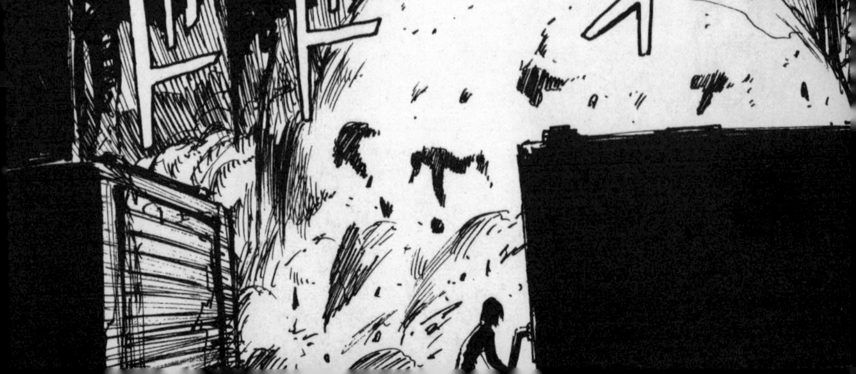

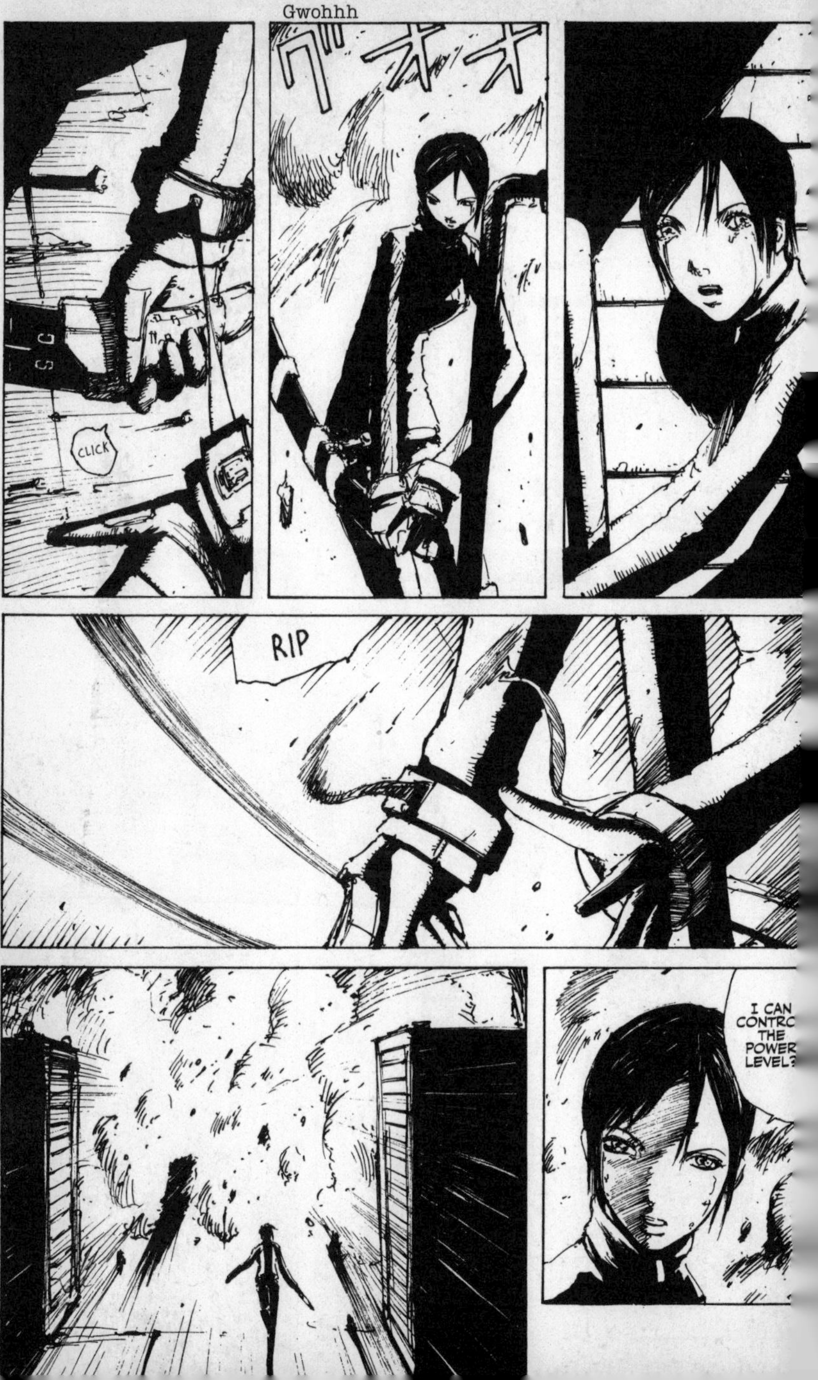
Gwohhh
グオオ
CLICK
RIP
I CAN CONTRO THE POWER LEVEL?

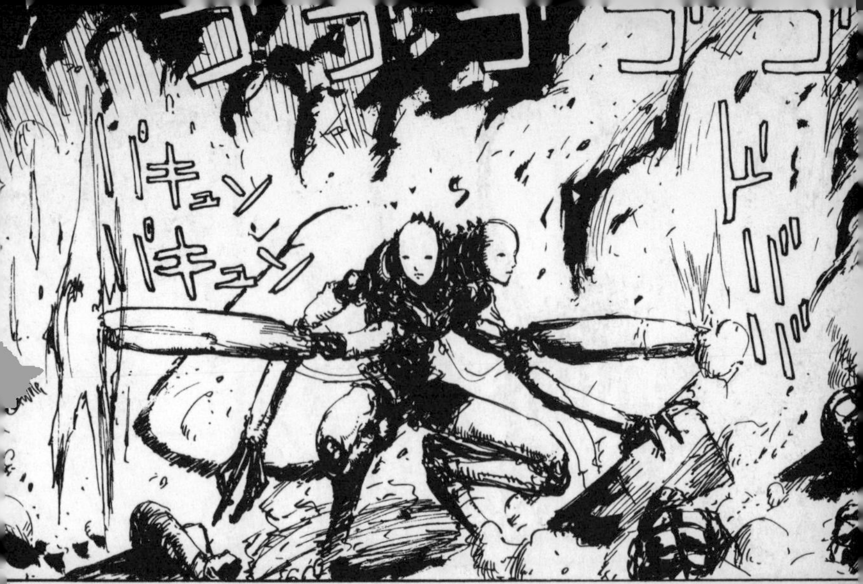
パキュン
パキュン

Pakow pakow

Boommmmm

Dabababa

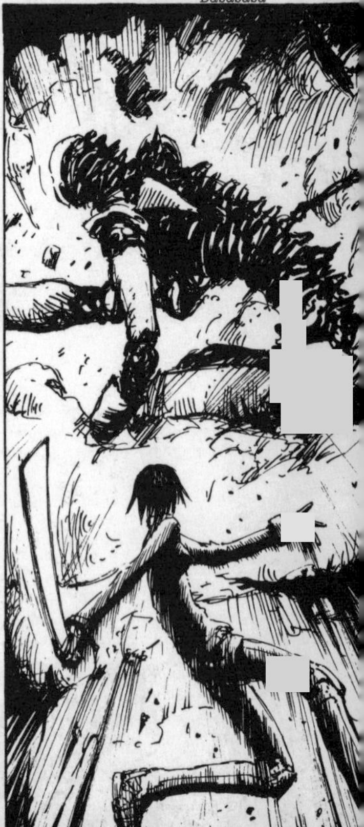

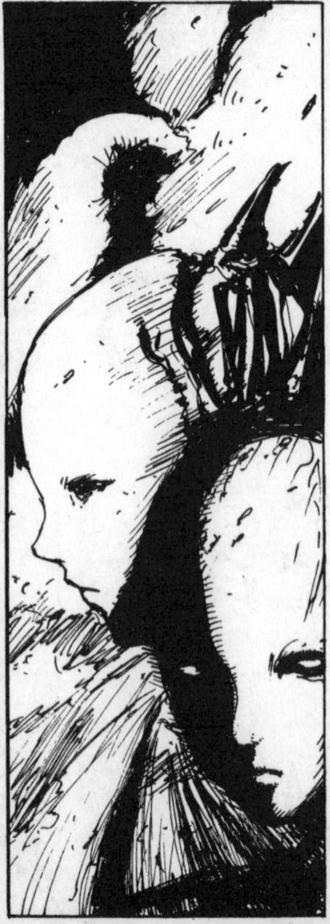

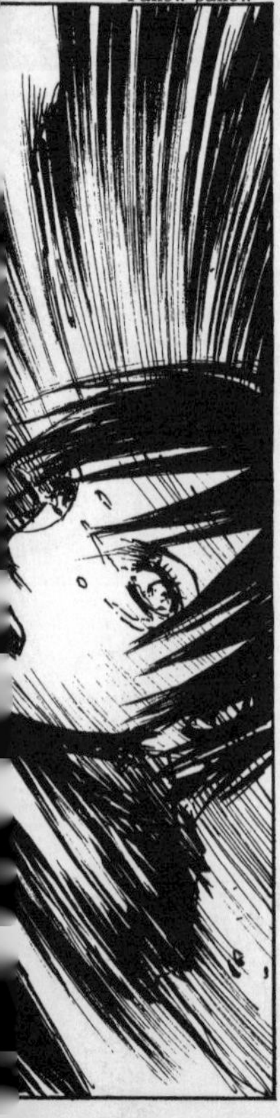

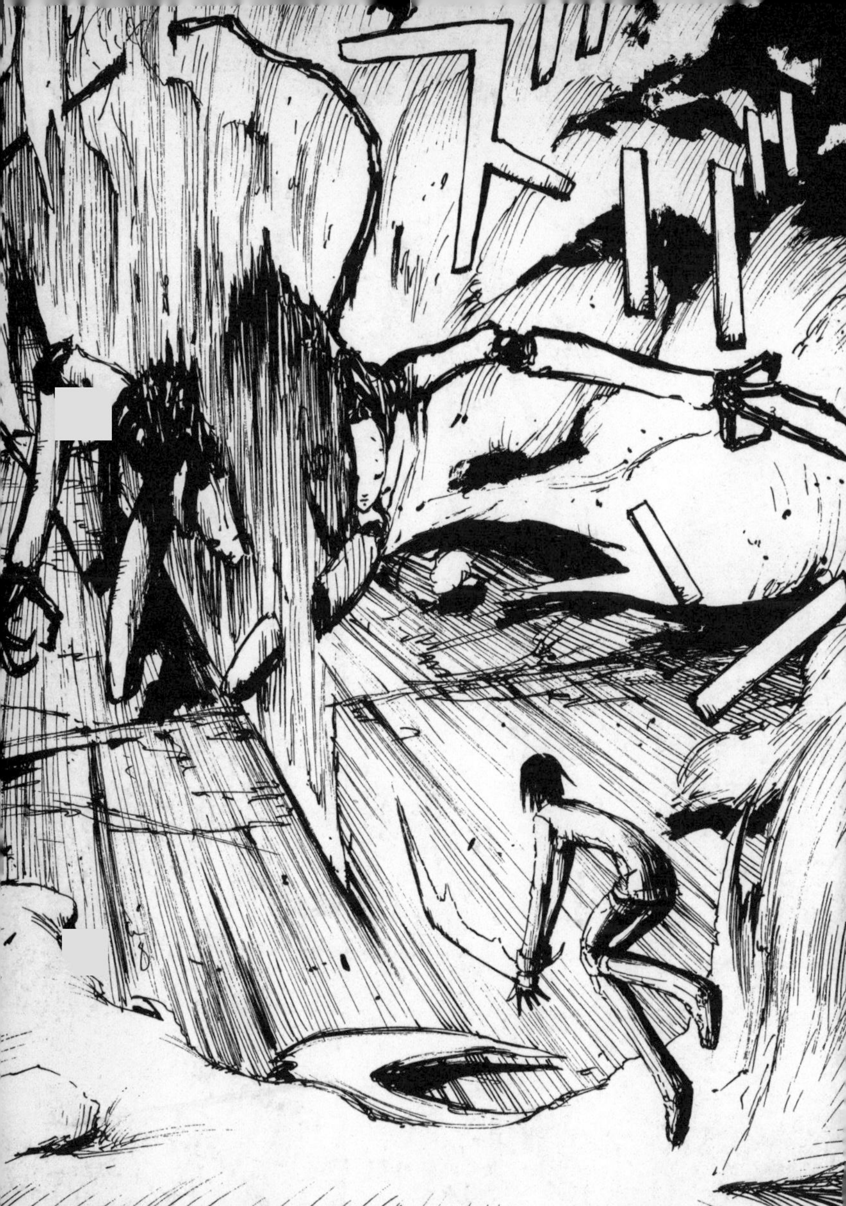
Slice
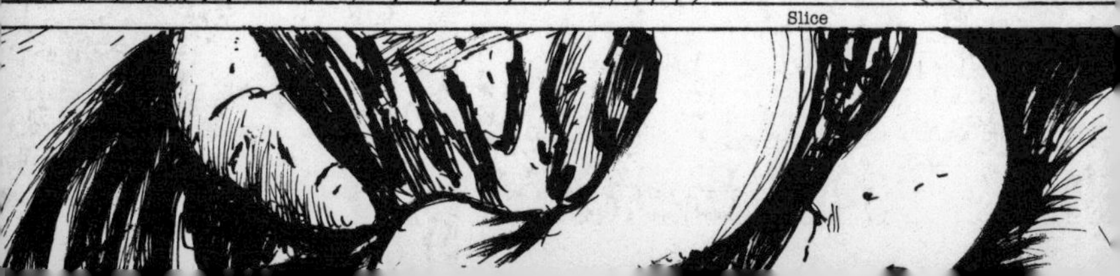

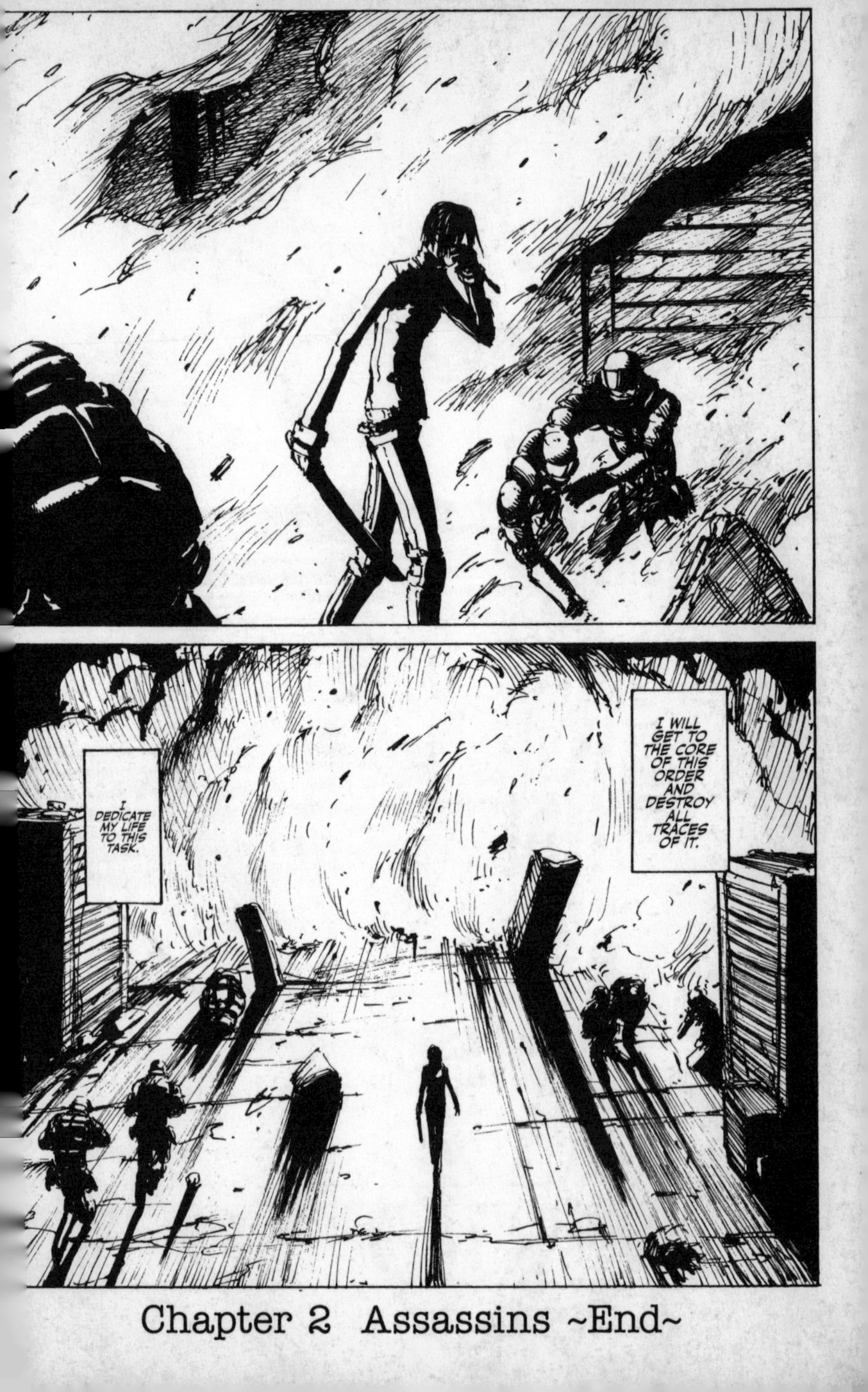
I WILL GET TO THE CORE OF THIS ORDER AND DESTROY ALL TRACES OF IT.
I DEDICATE MY LIFE TO THIS TASK.

Chapter 2 Assassins ~End~

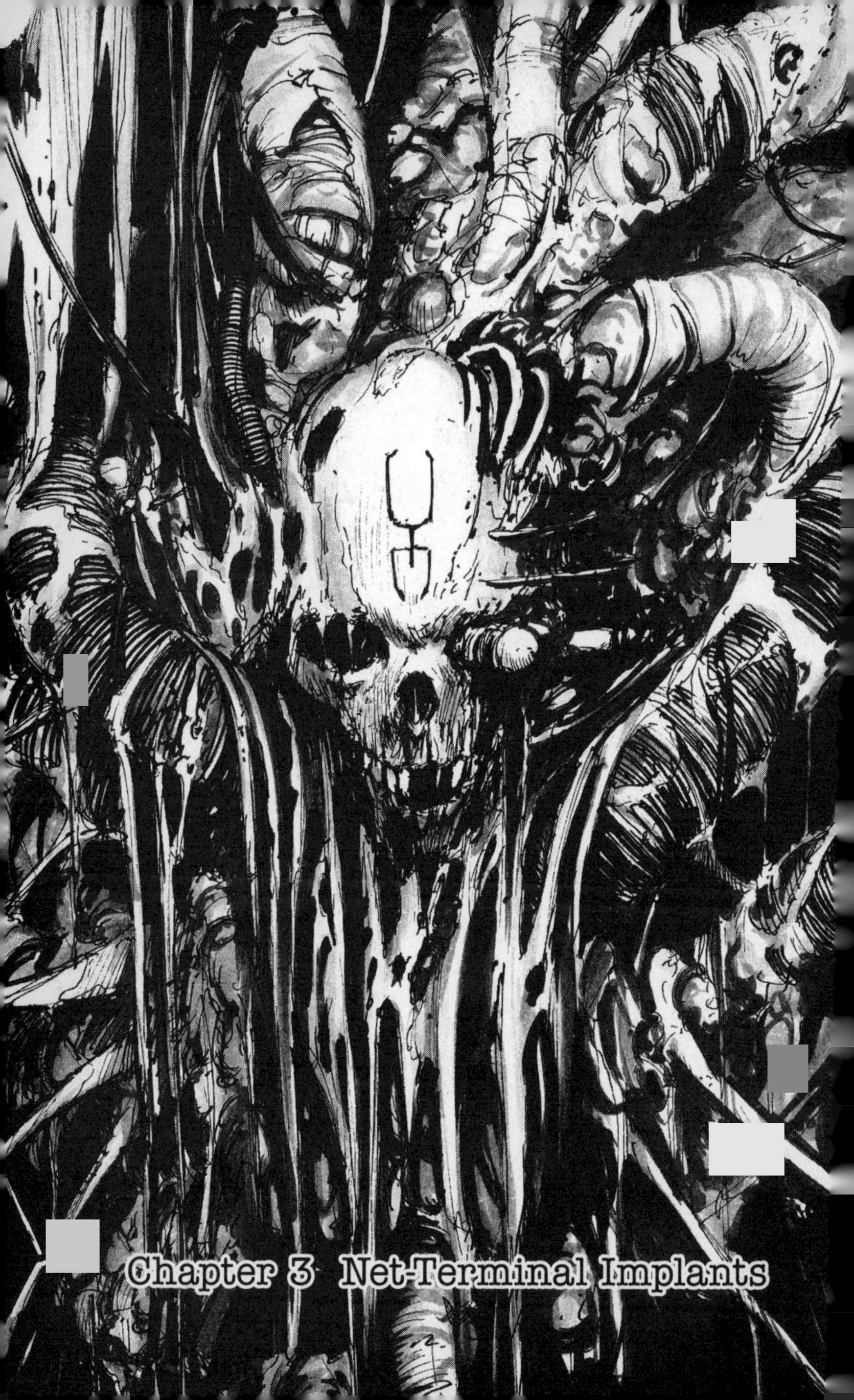

Chapter 3 Net-Terminal Implants

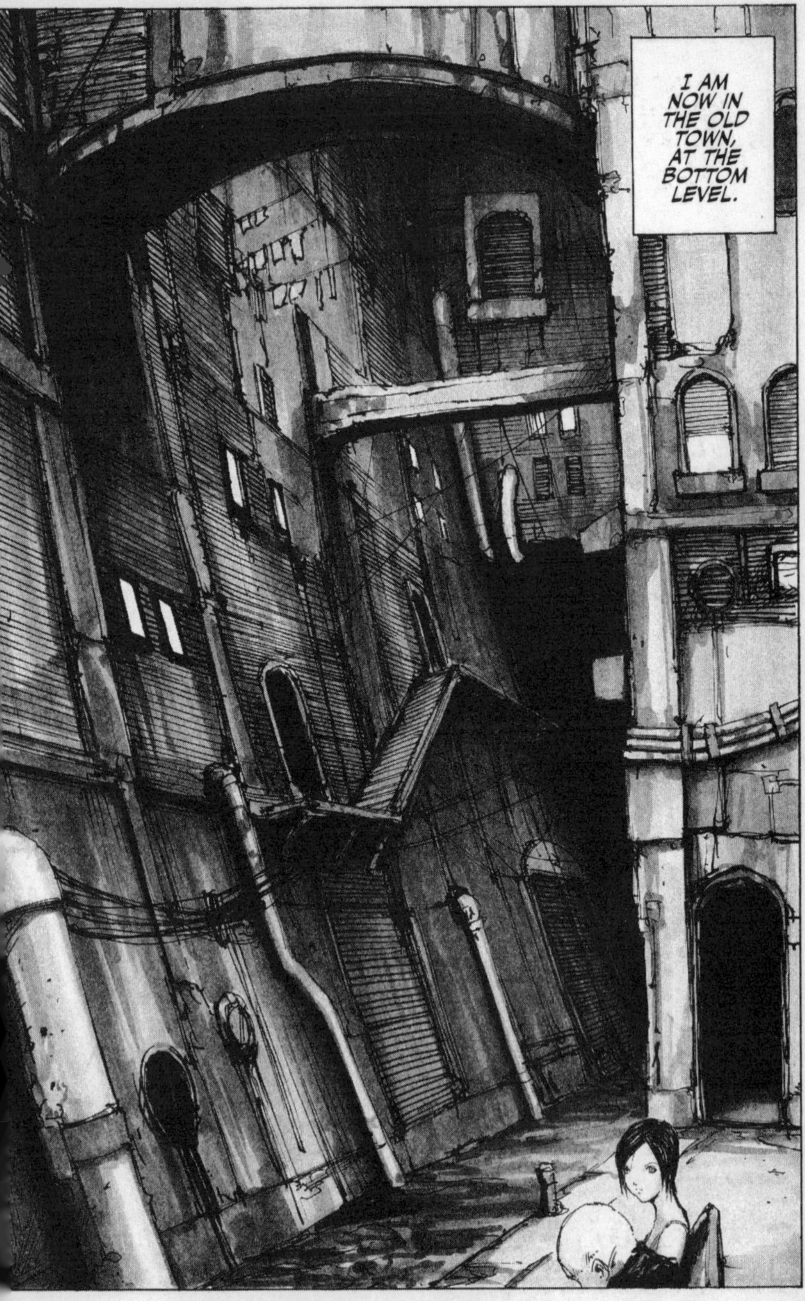
I AM NOW IN THE OLD TOWN, AT THE BOTTOM LEVEL.

AN OLD MAN HAS TOLD ME THAT THERE ARE CHILDREN HERE WHO WITNESSED ONE OF THE KIDNAPPINGS.

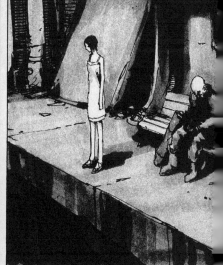

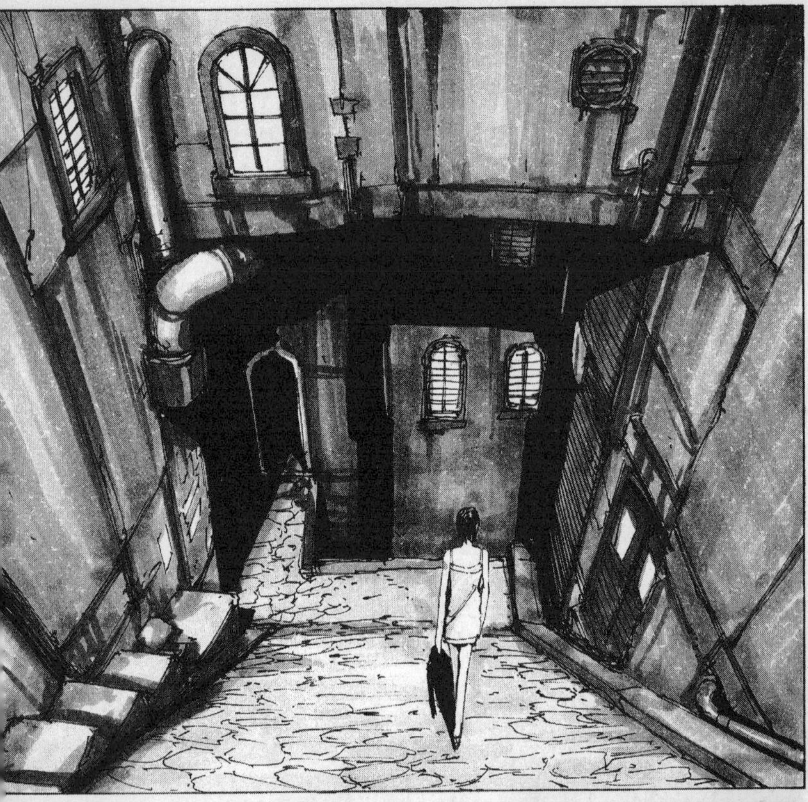
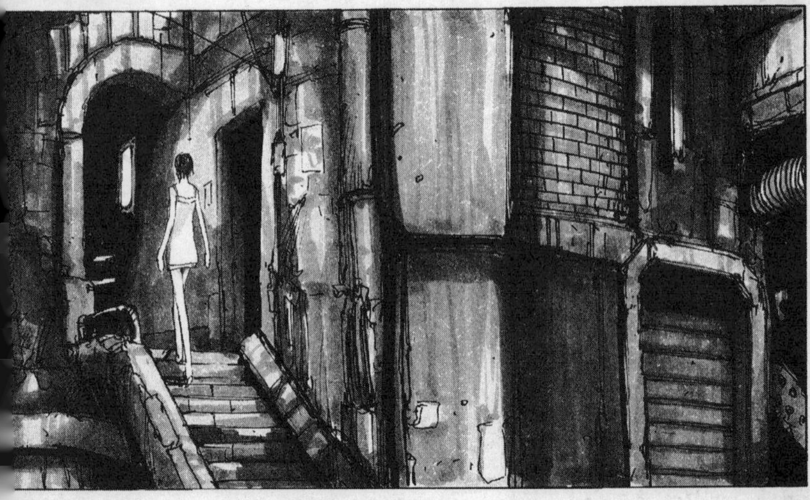

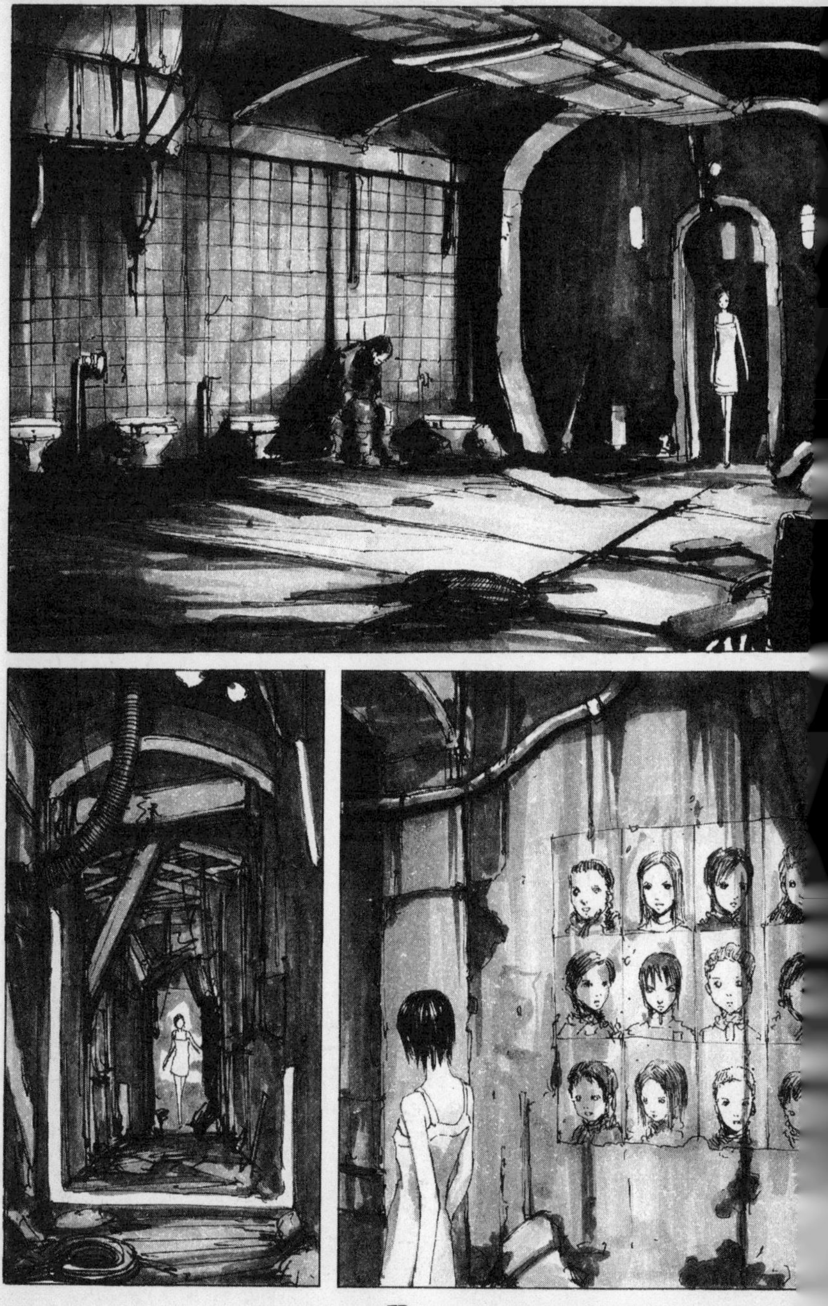

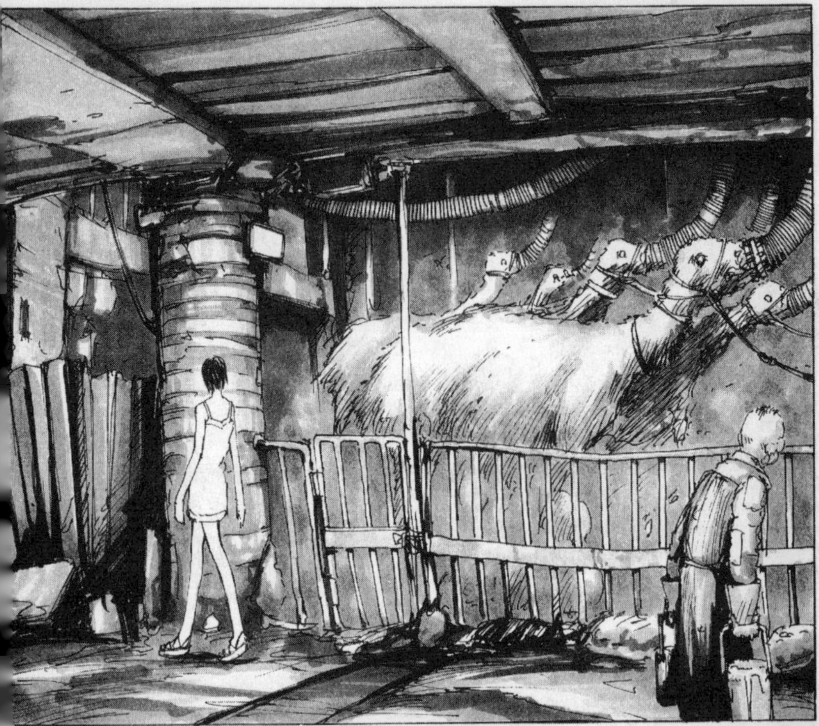

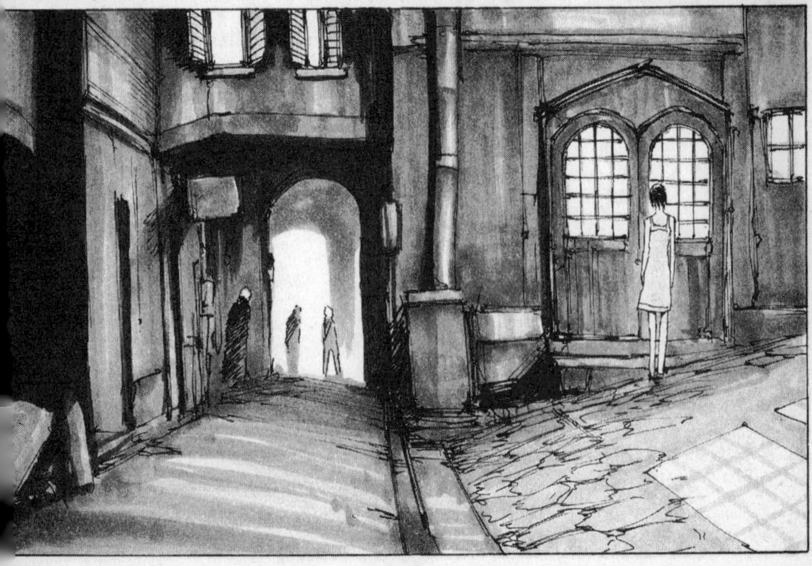

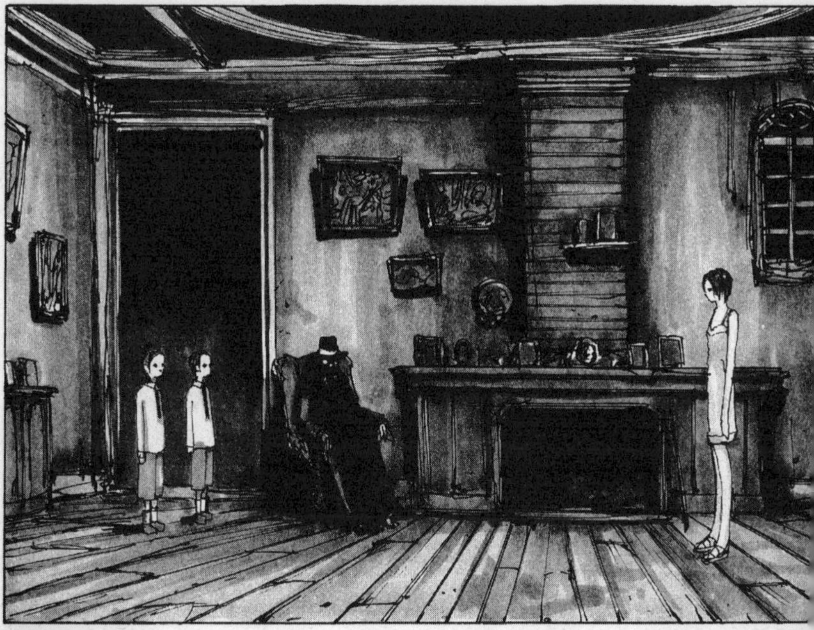

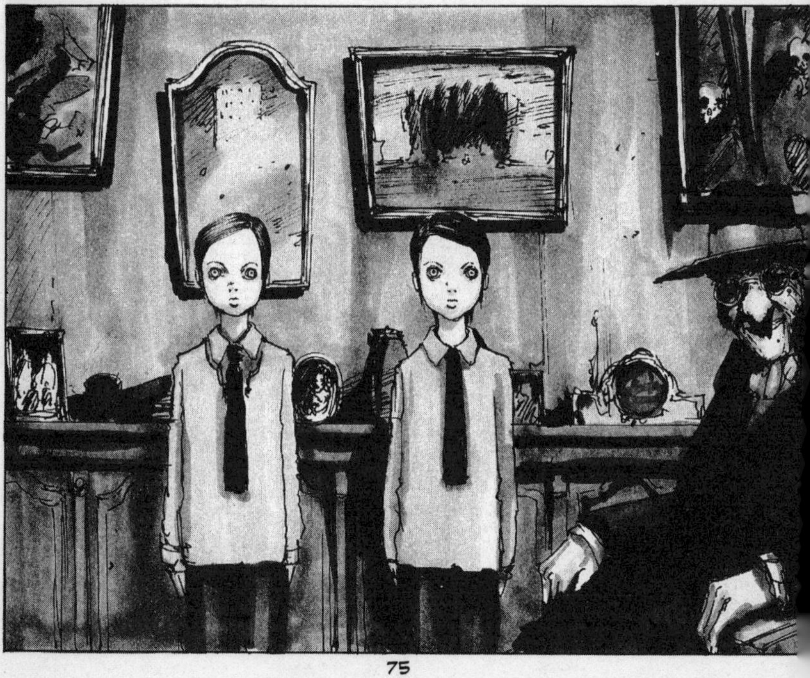

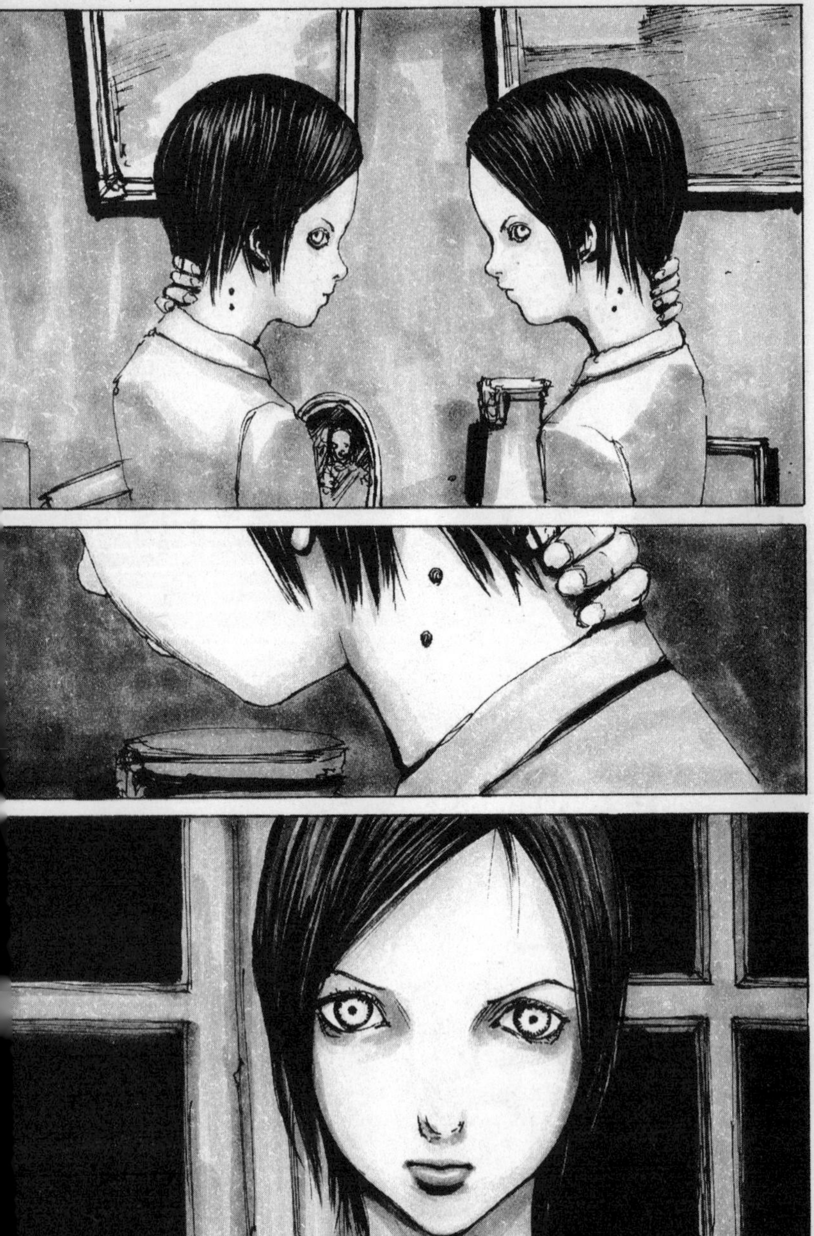

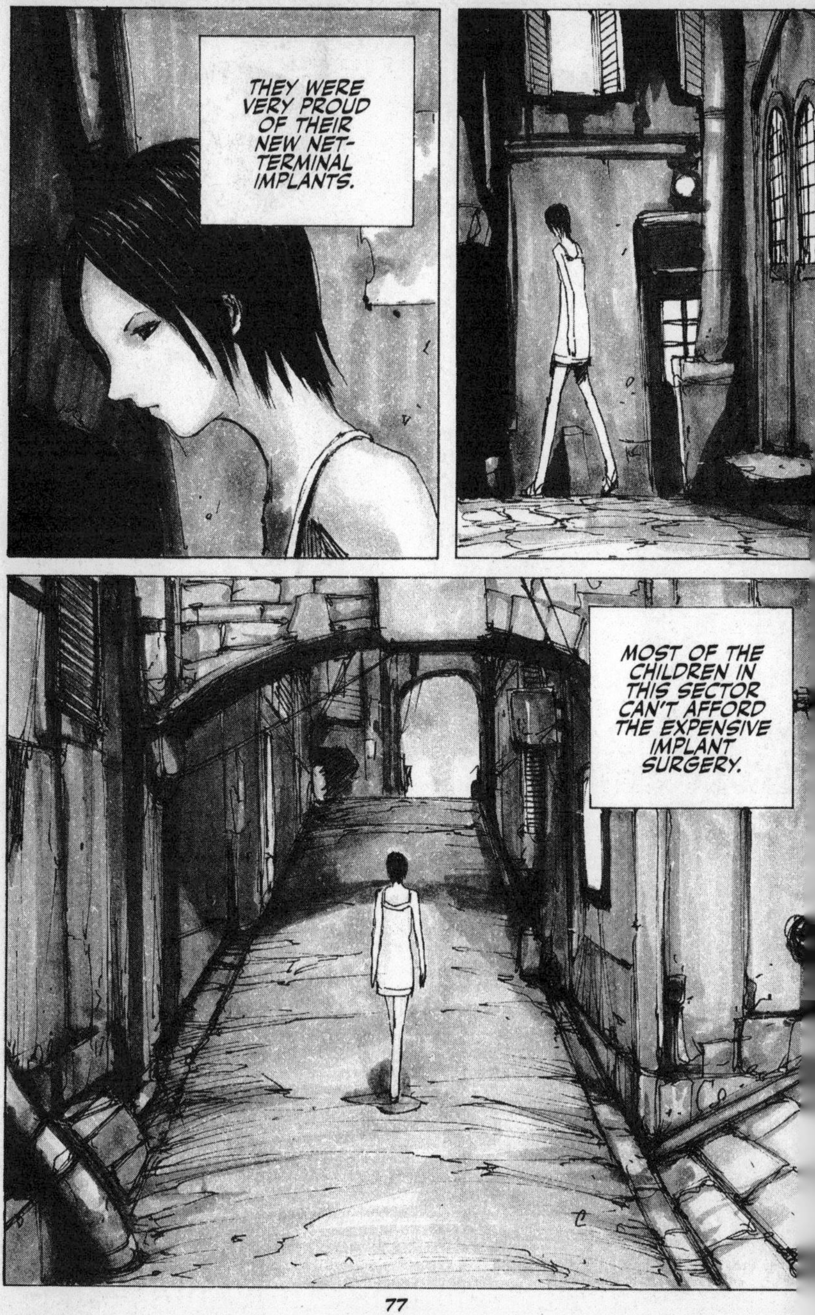
THEY WERE VERY PROUD OF THEIR NEW NET-TERMINAL IMPLANTS.
MOST OF THE CHILDREN IN THIS SECTOR CAN'T AFFORD THE EXPENSIVE IMPLANT SURGERY.

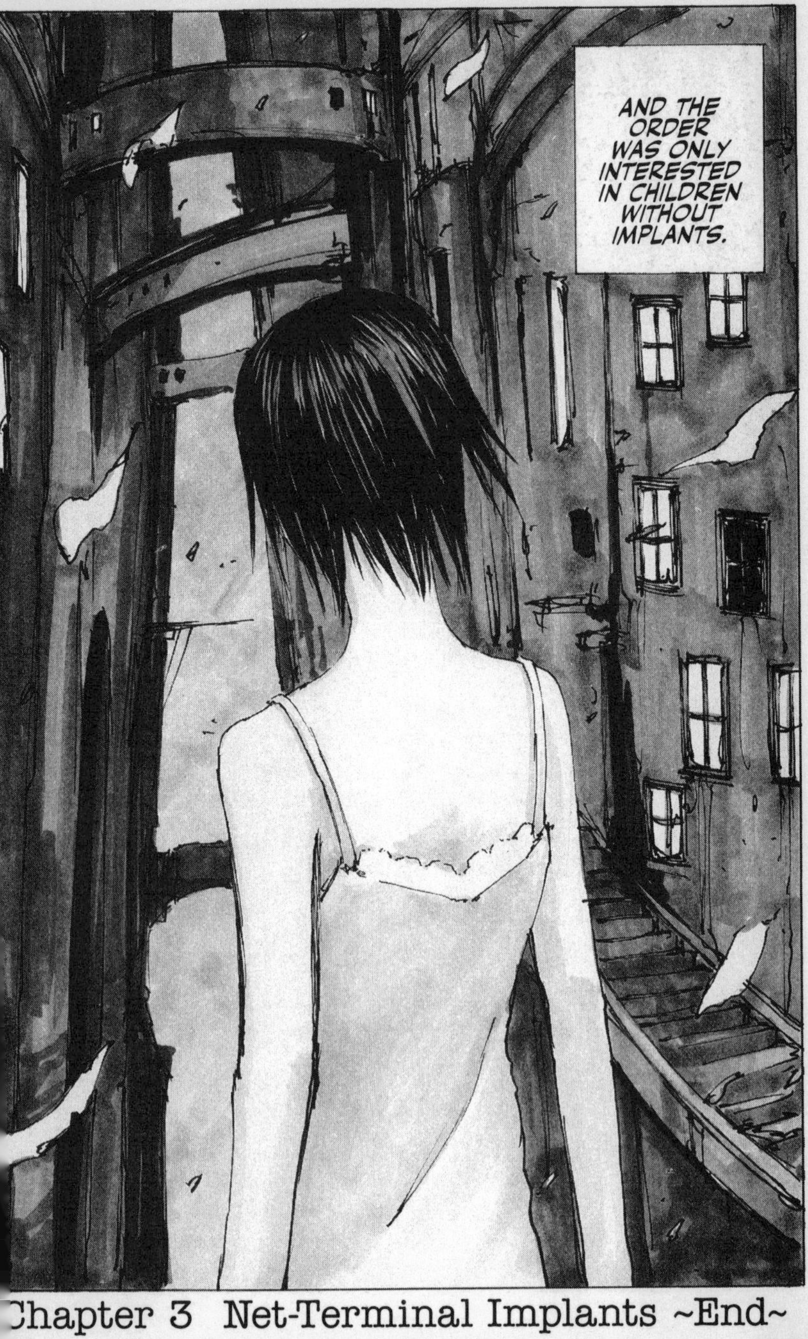
AND THE ORDER WAS ONLY INTERESTED IN CHILDREN WITHOUT IMPLANTS.

Chapter 3 Net-Terminal Implants ~End~

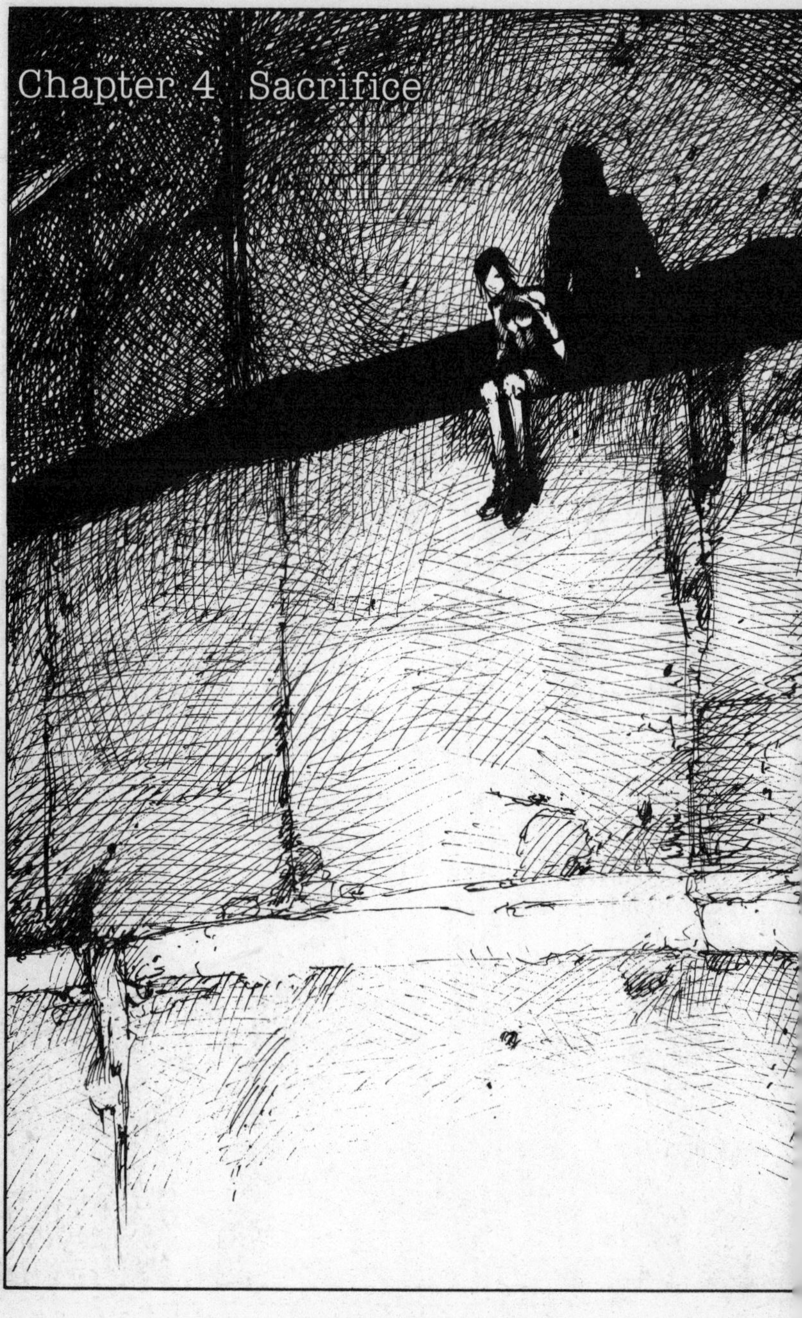
Chapter 4 Sacrifice

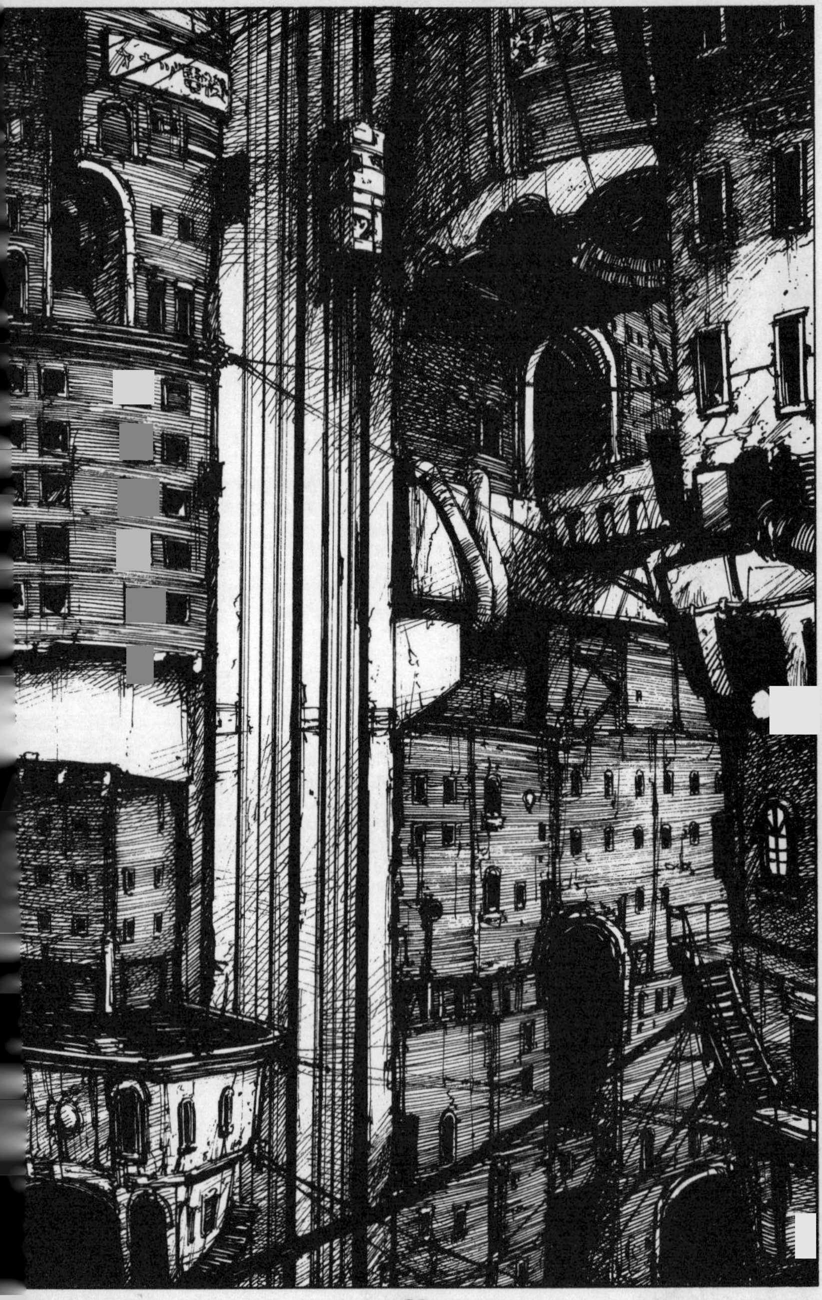

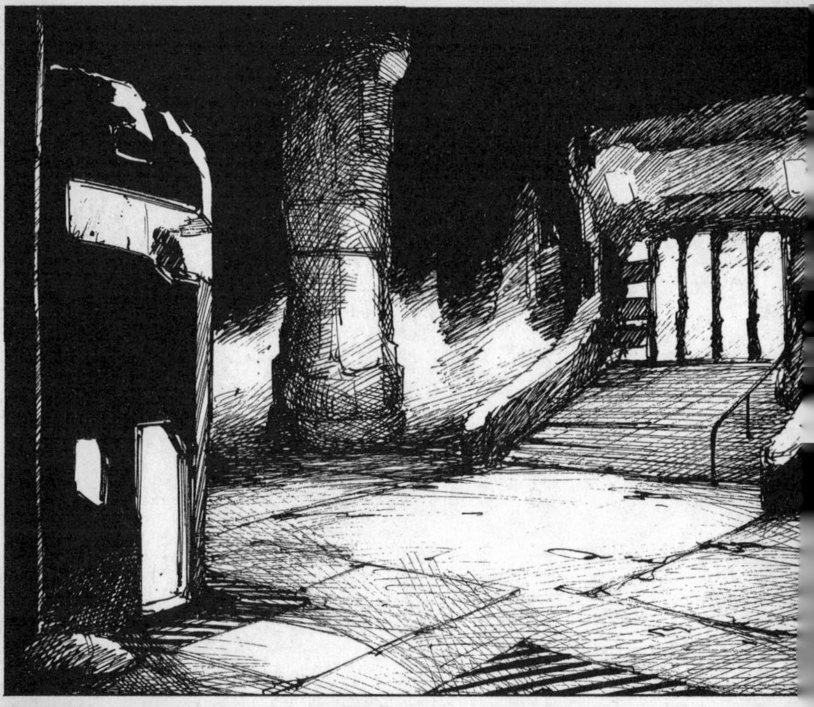
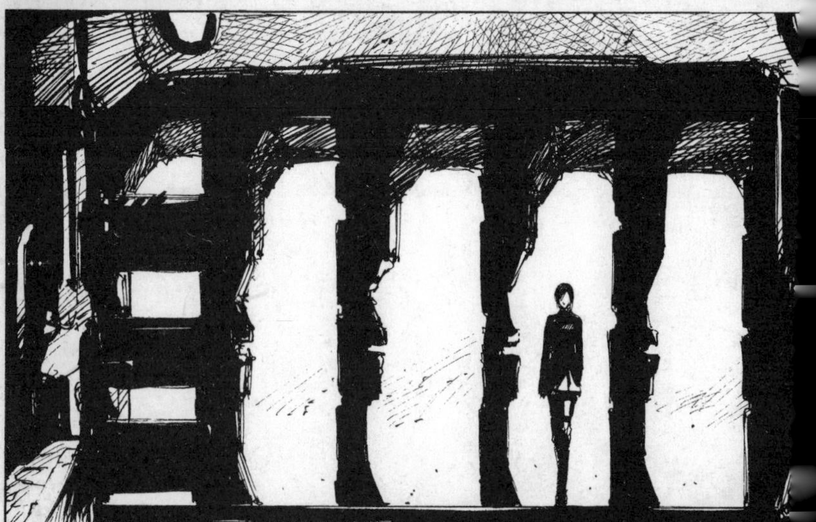

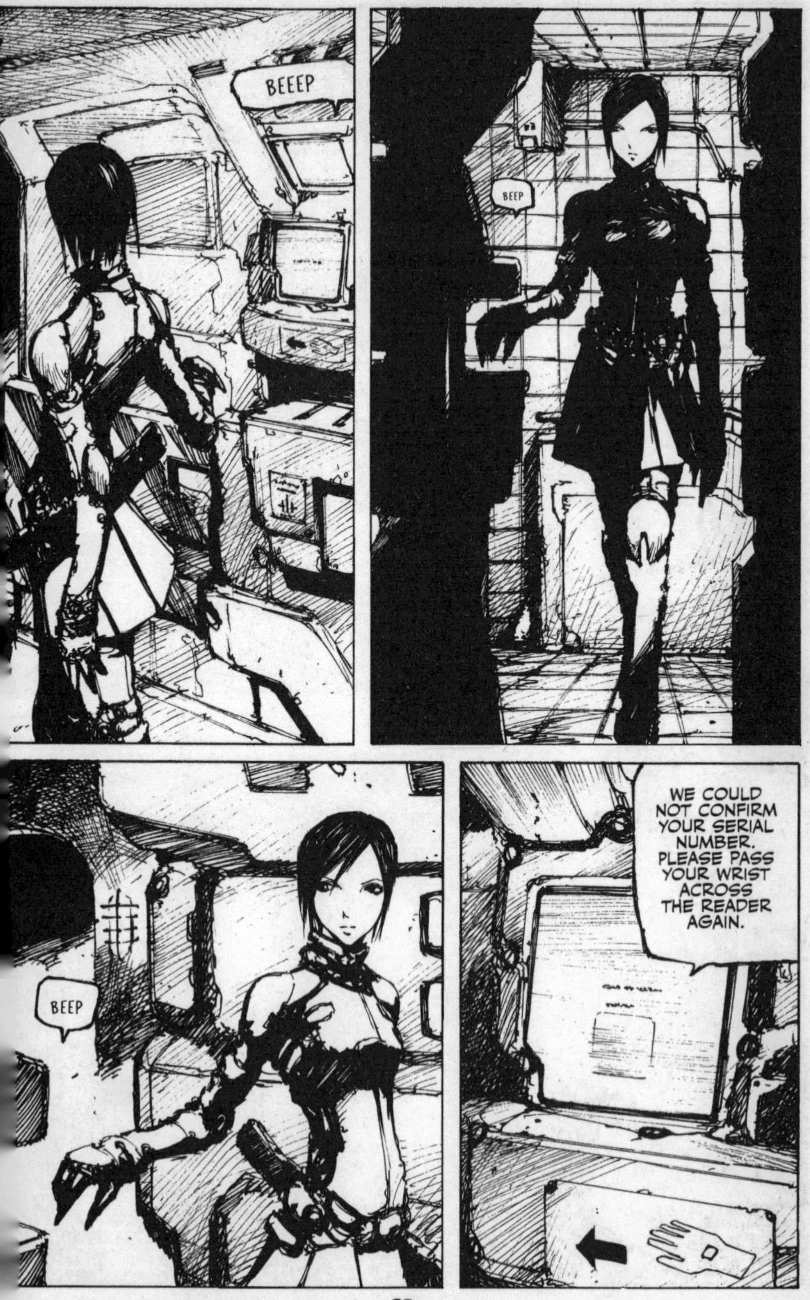
BEEP
BEEEP
WE COULD NOT CONFIRM YOUR SERIAL NUMBER. PLEASE PASS YOUR WRIST ACROSS THE READER AGAIN.
BEEP

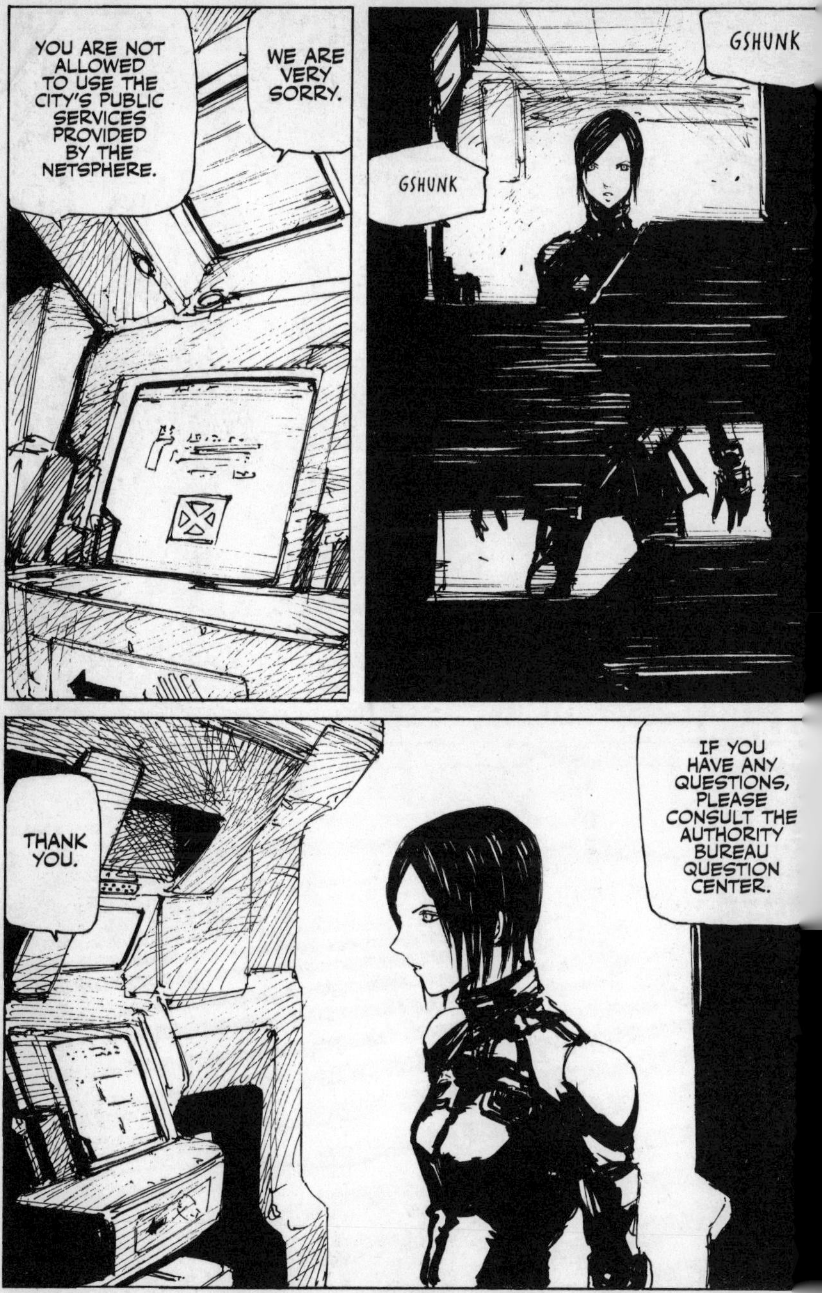
GSHUNK
GSHUNK
WE ARE VERY SORRY.
YOU ARE NOT ALLOWED TO USE THE CITY'S PUBLIC SERVICES PROVIDED BY THE NETSPHERE.
IF YOU HAVE ANY QUESTIONS, PLEASE CONSULT THE AUTHORITY BUREAU QUESTION CENTER.
THANK YOU.

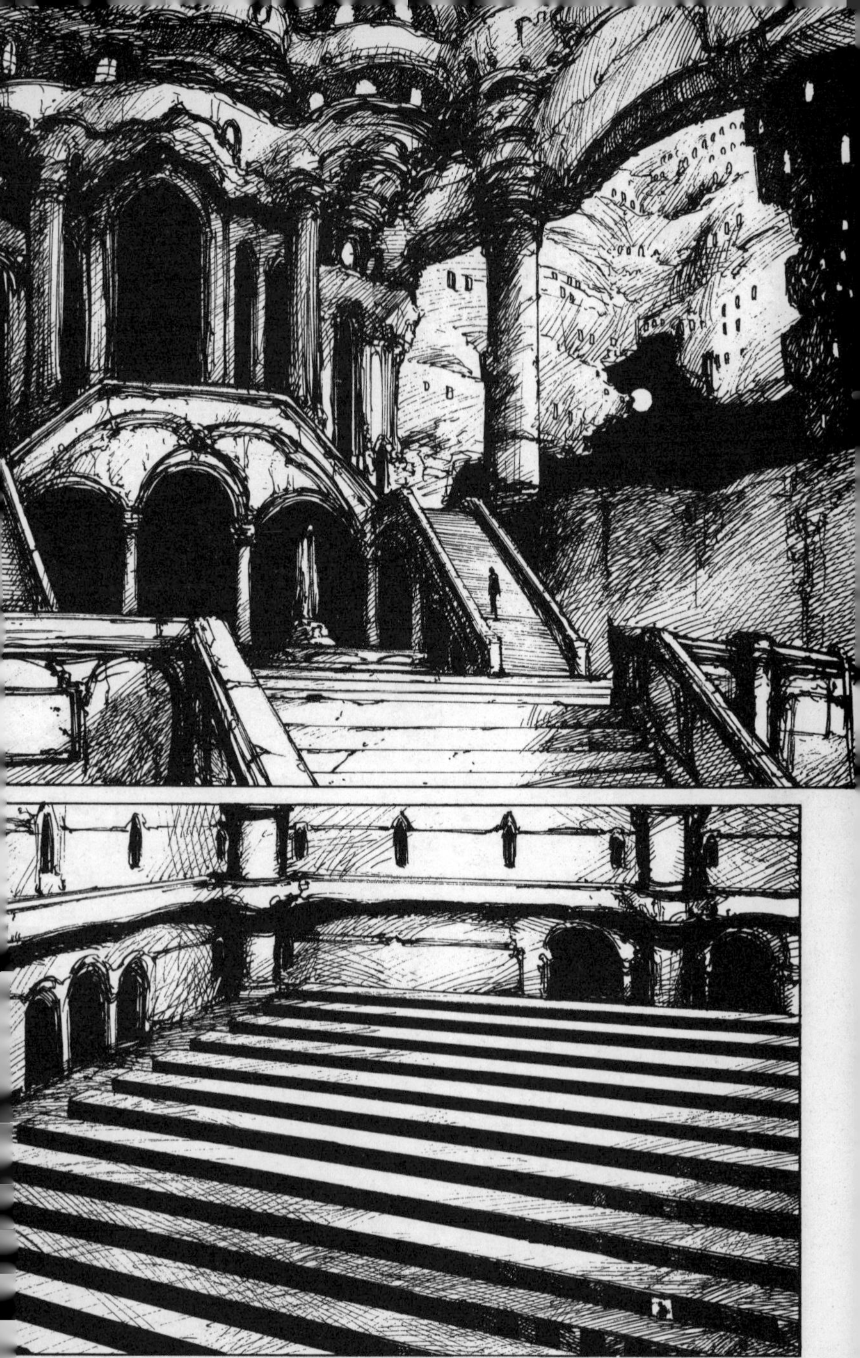

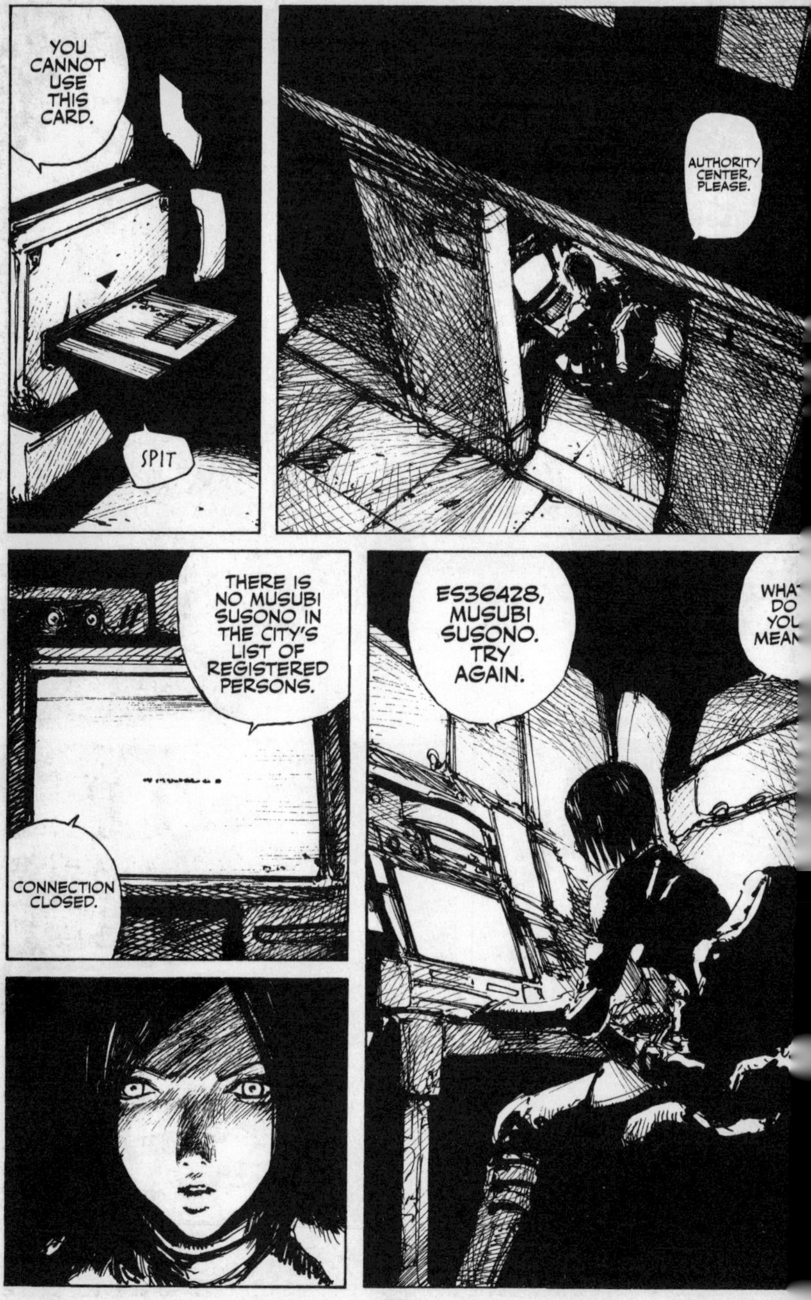
AUTHORITY CENTER, PLEASE.
YOU CANNOT USE THIS CARD.
SPIT
WHA DO YOU MEAN
ES36428, MUSUBI SUSONO. TRY AGAIN.
THERE IS NO MUSUBI SUSONO IN THE CITY'S LIST OF REGISTERED PERSONS.
CONNECTION CLOSED.

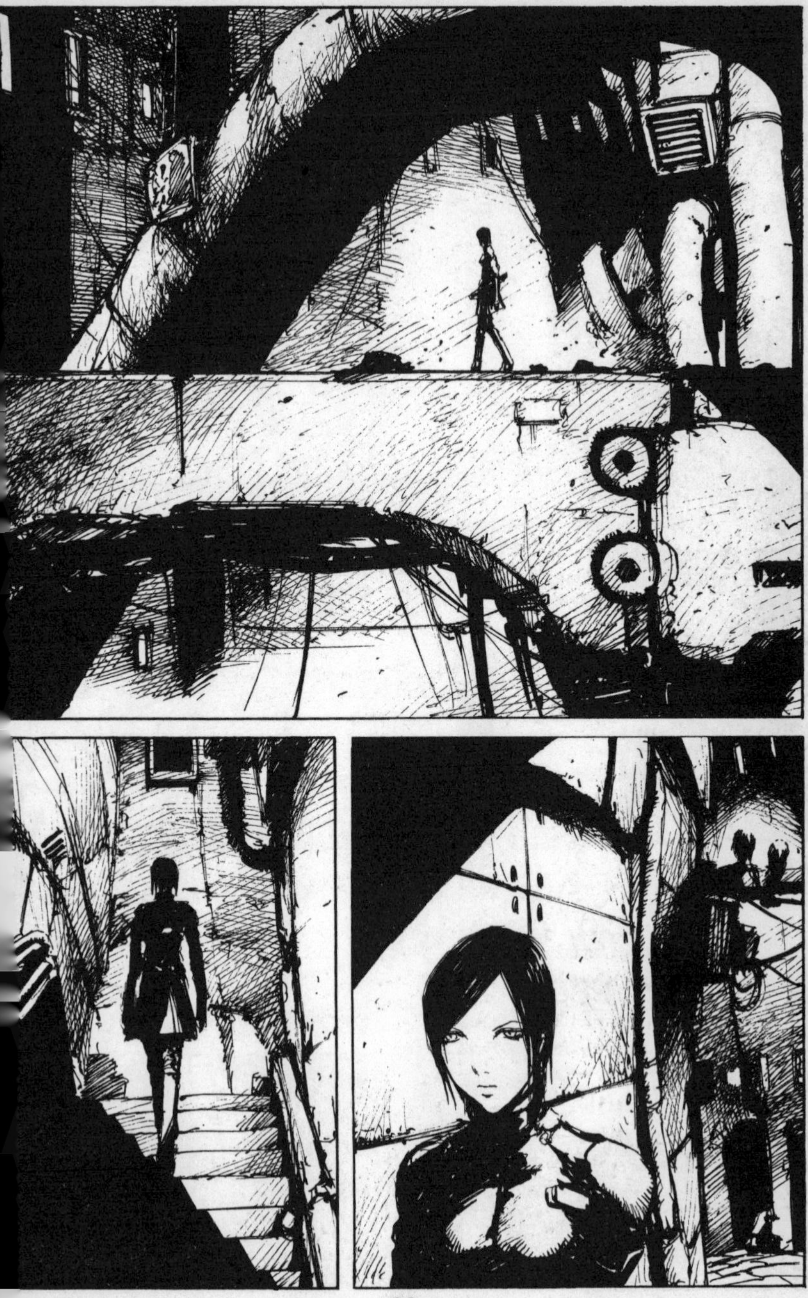

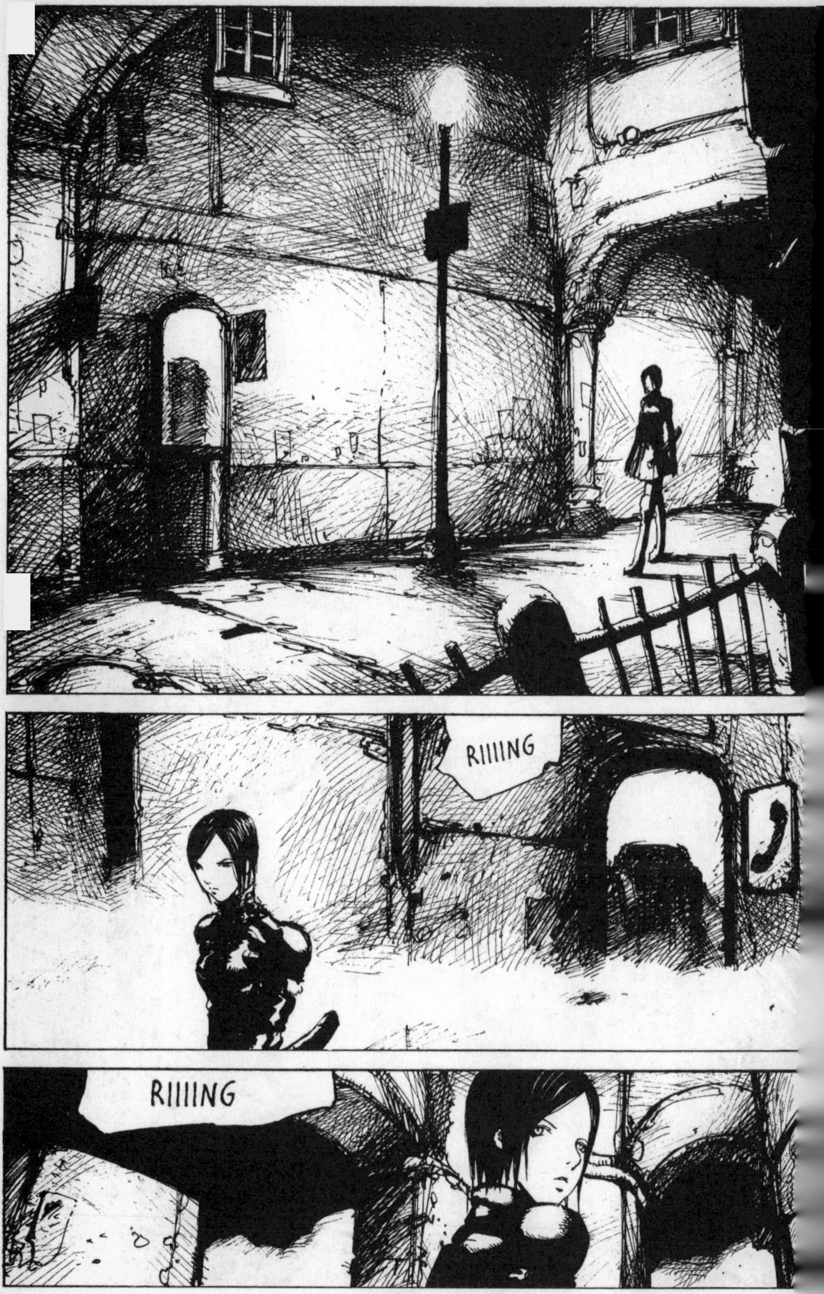
RIIIING
RIIIING

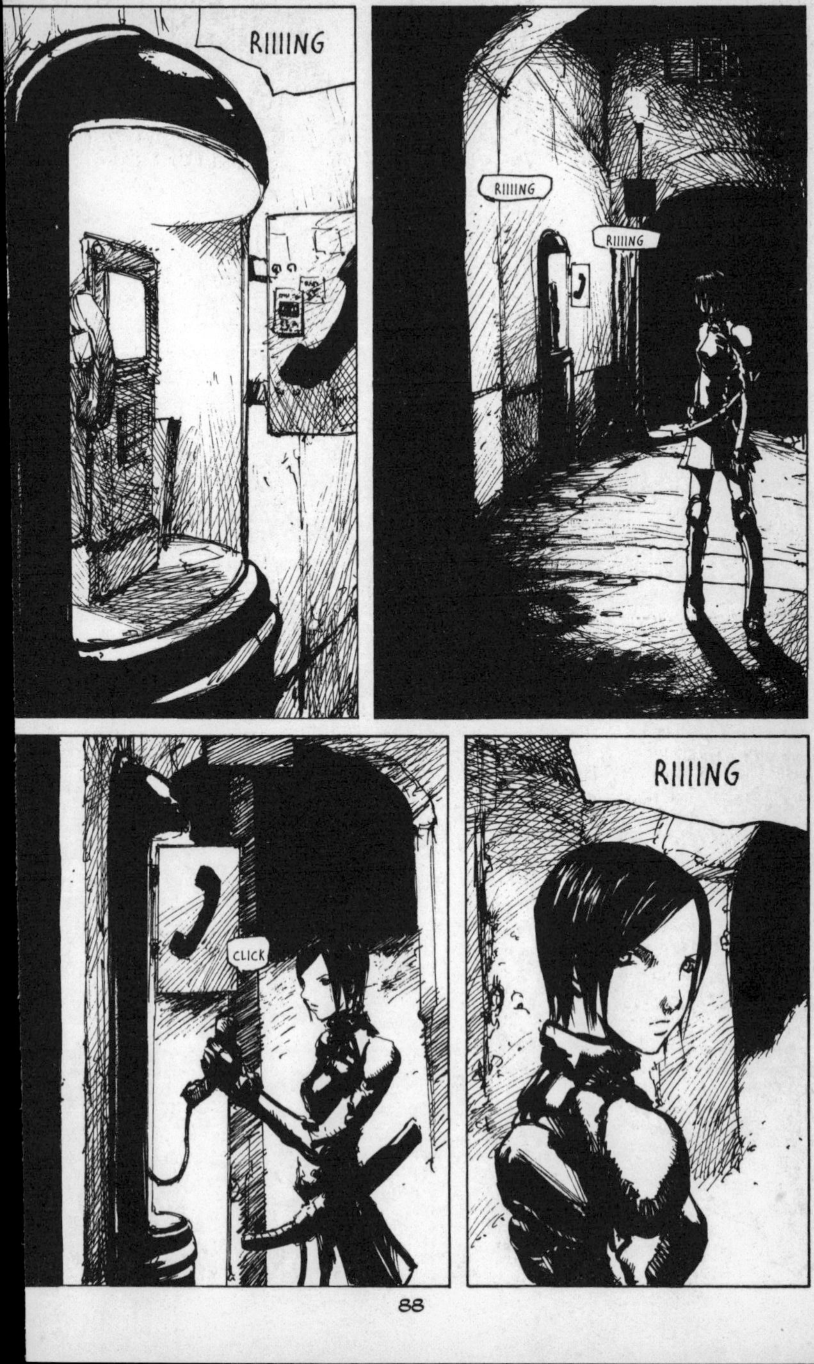
RIIIING
RIIIING
RIIIING
RIIIING
CLICK

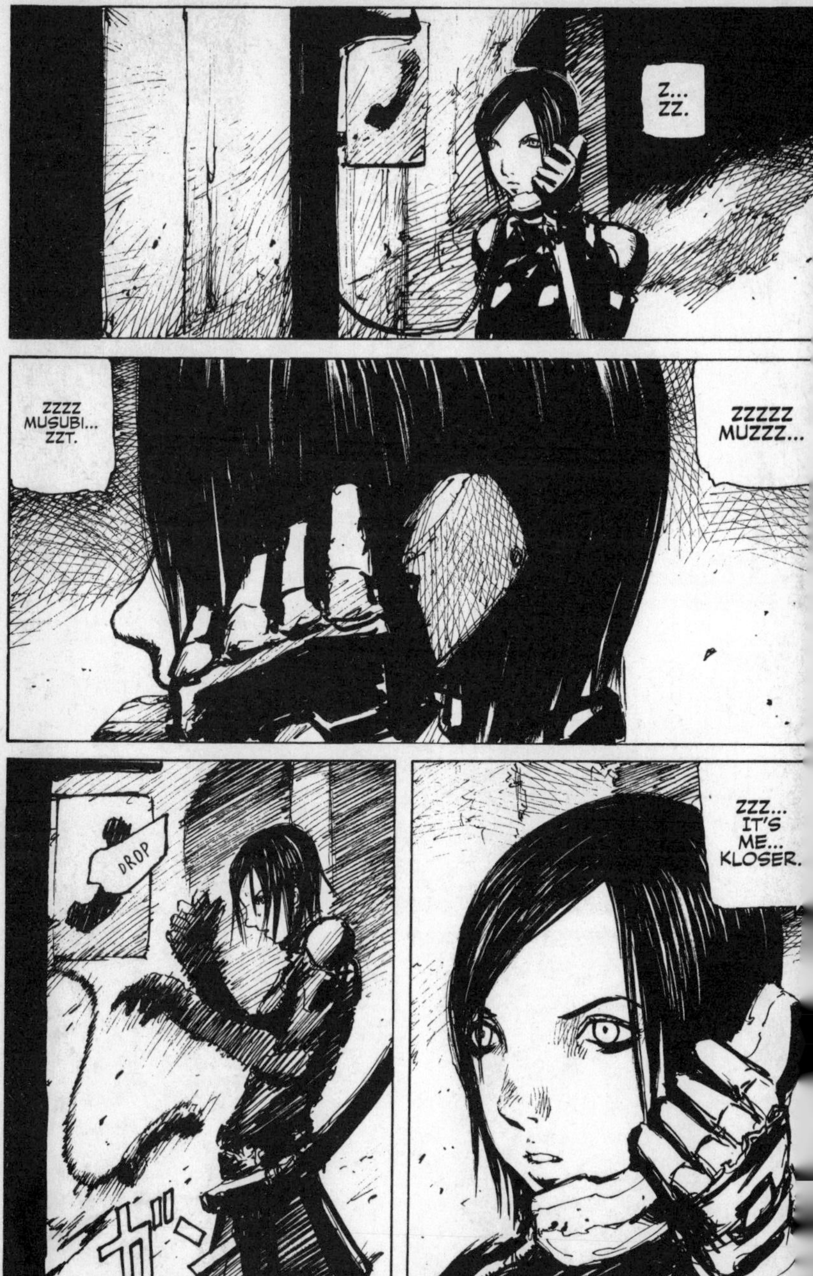
Z... ZZ.
ZZZZZ MUZZZ...
ZZZZ MUSUBI... ZZT.
ZZZ... IT'S ME... KLOSER.
DROP

Bang

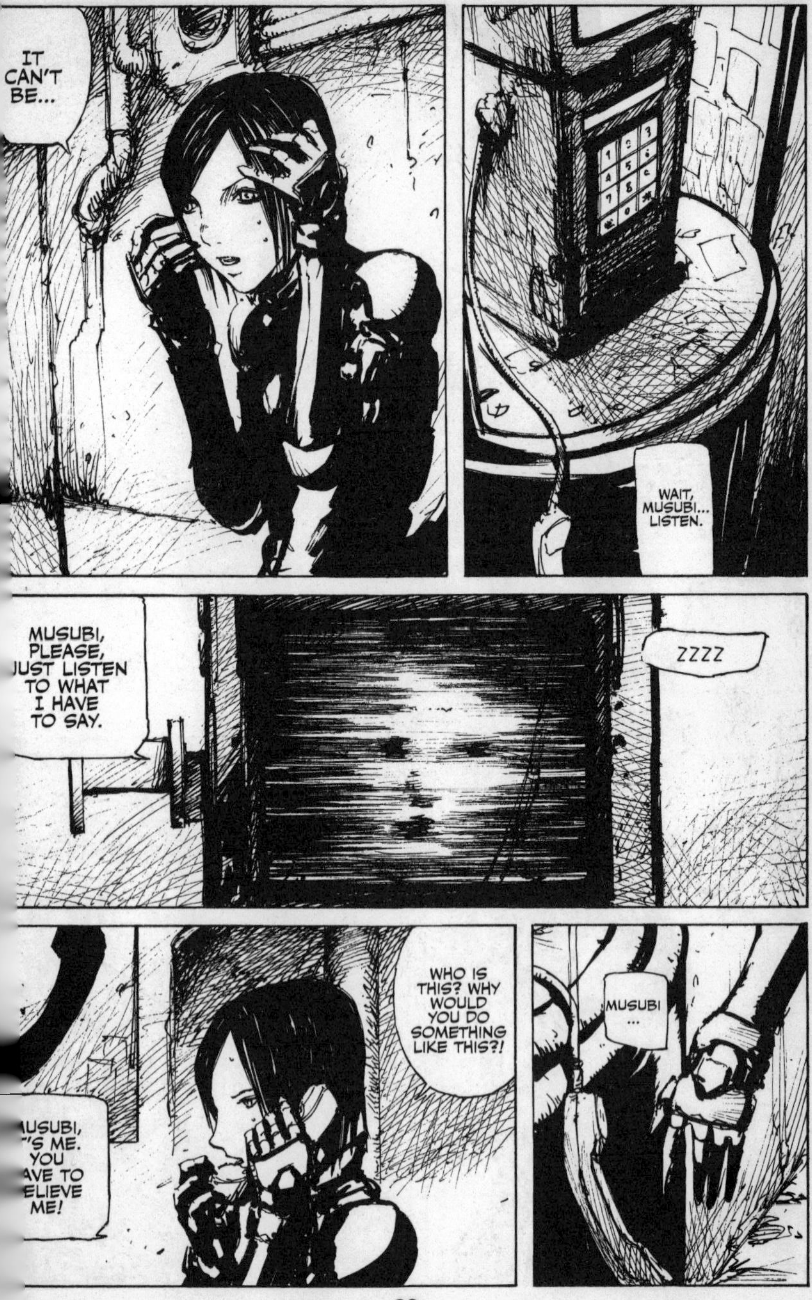
WAIT, MUSUBI... LISTEN.
IT CAN'T BE...
ZZZZ
MUSUBI, PLEASE, JUST LISTEN TO WHAT I HAVE TO SAY.
MUSUBI ...
WHO IS THIS? WHY WOULD YOU DO SOMETHING LIKE THIS?!
USUBI, 'S ME. YOU AVE TO ELIEVE ME!

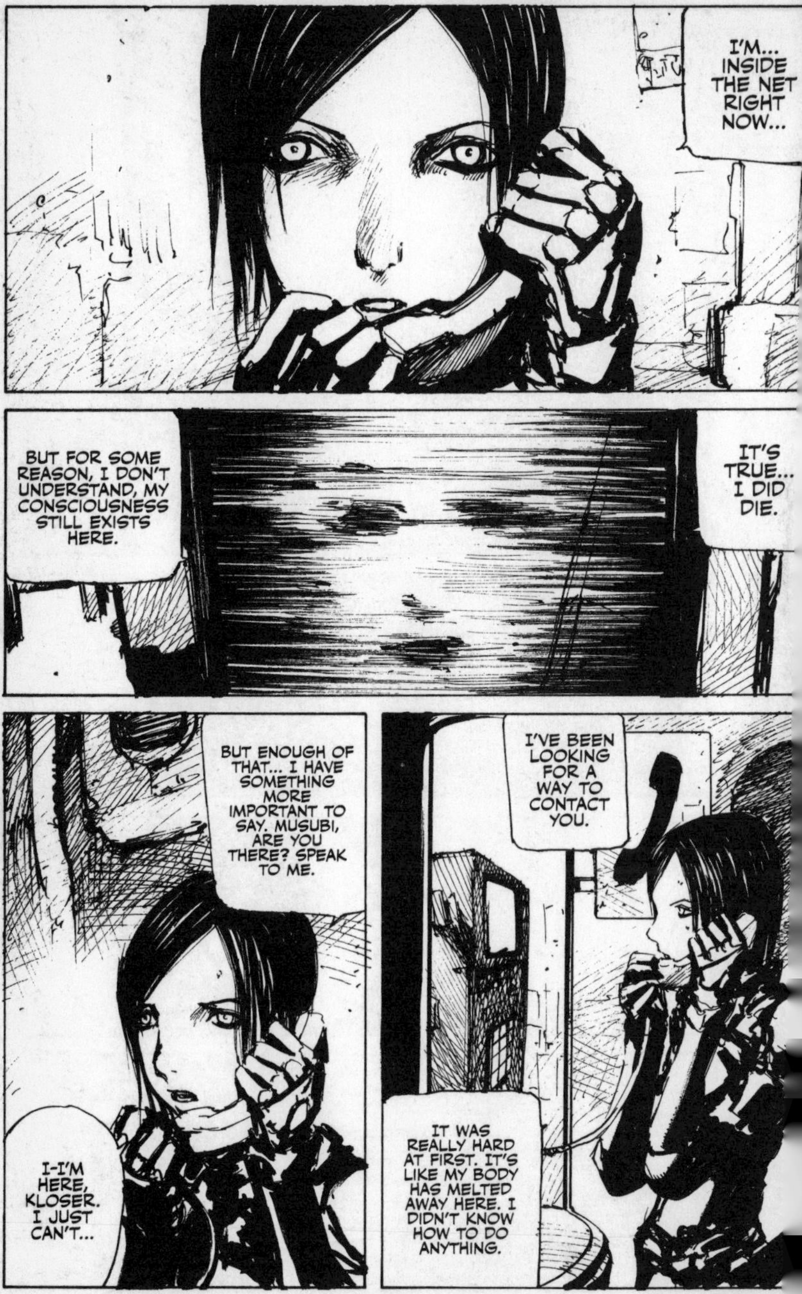
I'M... INSIDE THE NET RIGHT NOW...
IT'S TRUE... I DID DIE.
BUT FOR SOME REASON, I DON'T UNDERSTAND, MY CONSCIOUSNESS STILL EXISTS HERE.
I'VE BEEN LOOKING FOR A WAY TO CONTACT YOU.
IT WAS REALLY HARD AT FIRST. IT'S LIKE MY BODY HAS MELTED AWAY HERE. I DIDN'T KNOW HOW TO DO ANYTHING.
BUT ENOUGH OF THAT... I HAVE SOMETHING MORE IMPORTANT TO SAY. MUSUBI, ARE YOU THERE? SPEAK TO ME.
I-I'M HERE, KLOSER. I JUST CAN'T...

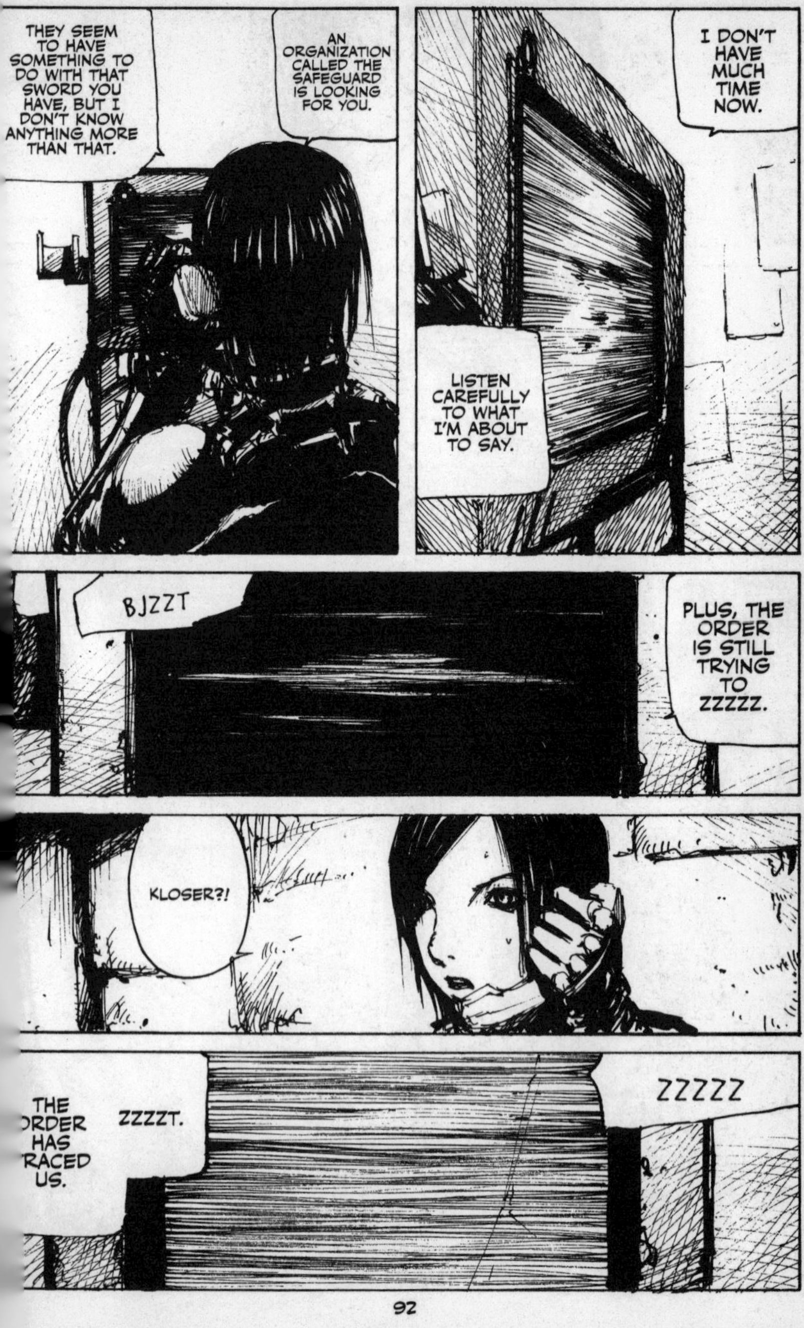
I DON'T HAVE MUCH TIME NOW.
LISTEN CAREFULLY TO WHAT I'M ABOUT TO SAY.
AN ORGANIZATION CALLED THE SAFEGUARD IS LOOKING FOR YOU.
THEY SEEM TO HAVE SOMETHING TO DO WITH THAT SWORD YOU HAVE, BUT I DON'T KNOW ANYTHING MORE THAN THAT.
PLUS, THE ORDER IS STILL TRYING TO ZZZZZ.
BJZZT
KLOSER?!
ZZZZZ
ZZZZT.
THE ORDER HAS TRACED US.

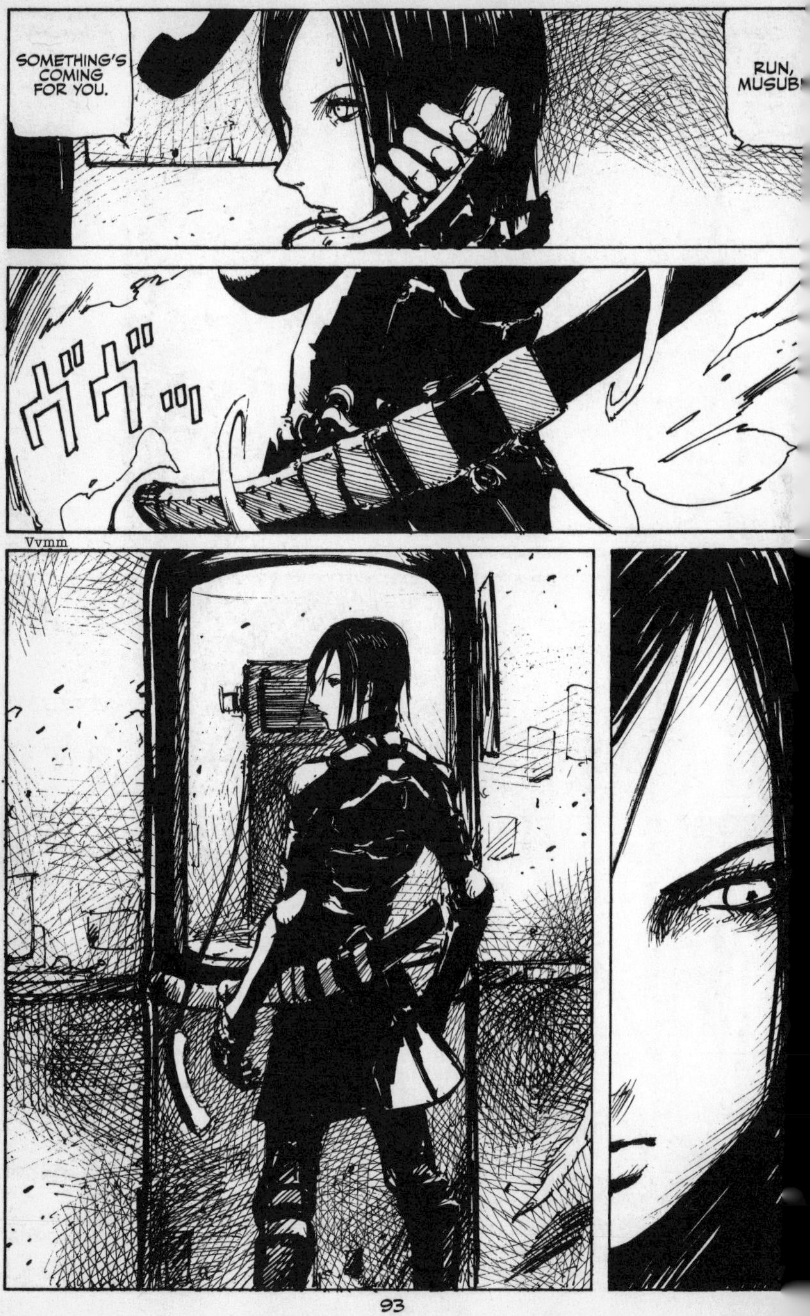
RUN, MUSUB
SOMETHING'S COMING FOR YOU.
Vvmm

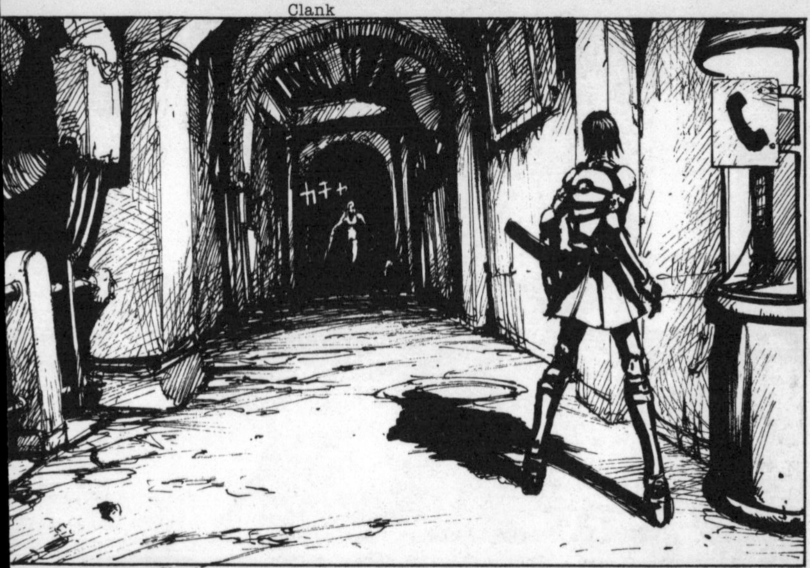
Clank
カチャ

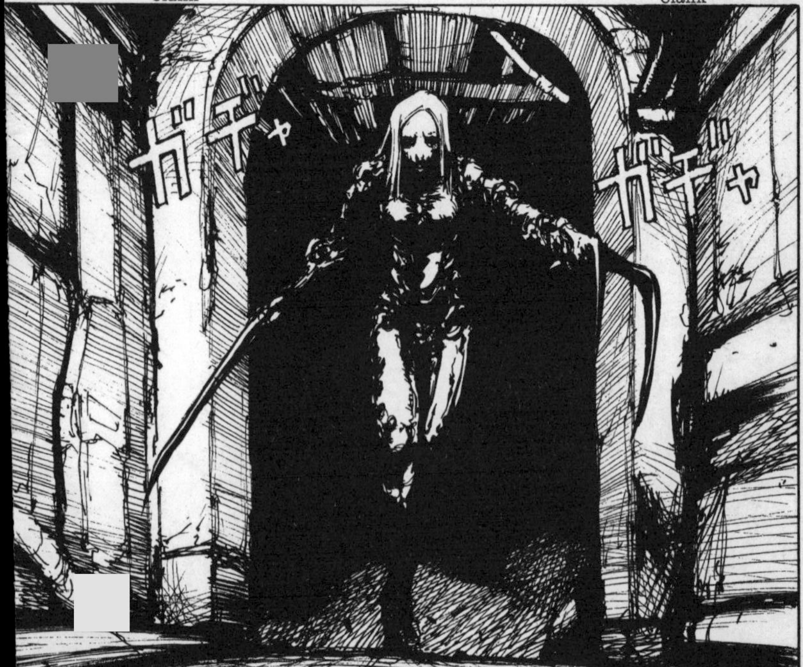
Clank
ガヂャ
Clank
ガヂャ

カキン

Kchnk

!

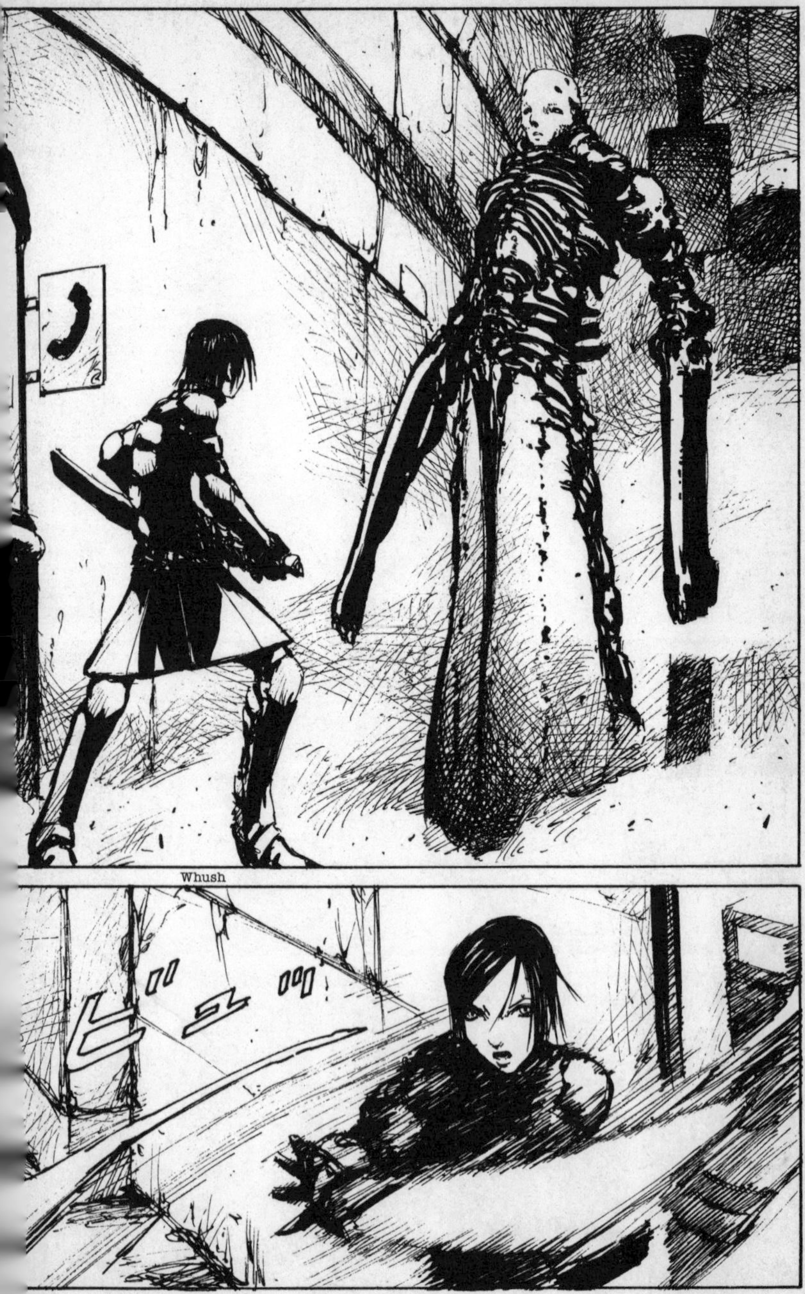
Whush

Boom

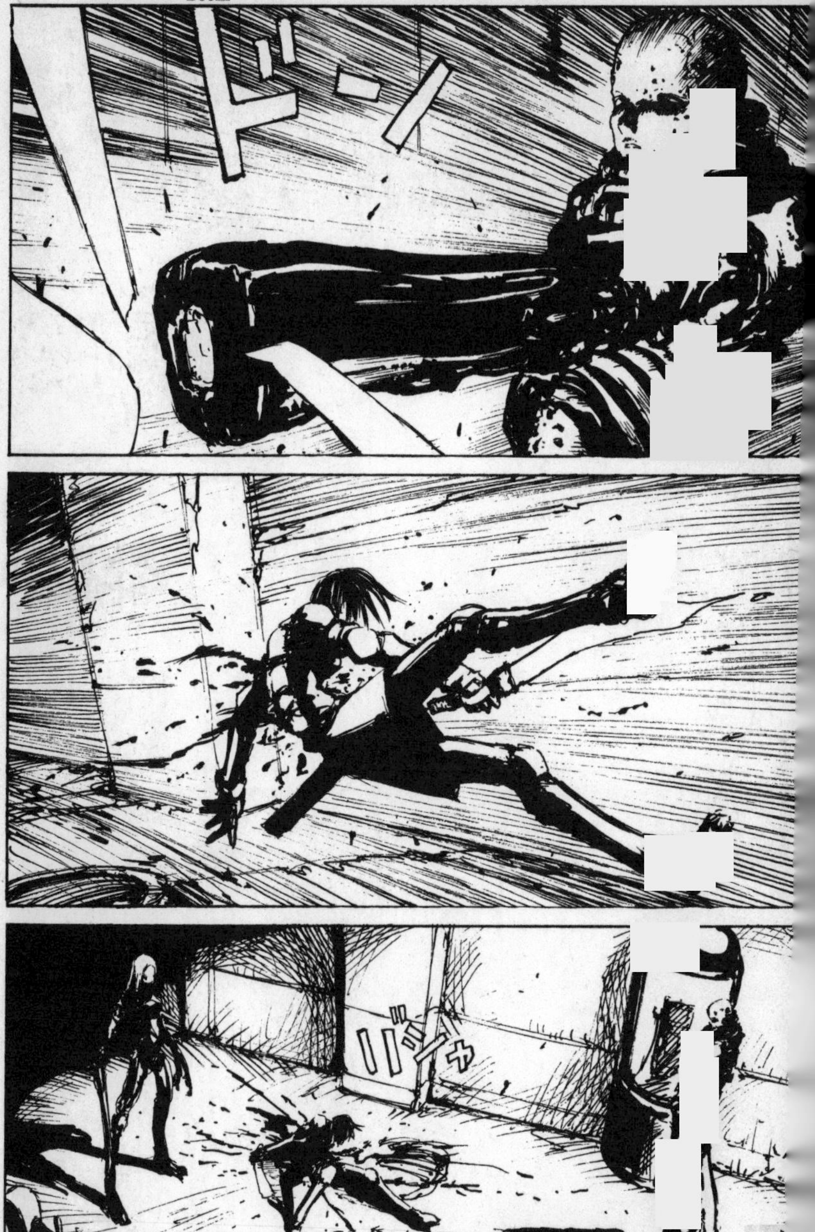

Splatch

Blubb

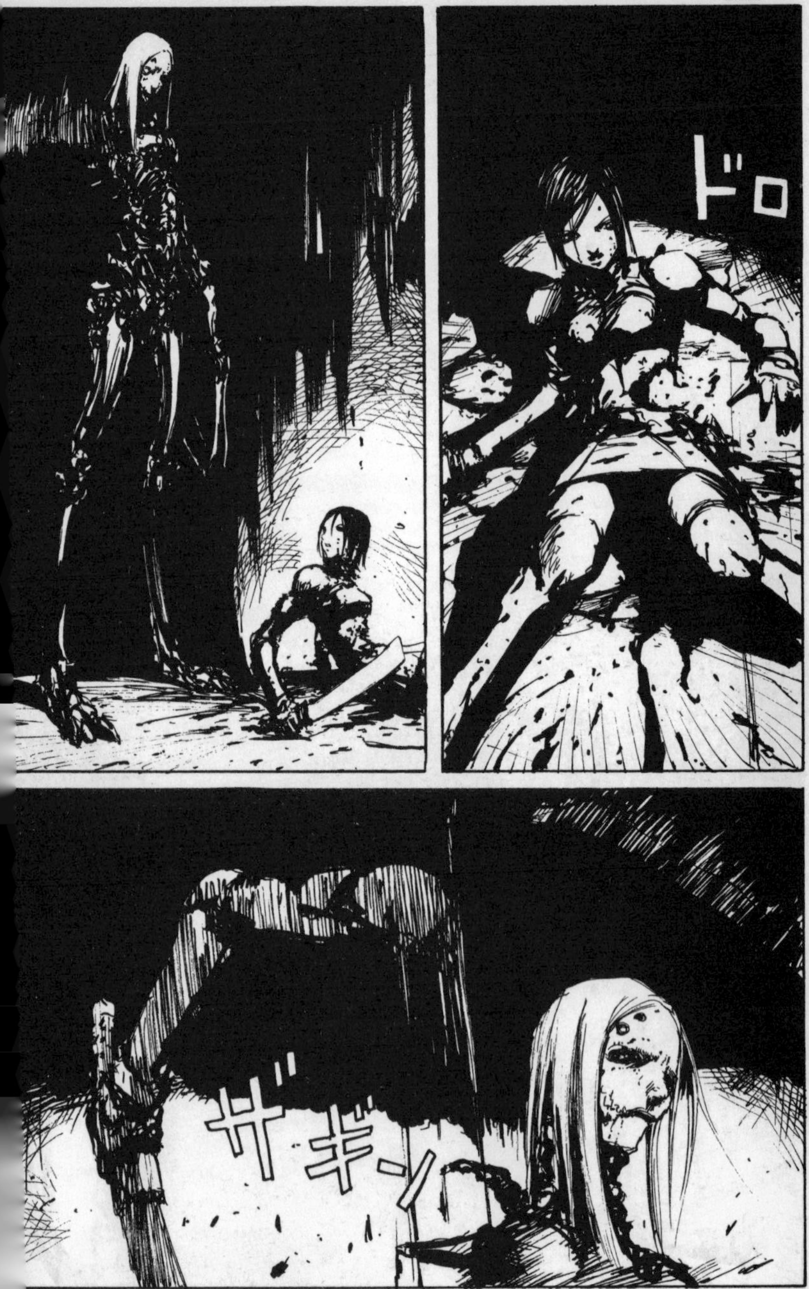
ドロ
ザギーン

Zchukk

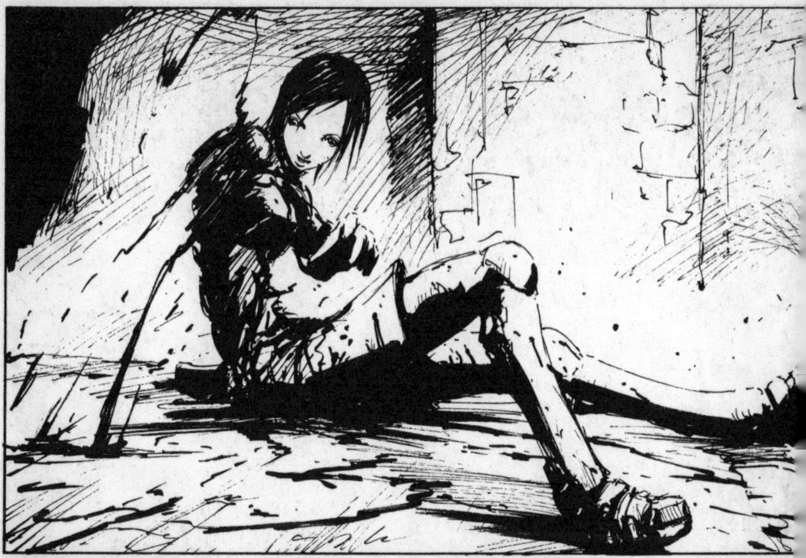

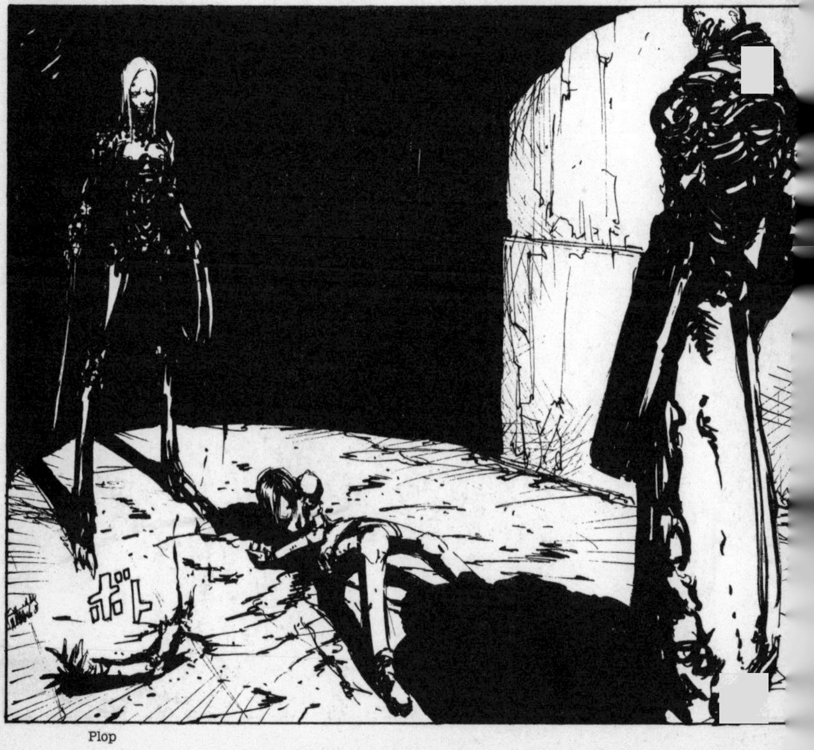
ボト

Plop

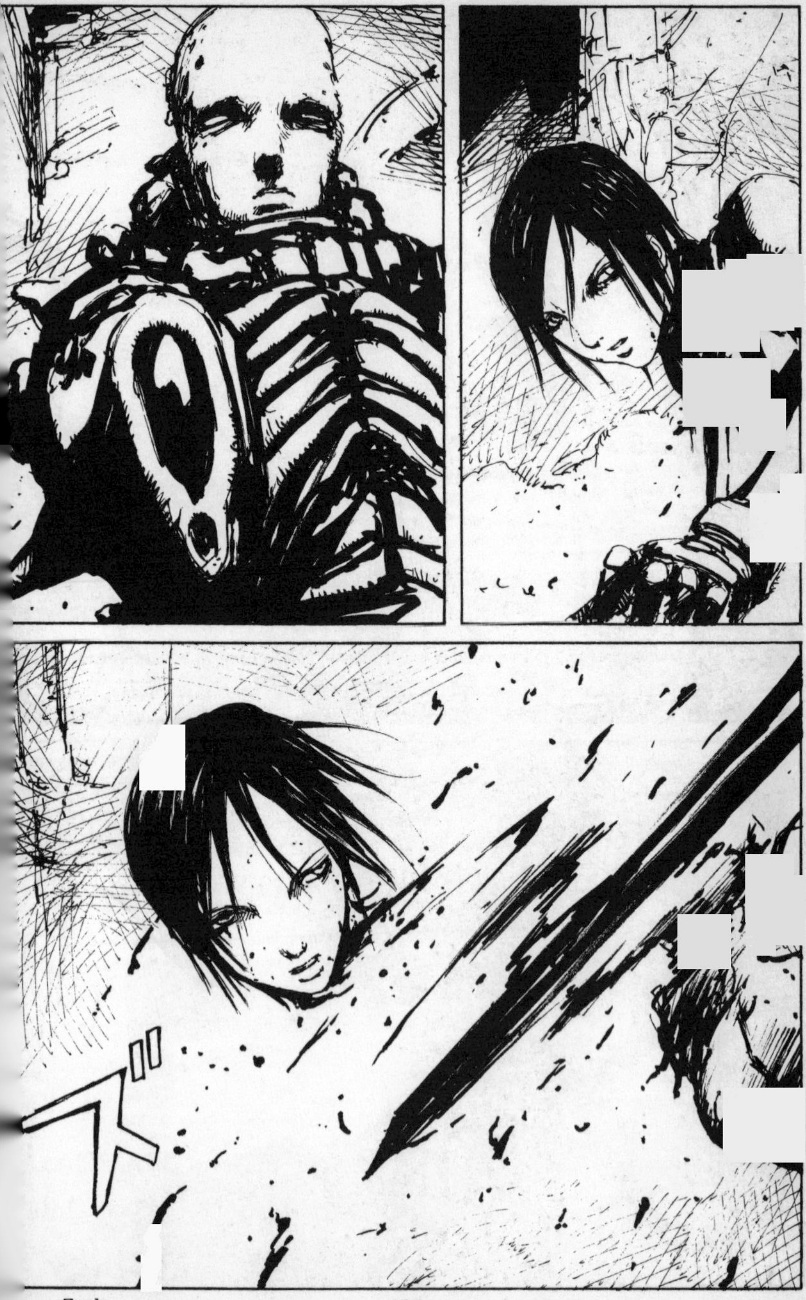
ズ

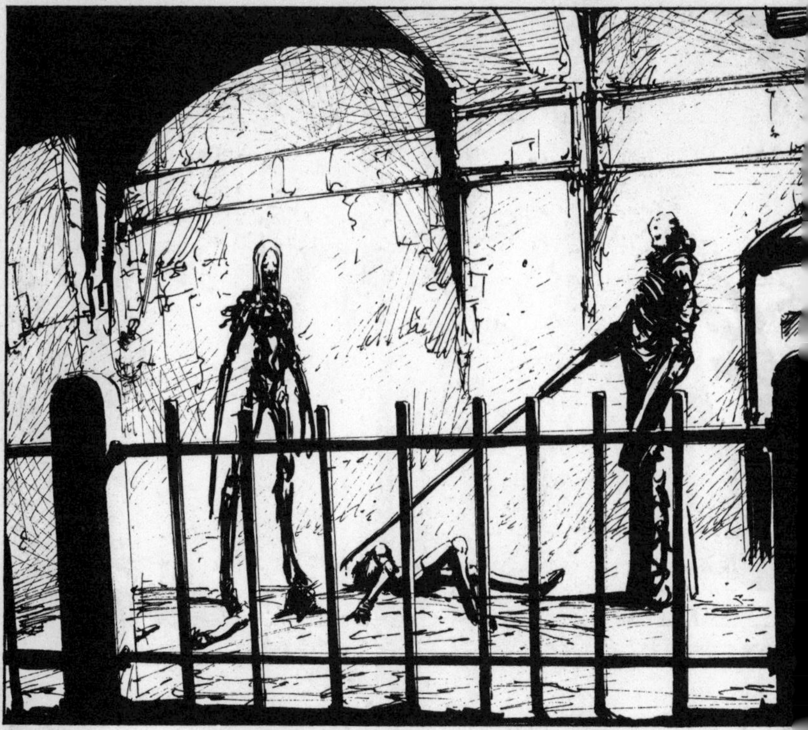

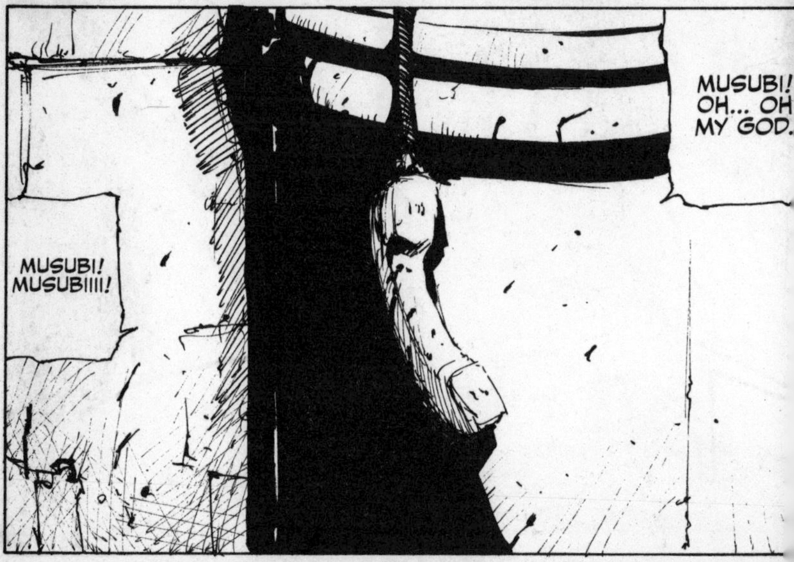
MUSUBI! OH... OH MY GOD.
MUSUBI! MUSUBIIII!

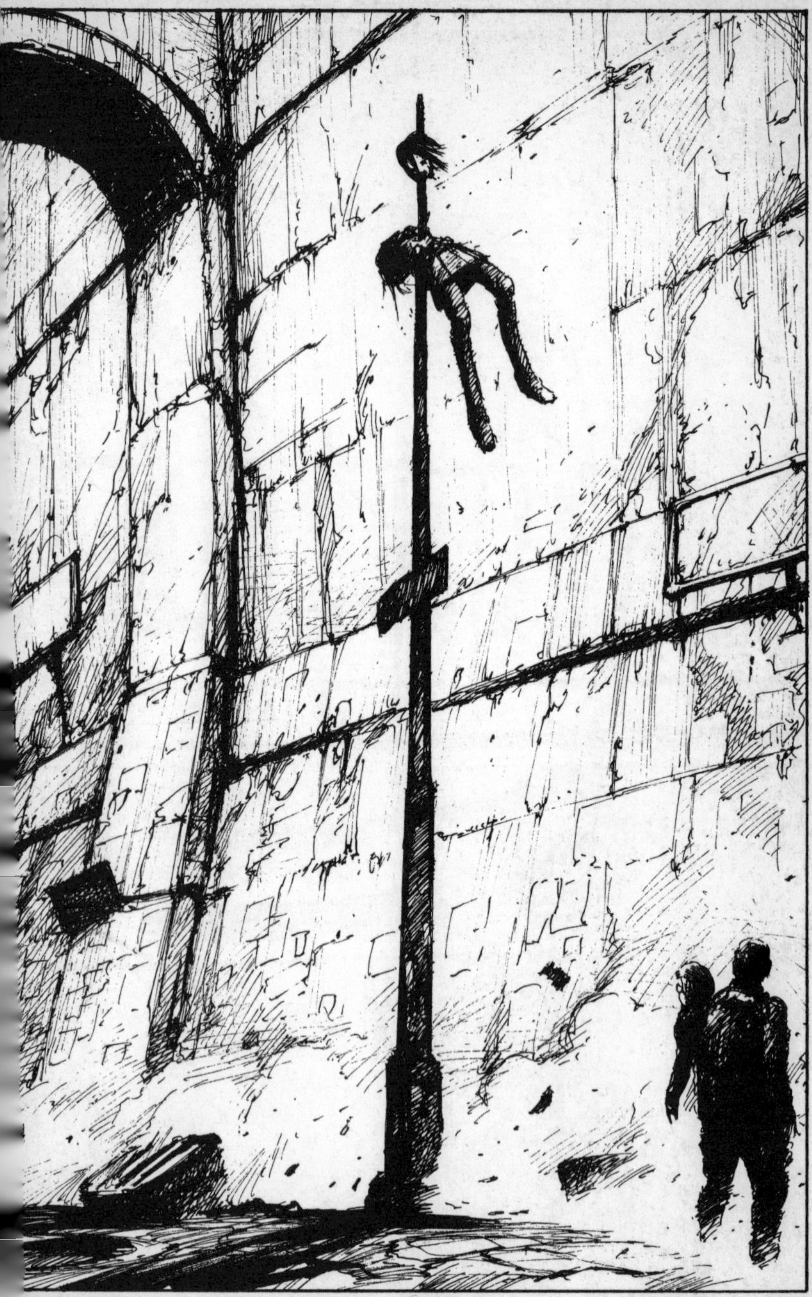

Chapter 4 Sacrifice ~End~

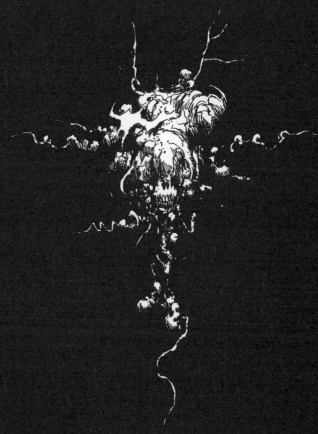

Chapter 5
Corpse Running Wild
第五章

しかばね
屍の暴走

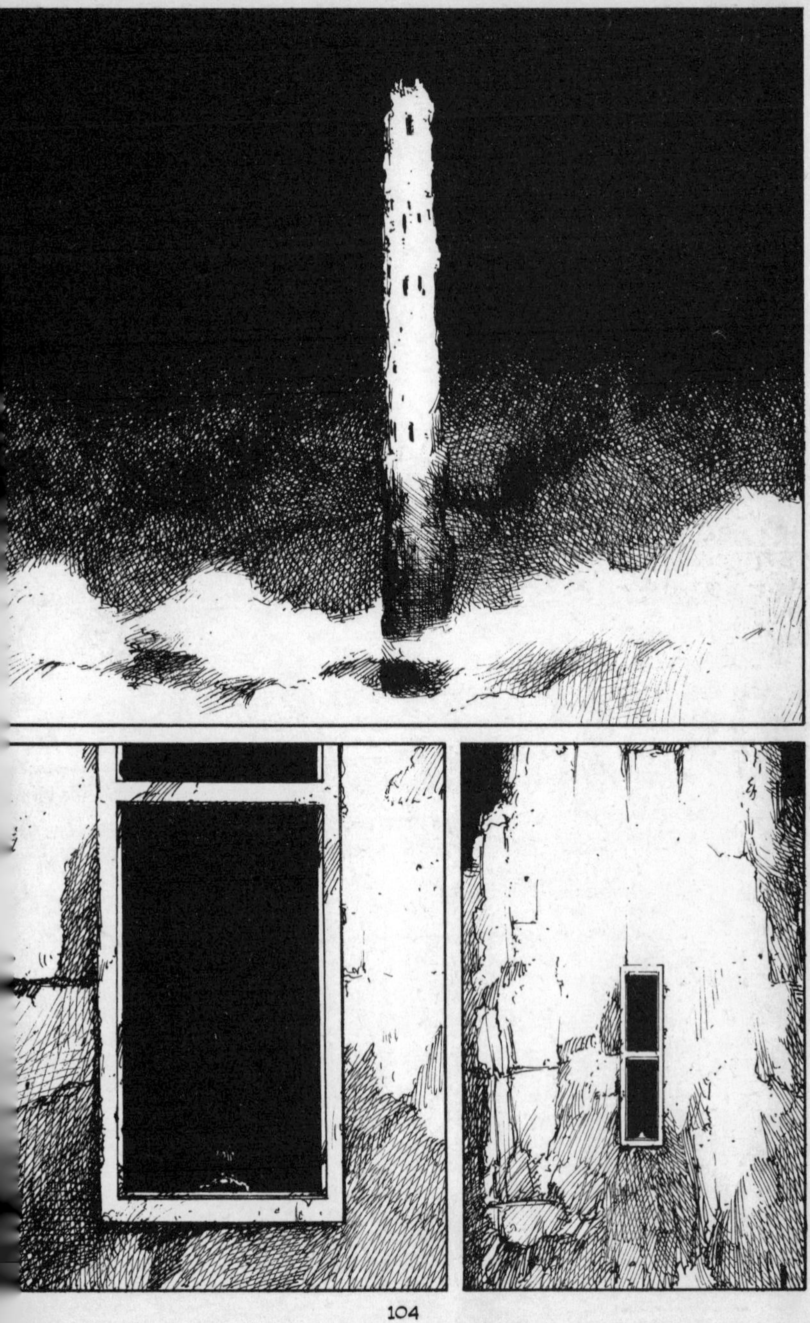

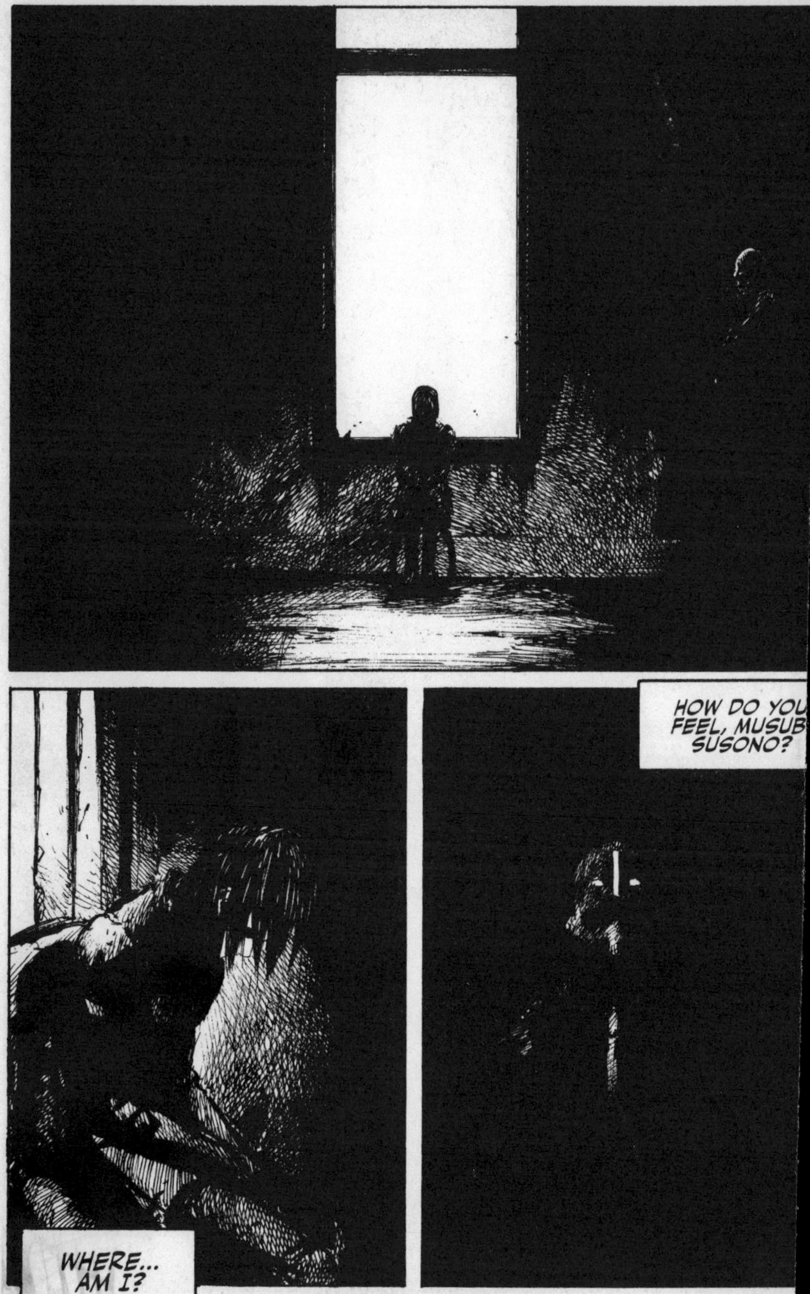
WHERE... AM I?
HOW DO YOU FEEL, MUSUB SUSONO?

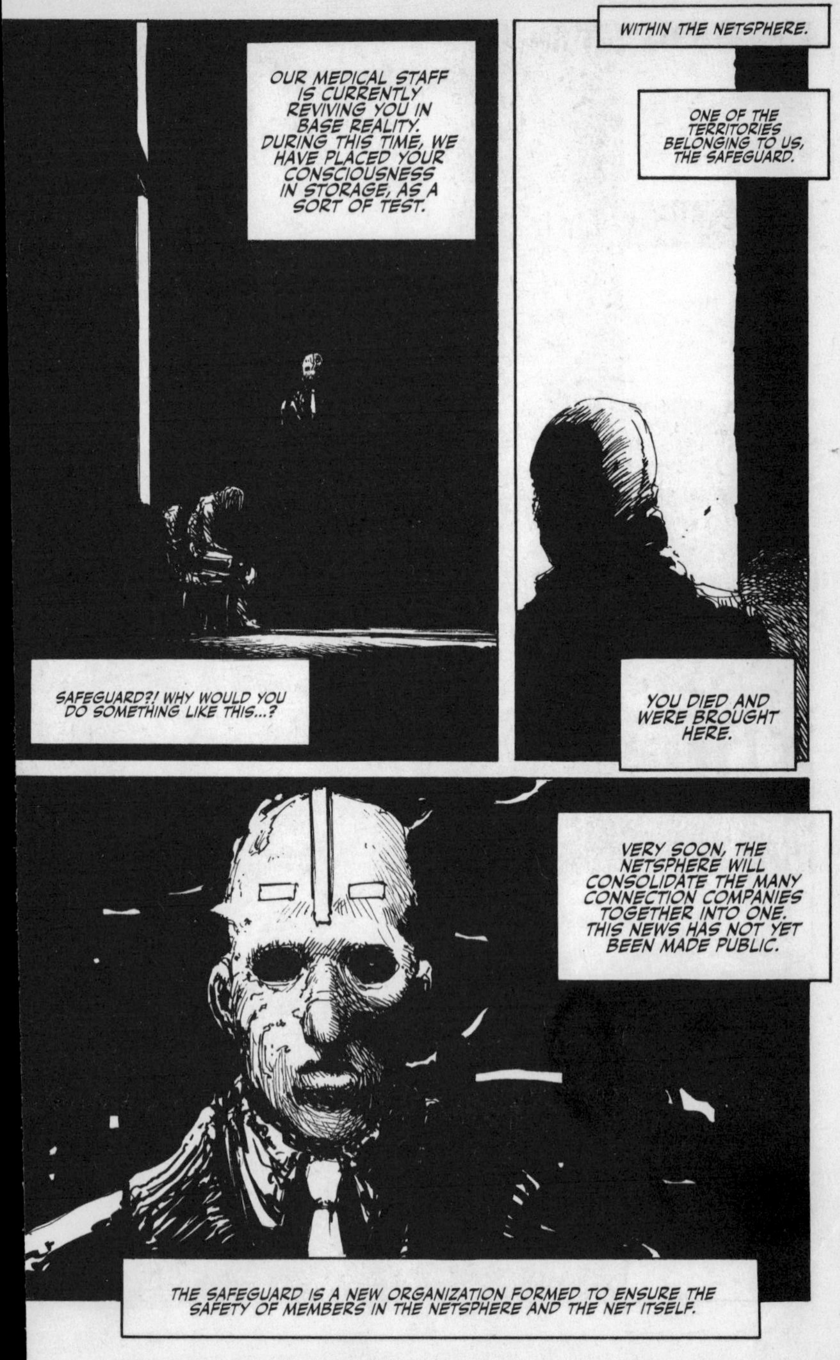
WITHIN THE NETSPHERE.
ONE OF THE TERRITORIES BELONGING TO US, THE SAFEGUARD.
YOU DIED AND WERE BROUGHT HERE.
OUR MEDICAL STAFF IS CURRENTLY REVIVING YOU IN BASE REALITY. DURING THIS TIME, WE HAVE PLACED YOUR CONSCIOUSNESS IN STORAGE, AS A SORT OF TEST.
SAFEGUARD?! WHY WOULD YOU DO SOMETHING LIKE THIS...?
VERY SOON, THE NETSPHERE WILL CONSOLIDATE THE MANY CONNECTION COMPANIES TOGETHER INTO ONE. THIS NEWS HAS NOT YET BEEN MADE PUBLIC.
THE SAFEGUARD IS A NEW ORGANIZATION FORMED TO ENSURE THE SAFETY OF MEMBERS IN THE NETSPHERE AND THE NET ITSELF.

THE SAFEGUARD WILL PURSUE AGGRESSIVELY THE ELIMINATION OF THOSE HUMANS WITHOUT NET-TERMINAL IMPLANTS.

IN THE NEWLY ENGINEERED WORLD OF THE NETSPHERE, NON-MEMBERS WILL HAVE NO RIGHTS.

WHAT ABOUT THE SAFETY OF NON-MEMBERS?

WE WOULD LIKE YOUR COOPERATION

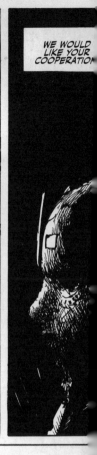

I WILL NEVER, EVER COOPERATE WITH YOU.

PUT ME BACK.

. . . .

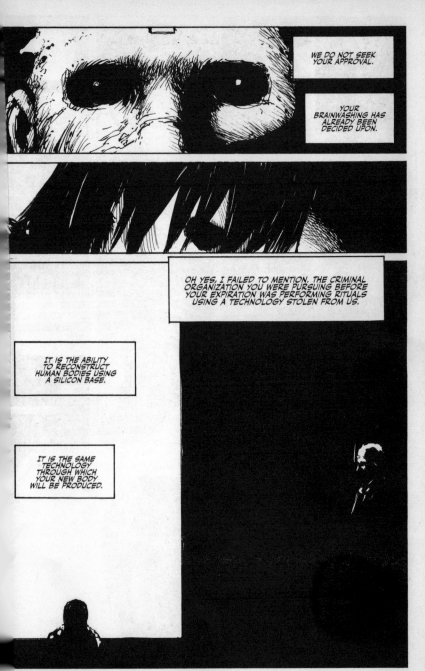

WE DO NOT SEEK YOUR APPROVAL.

YOUR BRAINWASHING HAS ALREADY BEEN DECIDED UPON.

OH YES, I FAILED TO MENTION. THE CRIMINAL ORGANIZATION YOU WERE PURSUING BEFORE YOUR EXPIRATION WAS PERFORMING RITUALS USING A TECHNOLOGY STOLEN FROM US.

IT IS THE ABILITY TO RECONSTRUCT HUMAN BODIES USING A SILICON BASE.

IT IS THE SAME TECHNOLOGY THROUGH WHICH YOUR NEW BODY WILL BE PRODUCED.

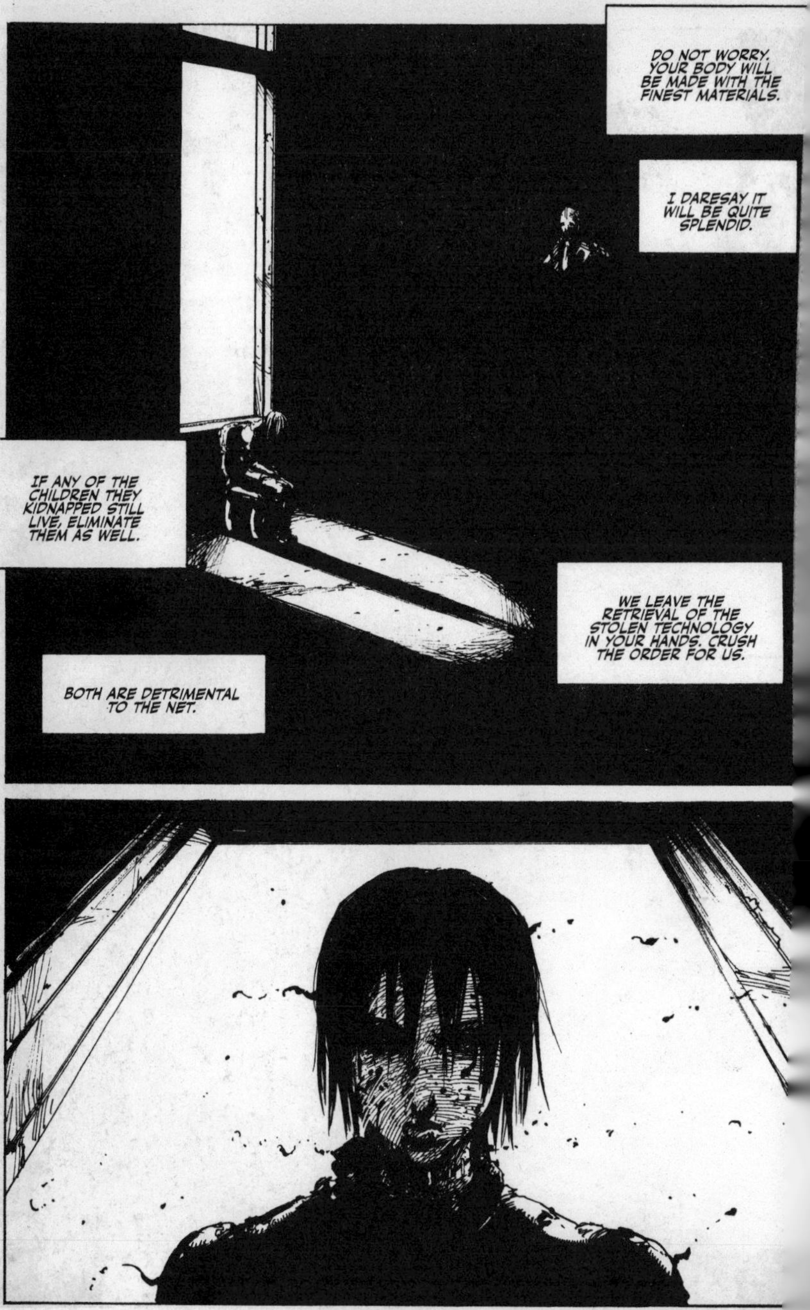
DO NOT WORRY. YOUR BODY WILL BE MADE WITH THE FINEST MATERIALS.
I DARESAY IT WILL BE QUITE SPLENDID.
WE LEAVE THE RETRIEVAL OF THE STOLEN TECHNOLOGY IN YOUR HANDS. CRUSH THE ORDER FOR US.
IF ANY OF THE CHILDREN THEY KIDNAPPED STILL LIVE, ELIMINATE THEM AS WELL.
BOTH ARE DETRIMENTAL TO THE NET.

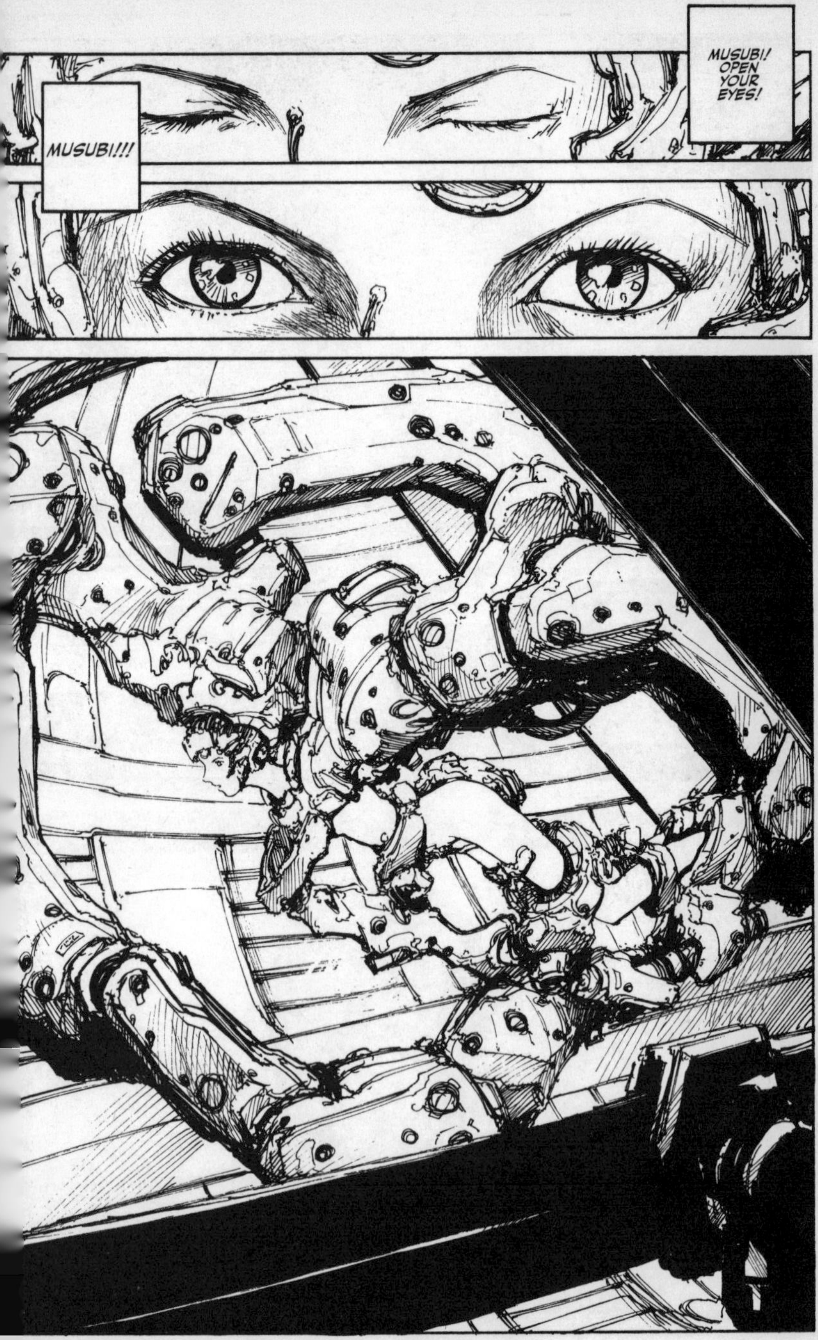
MUSUBI! OPEN YOUR EYES!
MUSUBI!!!

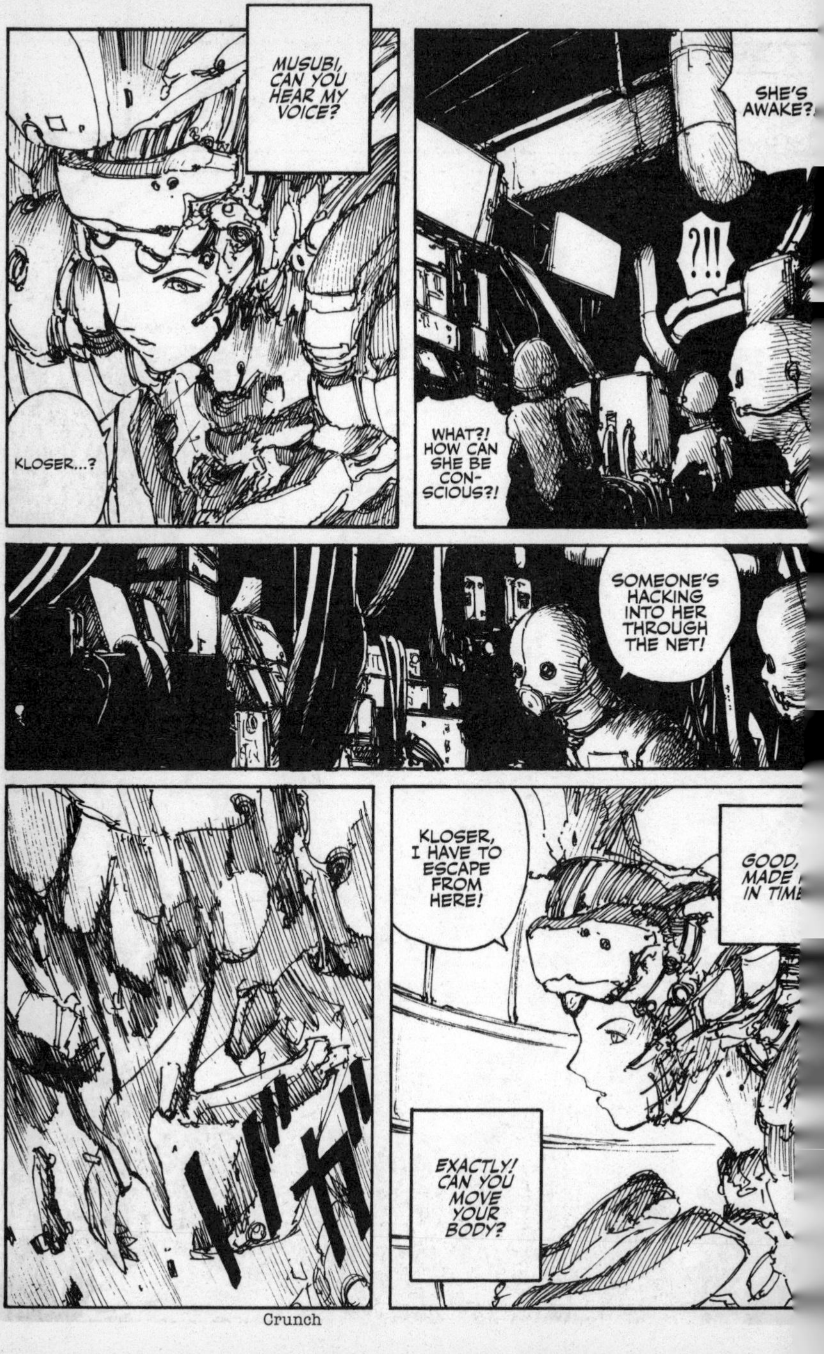
SHE'S AWAKE?!
?!!
WHAT?! HOW CAN SHE BE CON- SCIOUS?!
MUSUBI, CAN YOU HEAR MY VOICE?
KLOSER...?
SOMEONE'S HACKING INTO HER THROUGH THE NET!
GOOD, MADE IN TIME
KLOSER, I HAVE TO ESCAPE FROM HERE!
EXACTLY! CAN YOU MOVE YOUR BODY?
Crunch

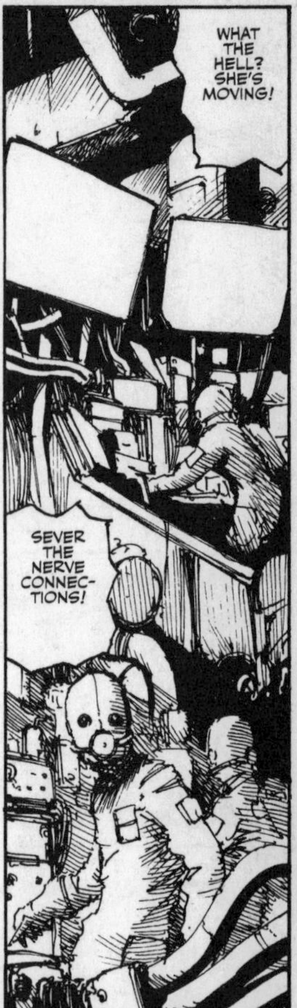
WHAT THE HELL? SHE'S MOVING!
SEVER THE NERVE CONNEC- TIONS!

Boom Boom

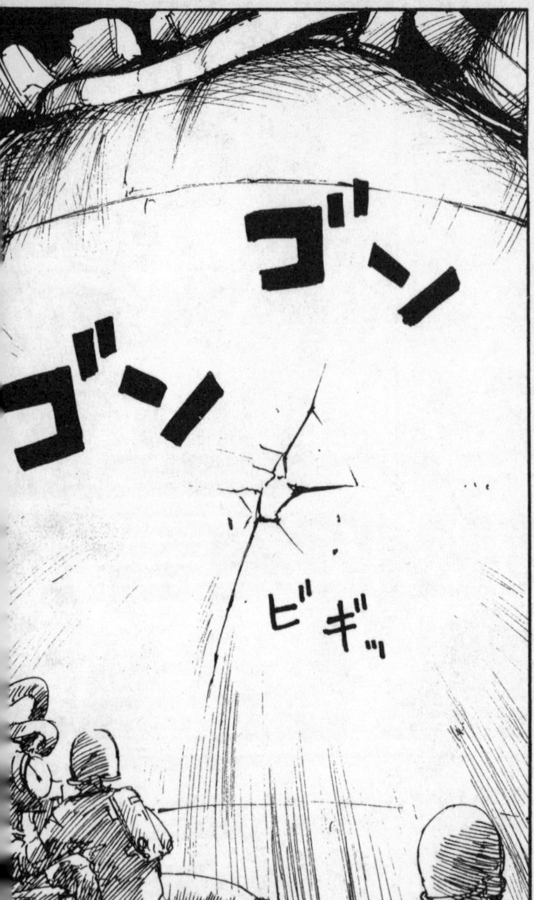
ゴン
ゴン
ビギッ
Crack

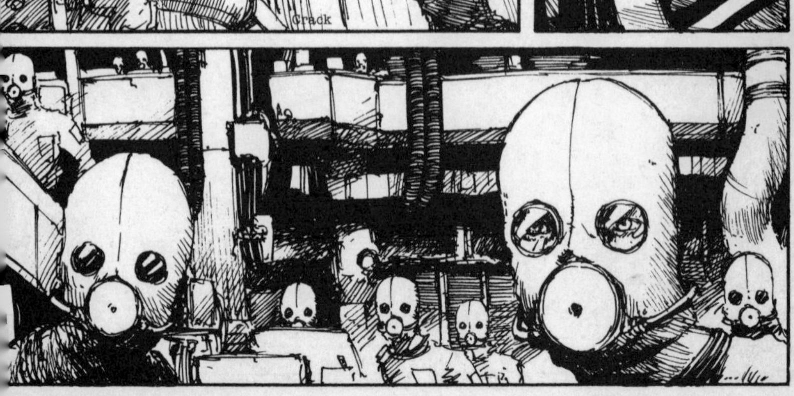

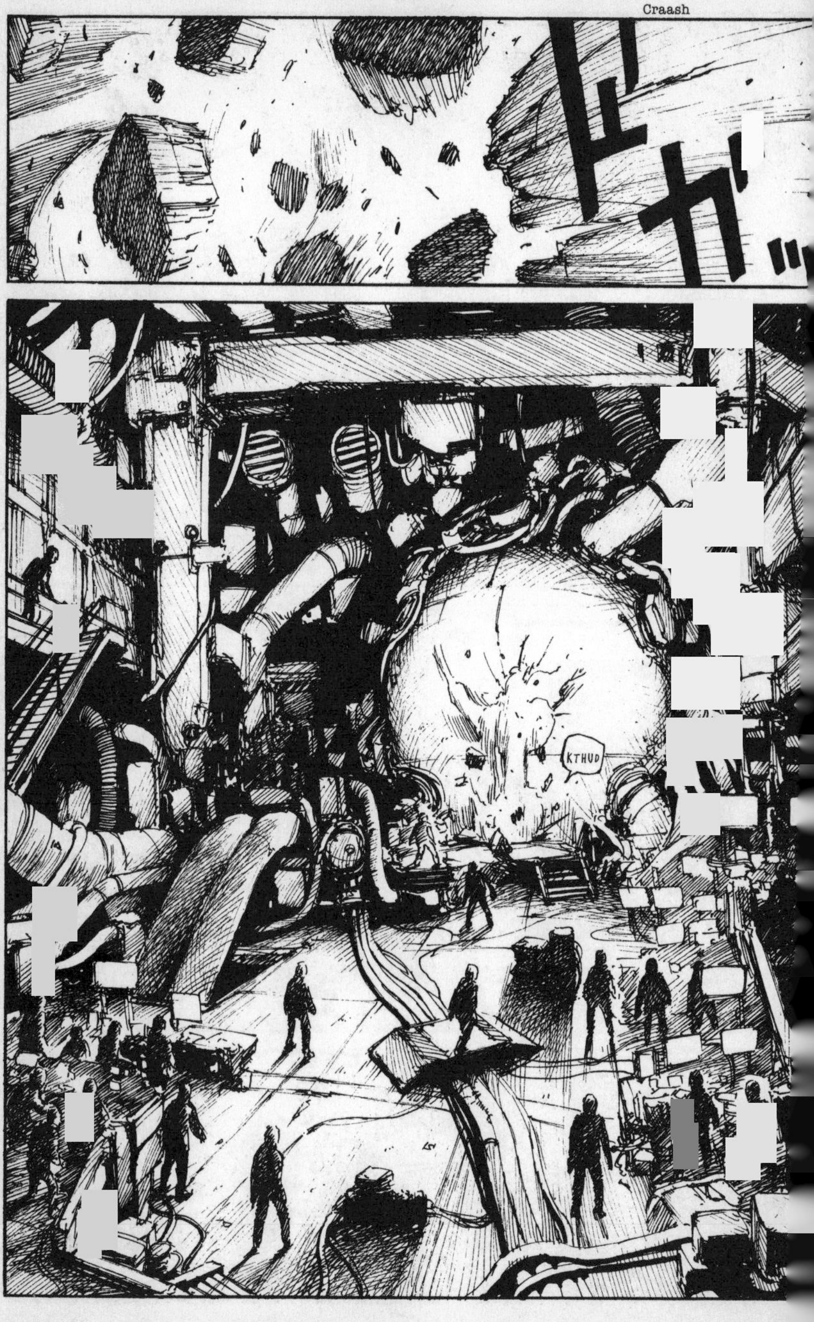
Craash
KTHUD

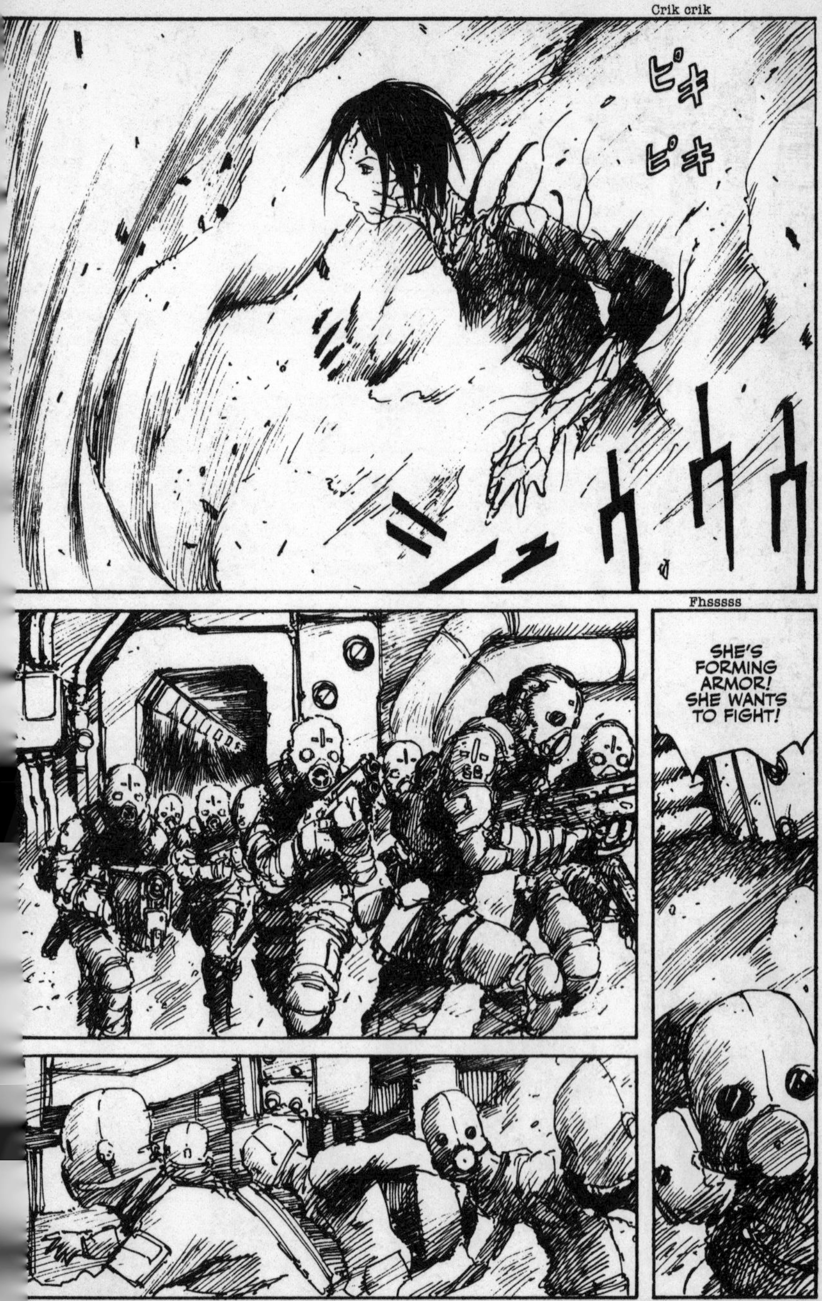
Crik crik
ピキ
ピキ
Fhsssss
SHE'S FORMING ARMOR! SHE WANTS TO FIGHT!

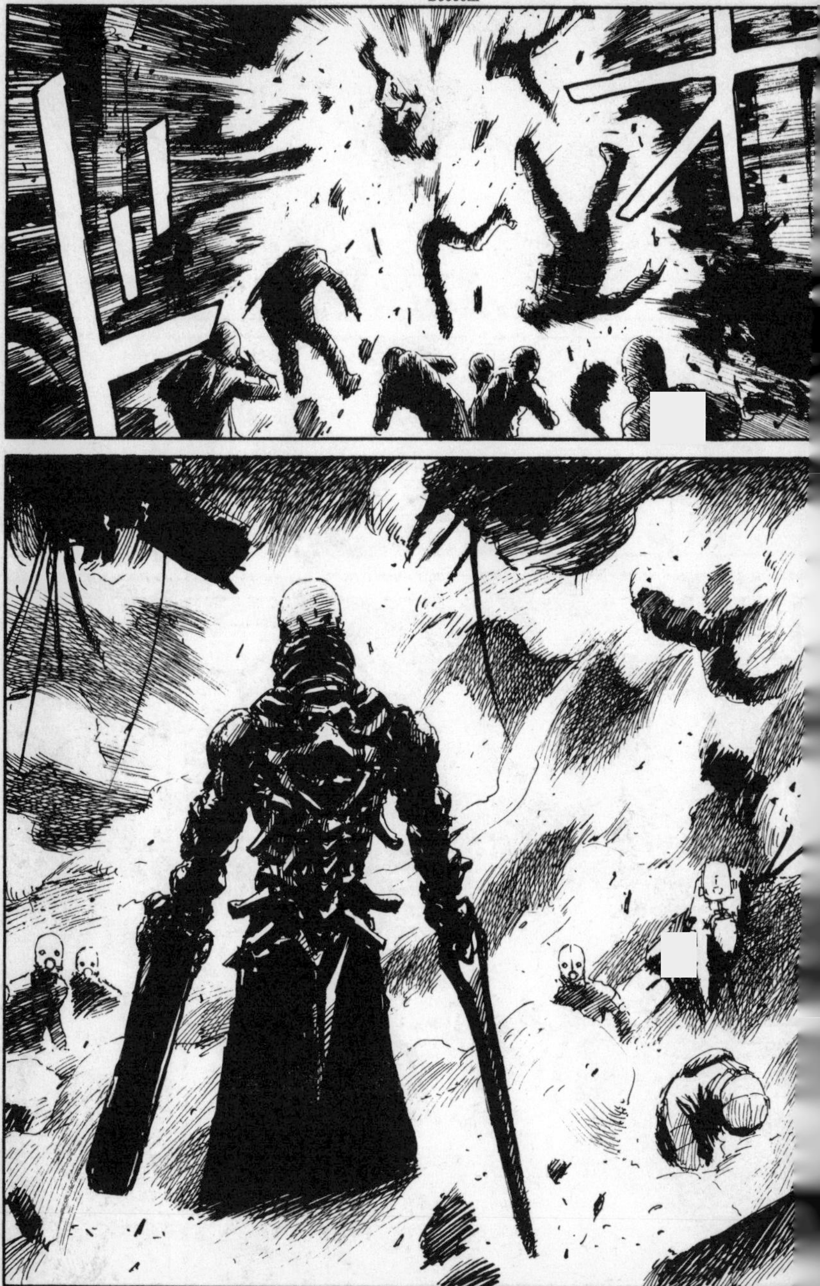
Boooom

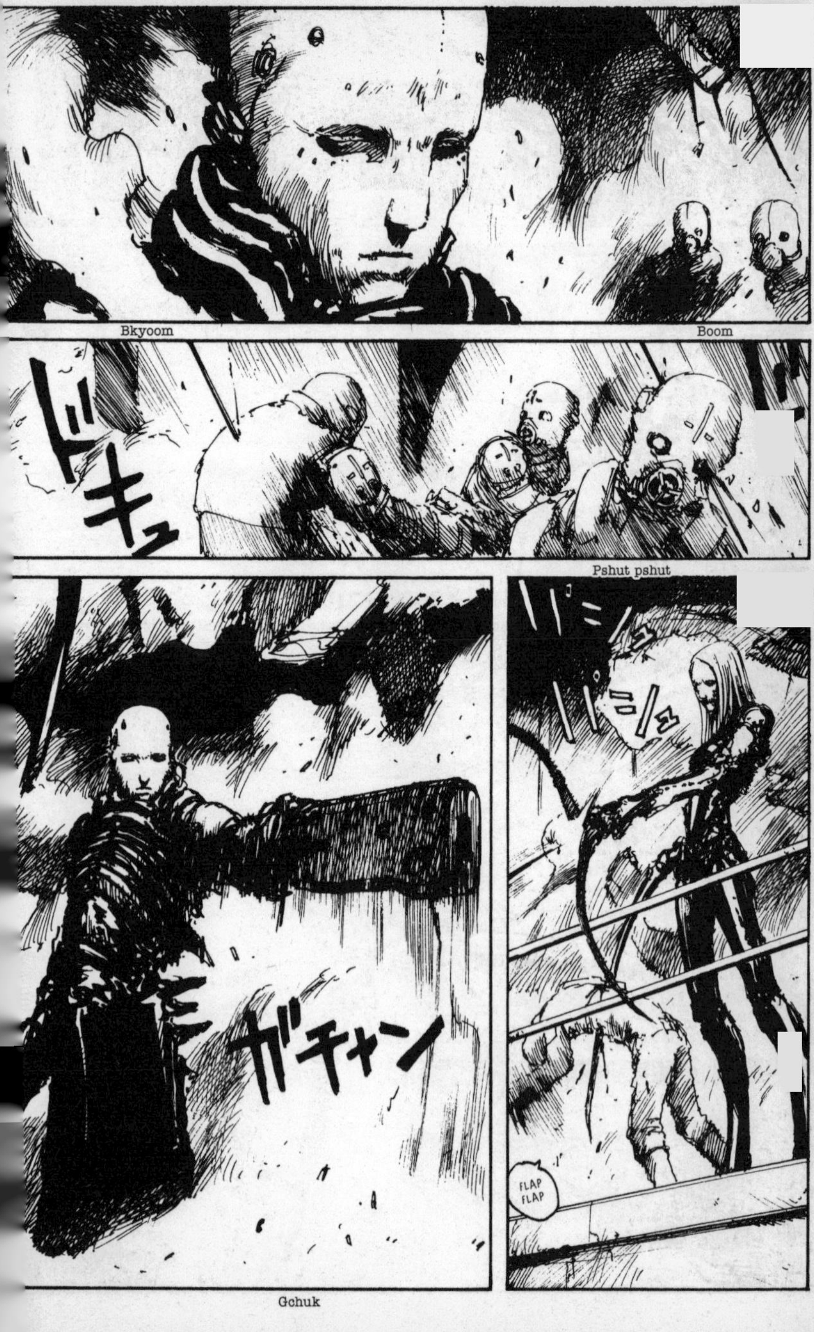
Boom
Bkyoom
ドキュ
Pshut pshut
FLAP FLAP
ガチャーン
Gchuk

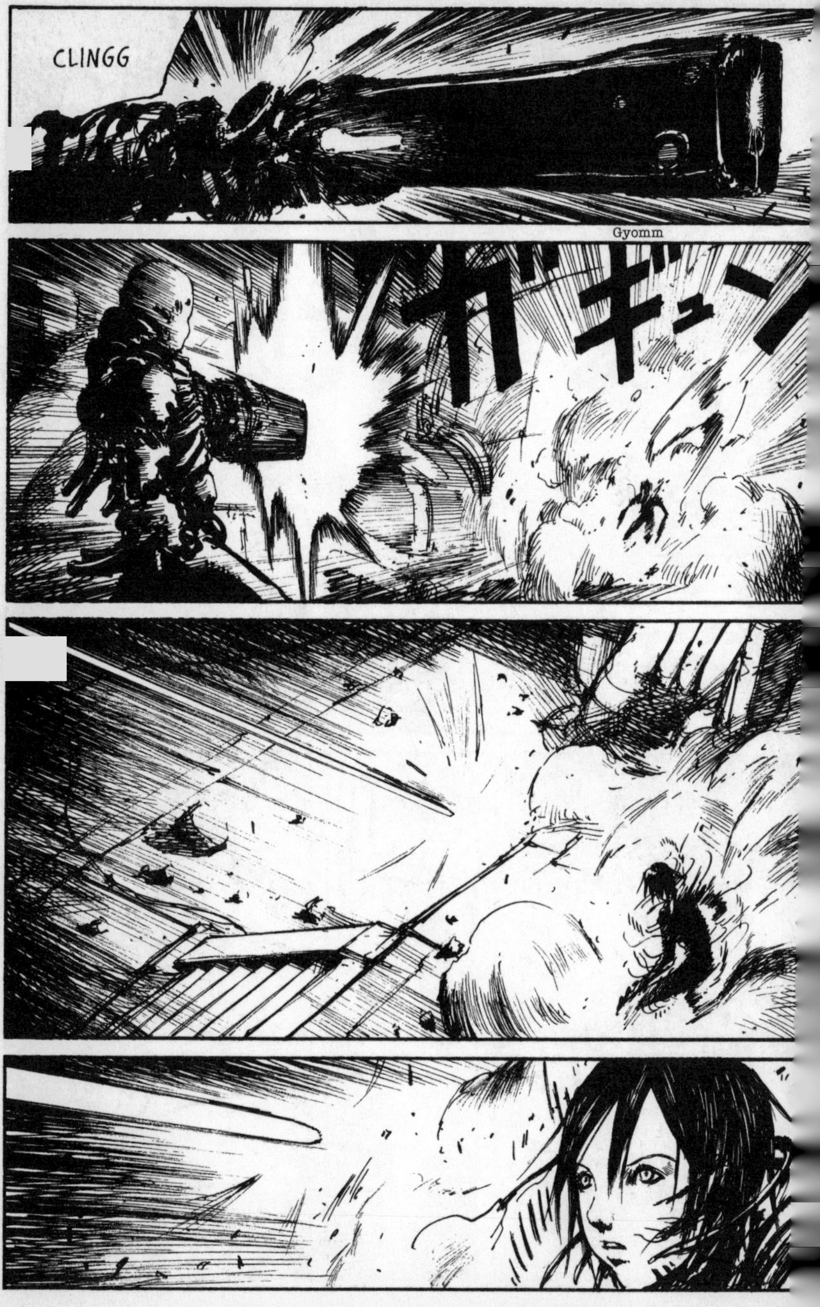
CLINGG
Gyomm
ガギュ

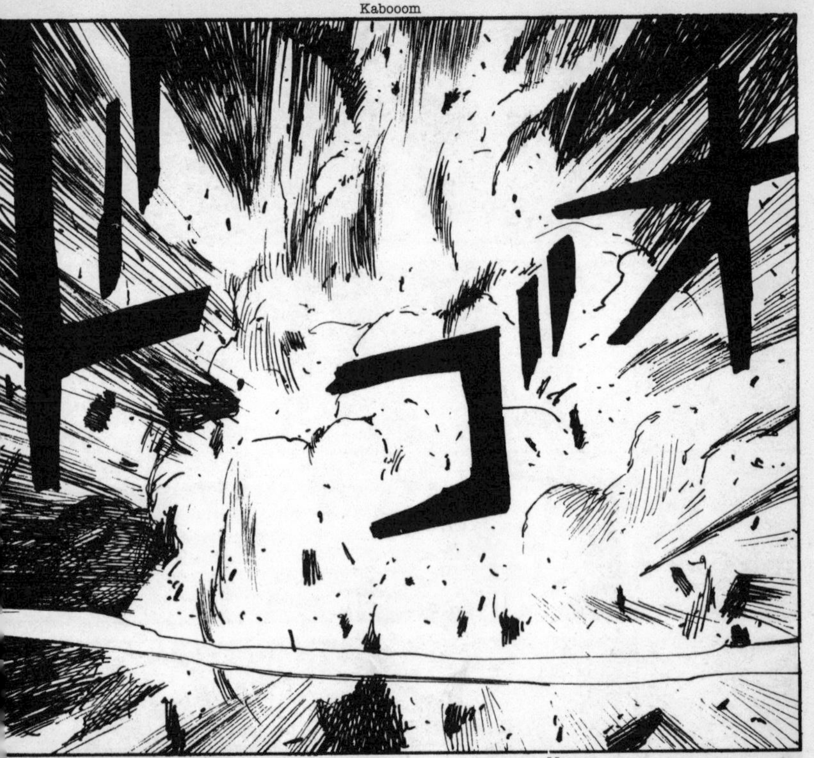
Kabooom

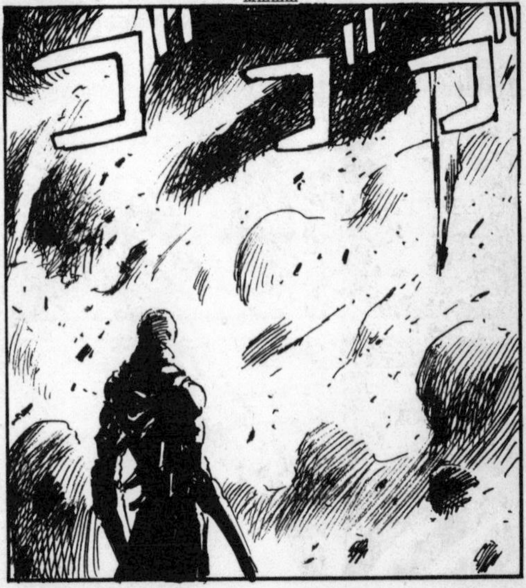
Mmmm

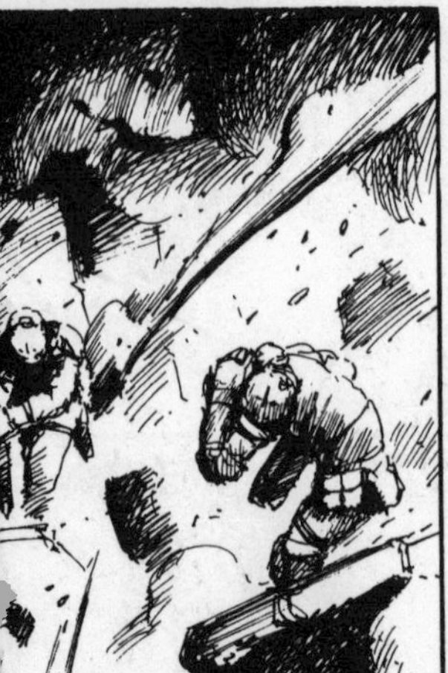

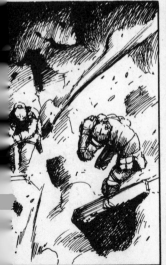

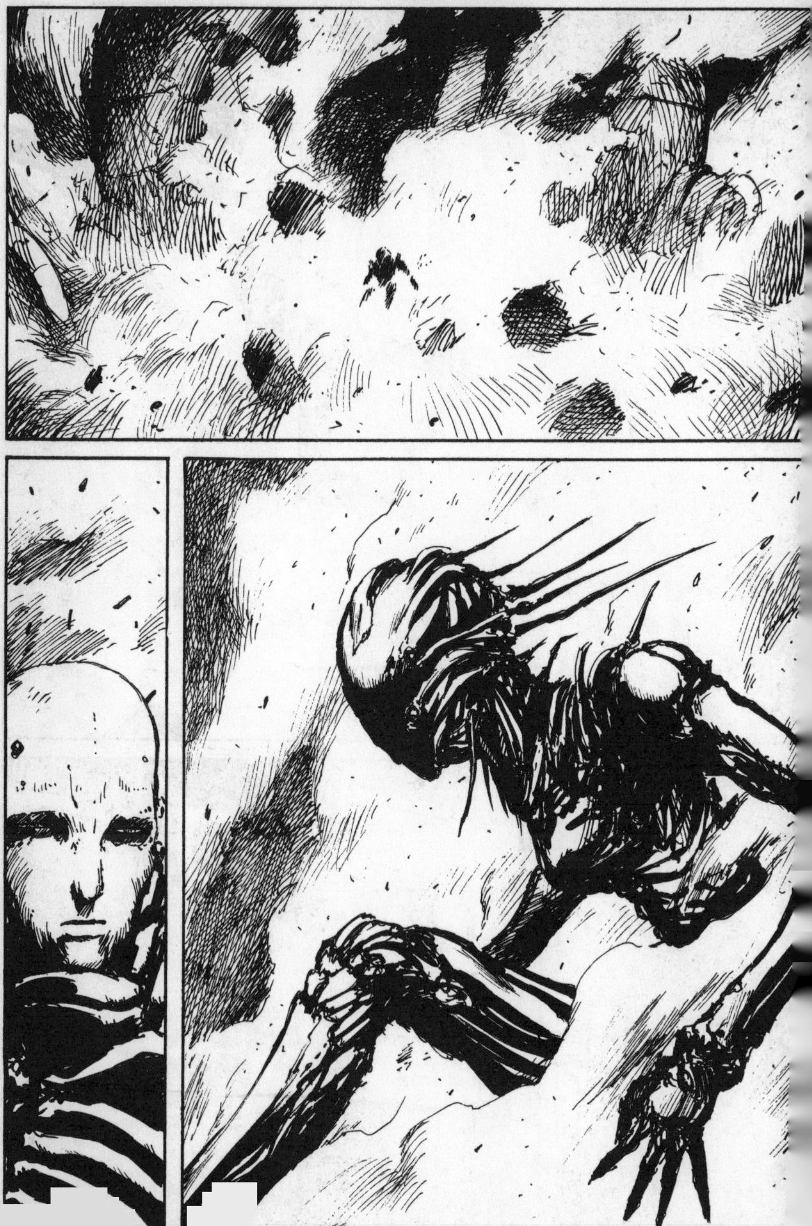

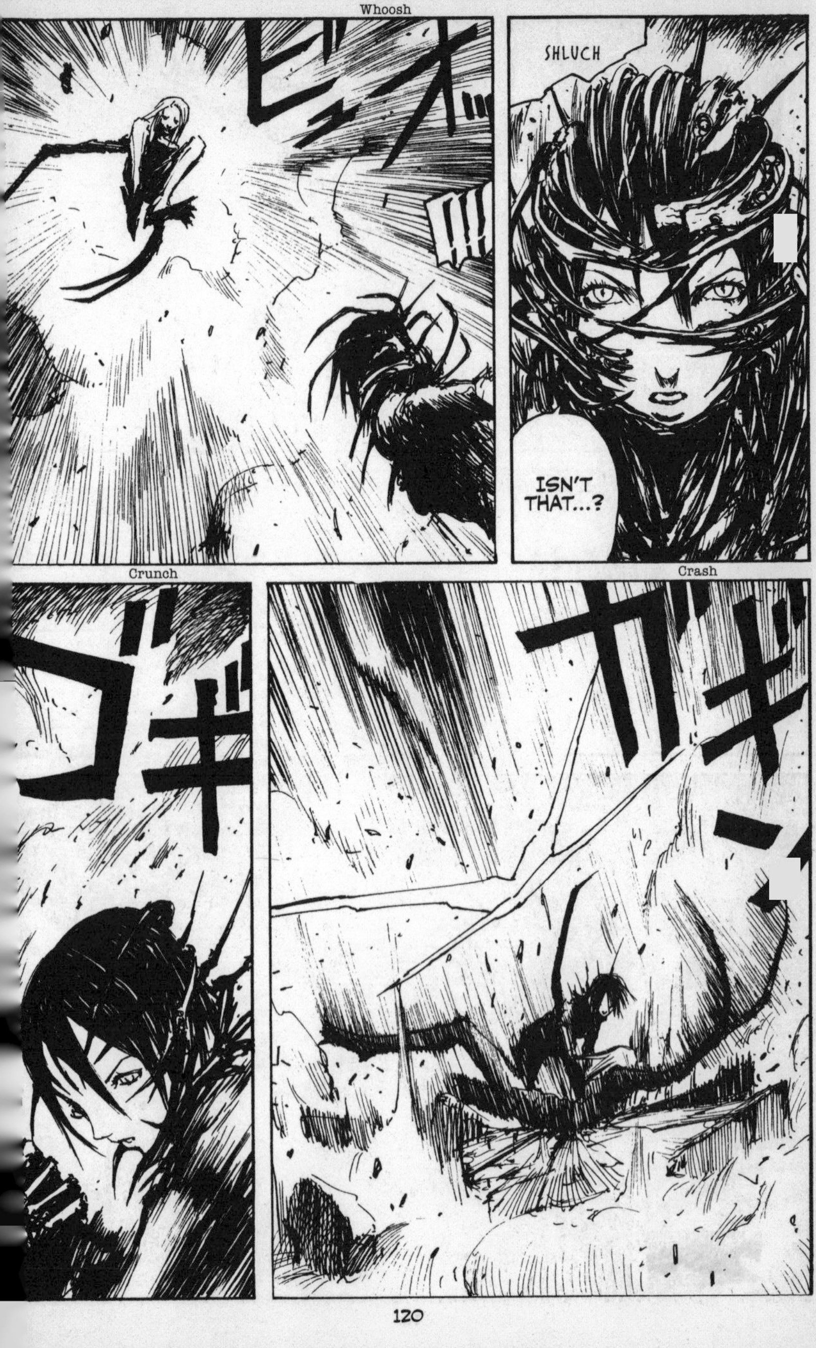
SHLUCH
ISN'T THAT...?
Whoosh
Crash
Crunch

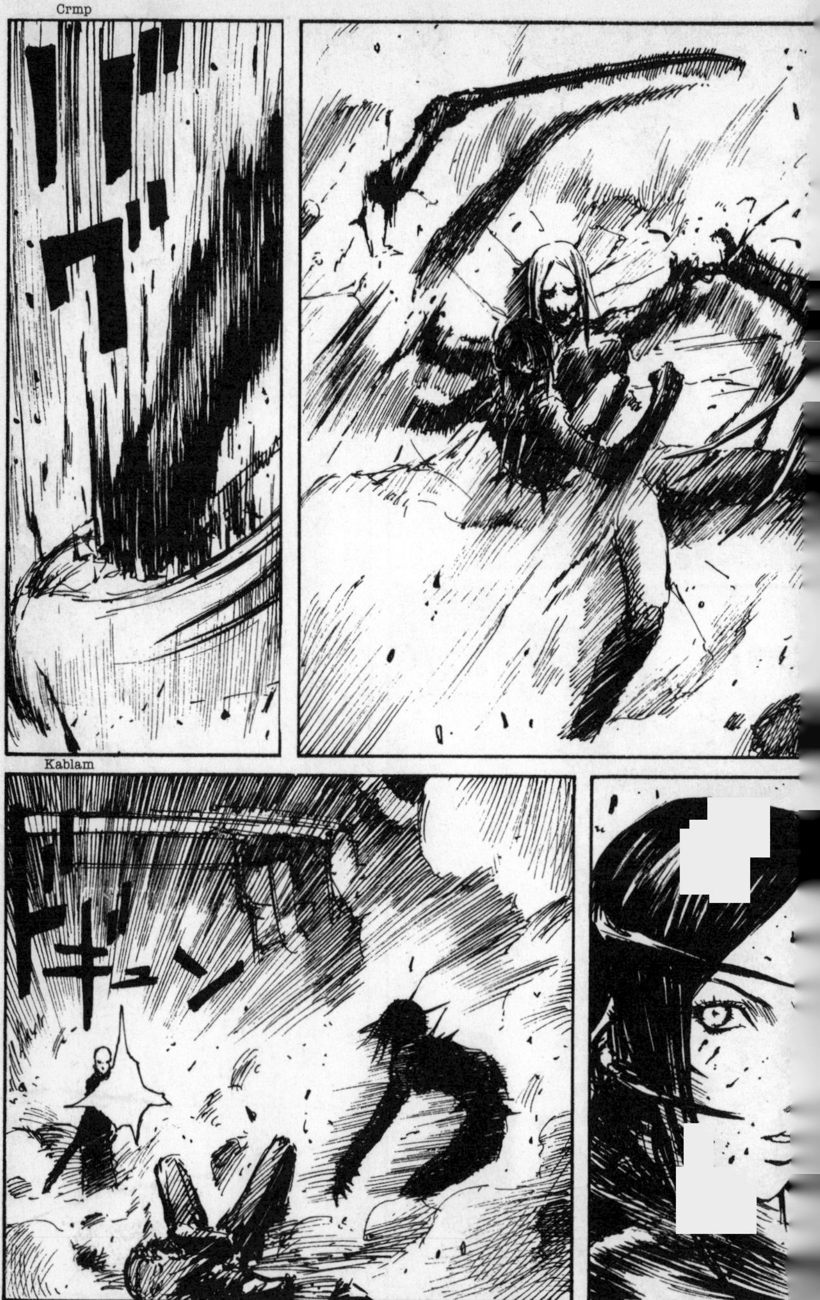
Crmp
Kablam

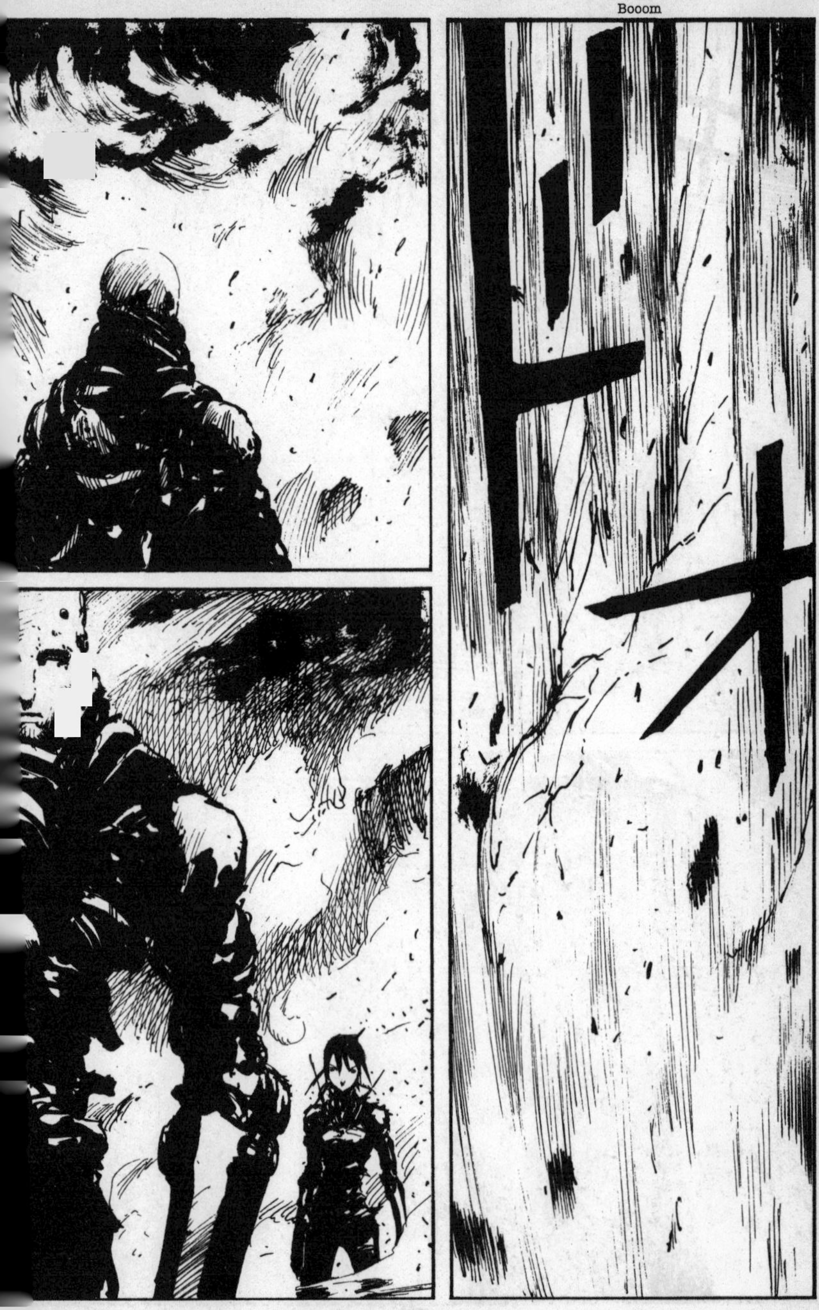
Booom
ドオ

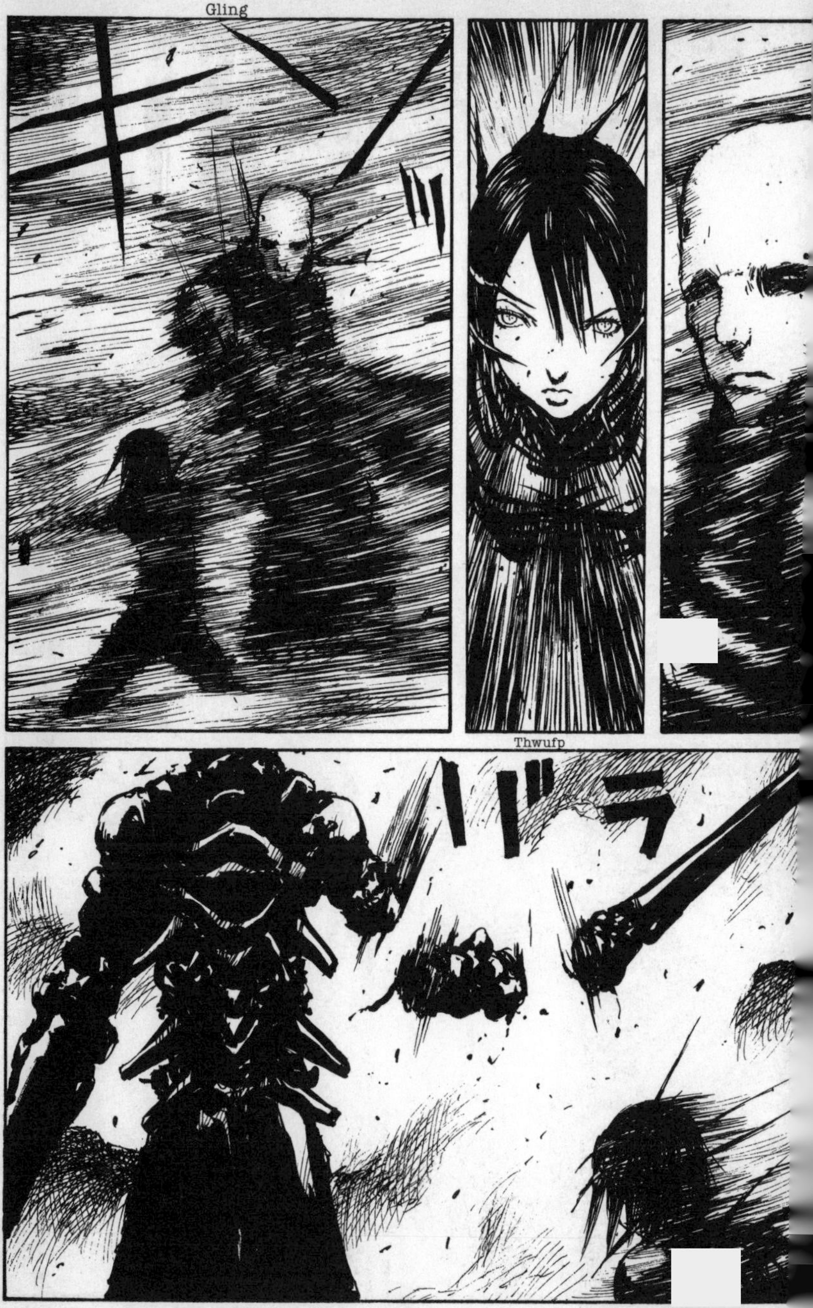
Gling
Thwufp
バラ

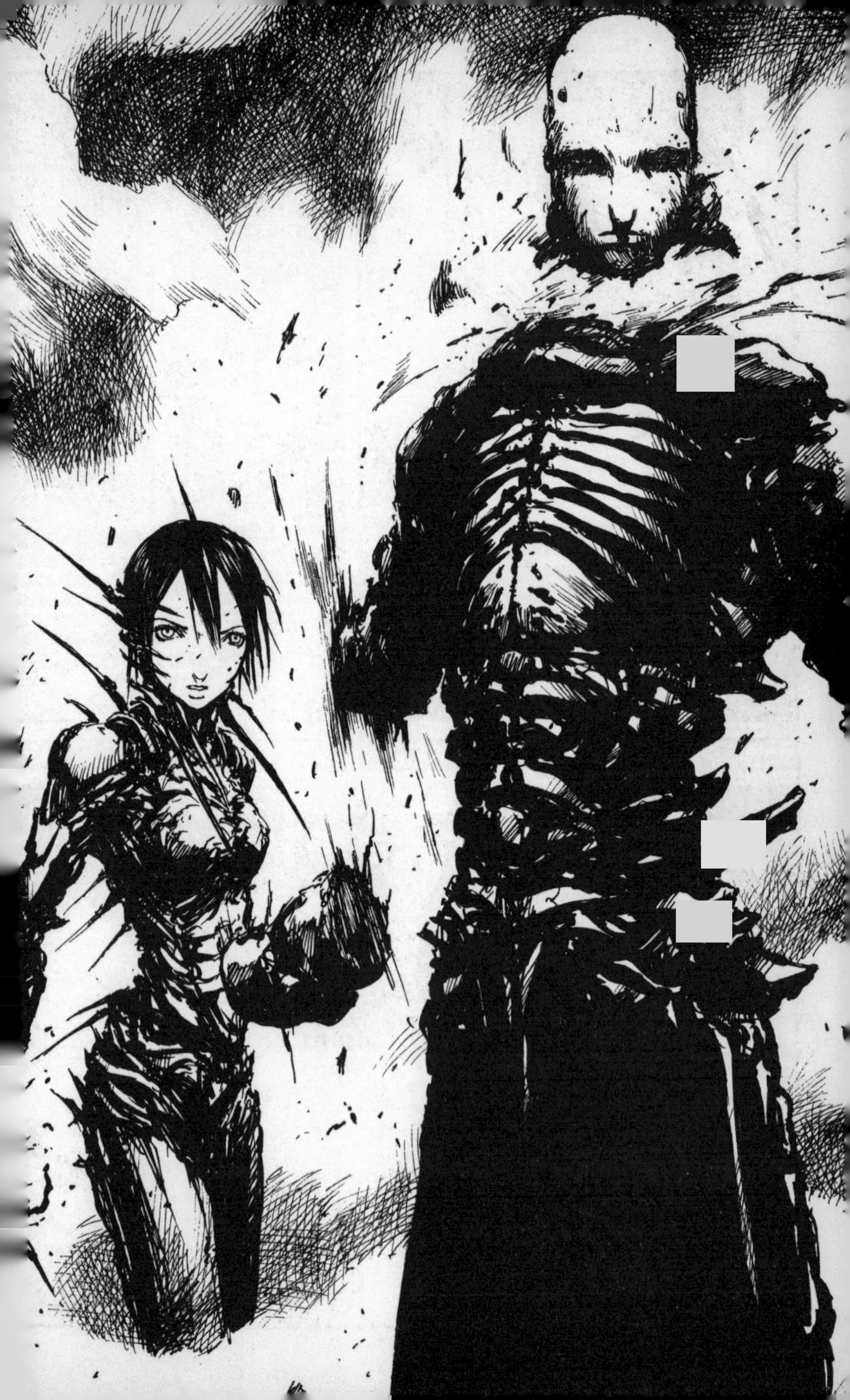

Thud

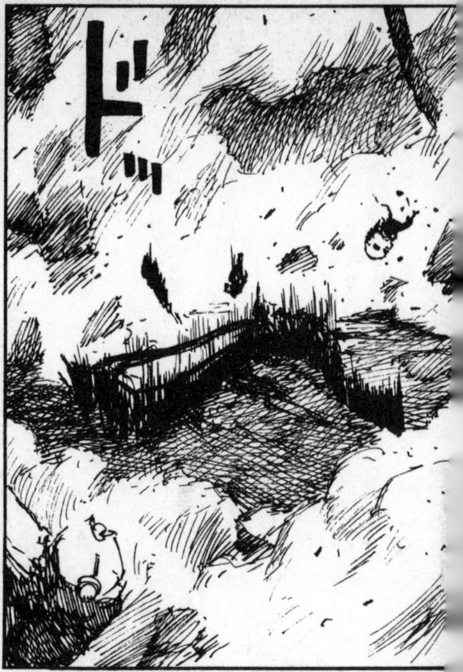
ドドッ

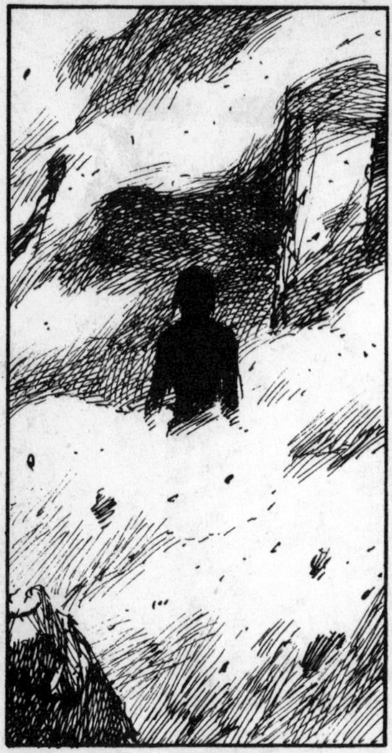

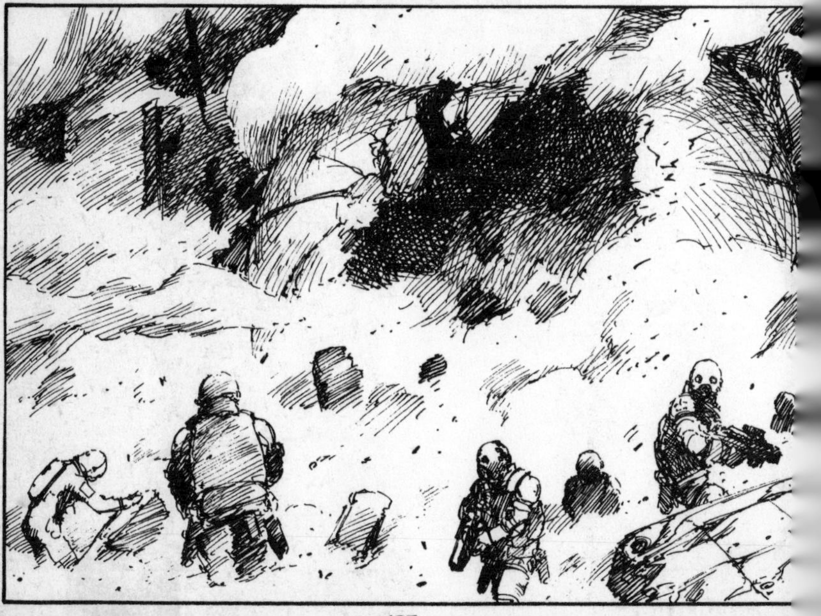

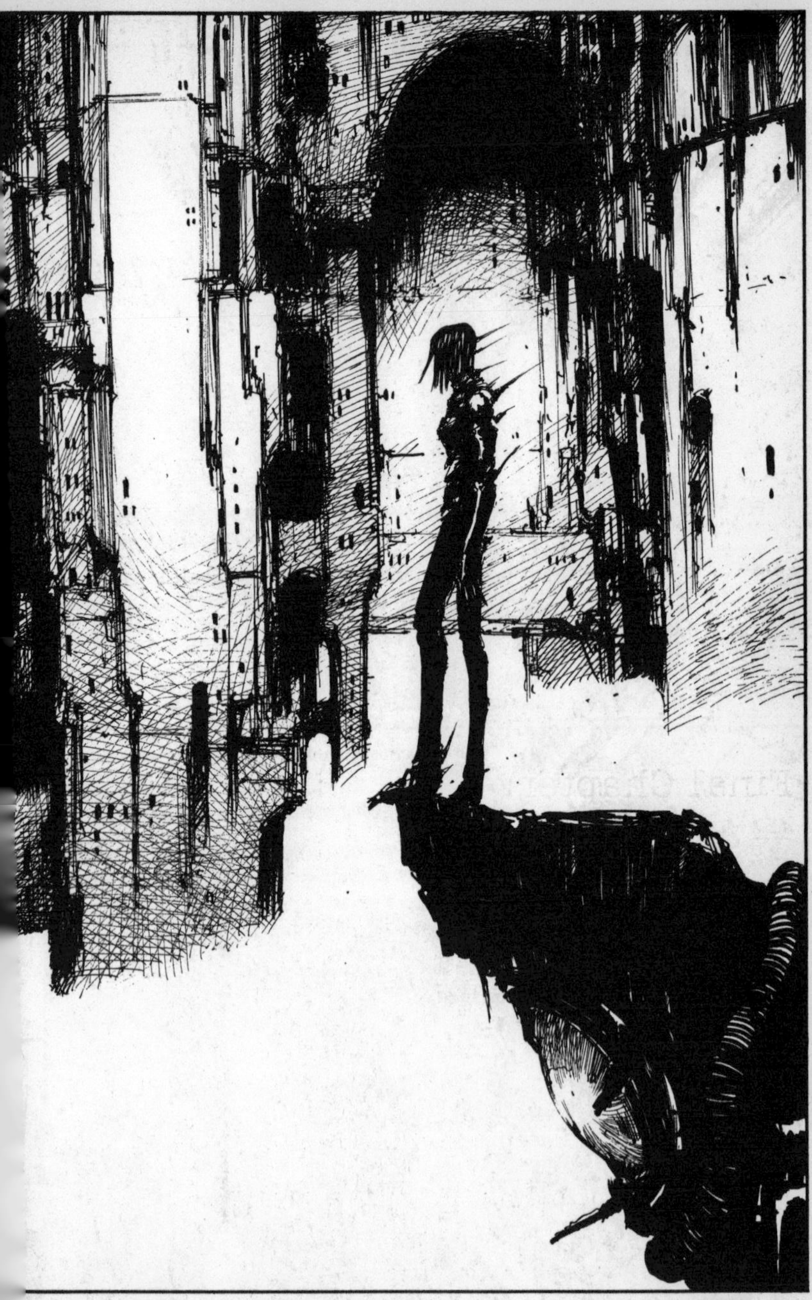

hapter 5 Corpse Running Wild ~End~

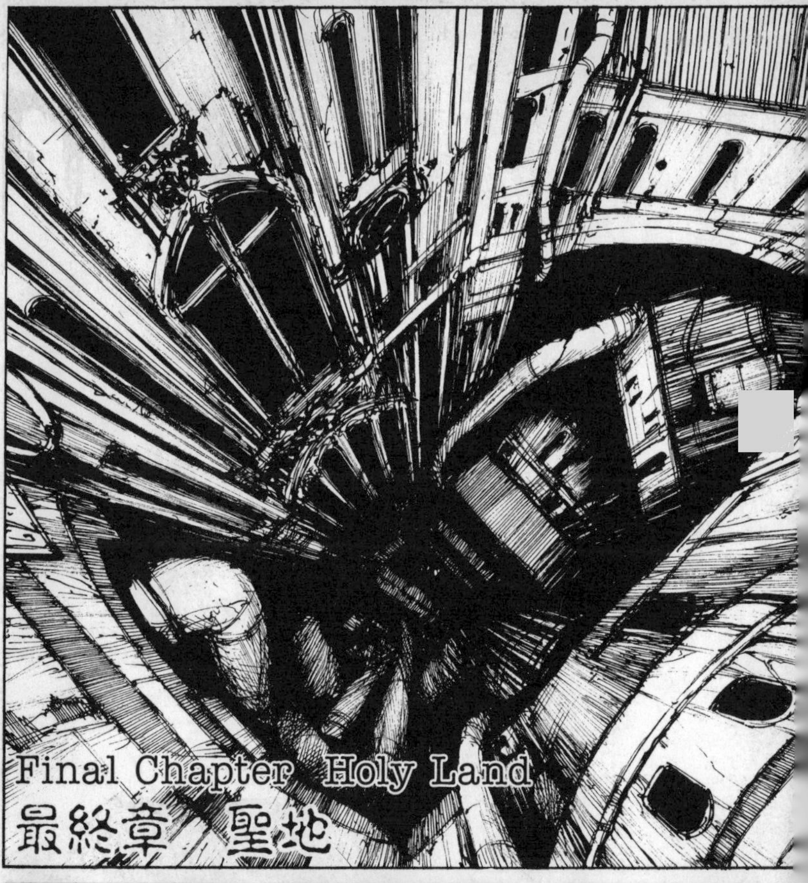
Final Chapter Holy Land
最終章 聖地

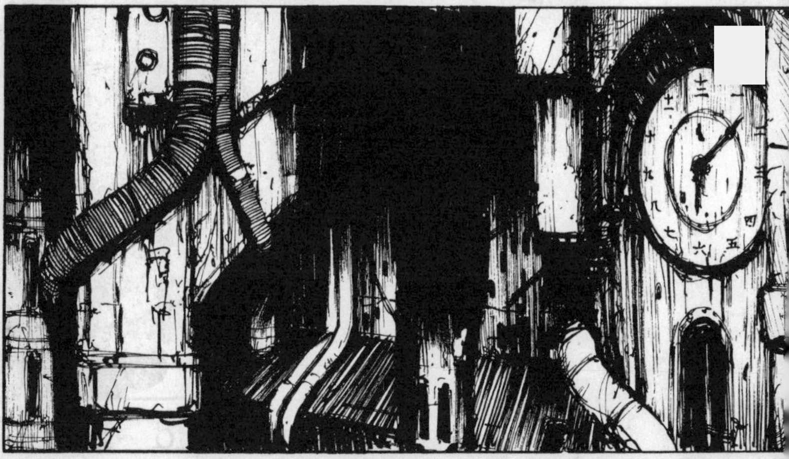

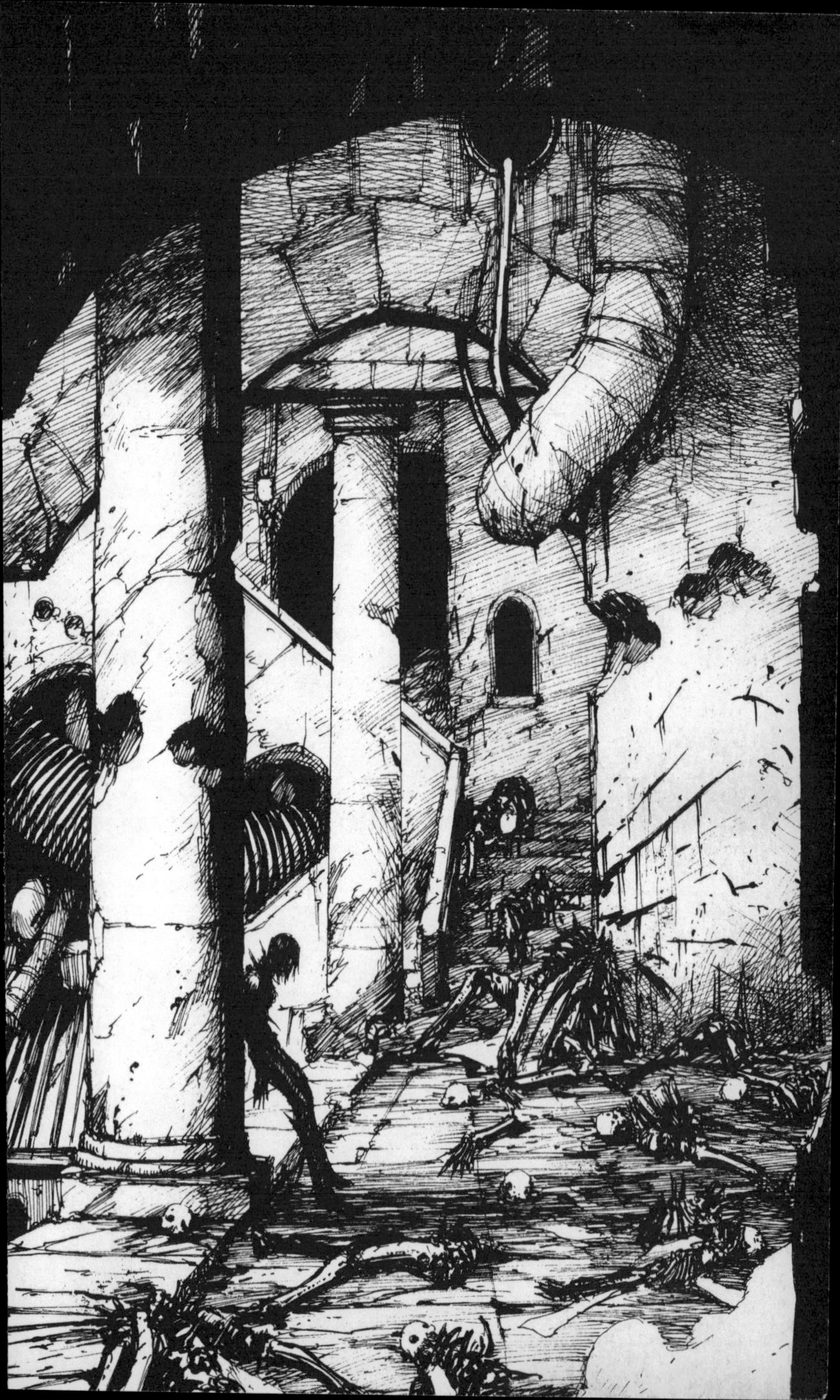

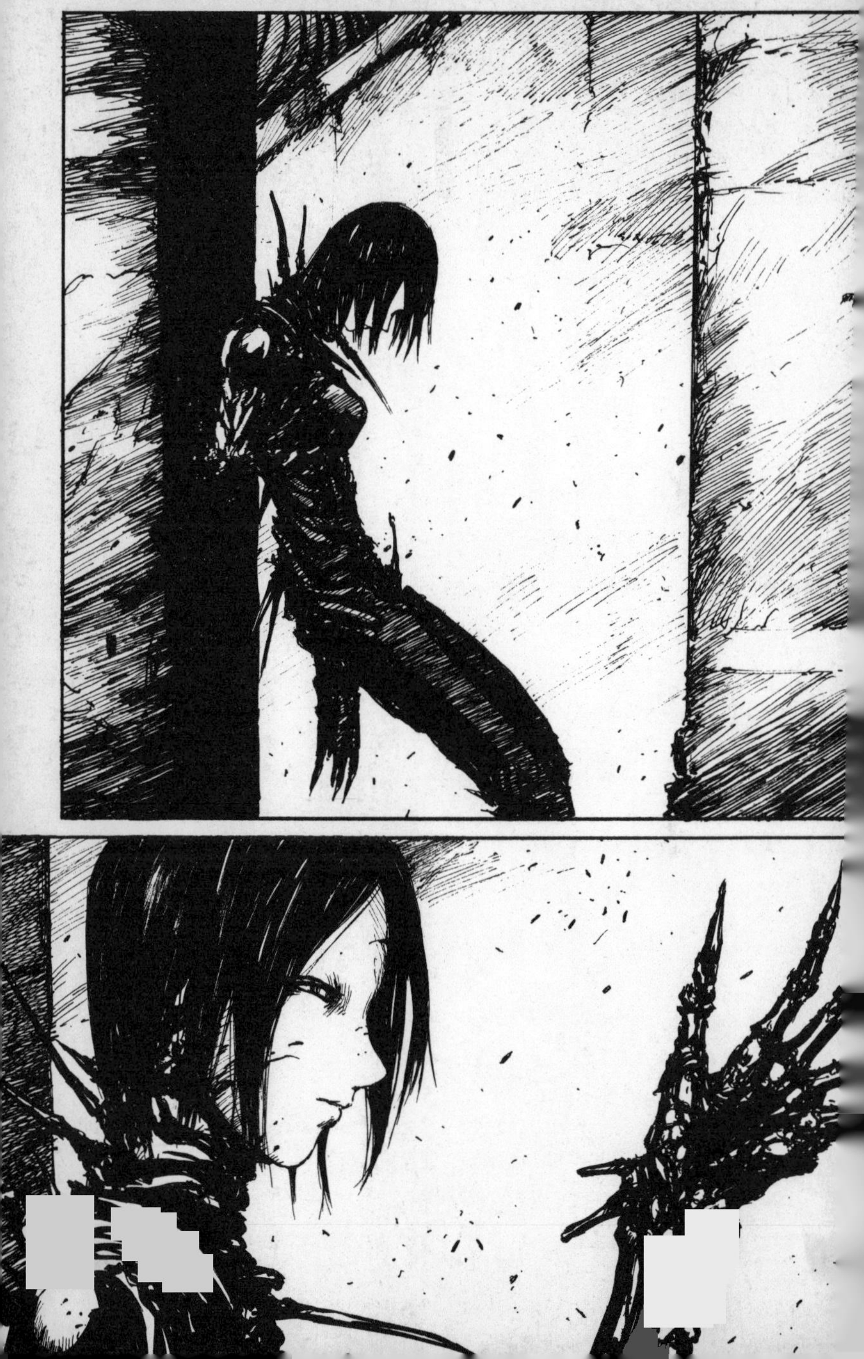

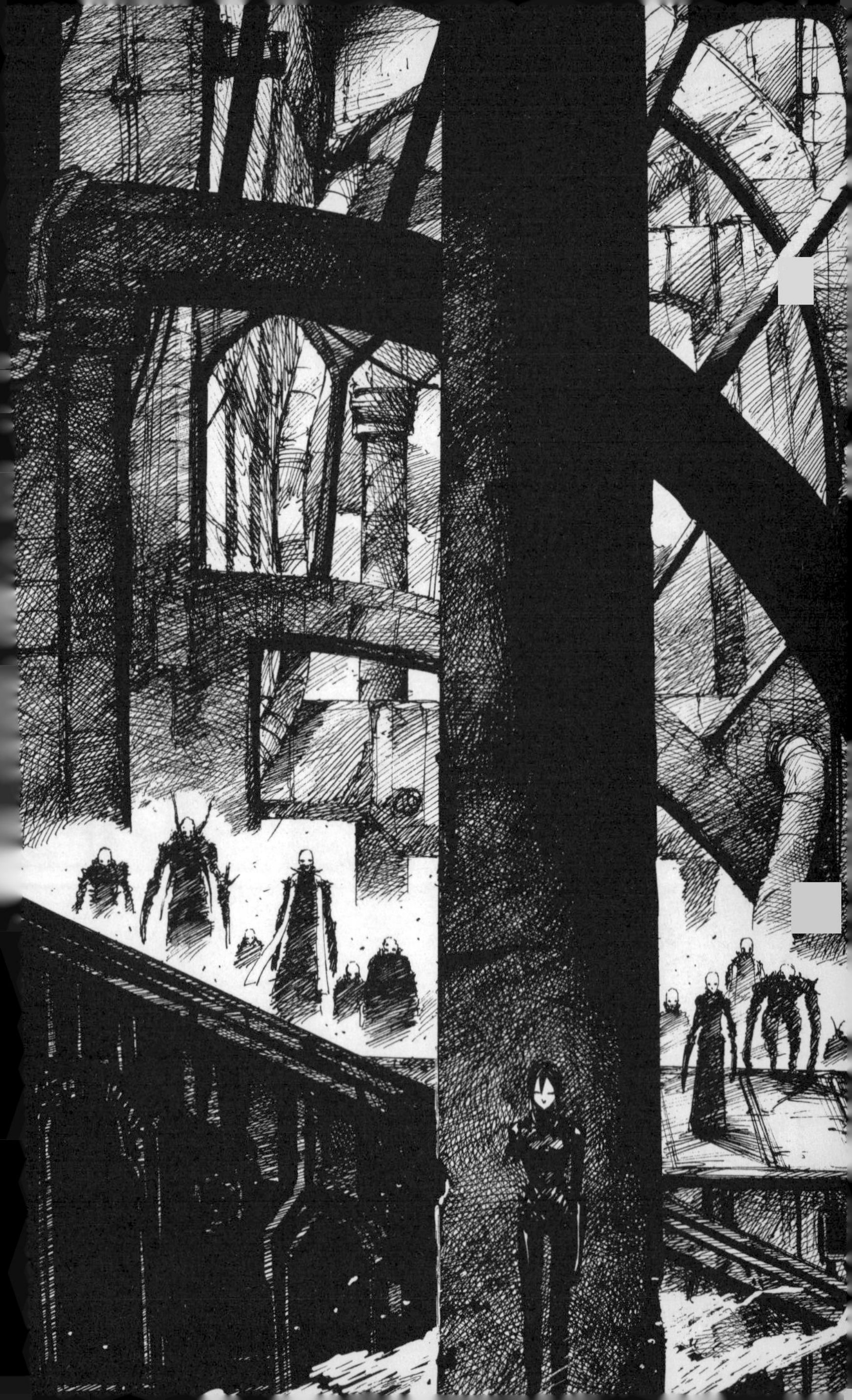

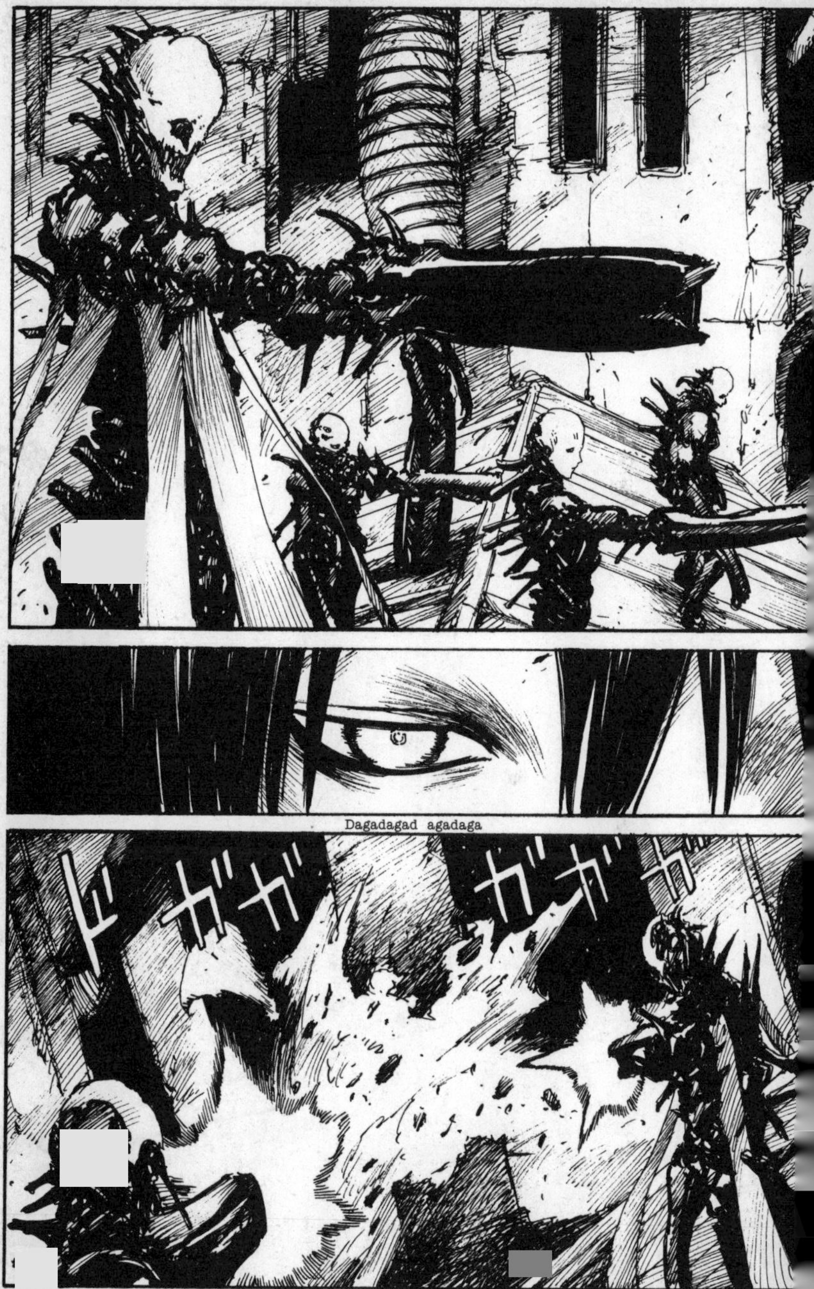
Dagadagad agadaga
ドガガ ガガガ

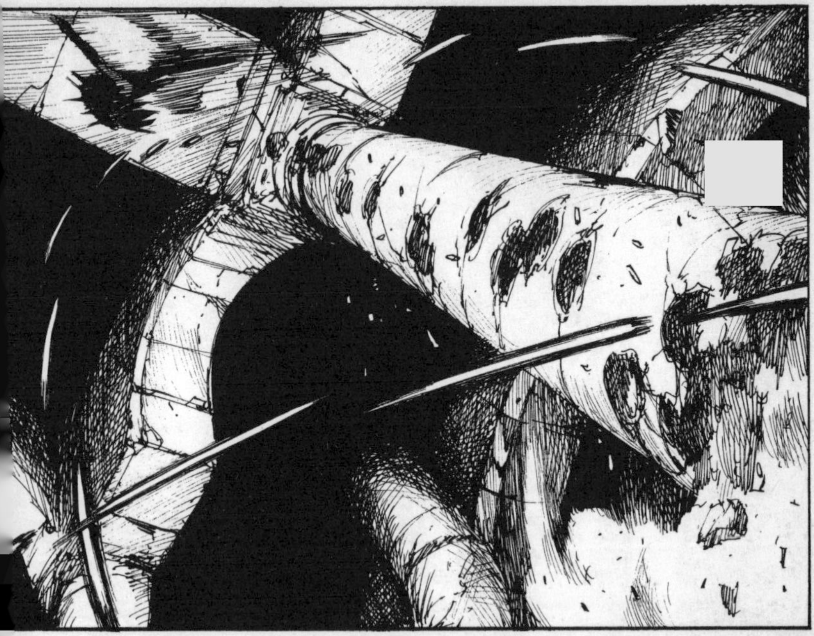

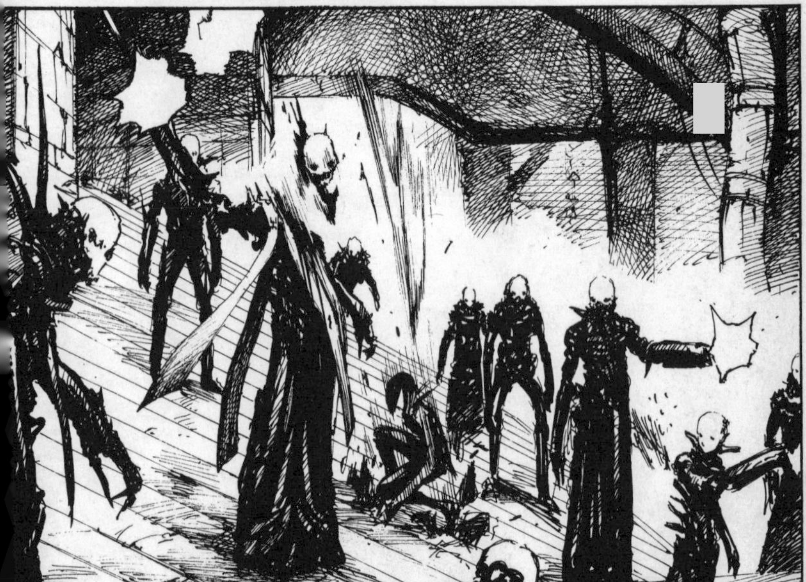

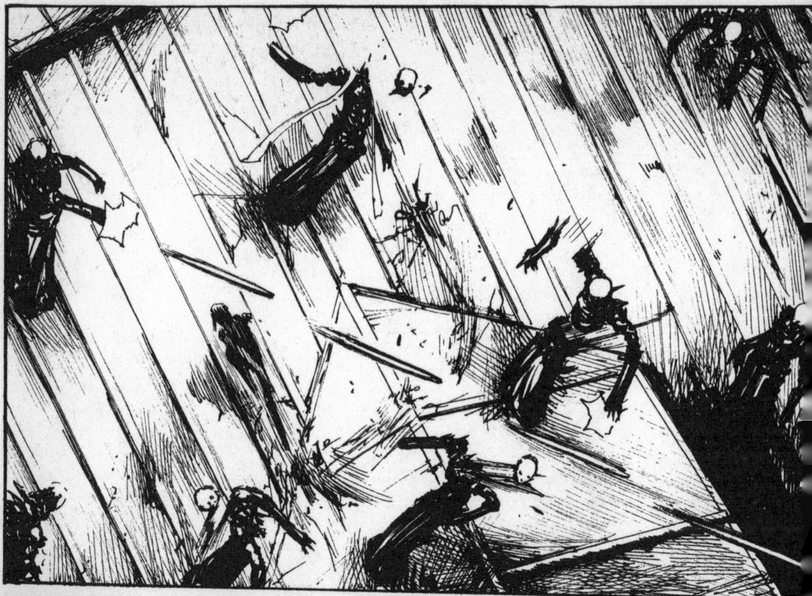

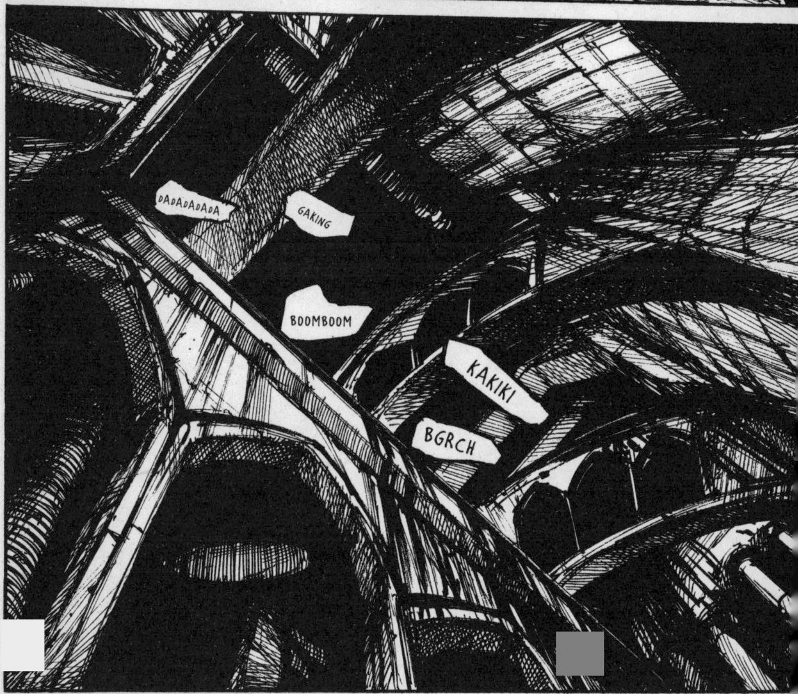
GAKING
DADADADADA
BOOMBOOM
KAKIKI
BGRCH

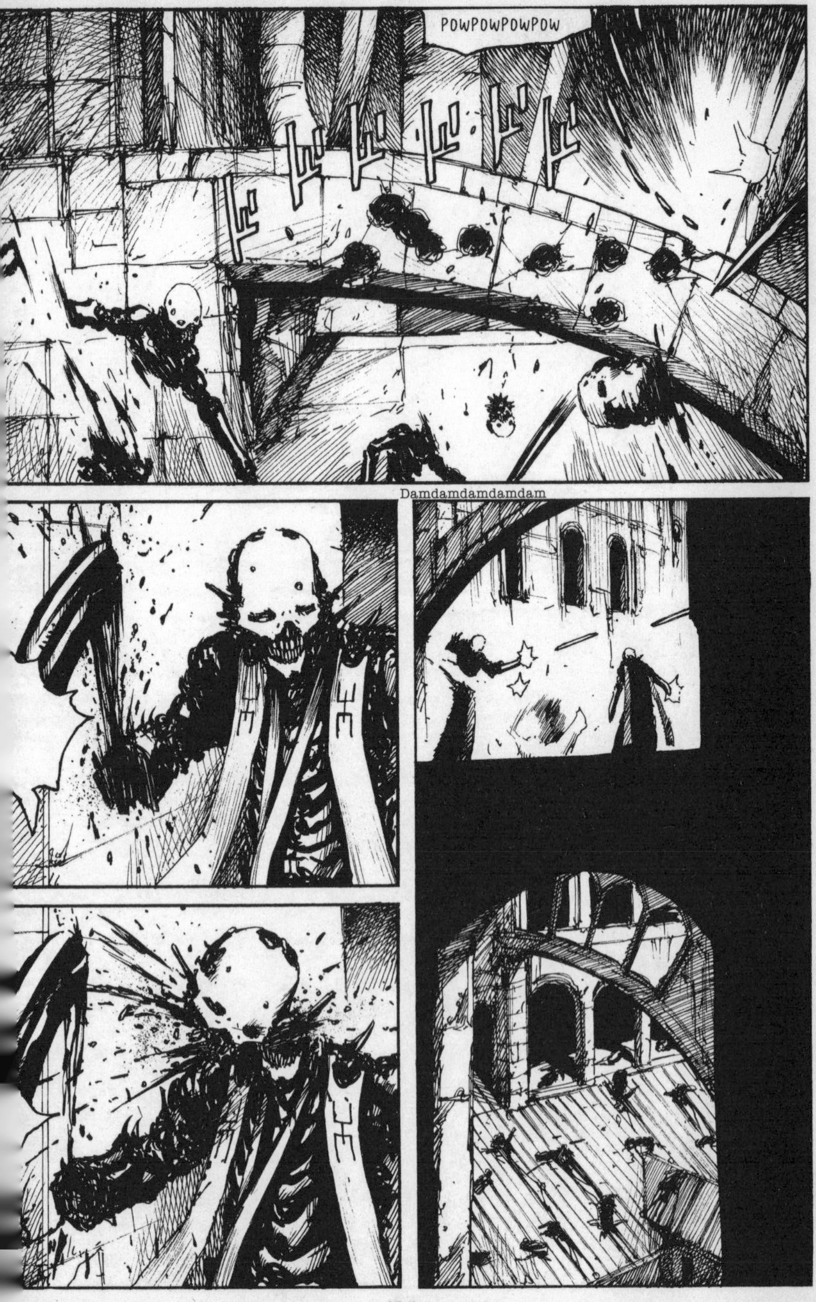
POWPOWPOWPOW
Damdamdamdamdam

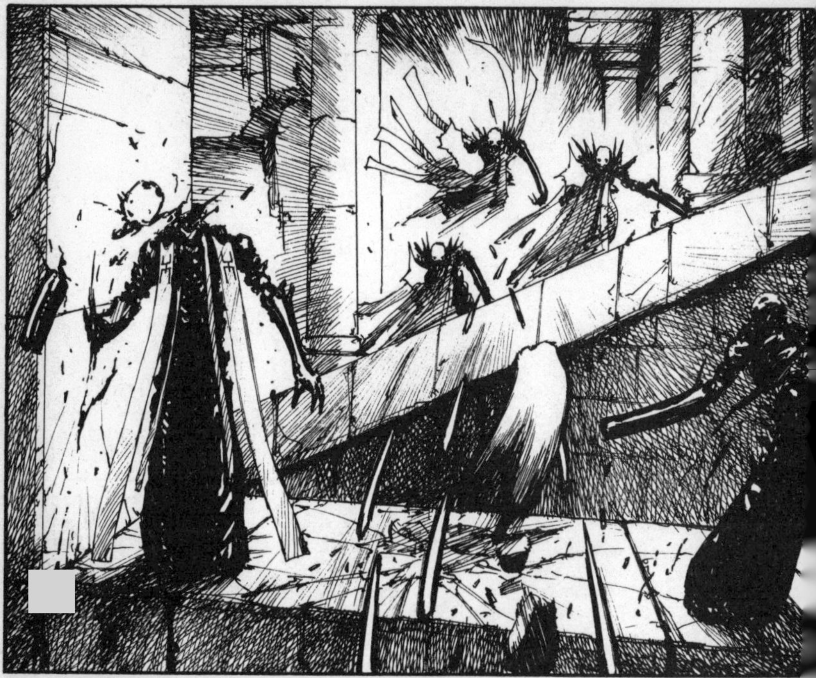
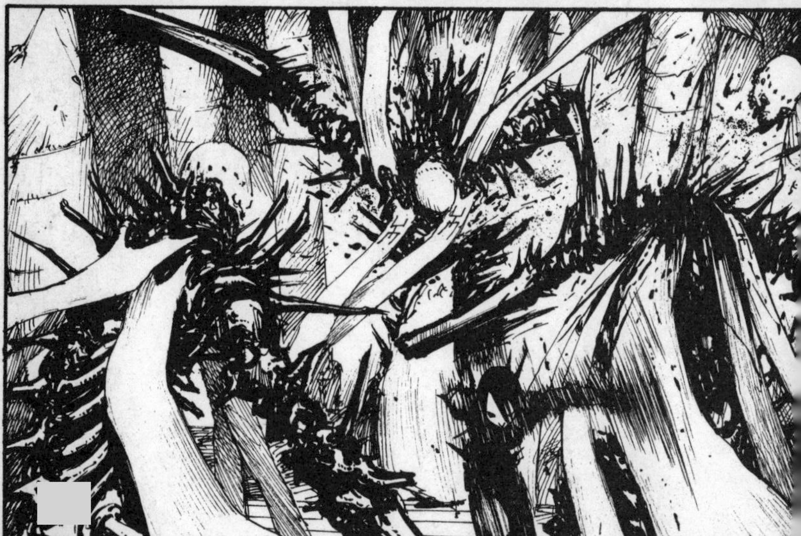

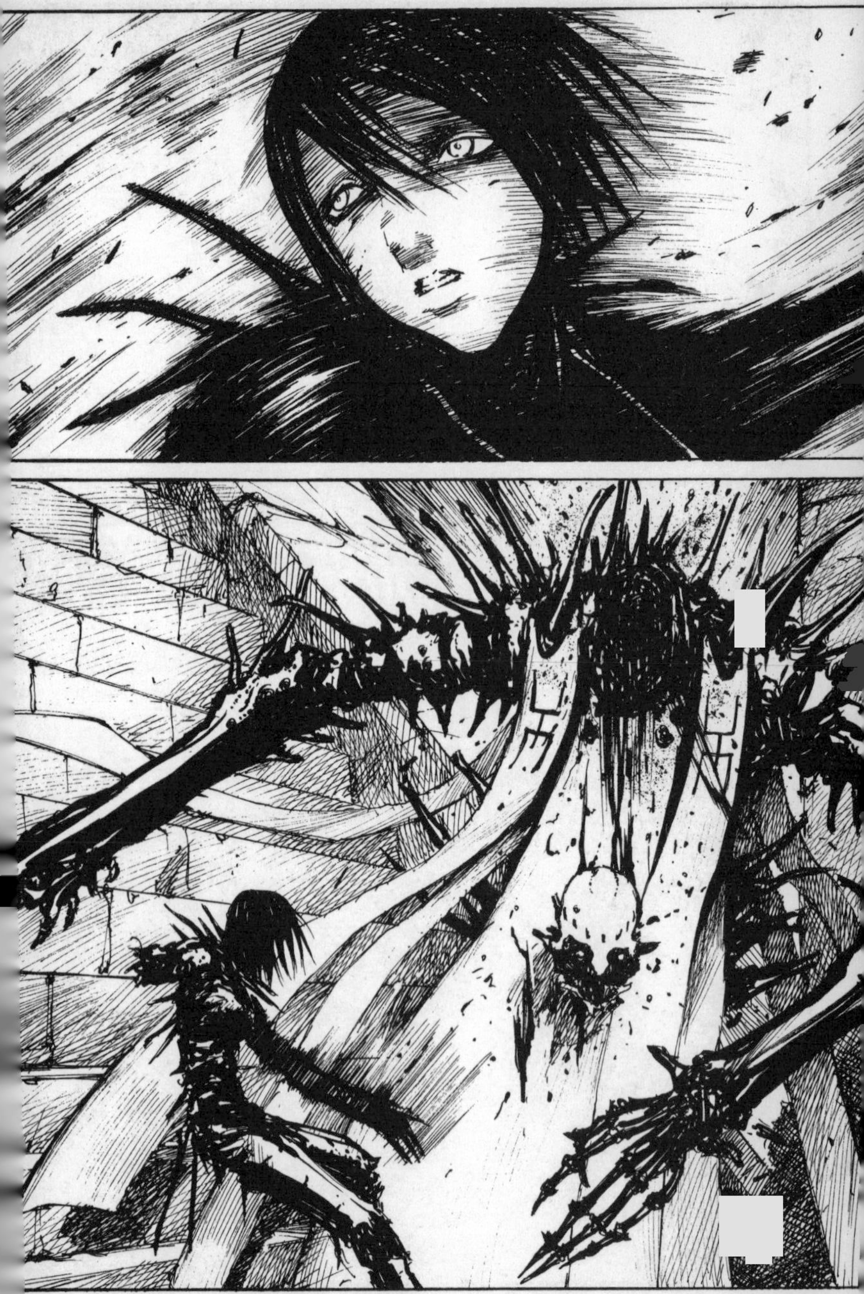

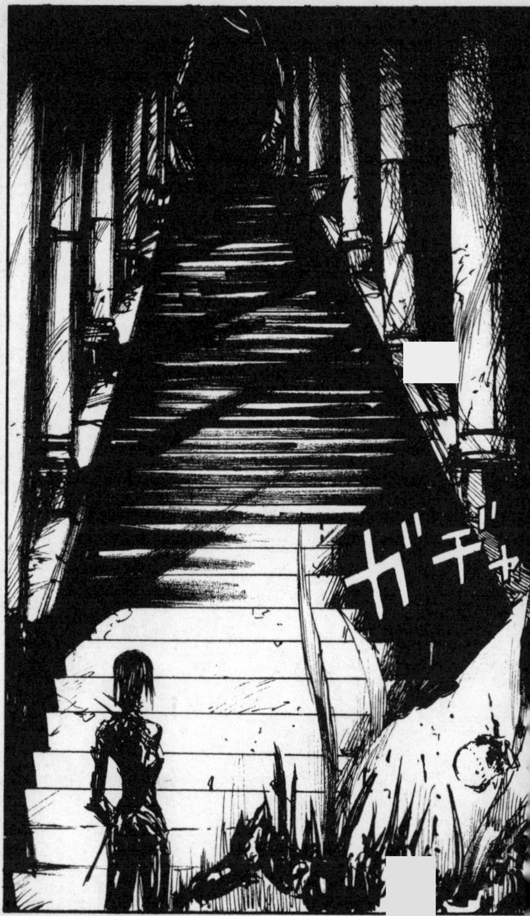
ガヂャ
Gchunk
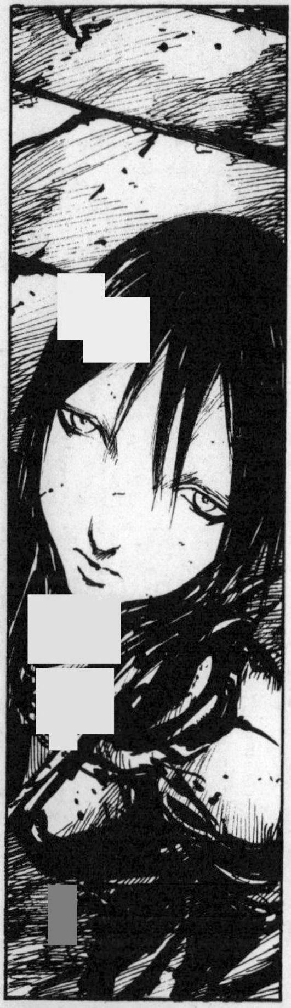
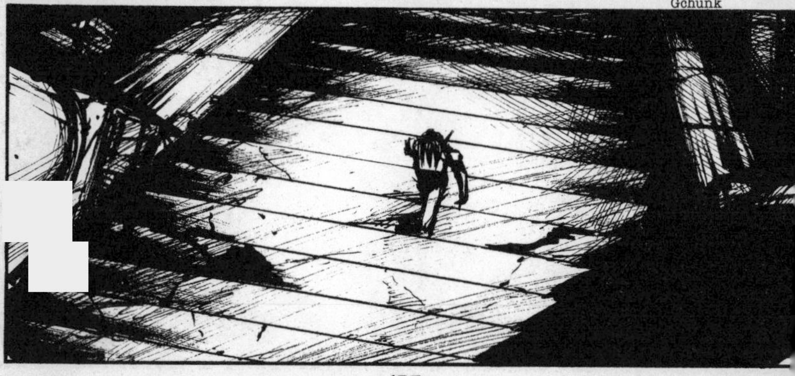

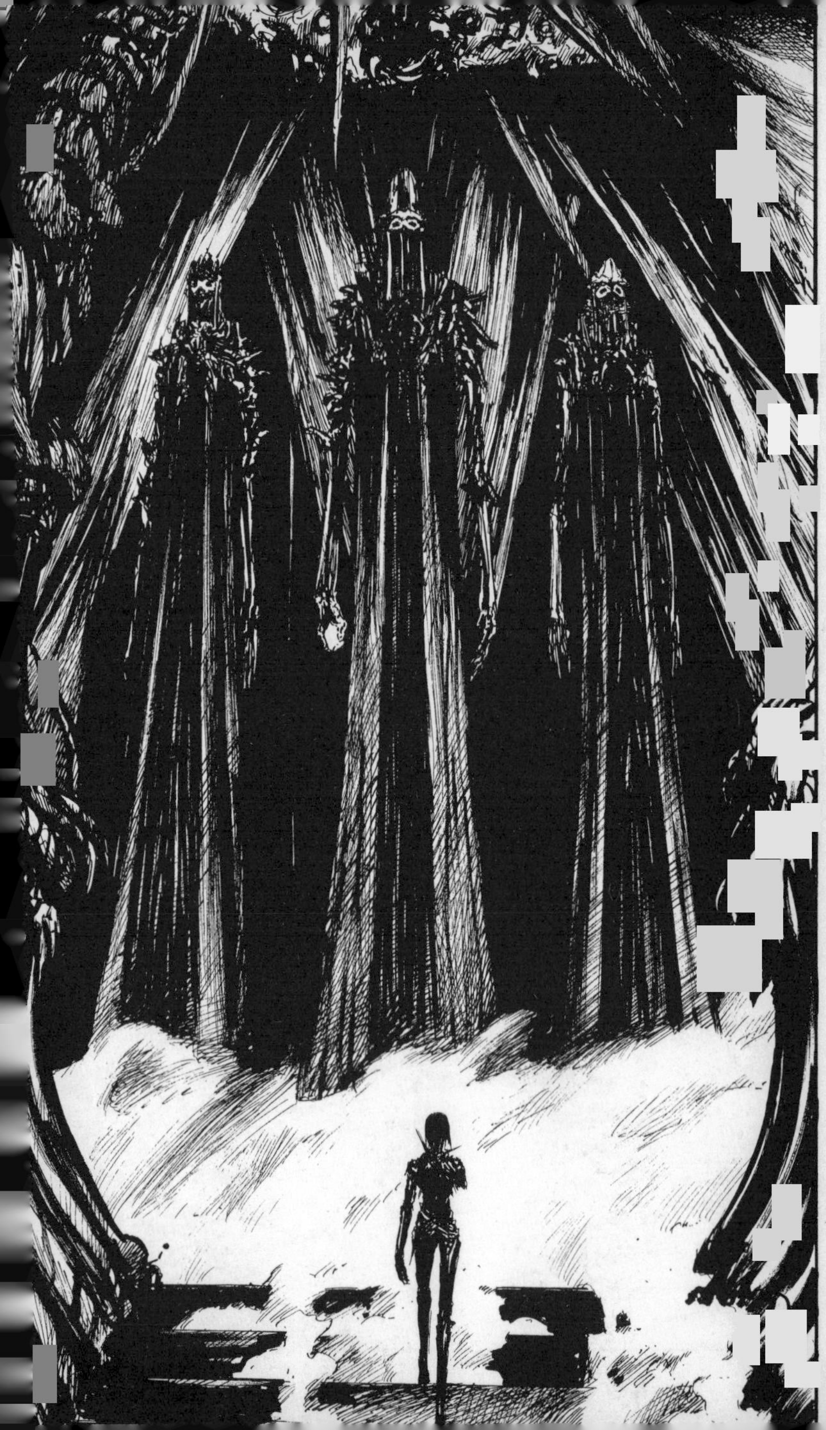

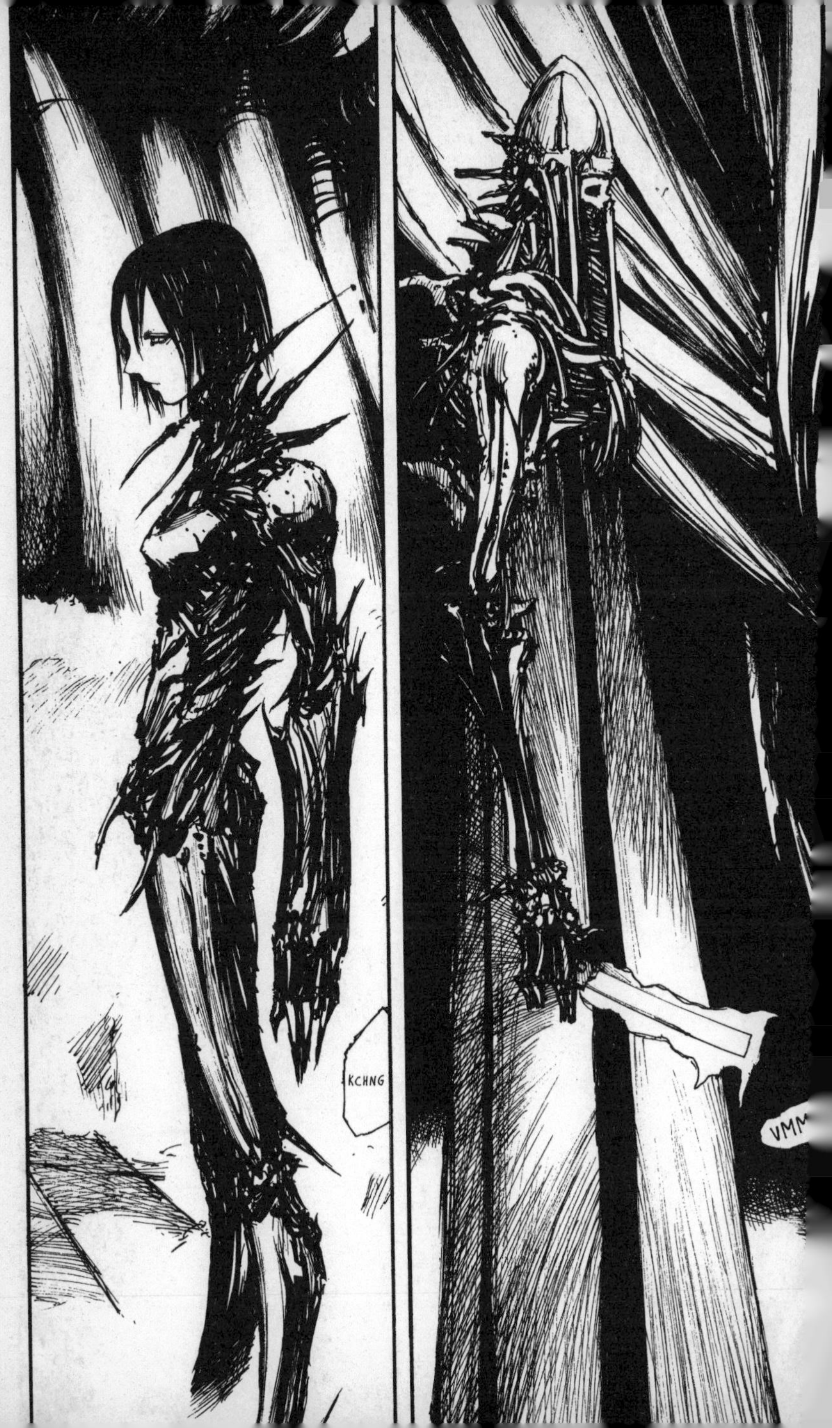
VMM
KCHNG

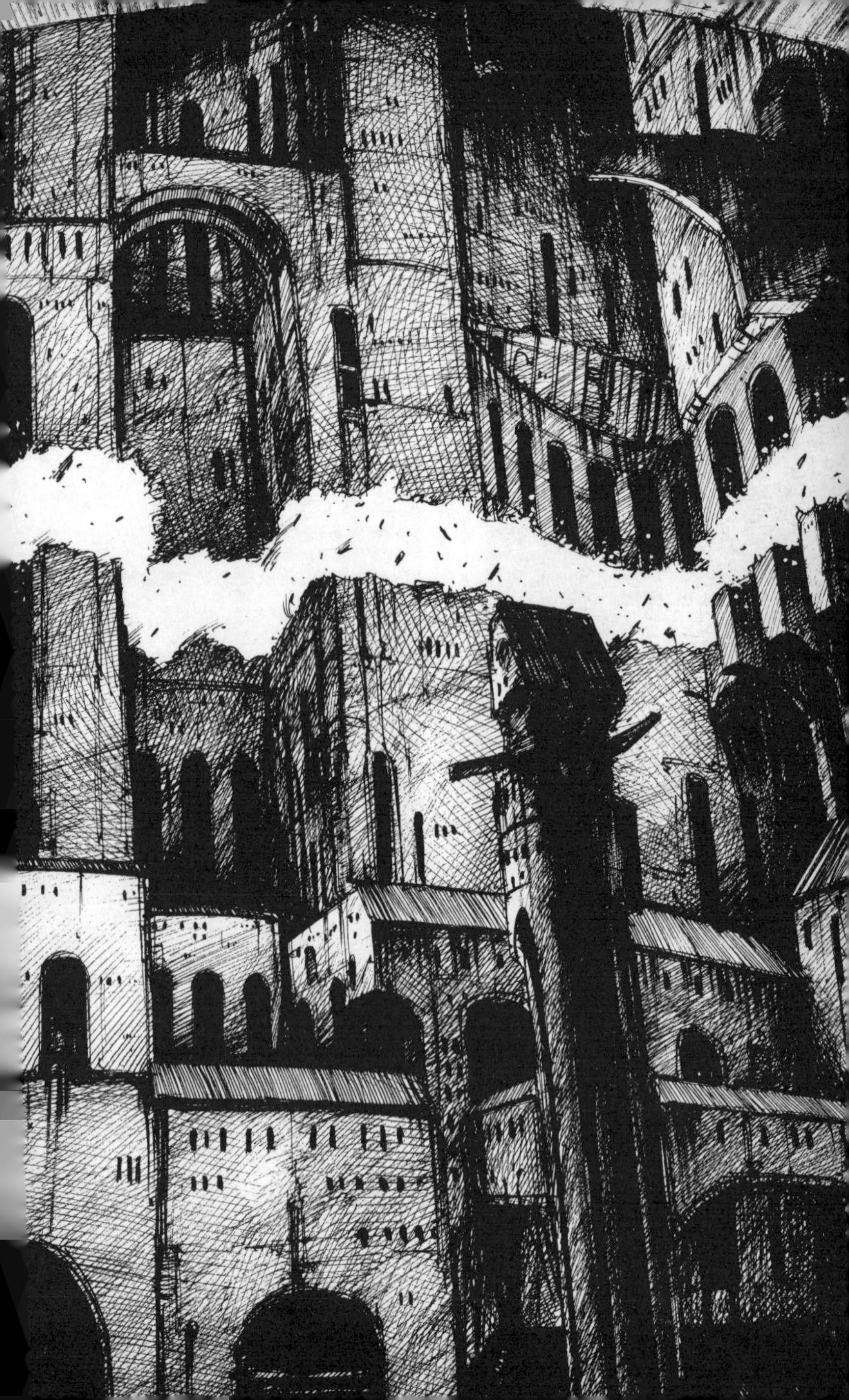

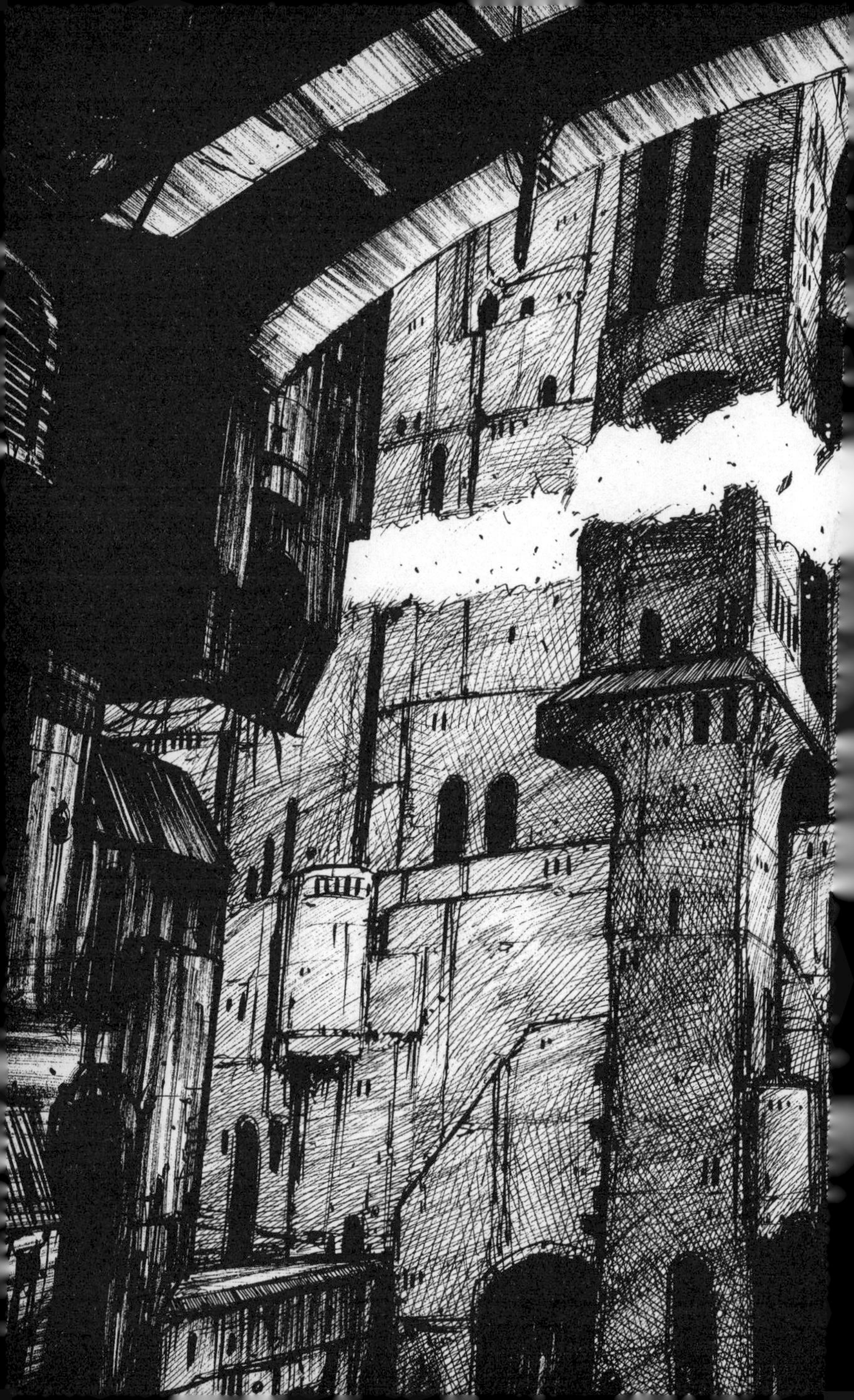

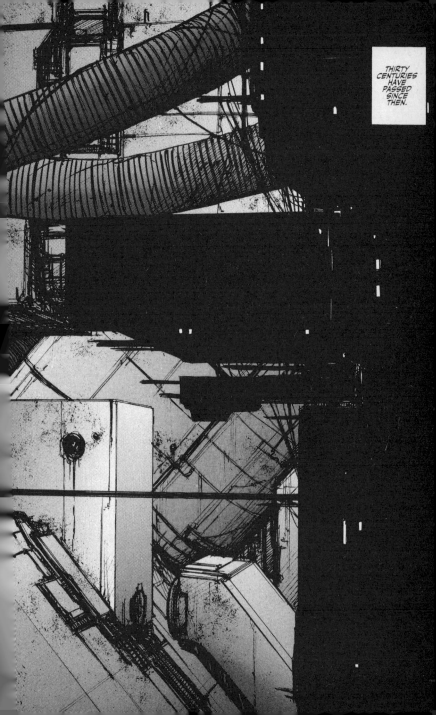

THIRTY
CENTURIES
HAVE
PASSED
SINCE
THEN.

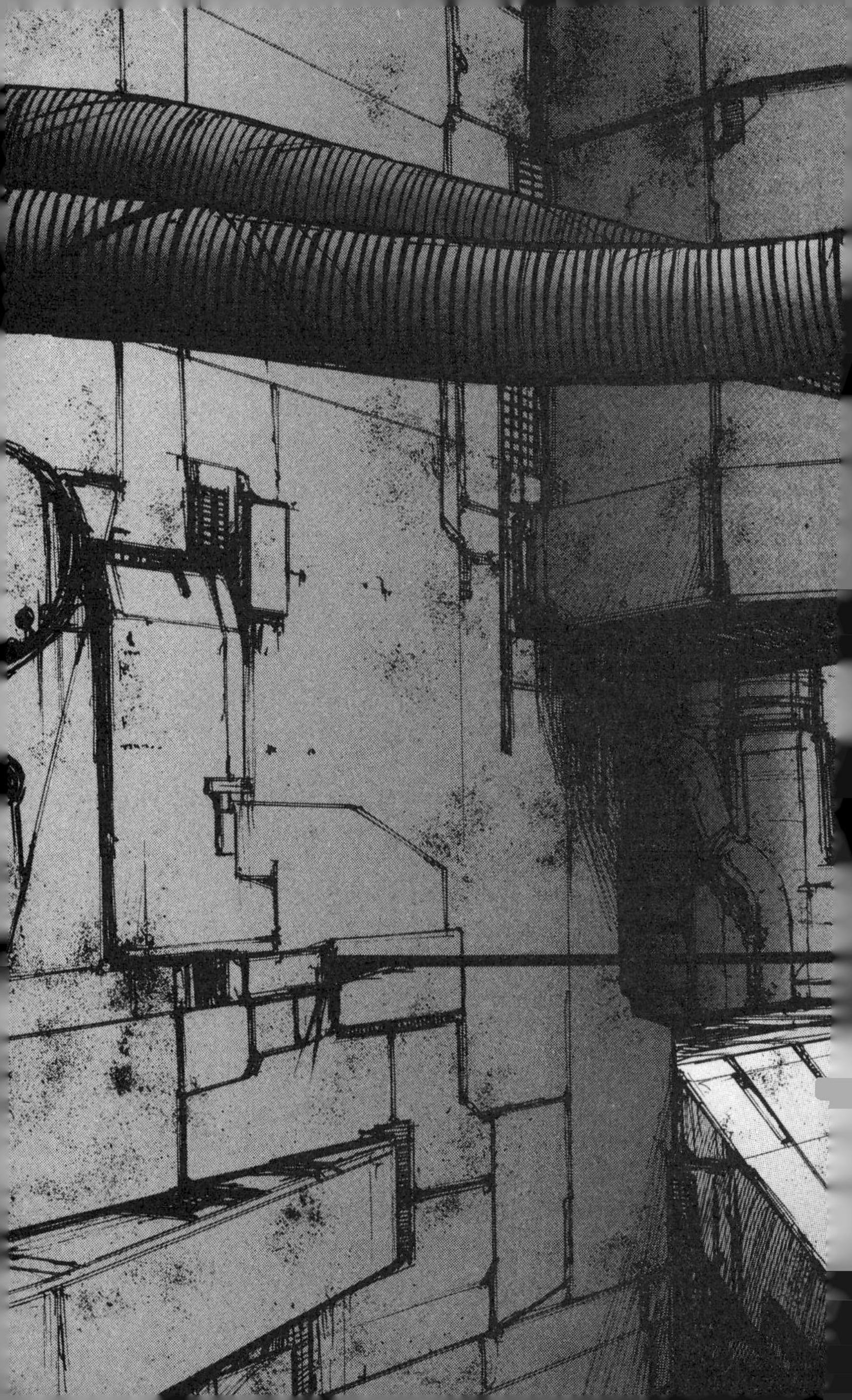

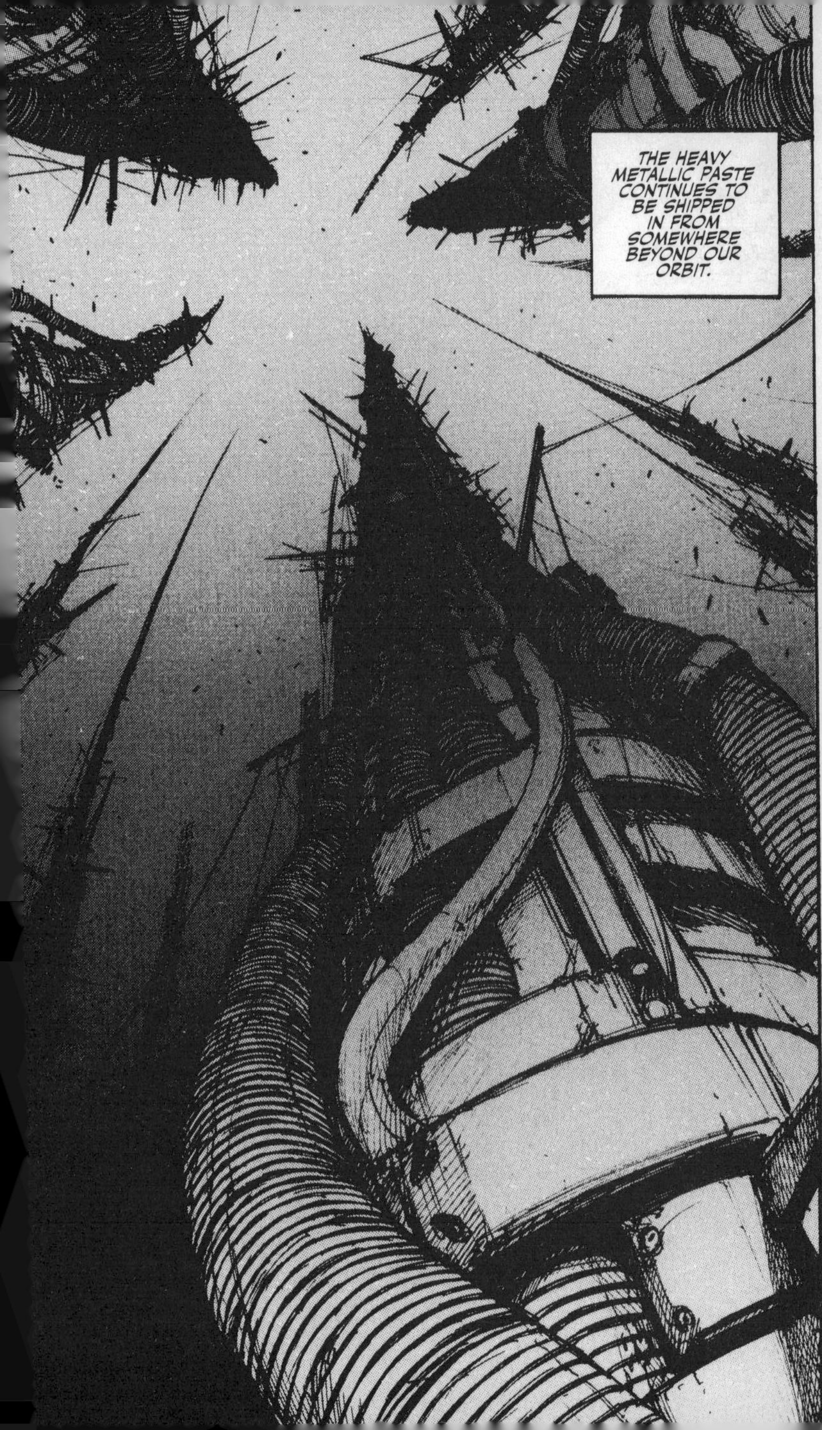
THE HEAVY METALLIC PASTE CONTINUES TO BE SHIPPED IN FROM SOMEWHERE BEYOND OUR ORBIT.

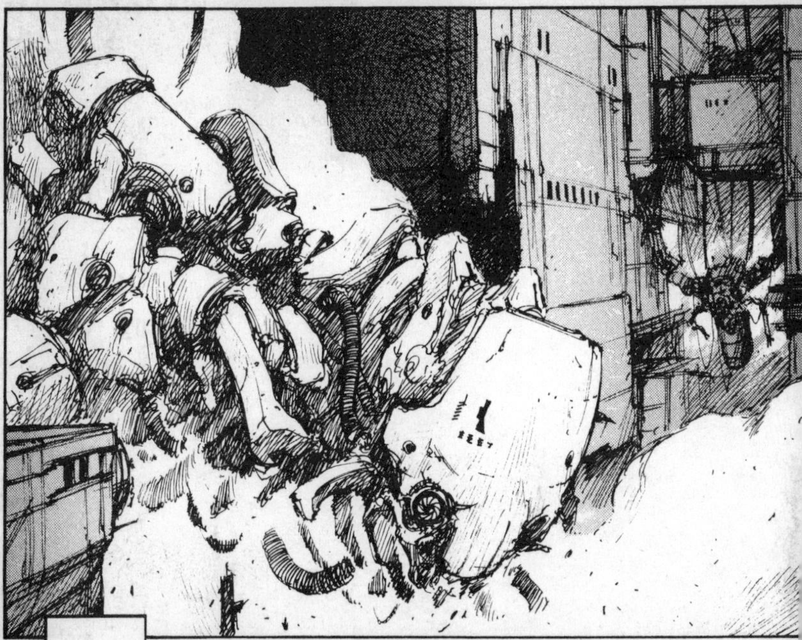

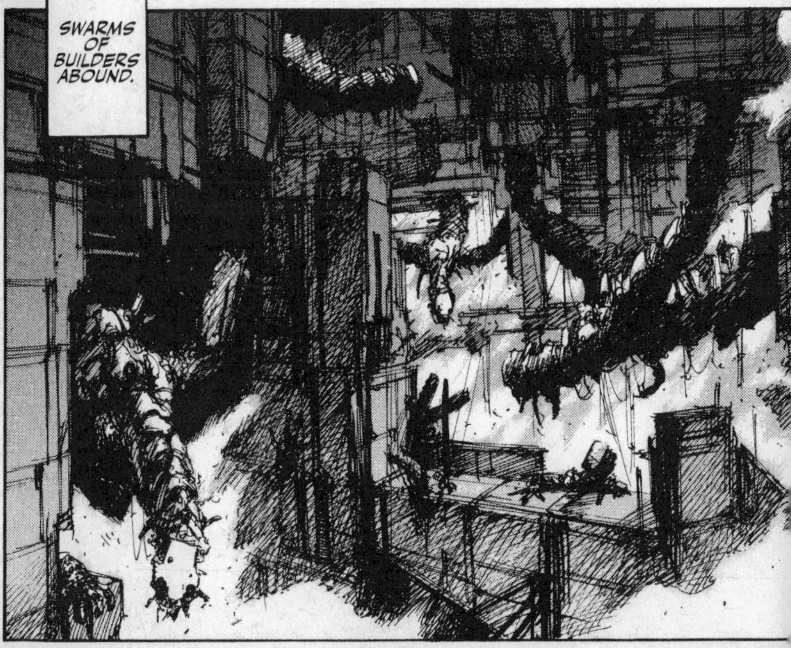
SWARMS OF BUILDERS ABOUND.

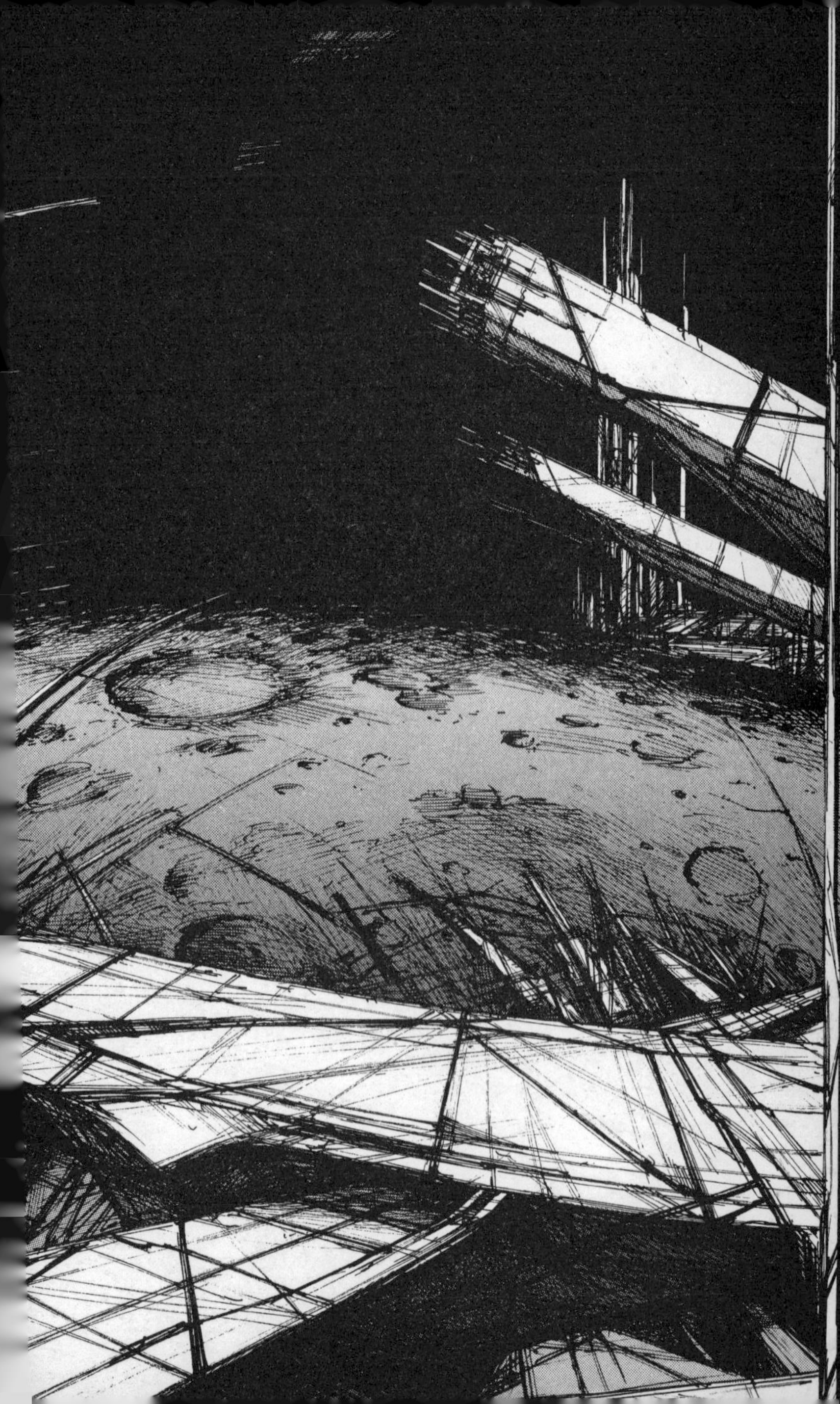

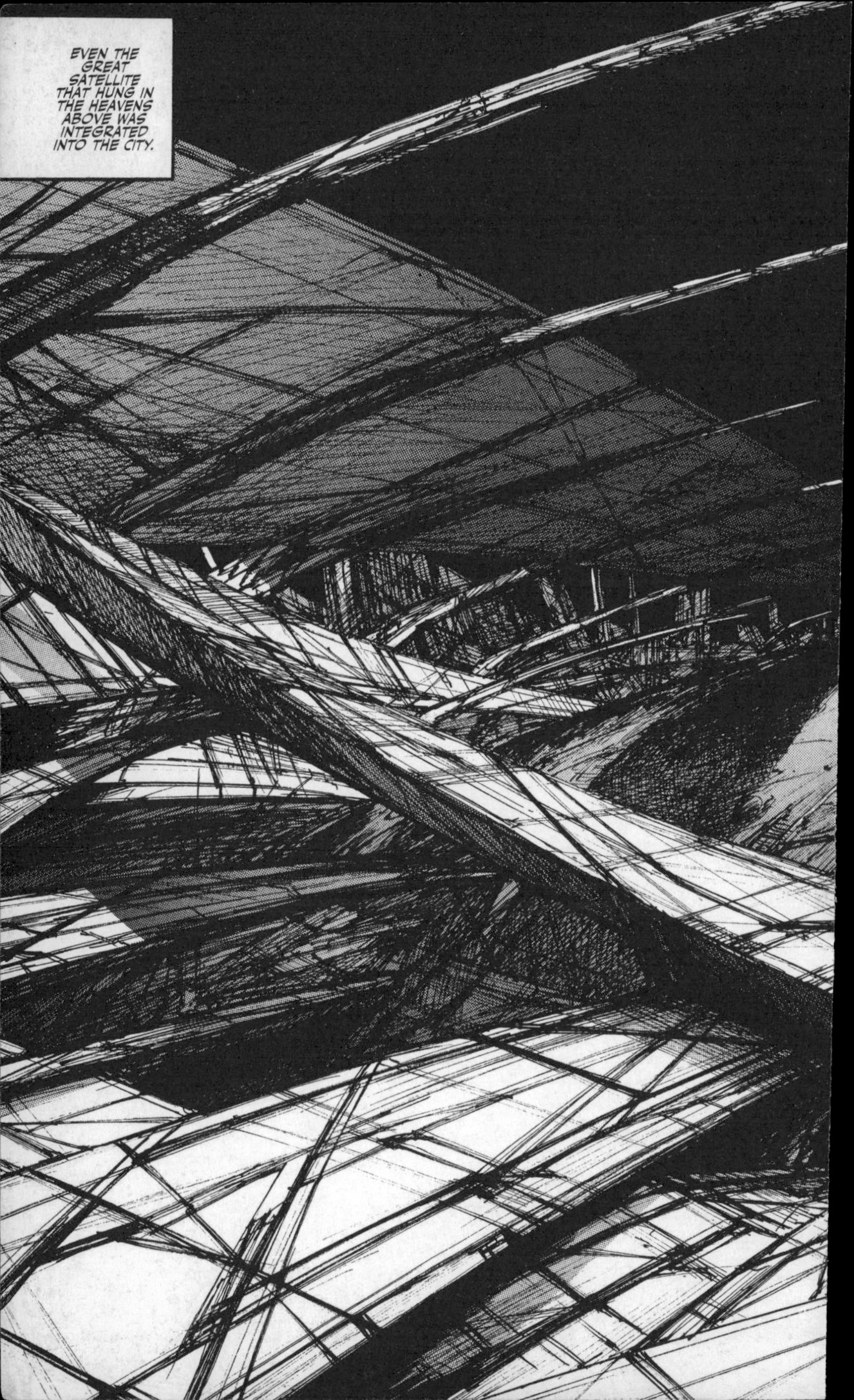
EVEN THE GREAT SATELLITE THAT HUNG IN THE HEAVENS ABOVE WAS INTEGRATED INTO THE CITY.

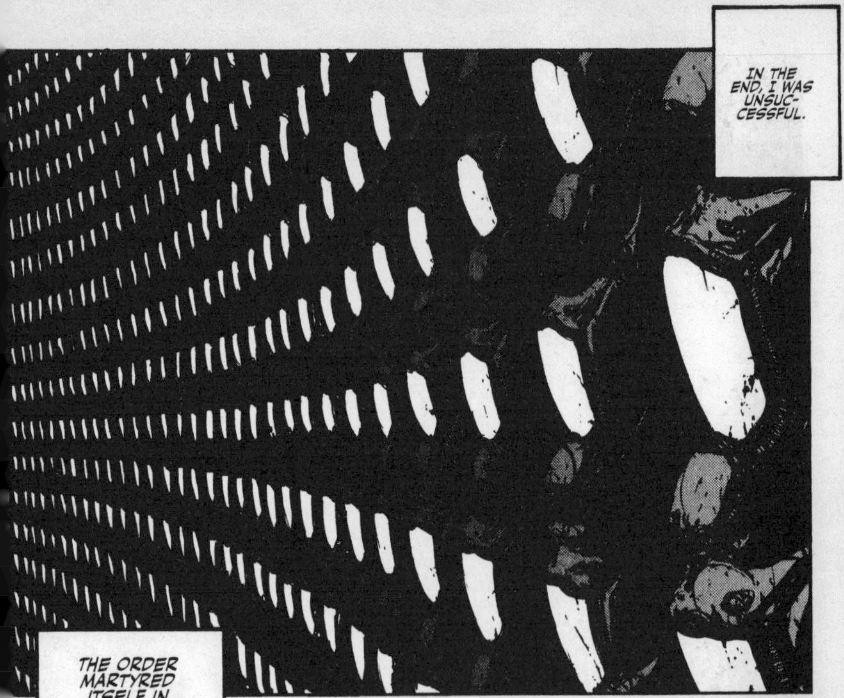
IN THE END, I WAS UNSUC-CESSFUL.
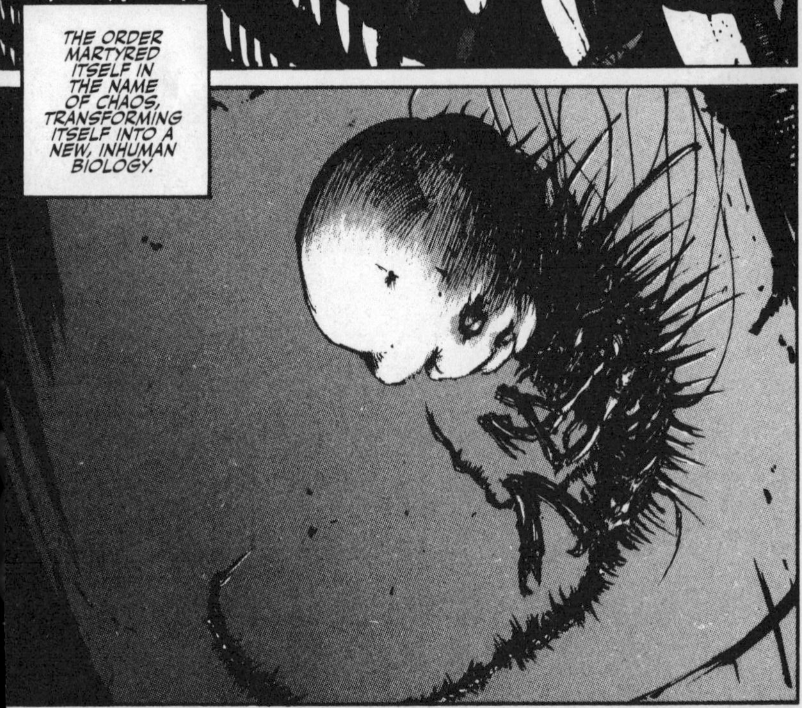
THE ORDER MARTYRED ITSELF IN THE NAME OF CHAOS, TRANSFORMING ITSELF INTO A NEW, INHUMAN BIOLOGY.

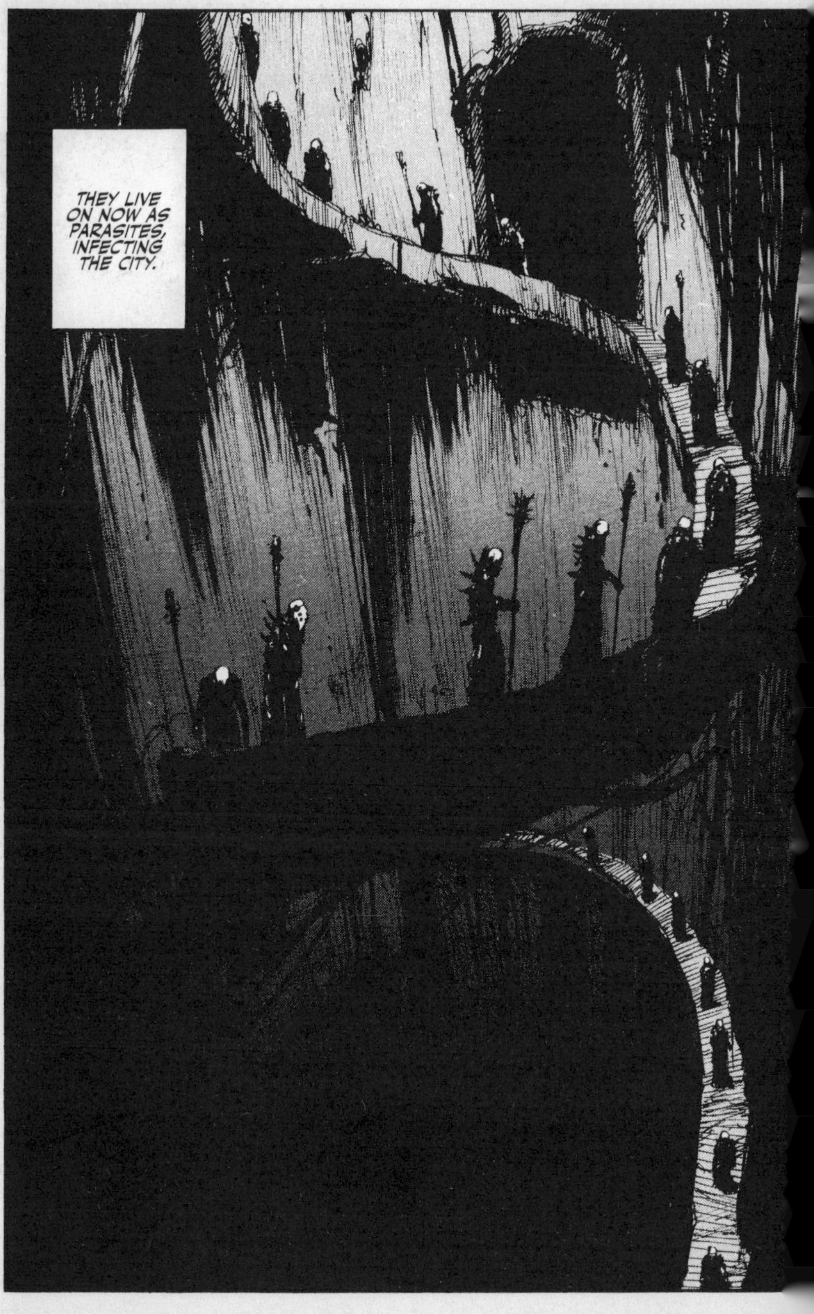
THEY LIVE ON NOW AS PARASITES, INFECTING THE CITY.

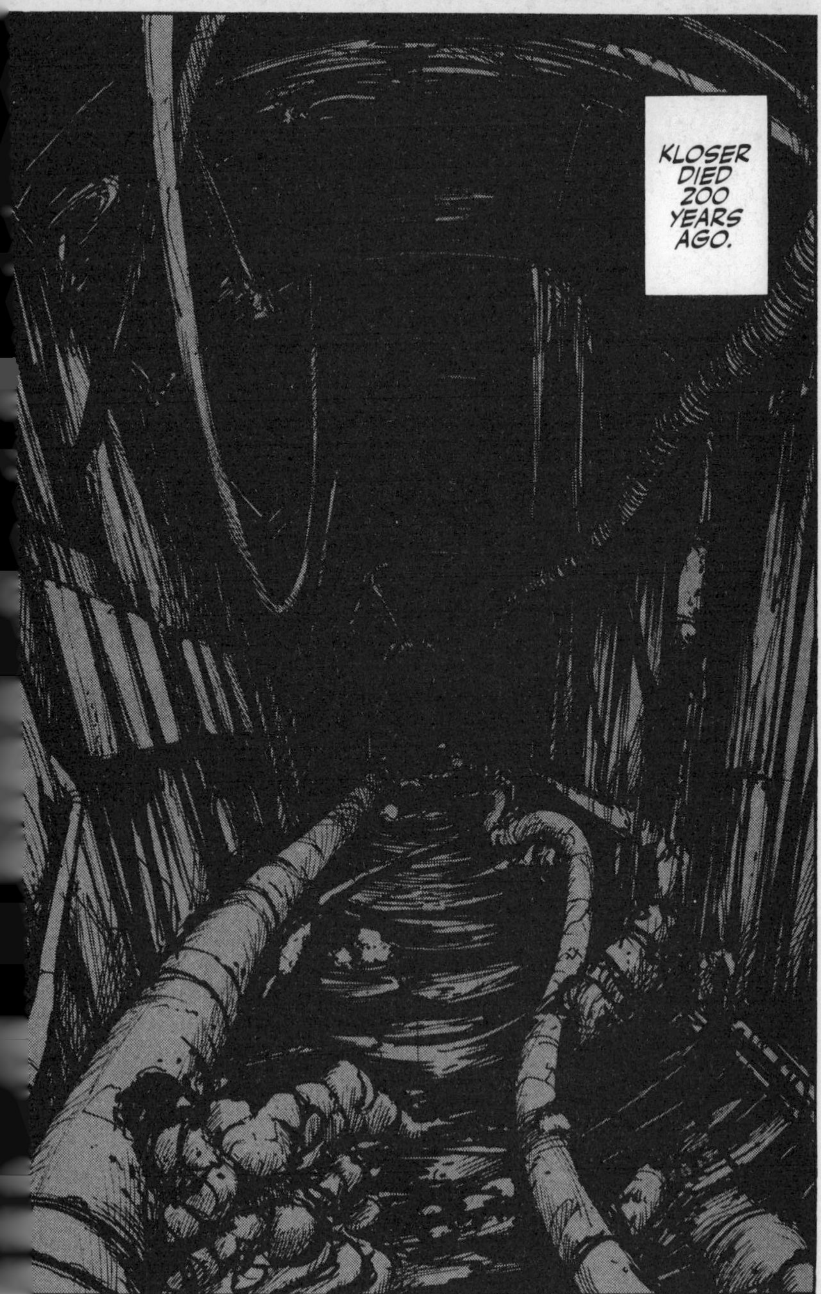
KLOSER DIED 200 YEARS AGO.

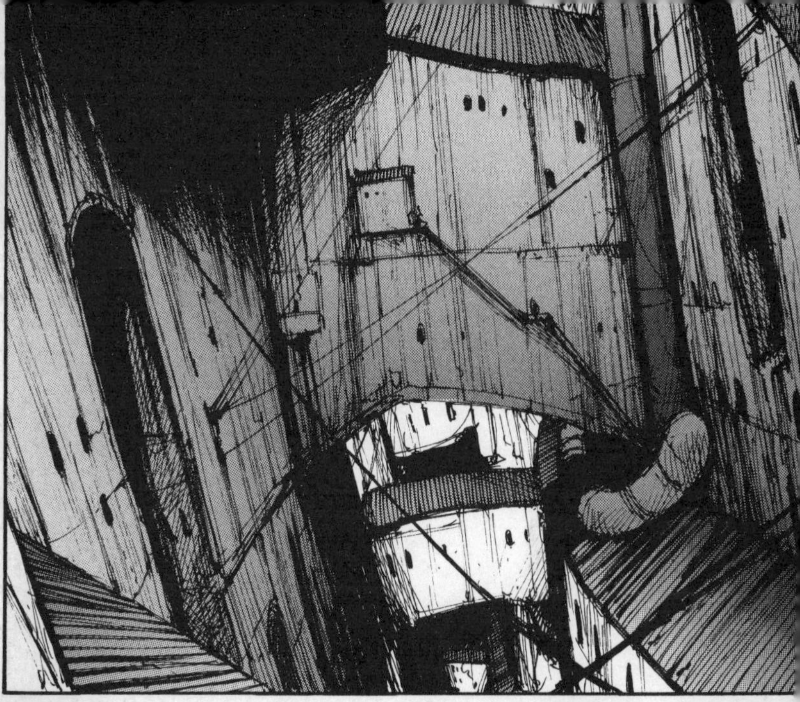
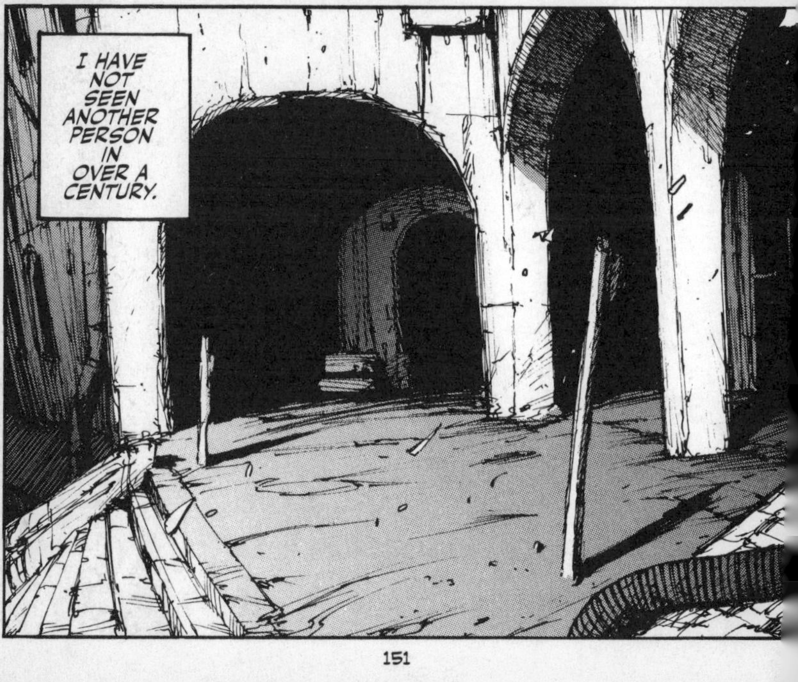
I HAVE NOT SEEN ANOTHER PERSON IN OVER A CENTURY.

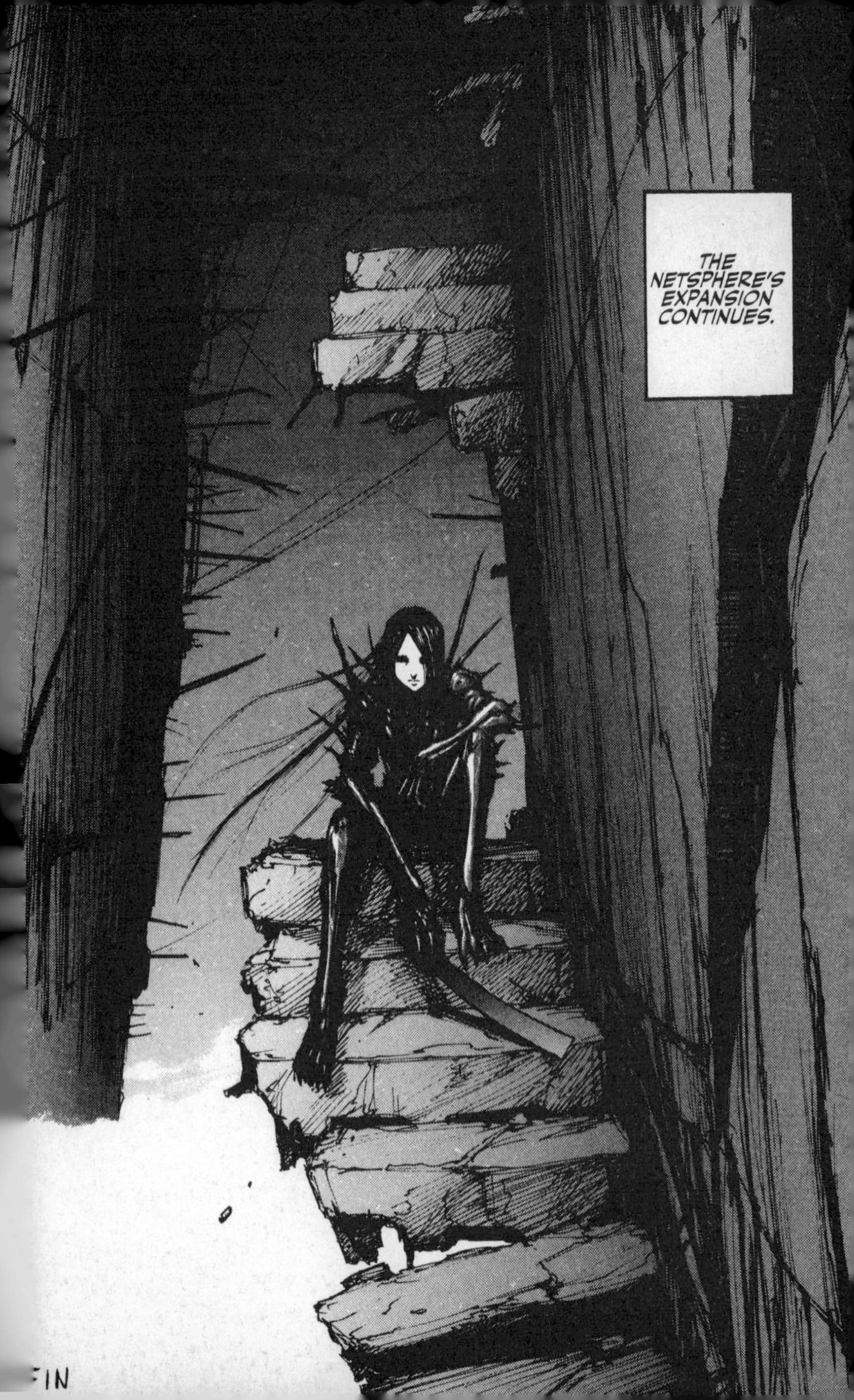
THE NETSPHERE'S EXPANSION CONTINUES.
FIN

「負の回廊」

Negative Corridor

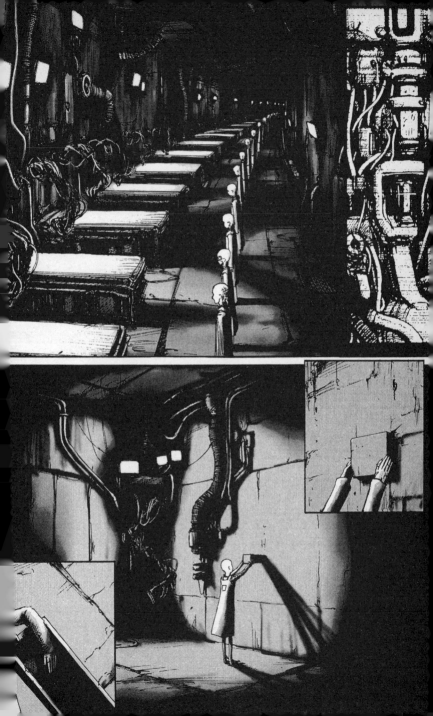

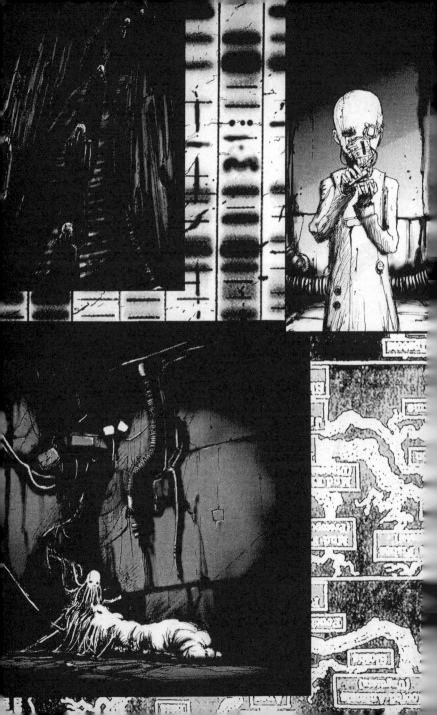

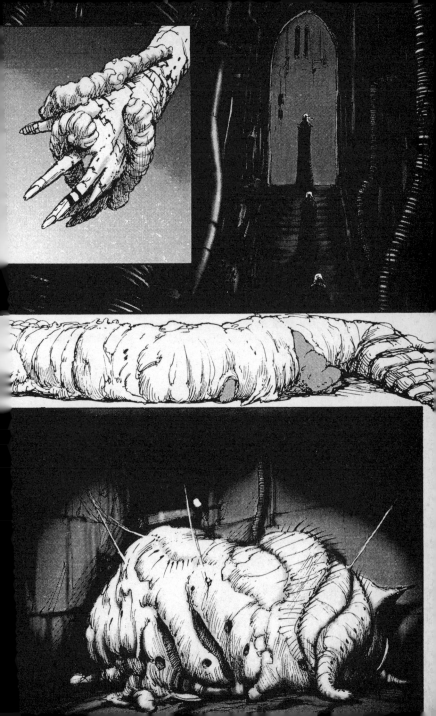

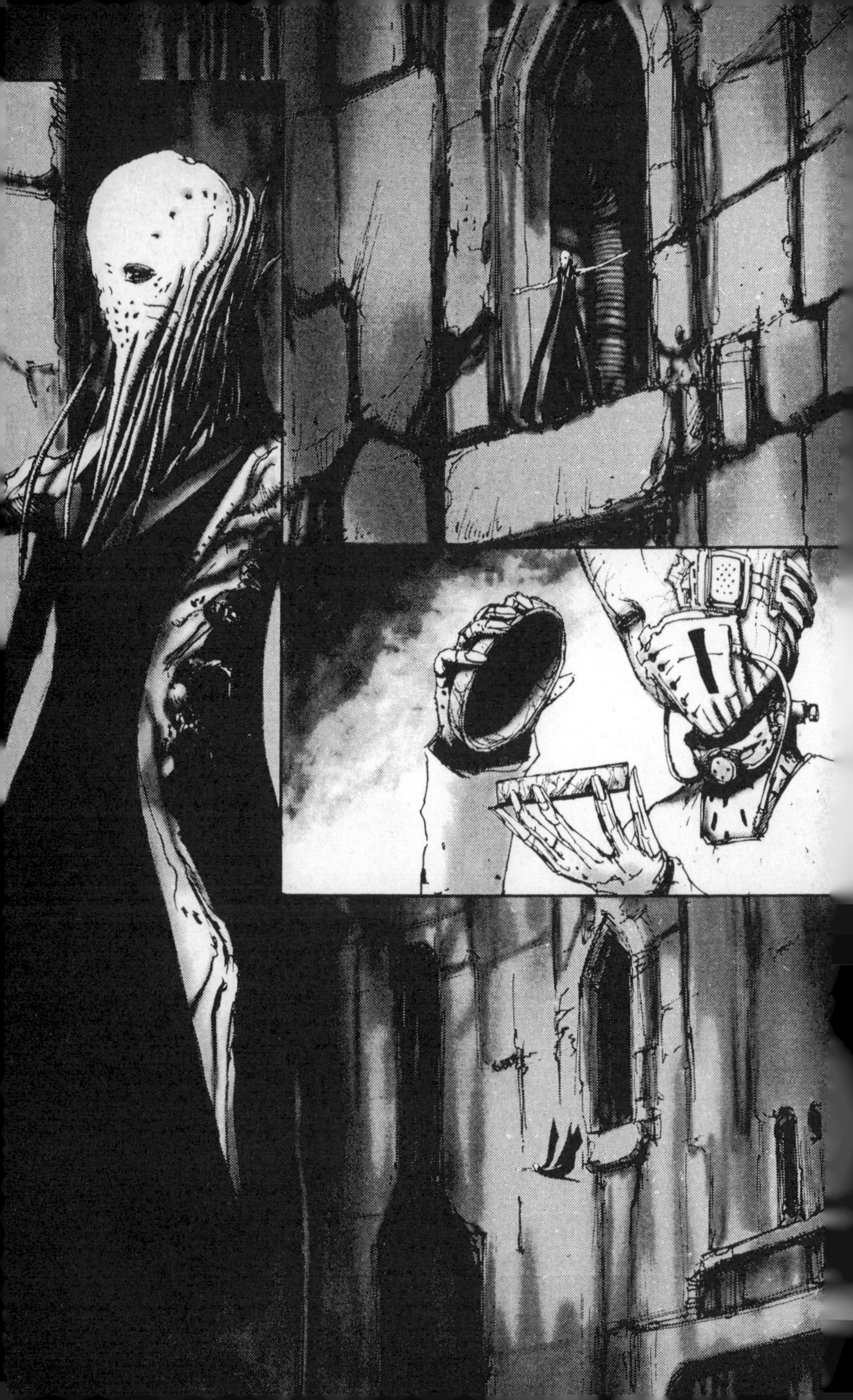

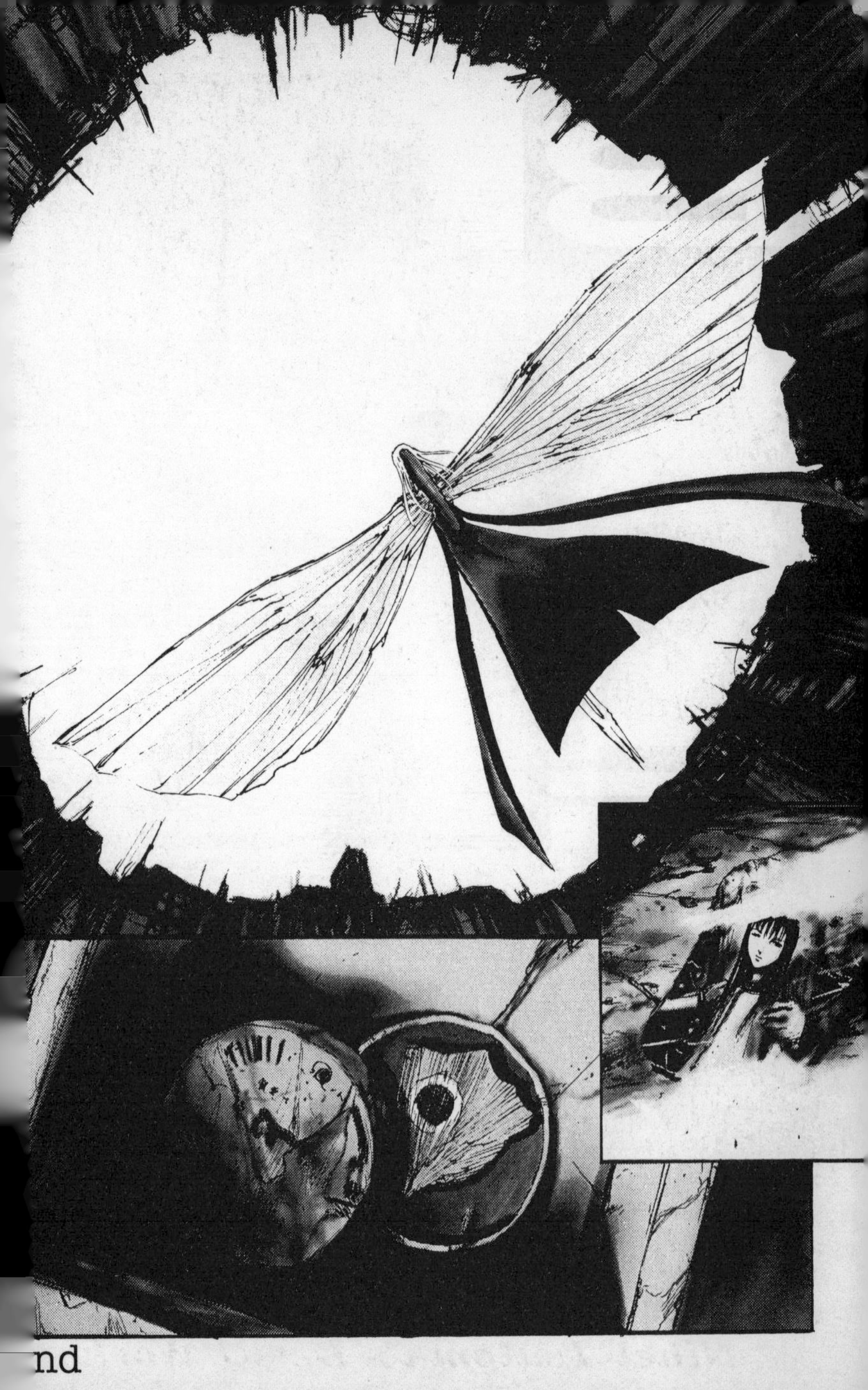

nd

Summer 1995 Four Seasons Contest Special Judges Award Recipien

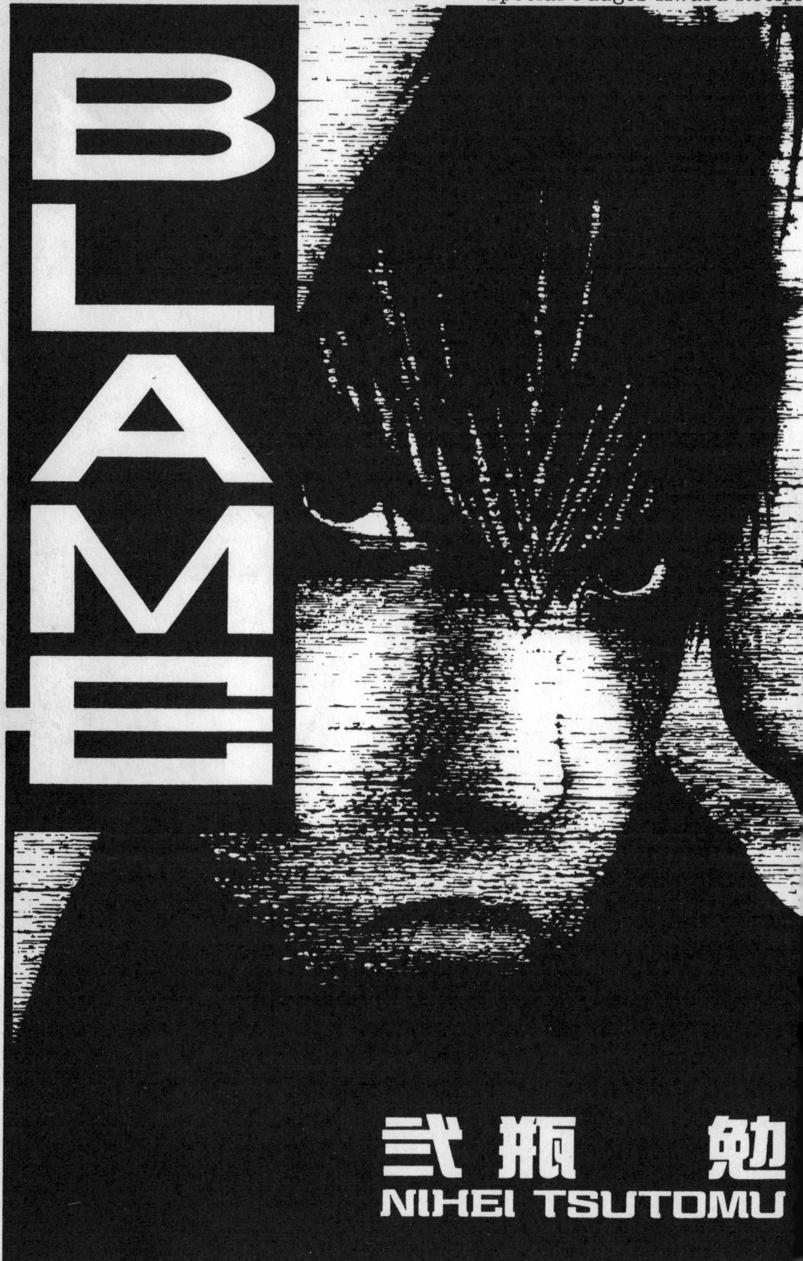
BLAME
弐瓶 勉
NIHEI TSUTOMU

Nihei Tsutomu's Debut Work

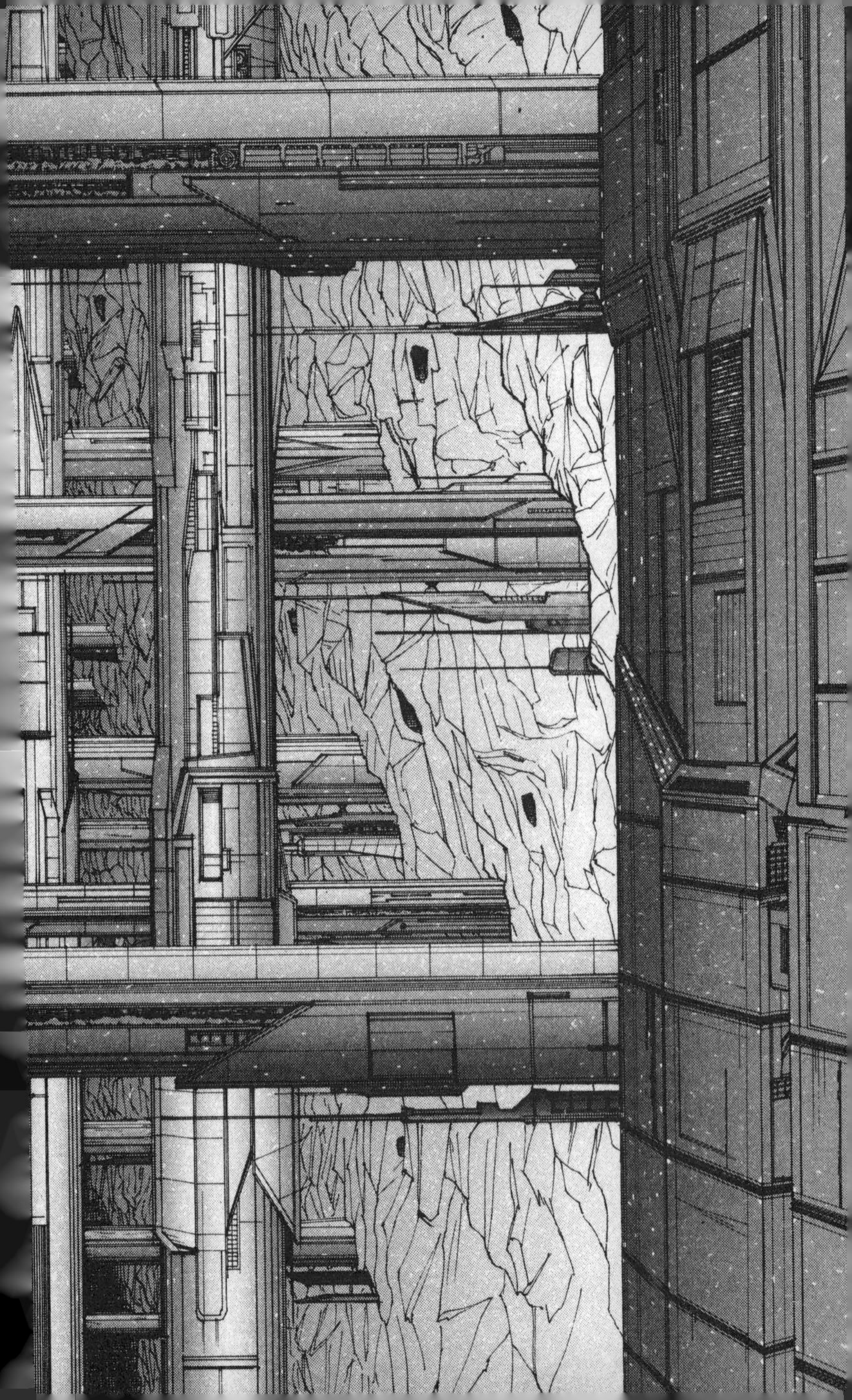

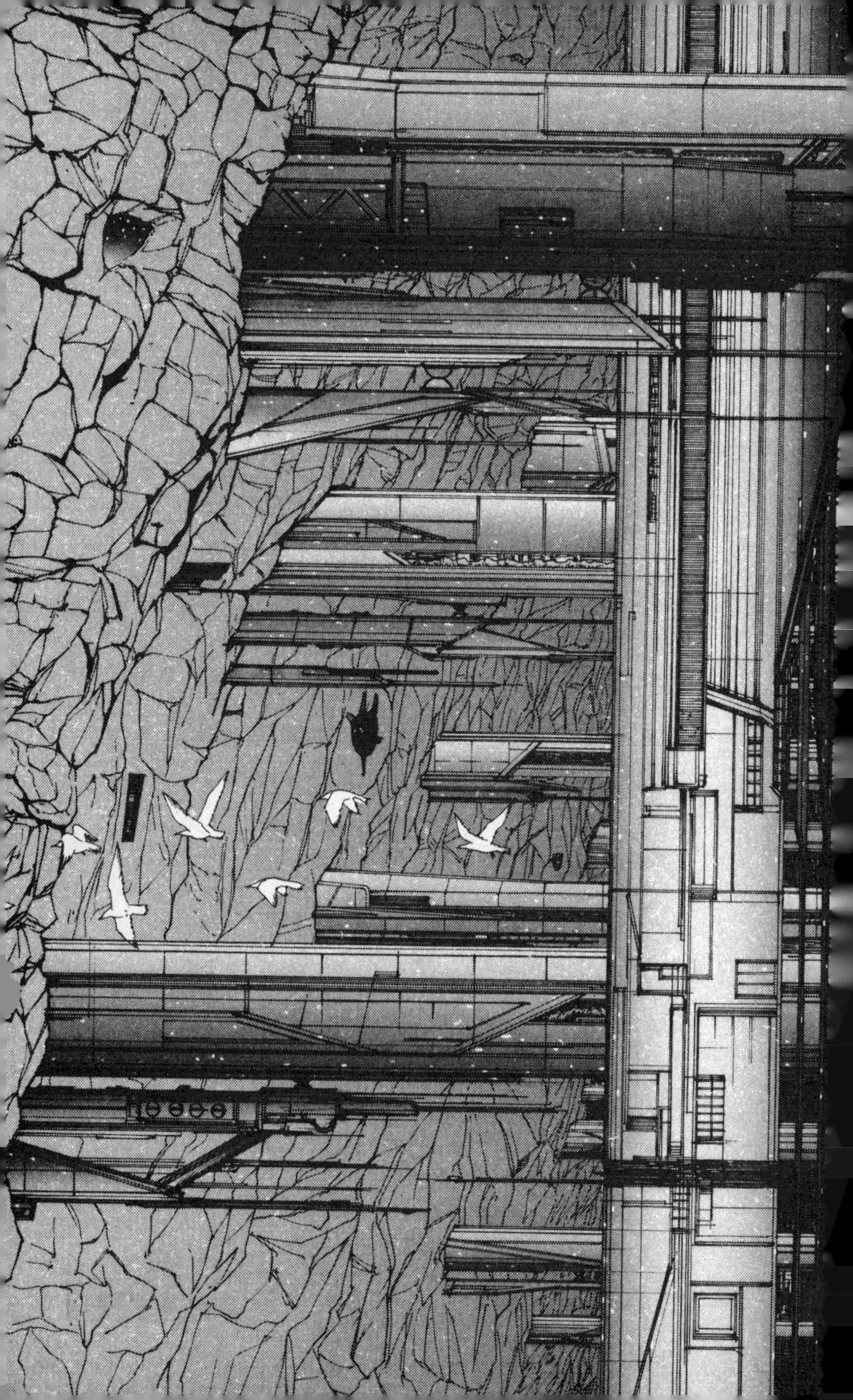

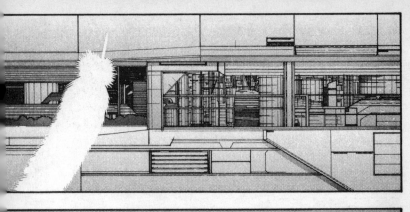

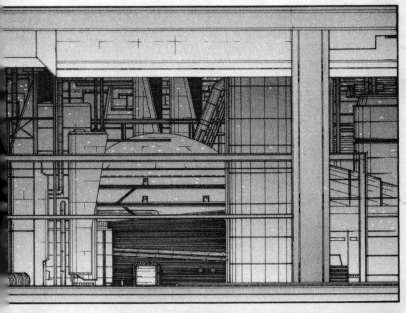

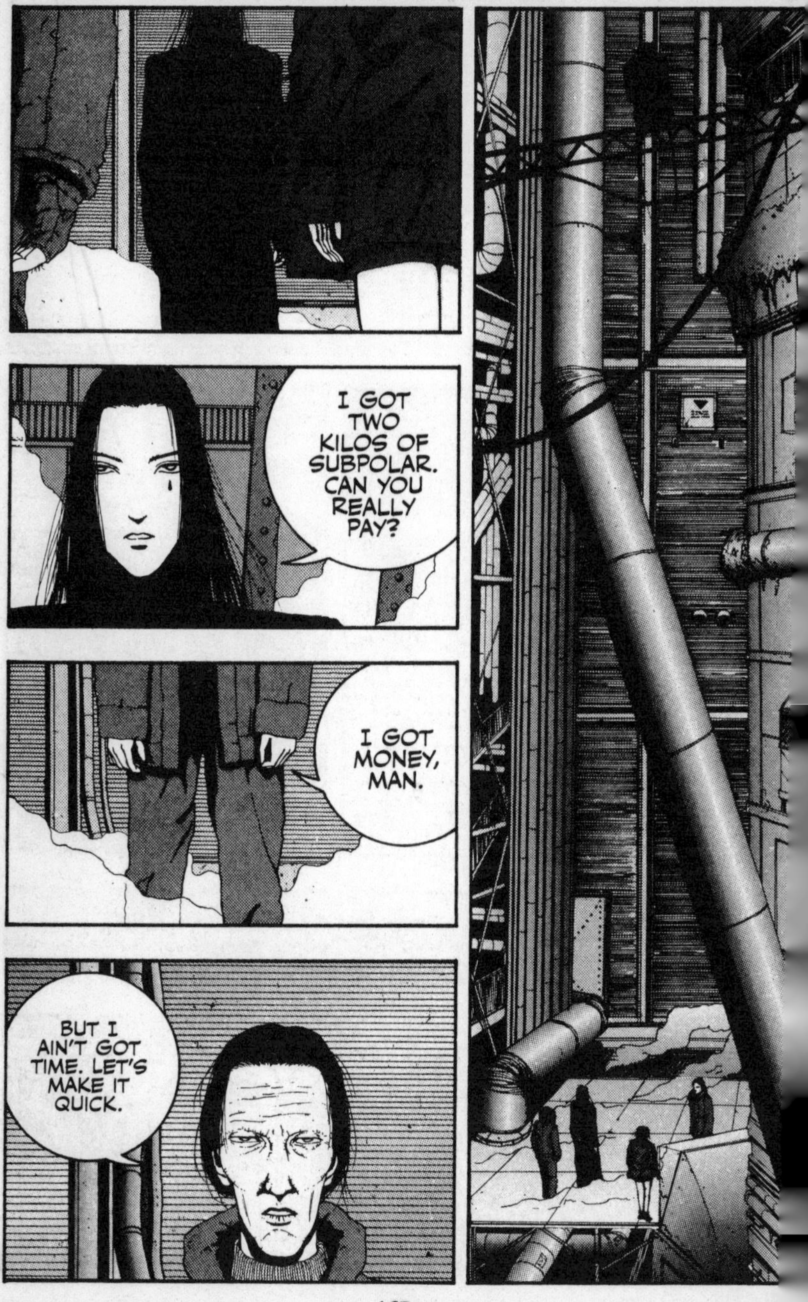
I GOT TWO KILOS OF SUBPOLAR. CAN YOU REALLY PAY?
I GOT MONEY, MAN.
BUT I AIN'T GOT TIME. LET'S MAKE IT QUICK.

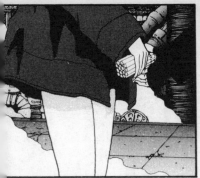

THUNK

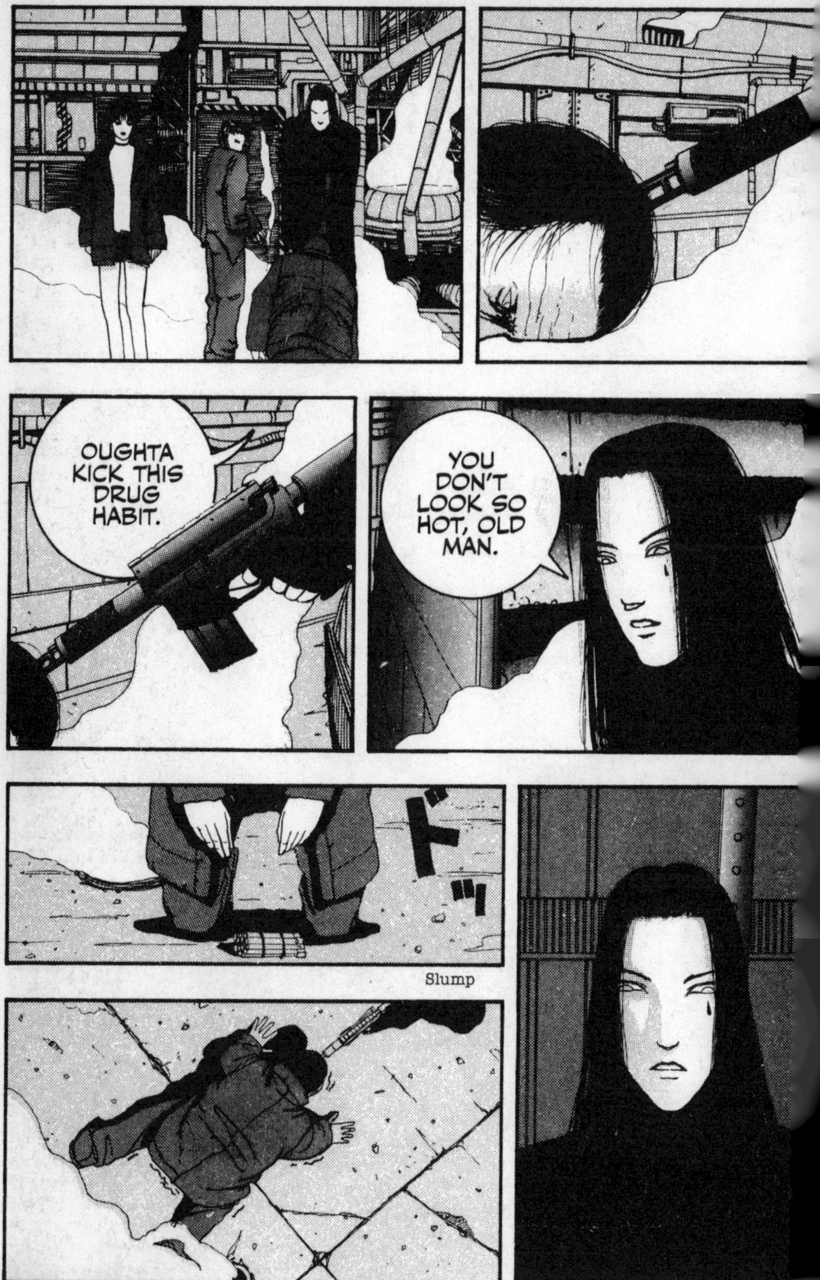
YOU DON'T LOOK SO HOT, OLD MAN.
OUGHTA KICK THIS DRUG HABIT.
Slump

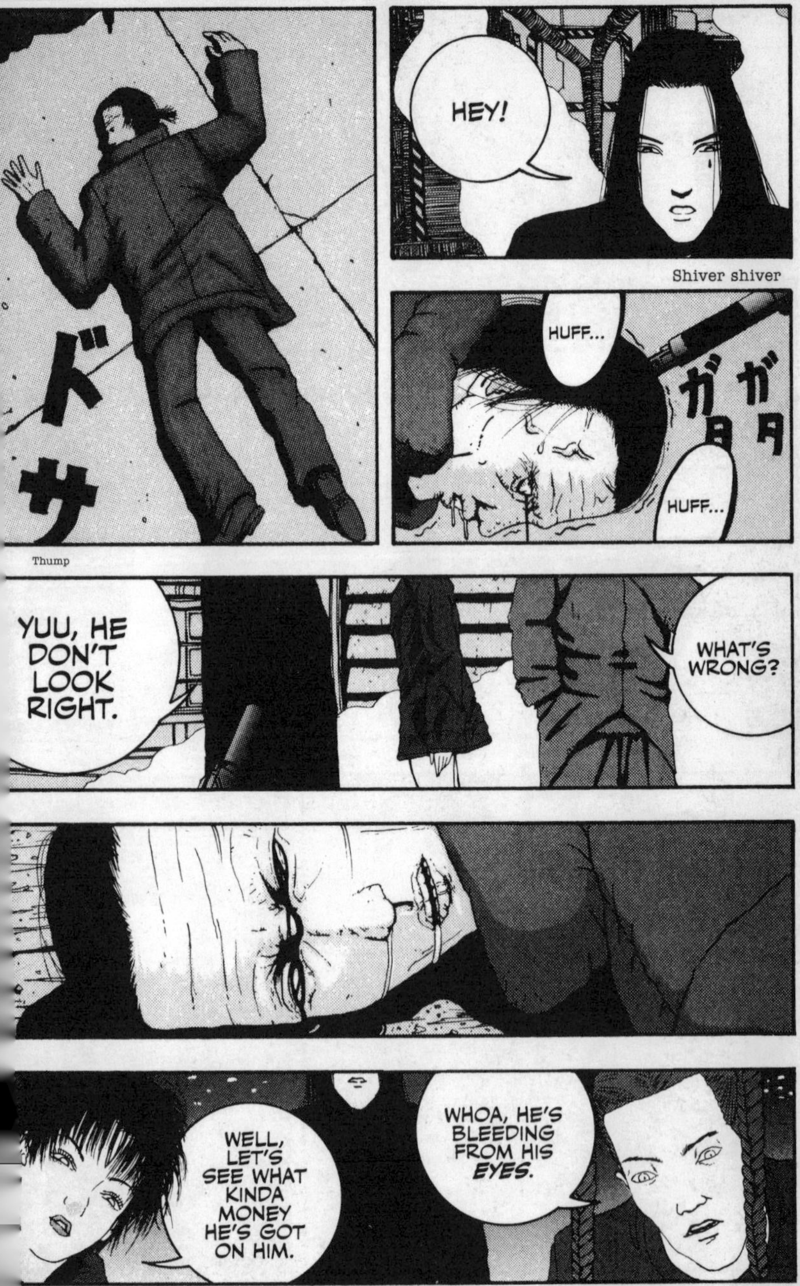
HEY!
Shiver shiver
HUFF...
ガタガタ
HUFF...
ドサ
Thump
WHAT'S WRONG?
YUU, HE DON'T LOOK RIGHT.
WHOA, HE'S BLEEDING FROM HIS *EYES.*
WELL, LET'S SEE WHAT KINDA MONEY HE'S GOT ON HIM.

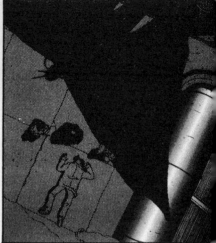

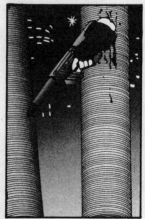

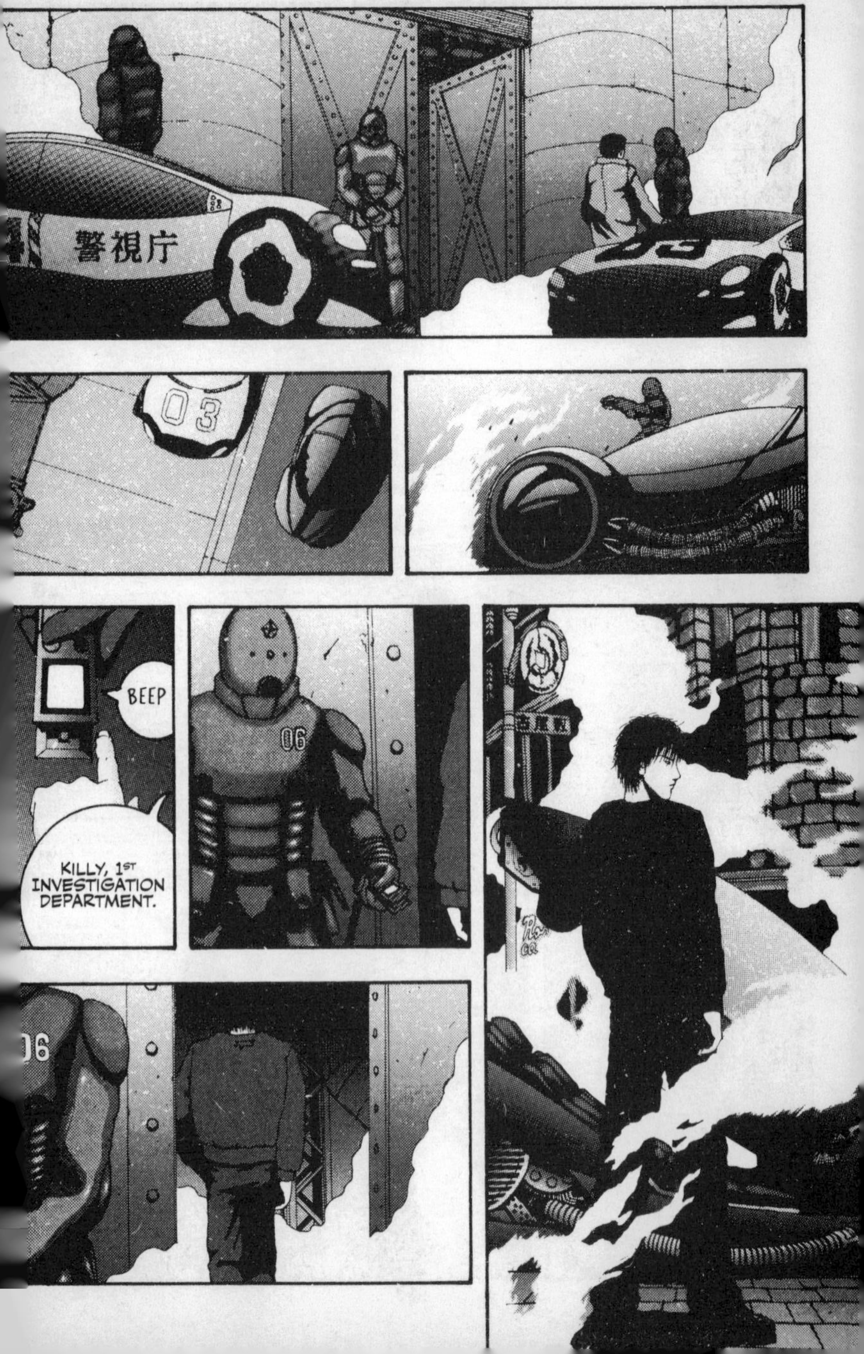
警視庁
03
BEEP
06
KILLY, 1ST INVESTIGATION DEPARTMENT.
06

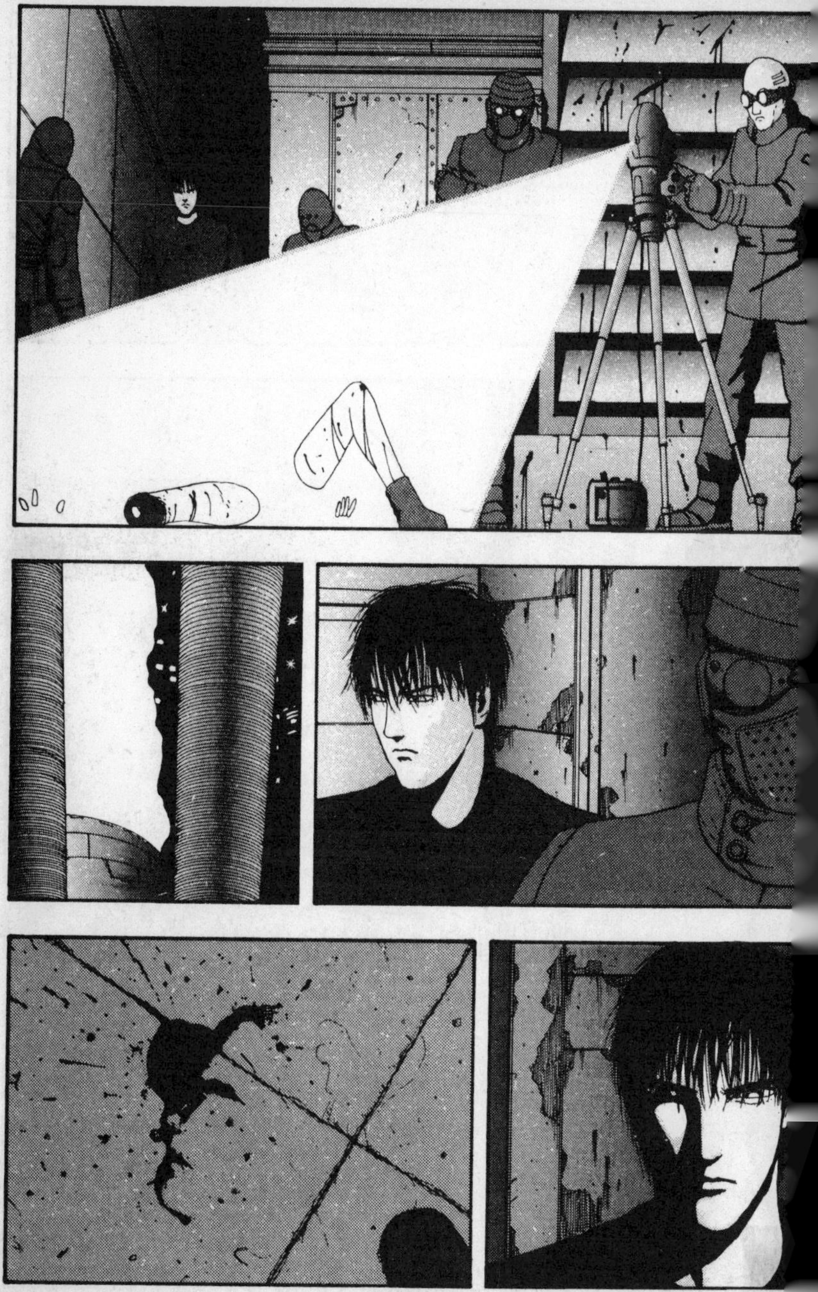

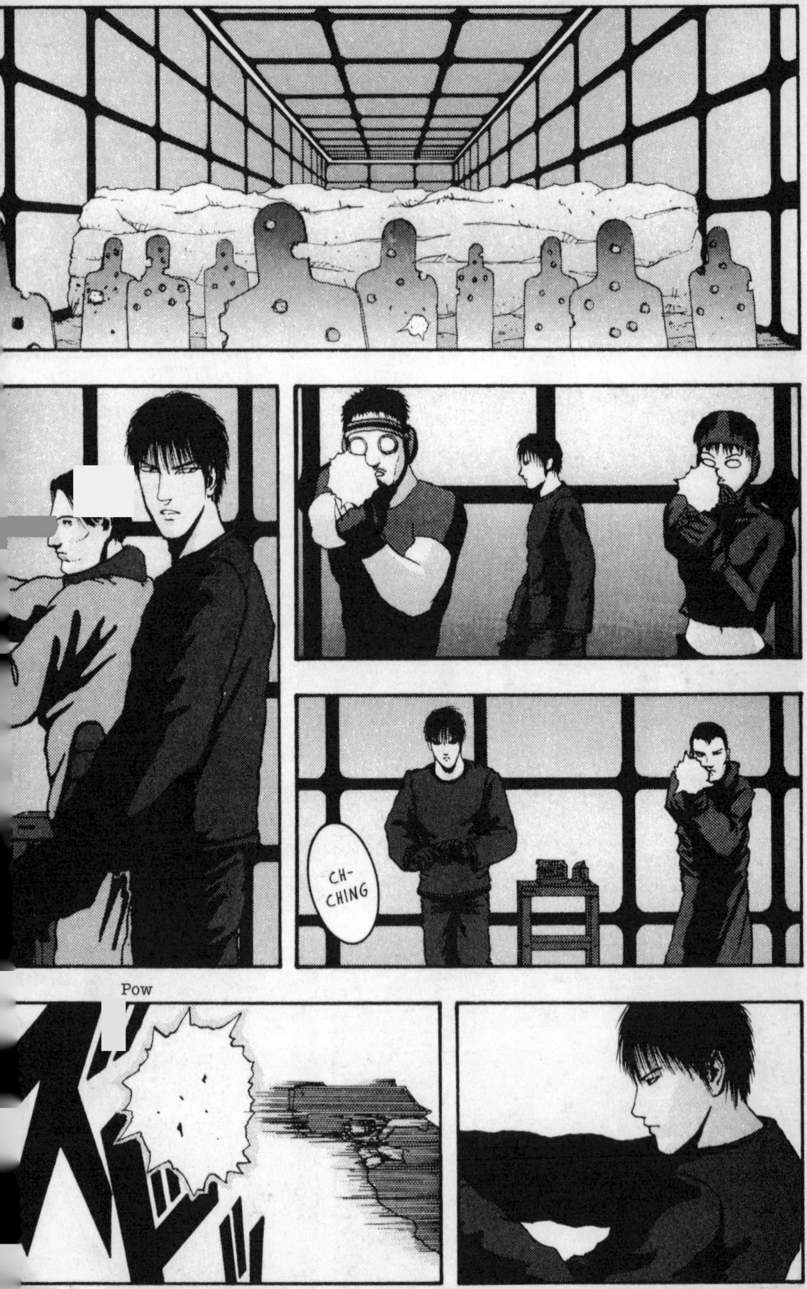
CH-
CHING
Pow

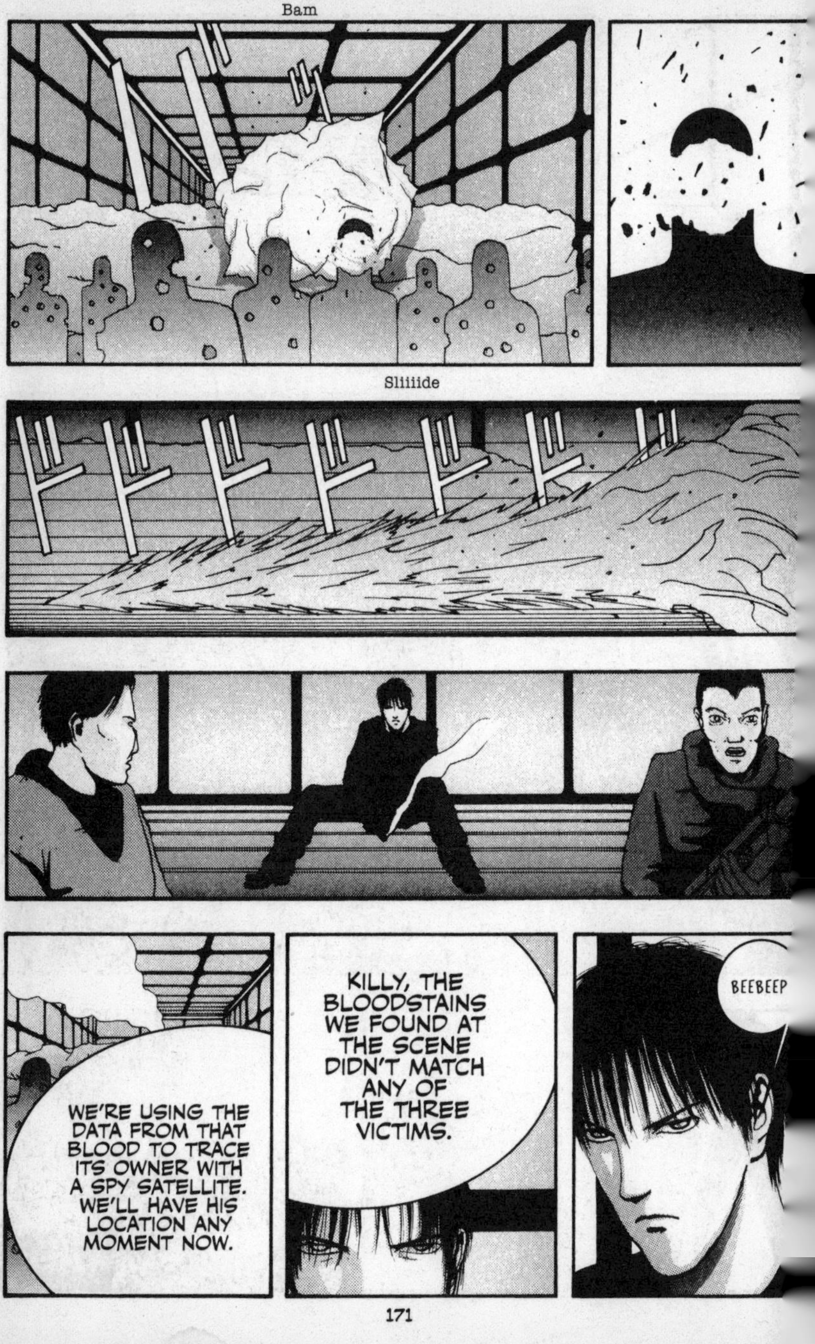
Bam
Sliiiide
BEEBEEP
KILLY, THE BLOODSTAINS WE FOUND AT THE SCENE DIDN'T MATCH ANY OF THE THREE VICTIMS.
WE'RE USING THE DATA FROM THAT BLOOD TO TRACE ITS OWNER WITH A SPY SATELLITE. WE'LL HAVE HIS LOCATION ANY MOMENT NOW.

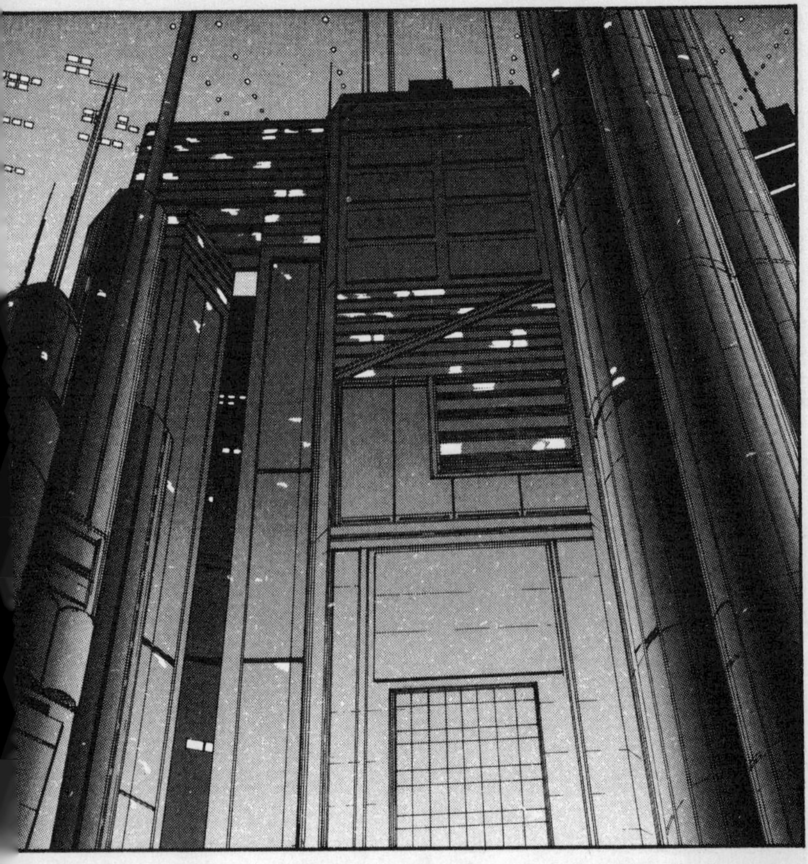
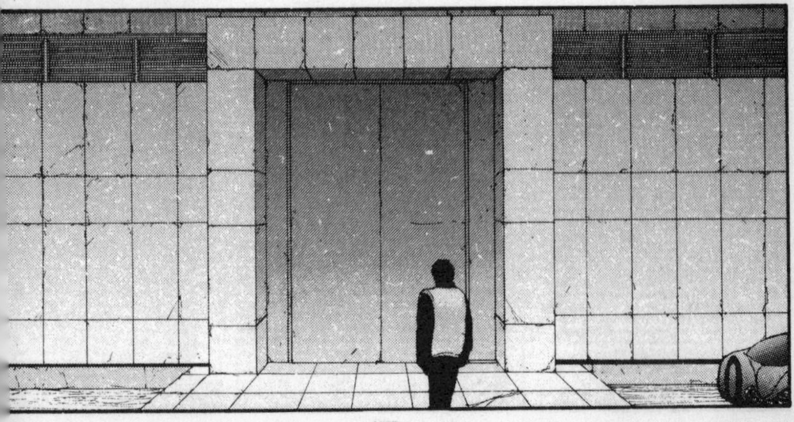

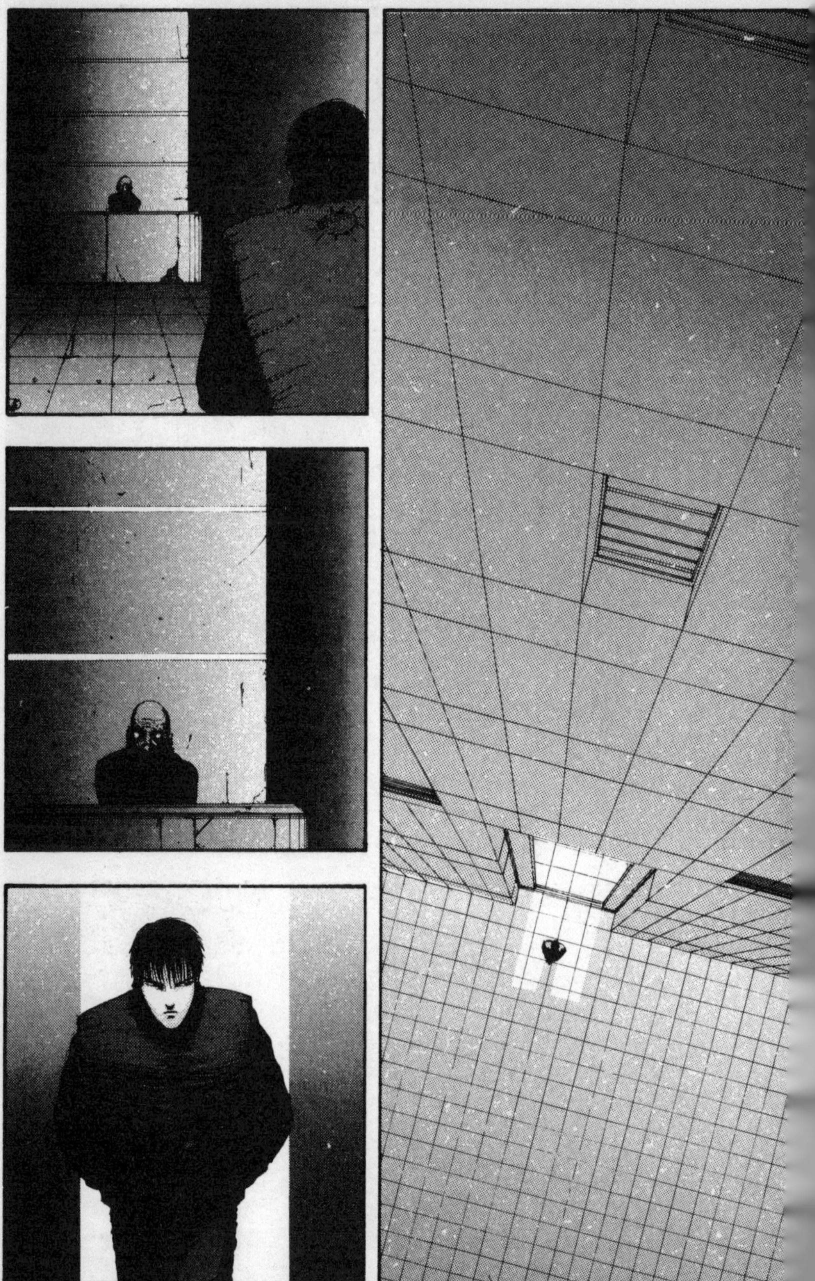

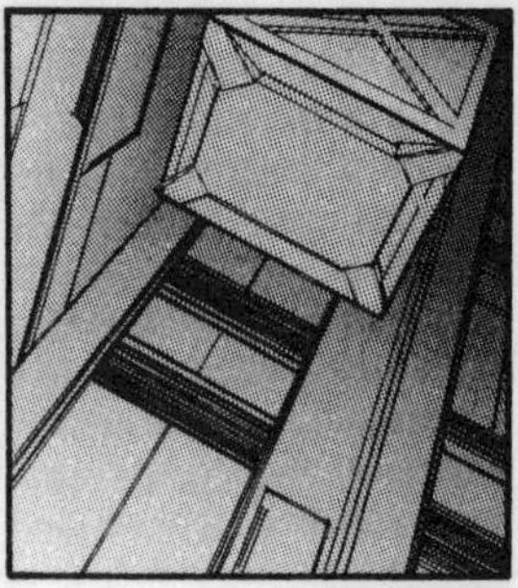
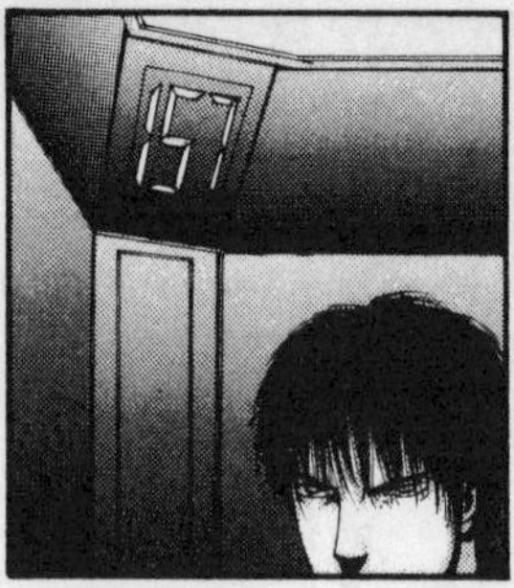
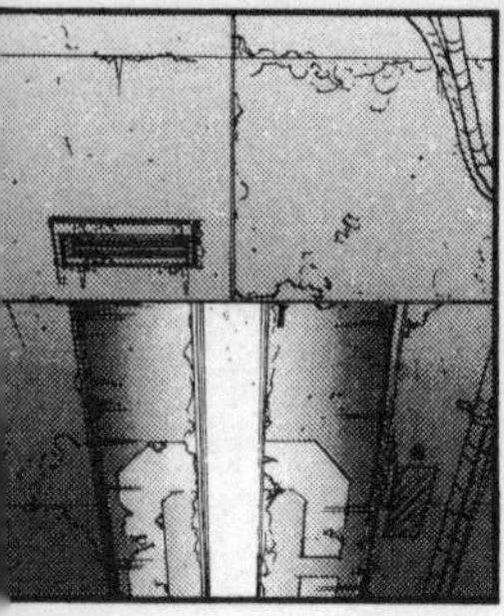
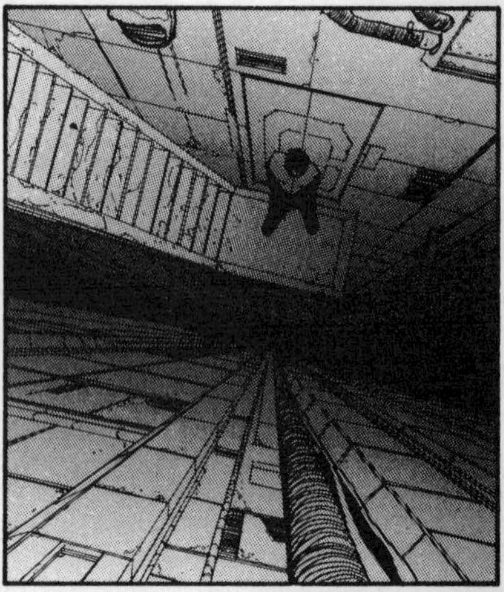
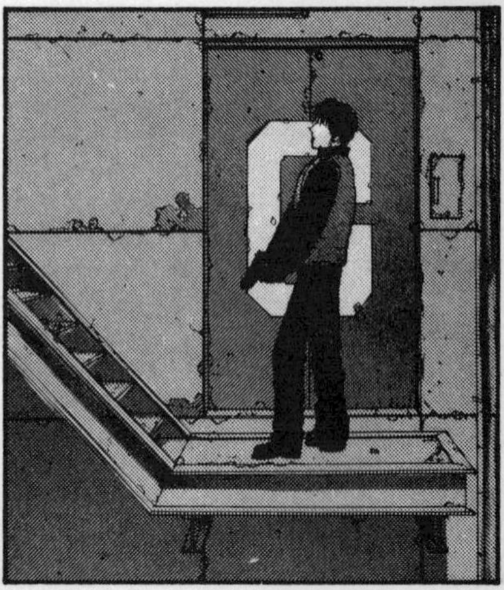
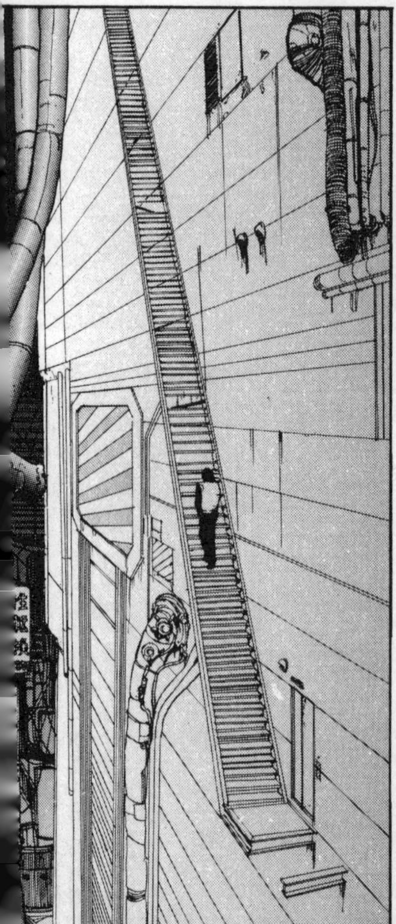

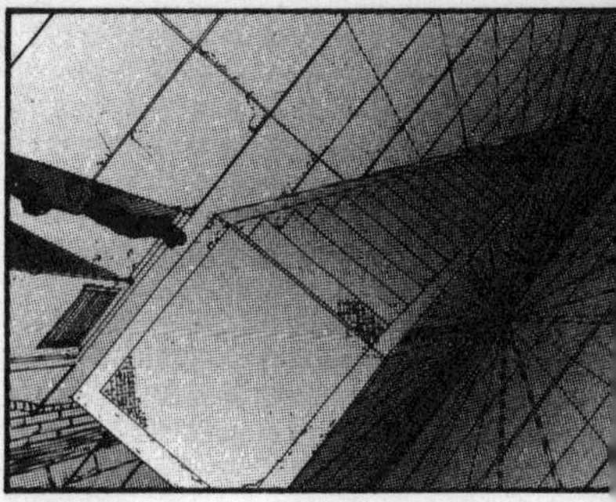
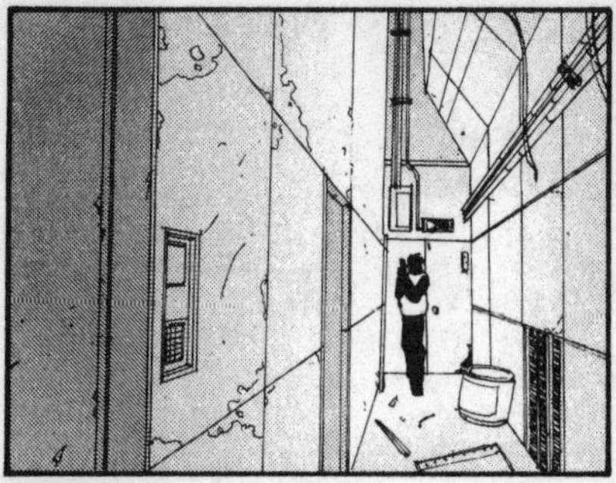
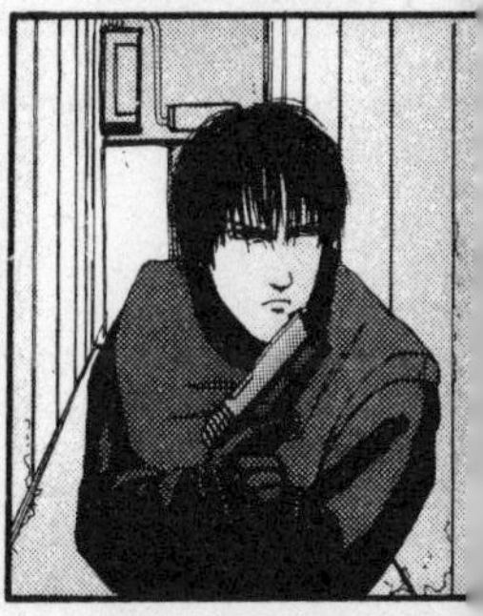
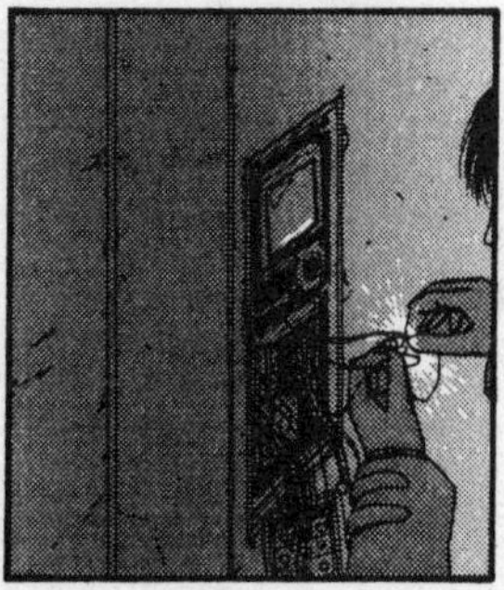
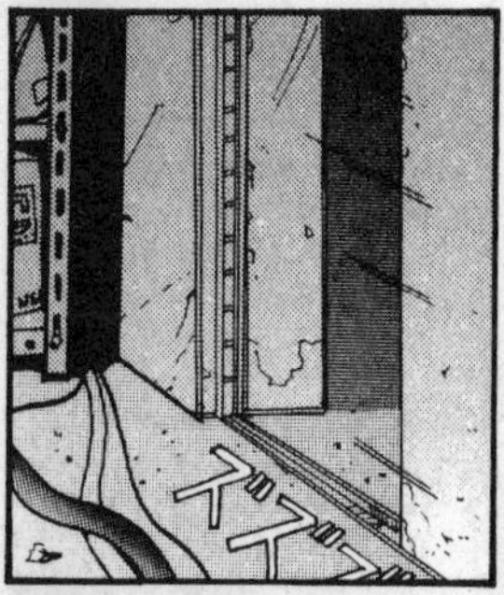
Zzzud
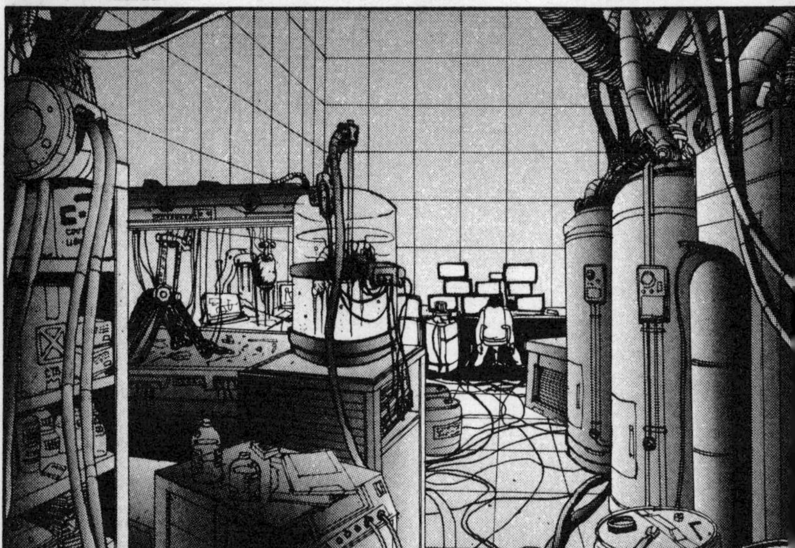

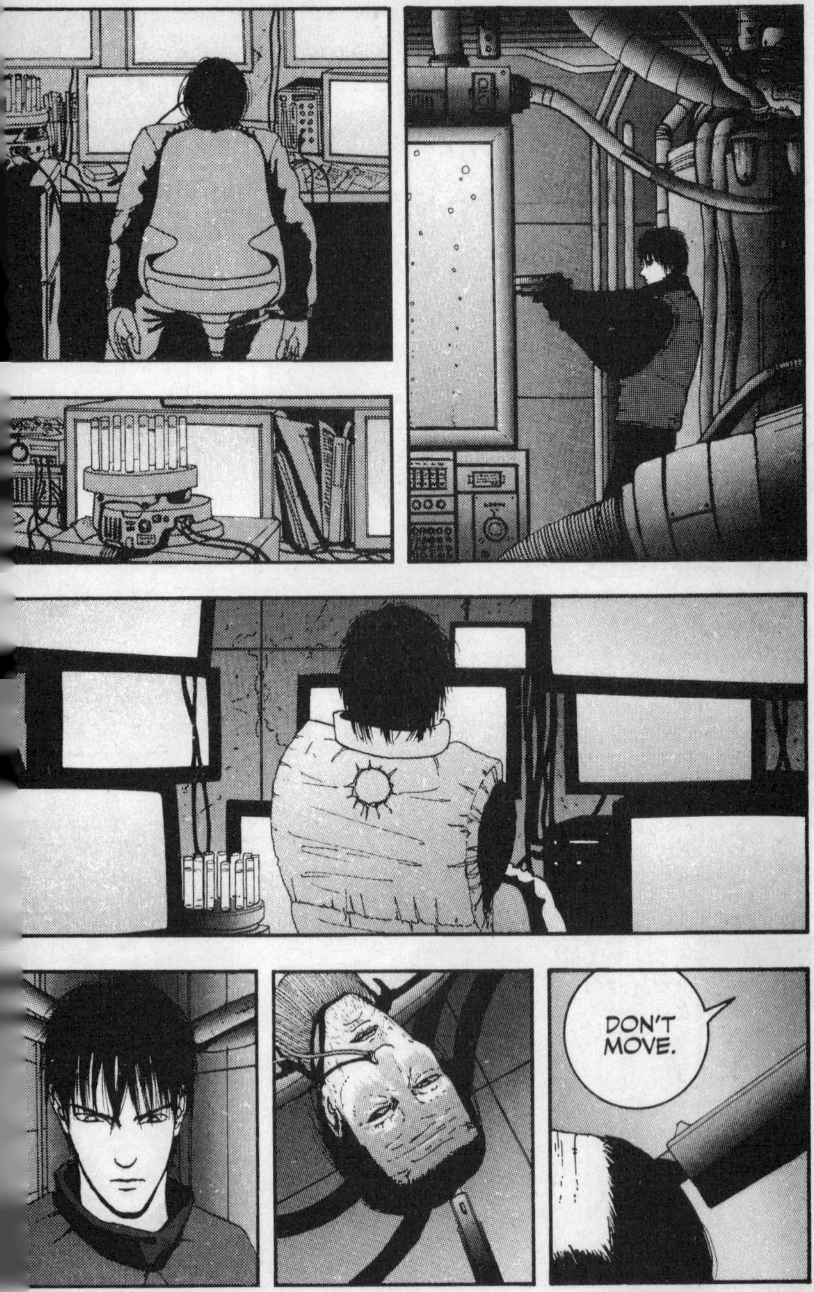
DON'T MOVE.

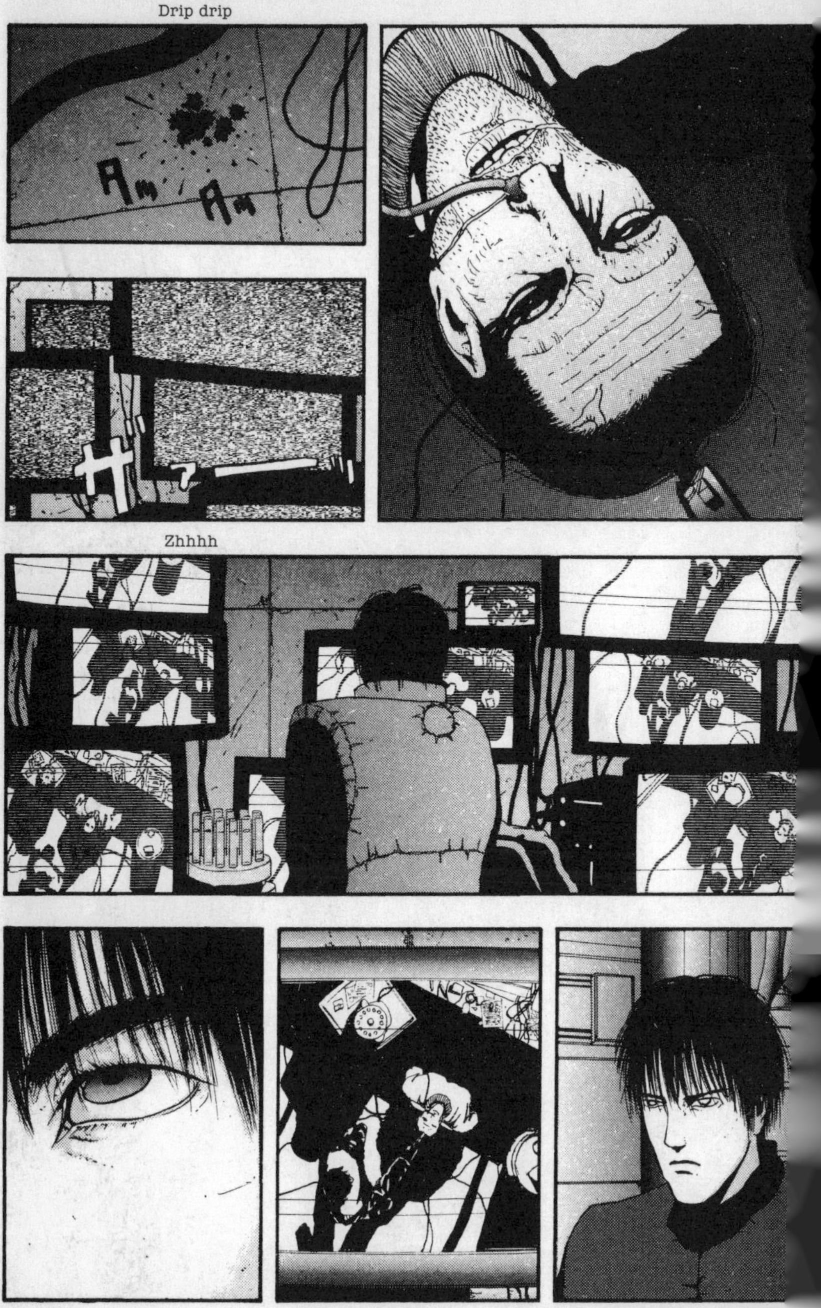
Drip drip
Zhhhh

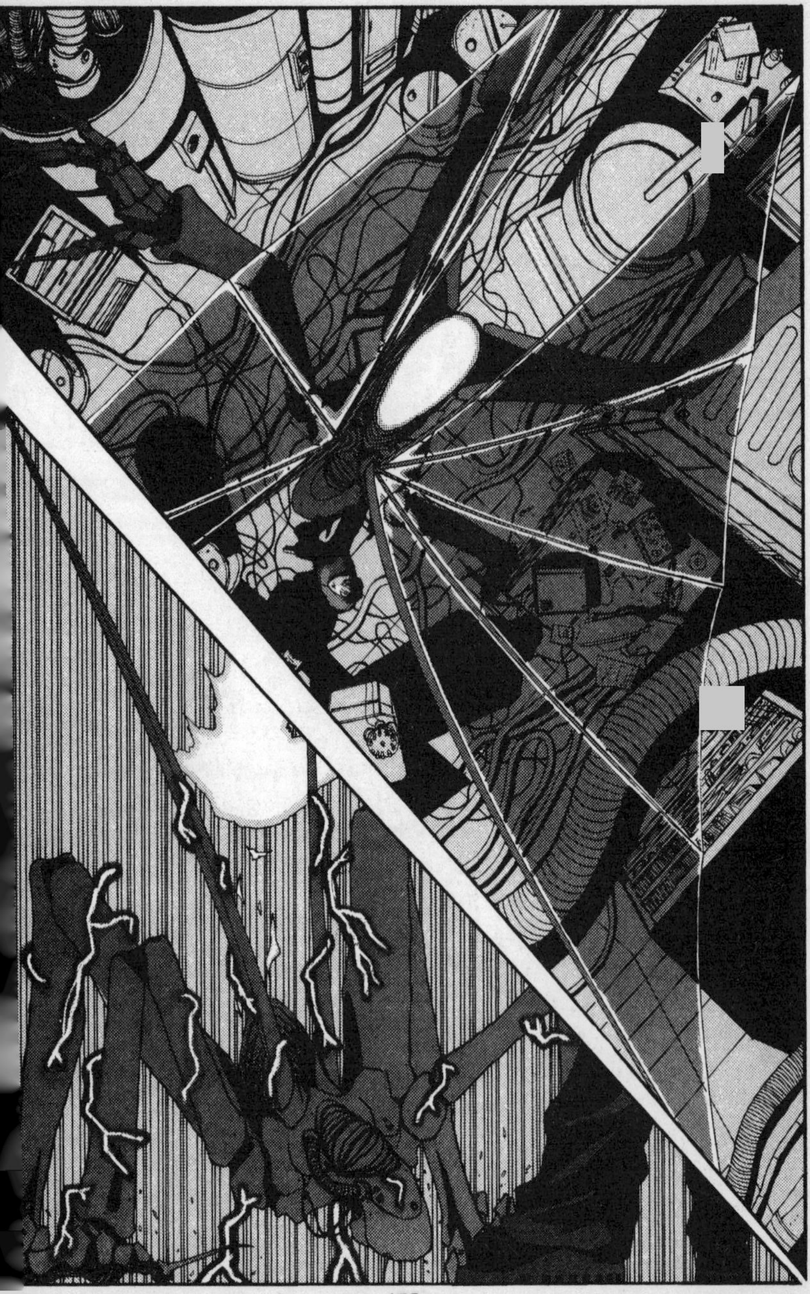

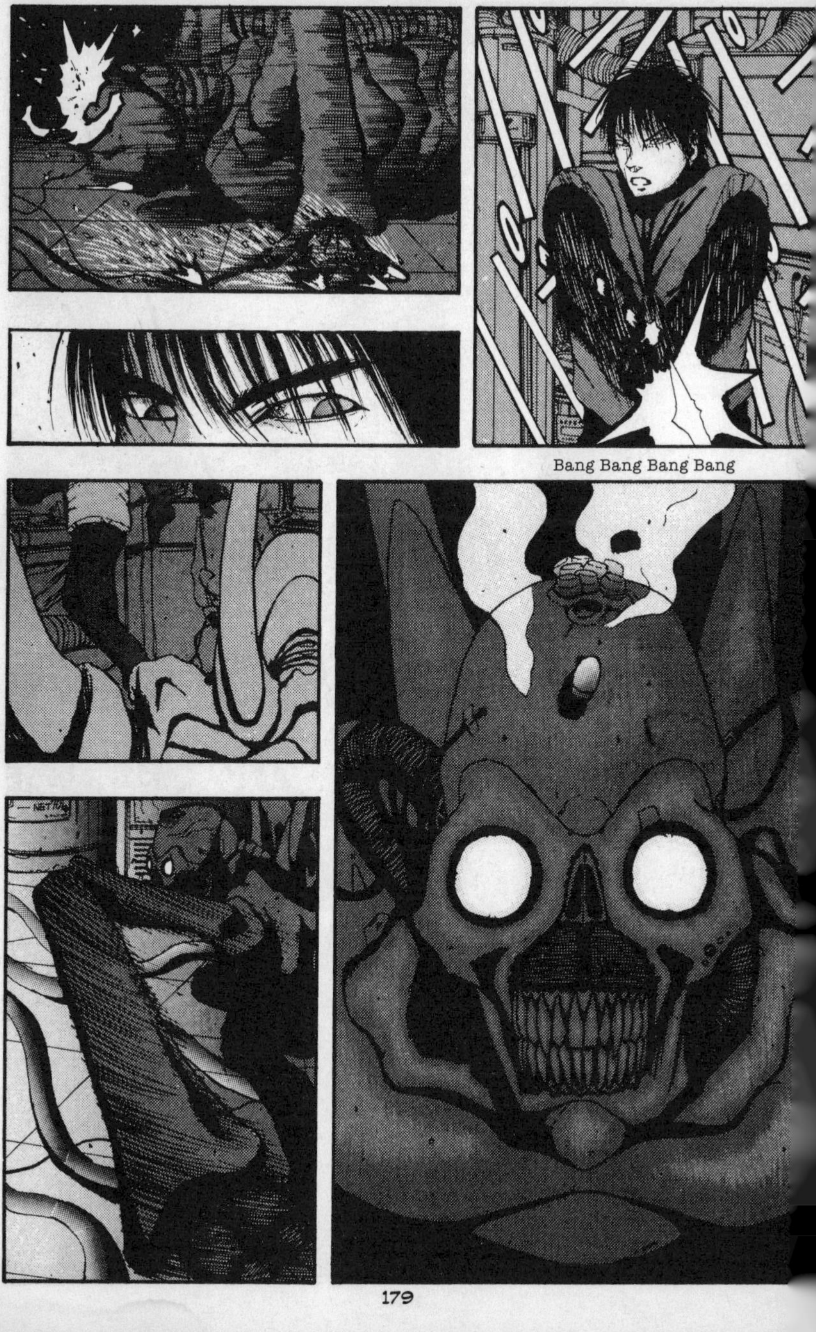
Bang Bang Bang Bang

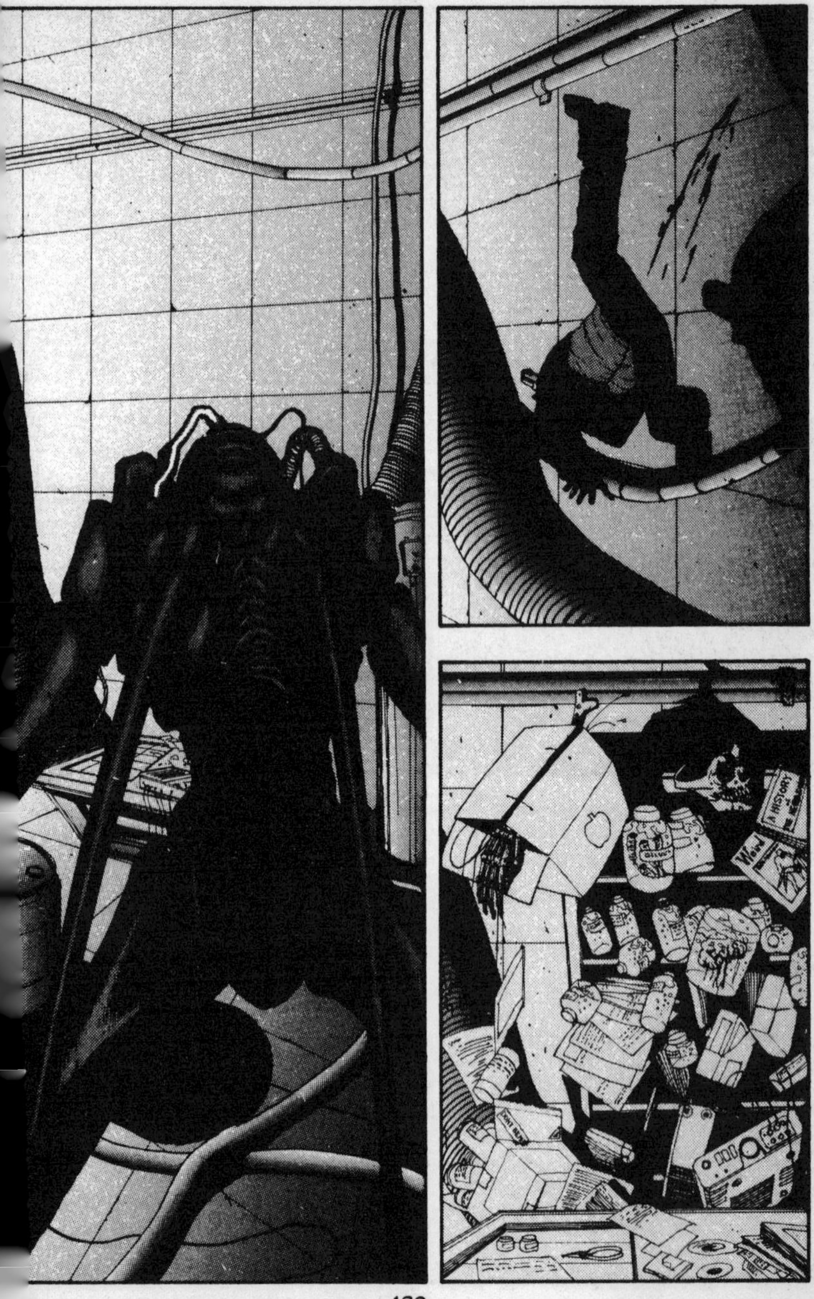

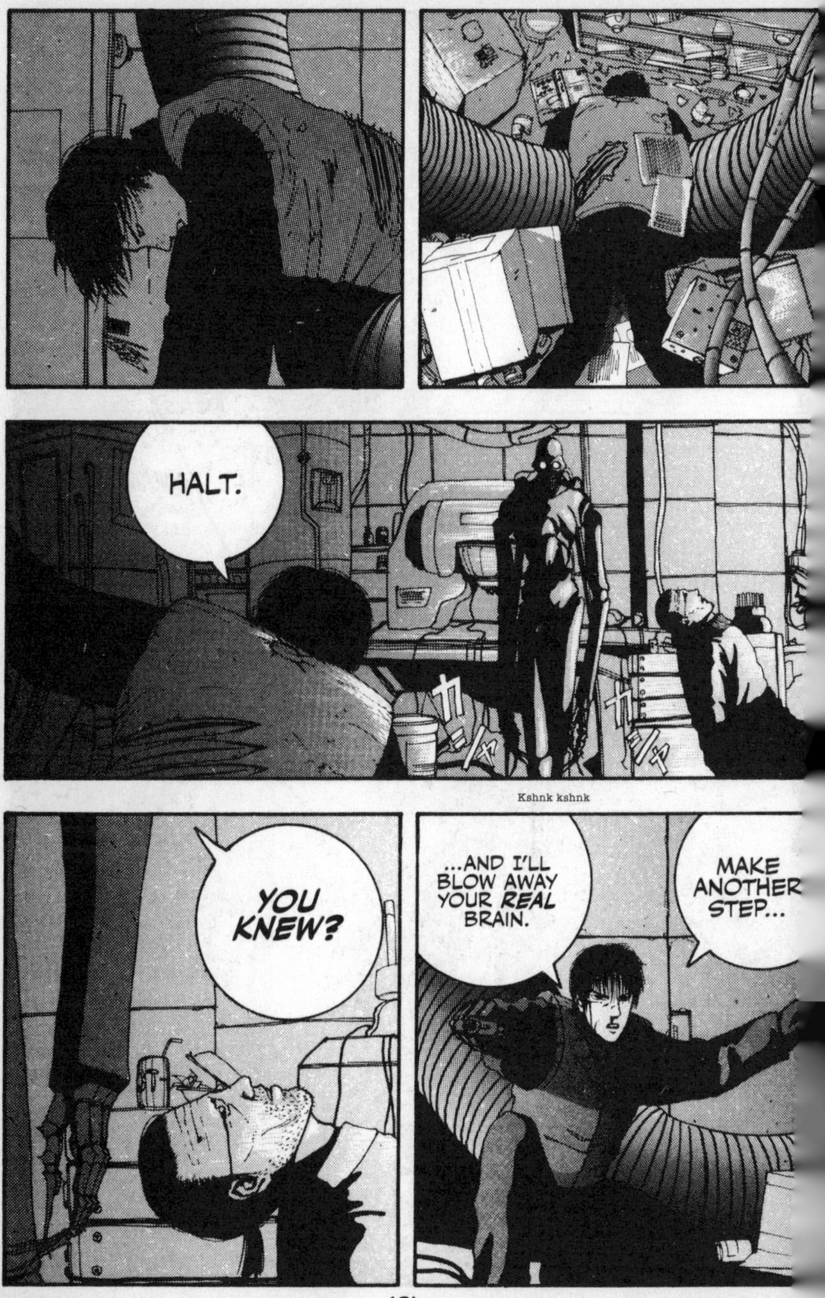
HALT.
Kshnk kshnk
MAKE ANOTHER STEP...
...AND I'LL BLOW AWAY YOUR *REAL* BRAIN.
YOU KNEW?

Pshhht

SHHT

I HAVE NO INTENTION OF RETURNING TO HIM, HOWEVER.

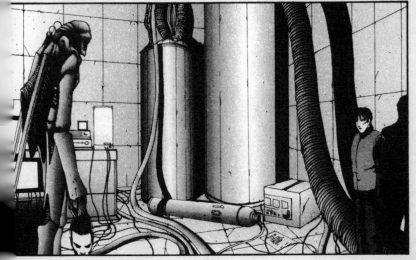

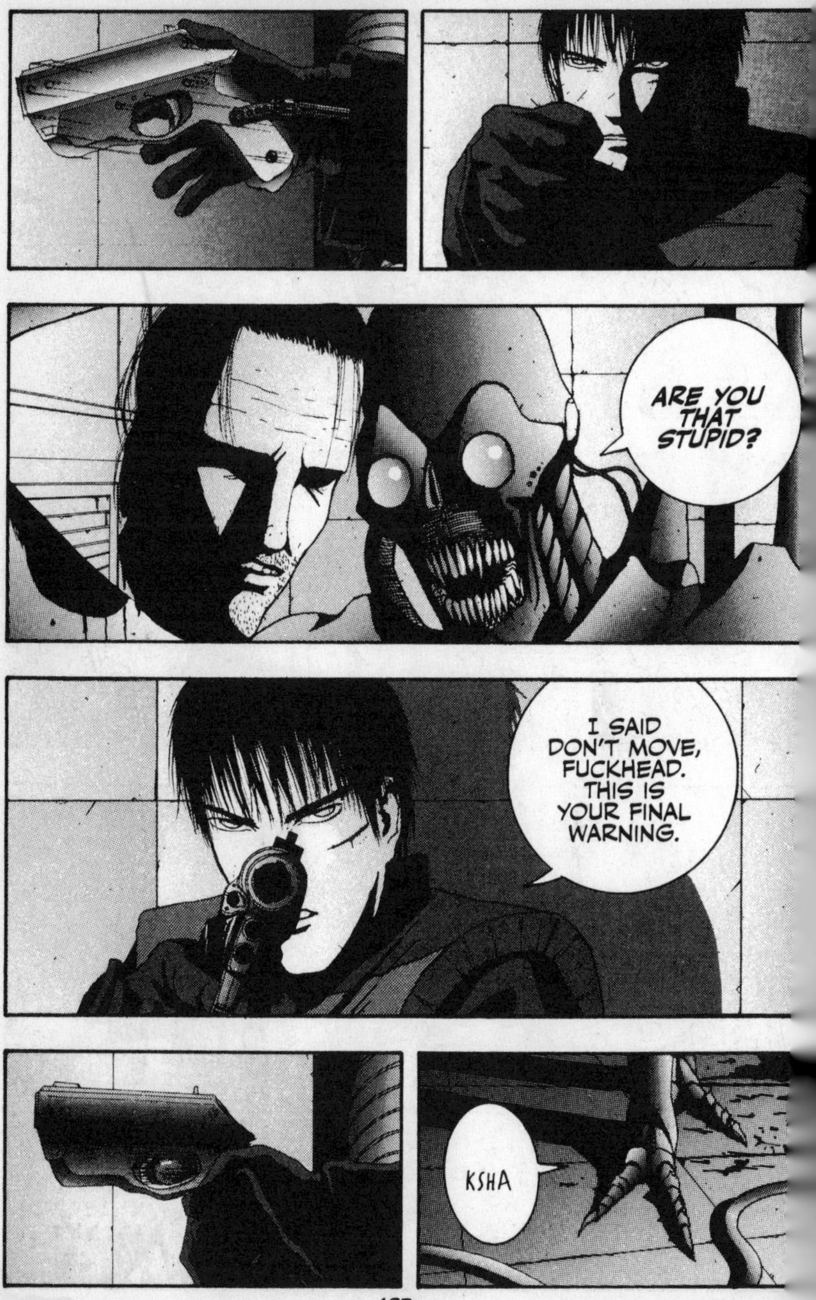
ARE YOU THAT STUPID?
I SAID DON'T MOVE, FUCKHEAD. THIS IS YOUR FINAL WARNING.
KSHA

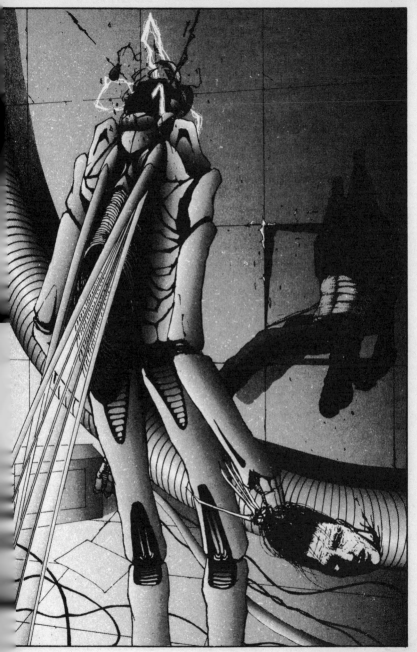

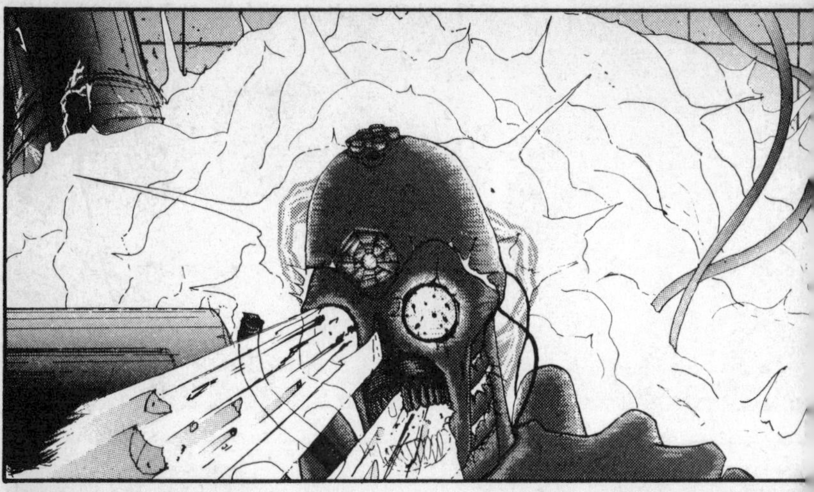
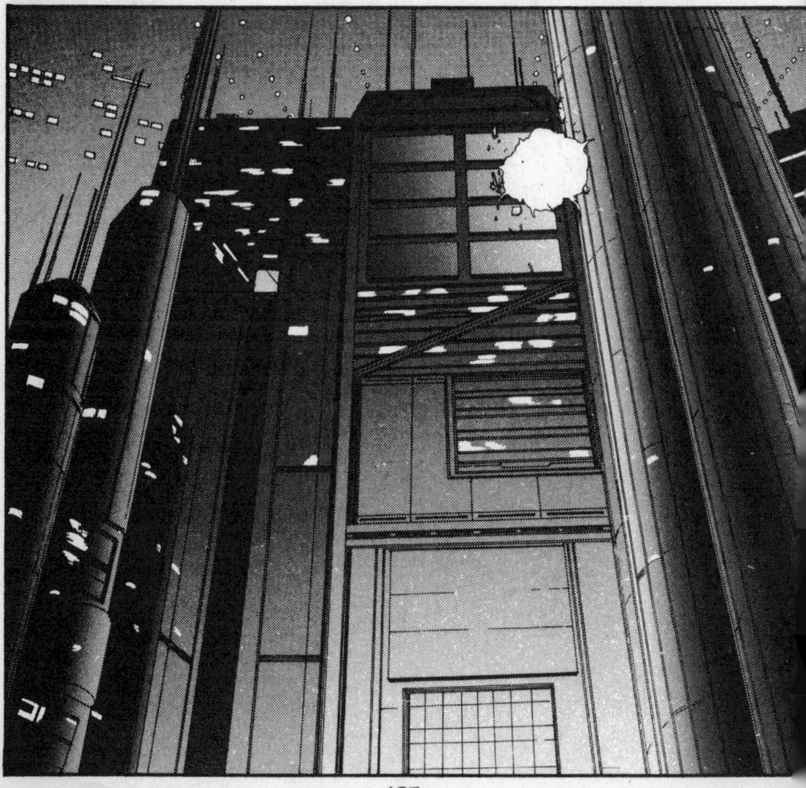

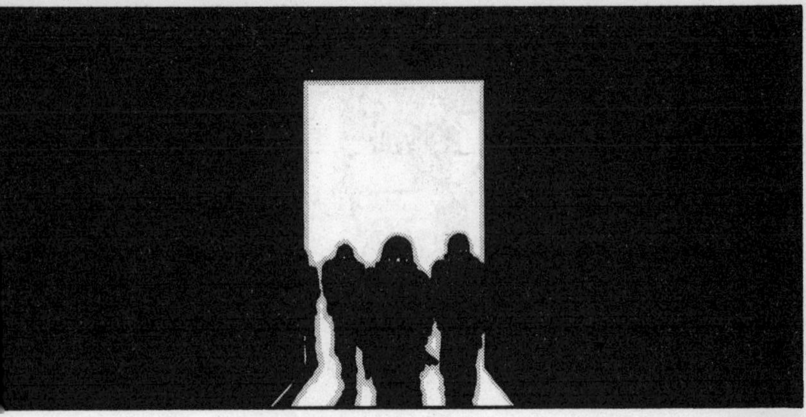
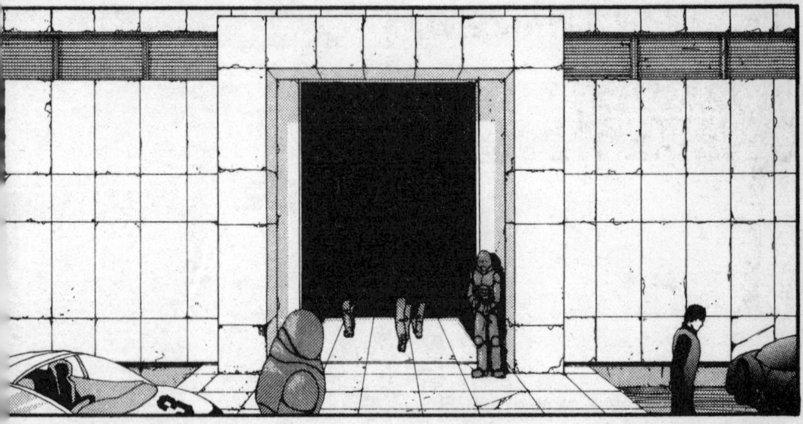
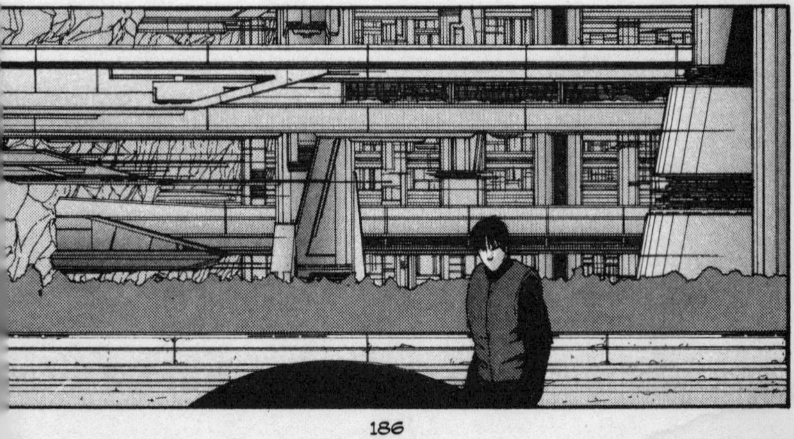

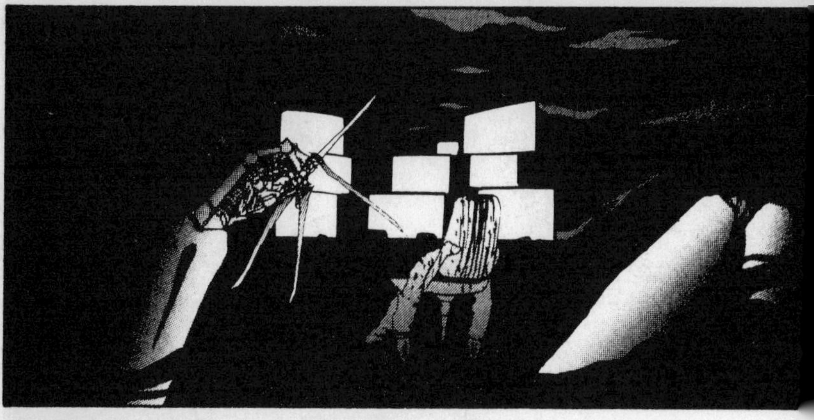

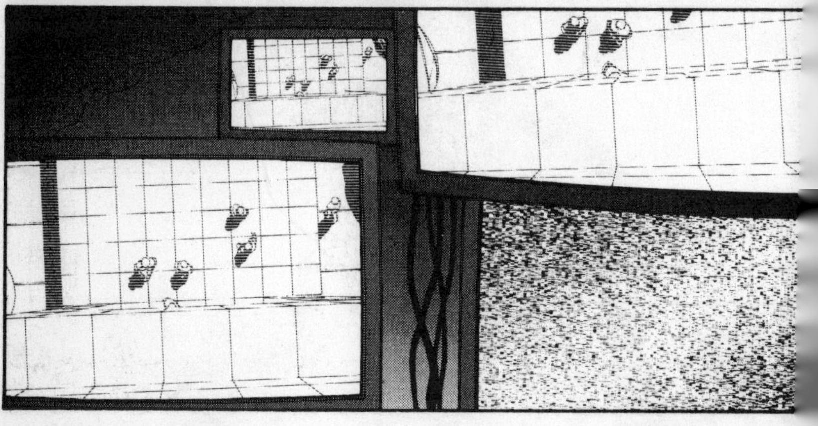

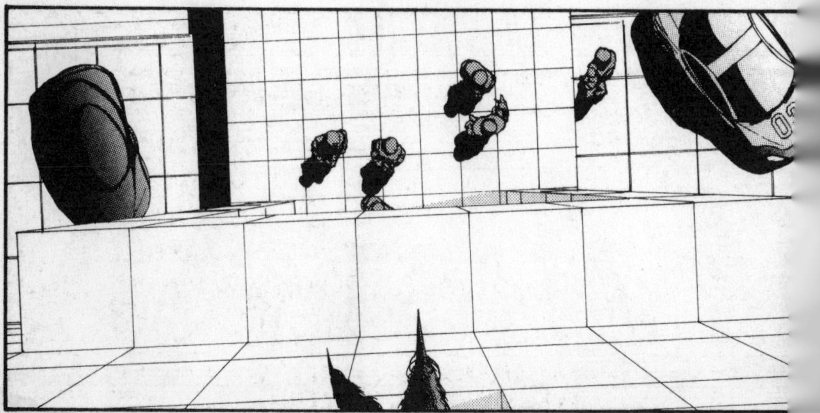

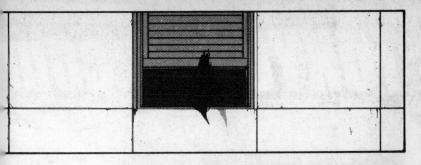

BLAME』@ END

VOLUME 2: SILENT NOISE

TRINITY BLOOD

RAGE AGAINST THE MOONS™

THE TRINITY BLOOD FRANCHISE RAGES ON!

Nothing is quite as it seems...

A mysterious weapon called Silent Noise destroys
Barcelona and threatens Rome... Abel Nightroad
battles personal demons... And the Duchess of Milan is in
more danger than she knows... The next volume of the
thrilling Pop Fiction series rages with sound and fury!

"INSTANTLY GRIPPING."
—*NEWTYPE USA*

© Sunao YOSHIDA 2000, 2001/KADOKAWA SHOTEN

POP
FICTION

STOP!

This is the back of the book.
You wouldn't want to spoil a great ending!

This book is printed "manga-style," in the authentic Japanese right-to-left format. Since none of the artwork has been flipped or altered, readers get to experience the story just as the creator intended. You've been asking for it, so TOKYOPOP® delivered: authentic, hot-off-the-press, and far more fun!

DIRECTIONS

If this is your first time reading manga-style, here's a quick guide to help you understand how it works.

It's easy... just start in the top right panel and follow the numbers. Have fun, and look for more 100% authentic manga from TOKYOPOP®!